2 JAN 2020

4 JAN 2022

7 SEP 2022

1 8 AUG 2023

2 7 MAR 2024

JUN 2018

118

10

KT-478-056

LIB/019

Neath Port Talbot
Libraries
Llyfrgelloedd
Castell-Nedd
Port Talbot

CLEMENTS, RORY
THE HERETICS

1 0 OCT 2019

2300061866

Neath Library
Victoria Gardens
Neath
Tel: 01639 644604

Books should be returned or renewed by the last date stamped above.
Dylid dychwelyd llyfrau neu eu hadnewyddu erbyn y dyddiad olaf a nodir uchod

NEATH PORT TALBOT LIBRARIES

2300061866

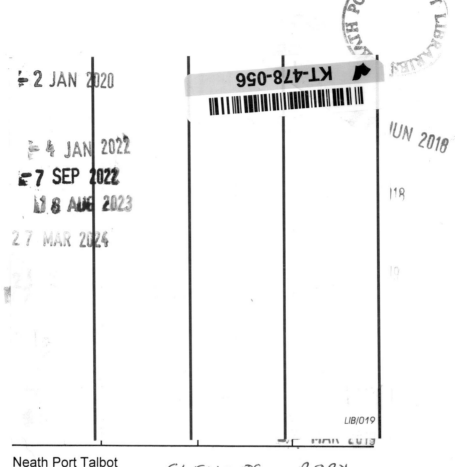

The Heretics

Also by Rory Clements

Martyr
Revenger
Prince
Traitor

The Heretics

RORY CLEMENTS

JOHN MURRAY

NEATH PORT TALBOT LIBRARIES	
2300061866	
Askews & Holts	26-Mar-2013
AF	£17.99
NEA	

First published in Great Britain in 2013 by John Murray (Publishers)
An Hachette UK Company

1

© Rory Clements 2013

The right of Rory Clements to be identified as the Author of the Work has been asserted by him in accordance with the Copyright, Designs and Patents Act 1988.

Maps drawn by Rosie Collins

All rights reserved. Apart from any use permitted under UK copyright law no part of this publication may be reproduced, stored in a retrieval system, or transmitted, in any form or by any means without the prior written permission of the publisher, nor be otherwise circulated in any form of binding or cover other than that in which it is published and without a similar condition being imposed on the subsequent purchaser.

All characters in this publication – other than the obvious historical figures – are fictitious and any resemblance to real persons, living or dead, is purely coincidental.

A CIP catalogue record for this title is available from the British Library

Hardback ISBN 978-1-84854-433-8
Trade paperback ISBN 978-1-84854-434-5
Ebook ISBN 978-1-84854-435-2

Typeset in 12.5/16 pt Adobe Garamond by Servis Filmsetting Ltd, Stockport, Cheshire

Printed and bound by Clays Ltd, St Ives plc

John Murray policy is to use papers that are natural, renewable and recyclable products and made from wood grown in sustainable forests. The logging and manufacturing processes are expected to conform to the environmental regulations of the country of origin.

John Murray (Publishers)
338 Euston Road
London NW1 3BH

www.johnmurray.co.uk

For Brian,
everyone needs a brother

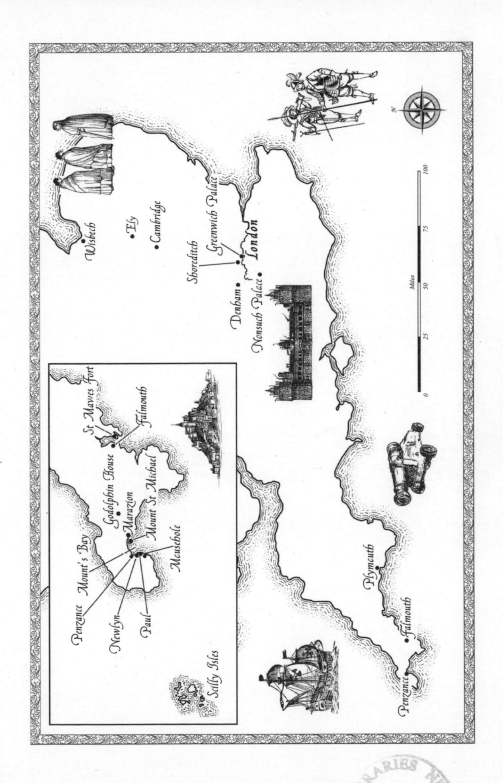

Wisbech
Ely
Cambridge
Shoreditch
Greenwich Palace
Denham
London
Nonsuch Palace

St Mawes Fort
Falmouth
Godolphin House
Mount St Michael
Penzance
Mount's Bay
Marazion
Newlyn
Paul
Mousehole

Scilly Isles

Plymouth
Falmouth
Penzance

Miles
100
75
50
25
0

NEATH PORT TALBOT LIBRARIES

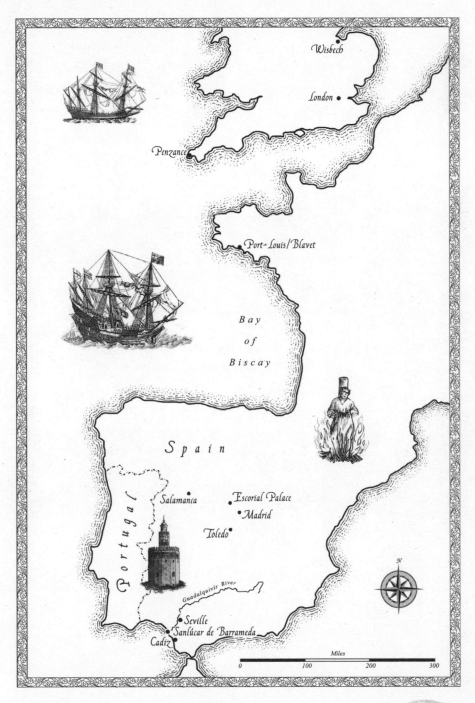

Wisbech

London

Penzance

Port~Louis/Blavet

*Bay
of
Biscay*

S p a i n

Salamanca

Escorial Palace
Madrid

Toledo

P o r t u g a l

Guadalquivir River

Seville
Sanlúcar de Barrameda

Cadiz

N

Miles

0   100   200   300

NEATH PORT TALBOT LIBRARIES

Chapter 1

NEATH PORT TALBOT LIBRARIES

T HE KNOCK AT the door came as John Shakespeare unhooked his sword belt from a nail in the wall. 'Come in,' he said.

His assistant Boltfoot Cooper limped into the comfortable library of his master's house in Dowgate, close by the river in the city of London, and bowed. 'You have a visitor, master.'

'Not now. I am expected elsewhere.' He began buckling his belt. 'Pass me my cloak, Boltfoot.'

Boltfoot picked up the old black bear fur from the coffer where it had been flung and held it up for Shakespeare to pull about his shoulders.

'It is a man named Garrick Loake, sir. He begs you to spare him two minutes. He says he has most urgent business, of great import to the safety of the realm.'

'Who is he?'

Boltfoot's coarse seafarer's brow twisted in a frown. 'I know not, but from the varied colours of his attire, I might guess him to be a player or a poet. He did mention that your brother William recommended him to come to you.'

Shakespeare sighed. 'Send him in. Tell him he has two minutes, no more.'

*

Loake did indeed wear colourful clothes. They were in the Italian style, including a hat with an enormous feather. Boltfoot was right: he could not be anything but a player.

'Mr Loake? Is it true that my brother sent you?'

Loake bowed with a dramatic flourish. 'He did, Mr Shakespeare. And I am most honoured to make your acquaintance for I have heard a great deal of your bold exploits.'

'*Why* did Will send you here?'

'I took the liberty of confiding in him that I had concerns about a certain matter and he said straightway that you were the man to talk with.'

'Mr Loake, I have little time to spare you. Perhaps you would return tomorrow when I am less pressed.'

'I beg you to listen for a brief moment. I know what a busy man you are.'

Shakespeare remained standing. The library fire was blazing away and soon he would overheat in this fur. But he kept the cloak on. He did not wish to give this man the impression that he would stay and talk with him.

'I know your distinguished brother from the Theatre, Mr Burbage's fine playhouse in Shoreditch,' Loake continued. 'If you are as straight dealing as he is, then I am certain I can trust you.'

Shakespeare, a tall man with long hair, waited, merely smiling. His presence alone was often enough to lure men into revealing their secrets.

'I sometimes play there myself,' Loake went on. 'I am not a member of the company, but there is usually work for me as a hired man in one capacity or another. Yesterday, I was working with the costumes.' He twirled to display his brilliant outfit. 'I borrowed this, Mr Shakespeare. It is Capulet's apparel. Do you not think it becoming? Am I not a noble Veronese gentleman?'

'The certain matter, Mr Loake—'

'Forgive me, I shall come to that straightway. I have a secret to impart, you see. A secret involving papist intrigue. I believe young Cecil will pay very well for such intelligence.'

'You mean Sir Robert Cecil.' Shakespeare was not about to let his chief man be referred to as 'Young Cecil' by a stranger.

'Indeed, not old Burghley. It is the young Caesar who runs the Privy Council these days, is it not? His father holds the purse-strings, but the boy spends the gold. Your brother mentioned that you might have a pathway to that purse.'

Shakespeare was losing patience. He could not imagine that Will had said anything of the sort. 'Tell me the matter, Mr Loake. And do not refer to Sir Robert Cecil as *the boy.*'

'My information is worth twenty sovereigns, I am certain of it. Twenty gold sovereigns.'

'I fear you are ill informed.' The figure was laughable. There were too many snouts in the trough already. 'Very little is worth even twenty shillings. Twenty sovereigns is out of the question.'

'Well, that is my price. I have great need of gold, and I need it in haste, which is why I have come to you. I cannot go a penny below my asking price.'

Shakespeare stepped away from the oppressive heat of the fire and moved towards the door. 'Tell me what you know. And be quick about it.'

'What I know,' Loake said, 'is that there is a most foul conspiracy unfolding. It wafts from the papist fastness of eastern England, gathers force in the seminaries of Spain, but it will blow into a tempest here.' He lowered his voice for dramatic effect. 'A conspiracy the like of which England has never seen.'

'How do you know this?'

'It is my business to listen well, for I sometimes hold the book and prompt the players.'

'Names,' said Shakespeare wearily. 'Give me names. What manner of plot is this? Tell me the circumstance.'

'I will, Mr Shakespeare, when you give me twenty sovereigns. For the present, I must hold my peace, for if I say more, then you will know as much as I do, and I will have no power to bargain.'

Shakespeare suddenly caught a whiff of sweat. This man was scared and desperate. 'You are wasting my time. Say what you know.'

Loake put up his right hand, which had a ring on each finger. It shook. 'I will tell you one thing, one thing only. The seminary involved is the College of St Gregory in Seville.'

'The English college of Jesuits?'

'The very same. So you will tell young Cecil to give me a purse of twenty gold sovereigns, as agreed?'

Shakespeare laughed. 'Mr Loake, I have agreed nothing. Now I must go. If you have something to tell me, then return in the morning.' He waved a hand in dismissal.

Many men came to Shakespeare's door, scratching like curs for coins in return for information; at times of want it was a daily occurrence. Most of the intelligence was worthless, scraps of tittle-tattle overheard in taverns and gaols. But it all had to be listened to and some of it, no more than a tiny portion, had to be investigated. There was something in the demeanour of this man that interested Shakespeare. He would like to see him again, to delve more deeply. But not now.

'Twenty, I must have twenty. Sovereigns.'

Despite himself, Shakespeare stayed. It was plain to him that Loake had no concept of how to conduct a negotiation; no idea that you must demand a high price so you can meet somewhere in the middle.

'Even if we could agree a figure, I would need to seek authorisation for the payment, and that would be impossible without first knowing the details of your intelligence. Trust is required on both sides in such a transaction. I promise you this: if you tell me a secret as valuable as you claim, then I shall obtain up to five pounds on your behalf. Is that not fair dealing, Mr Loake?'

'I cannot go so low.'

Shakespeare rested his hand on the hilt of his sword as if to underline who held the power here.

'You must bear in mind, Mr Loake, that you have now informed me that you have knowledge of some treachery directed at this realm. If you do not tell me all you know, then you will be laying yourself open to a charge that you are an accessory to that treason.'

Loake drew himself up to his full height, which was not great, and wiped a sleeve of gold and blue across his sweat-glistening brow and prominent nose. 'Did your brother then lie when he said you were to be trusted?'

Shakespeare shook his head. 'I will not listen to insults, Mr Loake.'

Should he have Boltfoot take the man to Bridewell or the Fleet prison for the night? He rejected the notion; it would be a betrayal of his brother.

'Come back when you have collected your wits. I may have an offer for you if you tell me enough of interest. Be here half an hour after first light and I will see you.'

Chapter 2

IT WAS DUSK by the time Shakespeare got to Newgate prison. He came in secret, wearing his hat low over his forehead, his body swathed in black fur, concealing his identity from the long lines of curious onlookers already gathering for the next day's entertainment. The gloom was lit by a dozen bonfires and blazing cressets. Makeshift stalls had been put up to sell food and ale to those who would camp out here in this long, cold night to ensure the best view in the morning. Some among the waiting crowds stared at Shakespeare, but he ignored their insolent gaze and walked on with purpose.

He stopped at the main entrance beside the gate in the city wall. The road beneath his feet was cobbled and slippery; the gaol, towering above him, rose five storeys high into the darkening London sky. The last of the day's carts and drays clattered through the archway into the city. A flock of geese, driven by a man in a smock, waddled in to meet their fate. Shakespeare hammered with the pommel of his dagger on the gaol's heavy oak door. The head keeper, who had been waiting, opened it to him, welcoming his visitor with a bow and a sweep of the arm. The ring of keys that hung from his broad oxhide belt jangled as he ushered Shakespeare inside.

'How is he faring, Mr Keeper?'

'He does well, master. Never have I met so rare a man.'

Shakespeare turned and pushed back his hat to look into the keeper's eyes, gratified by what he saw there: honesty and genuine affection. He was not surprised; the condemned prisoner had that effect on many people. Shakespeare held the keeper's gaze. 'Where is he? In Limbo?'

The keeper nodded, a pained expression curling his lips. Limbo was a dark pit in the lower reaches of the ancient gaol, lacking light and air, where the condemned prepared themselves for the hangman. Its meagre bedding of straw was clogged with the ordure of frightened men.

'But at least he is alone there, master. No other felons await death.'

'Bring him to an upper cell. Let him breathe before he dies.'

'Mr Topcliffe commanded me, master—'

'Damn, Mr Topcliffe. I am here under orders from Sir Robert Cecil. Bring the prisoner up.'

The keeper hesitated, but then uttered some sort of grunt and shuffled off into the rank depths of the gaol. Shakespeare pulled his hat back over his brow and waited.

Within a minute, the keeper returned. 'I have ordered him brought to a cell on the second floor. I will take you there now. You will not be disturbed.'

The single window was barred by a grating of iron rods, embedded into the stone walls. It was a small aperture, scarcely big enough to admit the last of the day's light. The cell was clean and the cold air as fresh as could be hoped for in such a dungeon.

Shakespeare had not seen Father Robert Southwell in eight years and the passage of time had not treated him well. The years of solitary confinement in the Tower and episodes of torture at the hands of Richard Topcliffe had broken his body. His once serene face was now gaunt and his slender back bent, yet his eyes shone in the grey light. It seemed to Shakespeare that he had the exquisite fragility of church glass.

Southwell, his palms together in prayer, sank to his knees at the sight of his visitor, but Shakespeare raised him to his feet and clasped his hands. He turned to the gaoler, still hovering by the iron-strapped door. 'Bring us a flagon of good wine, Mr Keeper.' He dug fingers in his purse and pulled out a coin. 'That will pay for it.'

The keeper bowed and departed, leaving the door open.

'I could overpower you, Mr Shakespeare, and make my escape.'

Shakespeare smiled at the sad jest. Southwell would be hard pressed to do battle with a kitten.

'Shall we sit down, Father?'

There was a table and three stools, but the condemned Jesuit shook his head and continued to stand. His breathing was fast. Thin trails of vapour shot from his mouth and nose and vanished in the cold air. 'There is time enough for these bones to rest.'

'Are you being treated well?'

'I count the keeper as my friend. Many good people have sent in offerings of food and he has brought it to me, along with their messages of support. I never ate so well in the Tower as I do here.'

'Well, that is something at least.'

'Their generosity of spirit gladdens my heart, Mr Shakespeare. And on the matter of kindness, will you not tell me of your beloved wife, Catherine? You have a child, I believe.'

Shakespeare stiffened. Long before he had met Catherine in the year of eighty-seven, she had been a friend of Southwell and had received the sacraments from him. But now Catherine lay in her grave.

Southwell saw his pain. 'I am sorry. I see I intrude on some grief. Is she with God?'

'I must pray that she is.'

'Forgive me, I had not heard of your great loss, Mr Shakespeare. In the Tower, I heard nothing of the world beyond my four walls. I loved Catherine as a daughter or sister. I will pray for you both . . . and the child.'

'The child is well. She is called Mary. Catherine did not suffer . . .'

Shakespeare's voice broke and he shuddered, for the word resonated icily in this room. *Suffer.* He knew what agonies Southwell would have to suffer on the morrow. Convicted of treason at the court of Queen's Bench this day, he would be collected from his cell at dawn and dragged on a hurdle along the jarring road to Tyburn. There he would be hanged in front of a crowd of thousands, then cut down while he lived so that the butchers could tear his belly open and rip out his entrails to burn before his eyes. And at last, he would be quartered and beheaded.

Southwell noticed his visitor's unease. 'I think you are right, Mr Shakespeare. I will sit down. Come, sit with me. There are things I must tell you, though I am sure you are a busy man. Does Mr Cecil know you are here?'

'Yes, Sir Robert knows.'

'Ah – so he has been knighted. You see, I hear nothing. Well, I am sure it is deserved. He is my cousin, you know.'

'Yes, I know that. And I know that he admires your courage, if not your religion. And I can tell you, in confidence, that the Queen also knows I am here. She wishes to be told the contents of your heart. She wishes to know why one so holy and poetical should strive to bring about the destruction of her estate.'

Southwell frowned, as if he did not comprehend the question. 'I fear she has been fed falsehoods. I never meant the destruction of Her Majesty, nor any harm to England. I sought

✝ 9 ✝

nothing but the eternal good of souls, including hers. Even now I call on the Lord God to enlighten her, and her Council, and not to hold them guilty for my death.'

'But your Church excommunicated her. The Jesuits support invasion by Spain—'

'Many errors have been made on all sides, Mr Shakespeare. You may tell Her Royal Majesty that I honour her as my sovereign lady. I have prayed for her daily.'

'I will tell her. Is that why you asked me to come here, Father?'

The keeper arrived with the wine and two goblets. Setting a tallow rushlight on the table between Shakespeare and the condemned man, he bowed and backed away to the door, without a word. Again, he left the door open. Shakespeare poured the wine.

'He watches and listens, Mr Shakespeare,' Southwell said quietly. 'He fears I will take my own life. He has been ordered to keep me alive so that my death is witnessed as a warning to others.' Southwell reached out and grasped Shakespeare's arm in his thin fingers. 'Did you ever hear of a Catholic priest that hurt himself so? Why should we add the destruction of our souls to the demise of our bodies?'

Shakespeare understood. He sipped his wine and waited.

'And so to your question. I asked for you, Mr Shakespeare, because there is something I must beg of you. One favour. If you will do this one thing for me, then I may go to my death in peace in the hope that I will be saved by the Passion of our Lord, Jesus Christ.'

'Then you had better tell me what it is, Father.'

The priest sighed, closed his eyes for a moment, then spoke, little more than a whisper. 'There is a girl, Mr Shakespeare. A girl named Thomasyn Jade. I want you to find her.'

Shakespeare got up and walked to the door. A figure shrank

back into the passageway beyond. Shakespeare shut the door, then returned to sit at the table.

'This harks back nine years to the dangerous days of summer in eighty-six,' Southwell said, his voice still low. 'It can be no secret to you that I was newly arrived in England, for I know that you were then working for Mr Secretary Walsingham, and his spies had told him of my coming.'

Shakespeare nodded. He recalled all too well those feverish, fearful days and weeks. It was the time of the Babington plot that had led to the downfall of Mary, Queen of Scots, and brought so many foolish young Catholic men to the scaffold, condemned for plotting to assassinate Elizabeth and put Mary on her throne.

'Within a month of my arrival the so-called plotters and others had been rounded up. Some were racked, many were executed. Among those held was Father William Weston of the Society of Jesus.'

'I know all this.'

London had been a cacophonous circle of the inferno. The bells of the city churches pealed all day long and into the night; the streets were ablaze with fires celebrating that the plot had been uncovered and foiled. And on the river, an endless procession of captured conspirators and priests was carried upstream, bound hand and foot, from the baleful Tower to the courts at Westminster, and then drawn to the place of execution. It had seemed as though the slaughter would never abate.

'Indeed, Mr Shakespeare. And I am sure, too, that you will know of the other dark events that occurred in those months, when certain Catholic priests carried out exorcisms on unfortunate souls possessed by demons.'

Shakespeare's mouth turned down in distaste. It had been a disgusting affair. Young women and men had been held for days and weeks on end, being subjected to the most repulsive treatment by a group of priests and their acolytes, all in the name of ridding them of supposed demons. Many who had been sympathetic to the popish cause had been turned against it by the whole foul story.

'Yes, I remember it, Father Robert, for I spoke with Weston himself, but I believe the practice stopped at about the time of your arrival in England.'

The priest's eyes were downcast. His fine features brought to mind the name he had been given by the townsfolk of Douai in Flanders when he had attended the English College there as a young man: *the beautiful English youth*. That youth was now long gone, worn away by pain and deprivation, yet Shakespeare could still see the strange, troubling beauty in his soul.

'Yes, the exorcisms were halted. But much damage had already been done, and not just to the Catholic cause. The real victims, I fear, were some of those whom the priests were trying to help.'

'Was Thomasyn Jade one of them?'

'She was. It is no secret now that I met my Jesuit brother William Weston soon after my arrival and not long before his arrest. I did not know it at first, but it seems he was the prime mover of these exorcism rites. We travelled together to a house in Buckinghamshire – I will not tell you more than that – to confer and rest. We stayed there a week. During that time, a girl of seventeen or eighteen – Thomasyn – was brought to us by certain priests to be rid of devils. She had already undergone many more such ordeals at Denham House, near by, which, as you must know, was the centre of these goings-on.

'I watched in horror as the ritual was played out. She was stuck with pins to catch the devils beneath her skin and she was made to drink concoctions of herbs. The holy thumb of the martyr Campion was thrust in her mouth. Brimstone was burnt beneath her nose so that I believed she would choke to death. I was affronted, Mr Shakespeare, for I saw that those who did these things were in mortal error. Those who witnessed the events were struck with such fear that they quaked and trembled and wept most bitterly. Within a short while, I brought the ceremony to a halt and, though Father Weston was my superior, I advised him that he would do well never to partake in such things again.'

Shakespeare was surprised to hear Southwell voice such open criticism of a fellow of the same order.

The priest waved his hand. 'Do not misunderstand me. I have nothing but admiration for the work and ministry of Father Weston. He is a saintly man. Perhaps too saintly sometimes, too unworldly. He did what he did out of fine motives, trying to save souls. But he was misguided in subscribing to the rite of exorcism, nor am I alone among the Catholic fraternity in thinking this way. I have sometimes wondered since whether the simple fact of his failing eyesight might have made him easily deluded by others less honest. I do not believe he saw evil spirits under the girl's skin, nor do I believe he truly saw them coming from her mouth and . . .' He hesitated, scarce able to say the shameful words. 'And from her privy parts. But *he* believed he did.'

'Why do you want me to find the girl?'

'Because she was ill used by us. When she came to the house, she was shaking with fear; she was halfway mad with frenzy and weeping. I should never have allowed the exorcism to proceed as far as it did.'

'And what became of her at the end of the day's torments?'

'She was given cordials and food, and I spoke soothing words to her. I tried to discover more about her, but she could not speak. I tried to pray with her, but she became yet more distressed. I was at a loss. I did not know what to do for her. With five sisters of my own, I understand women's ways, but I am aware that the years among men at the Society colleges have made me less easy in their company. Thomasyn could not stay at that house and I could not take her with me. Instead she was taken away by the priests who had brought her, back to the house near by whence she had come.'

'Denham House?'

'Indeed.'

Shakespeare gave a wry smile. He had heard much about Denham House, a putrid place, a dark hole of corruption and wickedness.

'I fear I did not do well by her, Mr Shakespeare. Three weeks later the priests who housed her were themselves arrested, as was Father Weston. Thomasyn Jade was taken away by the pursuivants, but her story reached certain courtiers and she was soon freed into the care of a great Protestant lady, the Countess of Kent. It was hoped that she would undo the priests' efforts to reconcile the wretched girl to the Church of Rome, and take her back to Protestantism. But within a few days I heard that she had disappeared. I prayed for her every day and worried for her, for she was an afflicted young woman and in need of proper care and spiritual nourishment. I sought her as best I could, but in the year of ninety-two, as you know, I was myself arrested. I have heard nothing of her since. Her memory haunts me, and I cannot go easily to my death.'

'And if I find her?'

'My family and friends have set aside money on her behalf. They will be as godparents to her and she will be well cared for. There is nothing sinister, no more exorcisms. Nor will they seek to influence her choice of faith. I ask only that you find her . . . if she is alive.'

'Why should I do this for you, Father Southwell? You came to England as a traitor. Since then you have longed for martyrdom. You must see that you are my enemy.'

Robert Southwell crossed himself. 'You know that is not so, Mr Shakespeare.'

It was true. They were not enemies. And while Shakespeare could never comprehend Southwell's quest for death, nor like the way he held to the superstitions of Rome, he admired his courage, his piety and his poetry. If it was true, as the English state insisted, that some Jesuits contrived the death of princes, then Southwell was not one of them. Either way, though, he was about to have his martyrdom.

Shakespeare nodded slowly. This man had once risked life and liberty to help him; he could not refuse him now. 'I will do what I can, Father. You had better tell me every detail you know.'

Just over a mile north-east of Newgate, near Bishopsgate, Garrick Loake sat alone in an alehouse booth. He had downed four pints of strong beer and was beginning to feel hazy. Yet he was not drunk, not enough to ignore the uncomfortable feeling that his meeting with John Shakespeare had gone badly. Would it go any better on the morrow? A fresh tankard was slopped down in front of him. He paid the maid a penny, then picked up the vessel and drank deeply.

The problem was there was no going back now. He had told Shakespeare too much to shirk their next meeting, and so he would be at his house in the morning. What about tonight, though? He couldn't go home; it wasn't safe there. Not now. He looked around at the other drinkers in the taproom. Every man seemed a threat.

He fished out his purse and saw that his hand was shaking. Counting the meagre contents, he gauged that if he drank no more, there might just be enough for a room for the night at one of the cheaper inns. And he would say a prayer that Mr Shakespeare would save his skin.

Chapter 3

IT WAS ALMOST eleven o'clock when Shakespeare reined in at the brick-built gatehouse facing the green on the north side of Richmond Palace. In the distance, way beyond the outer wall, lights flickered behind a multitude of windows in the fourteen towers of the royal lodgings, clustered around the inner quad. Shakespeare patted the horse's neck. It had been a hard ride from Newgate along eleven miles of treacherous roads.

A squad of six halberdiers approached and barred his way. He showed them his papers and one of them disappeared beneath the archway into the echoing spaces of the outer courtyard.

Soon, an elegant, white-bearded man appeared, attired in black except for a crisp white falling band about his neck, and carrying a lantern. Shakespeare nodded in recognition; it was Clarkson, most trusted retainer to Sir Robert Cecil.

'Mr Shakespeare, sir, you are expected straightway.'

Clarkson held the lantern forward and studied the new-comer's mud-and-sweat-stained fur cloak, hesitating, as though worried that such poor clothes would not be acceptable in the royal chambers. Finally he dismissed his concerns. 'Please dismount and follow me. The guard will take your horse to the stables.'

Cecil, who was waiting in his apartments, did not bother with pleasantries. 'Well, John, what did Mr Southwell have to say for himself?' His voice was brisk and businesslike. 'I take it he did not offer to recant and plead for his life?'

'No, he desires martyrdom.'

'Then we shall not disappoint him. Will he make a good death?'

'I believe he will. He shows no fear.'

Cecil seemed disappointed. 'Why did he wish to see you?'

'He asked me to tell Her Majesty that he is, and always has been, a loyal subject.'

Cecil emitted a dry laugh. 'Yet like all his order he condemns her as a heretic. And we well know what the Inquisition does to those they accuse of heresy. Anyway, how can we believe a single word he says, now we know of this Jesuit policy of equivocation? He might be saying out loud, "I am loyal to the Queen," while in his heart are the words, "*though my first loy-alty is to the Pope and King Philip, and therefore I will conspire to kill her*".' Cecil almost spat the words. 'Is that all he said?'

'No. He wants me to find a girl. She is on his conscience. I think he fears he will not be saved if I do not do this.'

'What girl? I had thought him Christ's fellow.'

'Thomasyn Jade, one of those ill used by the exorcists back in the year of eighty-six.'

'Who is she?'

'I know nothing more than her name – and that she was brought to a house in Buckinghamshire to be exorcised by Weston in the few days that he was with Southwell. When Weston and others were arrested, she was taken by pursuivants. By then she was insane, which is why Southwell feels such guilt. He fears their rites helped destroy her mind. Lady Susan Bertie, the Countess of Kent, took the poor girl under her wing, but then she vanished.'

NEATH PORT TALBOT LIBRARIES

'God's wounds, Southwell and his like will have much to answer for at the day of judgment.'

Shakespeare did not point out that it was Southwell who had brought the girl's torments to a halt. He was aware that Cecil did not wish to hear a good word said about his condemned Jesuit cousin – not this night. Tonight Cecil had a heavy conscience of his own to contend with.

Southwell had become a forgotten man during his thirty months of isolation in the Tower and Gatehouse prisons, and he might have seen out his days in squalid obscurity, had he not drawn attention to himself by writing to Cecil's father, Lord Burghley, begging either to be allowed visits from friends or, failing that, to be brought to trial to answer charges. Old Burghley's response had been brutal and terse: *if Southwell is in such haste to be hanged, he shall quickly have his desire.*

It had been an uncharacteristically impatient and ill-judged response, but perhaps the Lord Treasurer's chronic gout had been the true irritant. Once the decision had been made, however, the younger Cecil had no choice but to issue the order for Southwell to be transferred from the Tower to Newgate to meet his fate.

The trial in the court of Queen's Bench, before Chief Justice Sir John Popham, had been swift and vicious. Attorney-General Edward Coke had led the prosecution, but it was the torturer Richard Topcliffe whose voice had been loudest. His ranting and raving had been such that Popham had had to silence him.

The worst part was the unexpected arrival of the one witness for the prosecution: Anne Bellamy, a young woman whom Southwell had once called friend and whose betrayal had led to his arrest. Now she was married to Topcliffe's young apprentice, Nicholas Jones. As she stepped up to the witness stand and testified how she had been taught to equivocate – to lie – by Southwell, he hung his head, crushed. How, shouted

Topcliffe, could any man or woman believe a word a priest said if he spread a doctrine of deliberate falsehood? The jury took fifteen minutes to find him guilty and sentence was pronounced.

Shakespeare knew, however, that the Queen and her Council were rattled. A week ago, Father Southwell had languished unremarked in his Tower cell. Now his name was on everyone's lips and the whole of London would be there to see him brought to his doom. It would be a huge spectacle and one that would not show the Queen or her government in a good light.

'Well, John, what was your reply to the Jesuit's request?'

'I said I would seek her, Sir Robert.'

'Did you so?'

Cecil stretched his aching neck. He was a man of small stature, with a slight hunch to his shoulder that he tried in vain to disguise by altering his posture. These days, he was increasingly exhausted by the burdens of state. His bed called out to him, but as long as the Queen was awake, so must he be.

'And do you think you have the time for such trifles? Do you not think we have rather more important matters to contend with?'

Shakespeare knew that he did. Listening to informants such as Garrick Loake, for instance. But he said nothing. He and Cecil both knew that his work as chief intelligencer left him little enough time to hunt for a maddened girl who could be anywhere, or dead. How could he find room for such a quest when the threats from the Escorial Palace of Spain and the Vatican increased day by day, when plots to kill the Queen were a constant threat, and when King Philip had made no secret of his plan to avenge the Armada defeat of the year eighty-eight by sending a yet greater war fleet against England?

'Well,' Cecil said, the curtness of his tone beginning to dissipate, 'Her Majesty awaits you, so let us hasten to the Privy

Chamber. The sooner this is done, the sooner I shall slumber. Come.'

With Clarkson and another retainer following them, the two men walked out into the inner quad. Shakespeare glanced up at the vast turreted confection that enclosed the night sky. They mounted a flight of steps to the hall, then traversed an ante-room, past the guards and into the Presence Chamber. A group of courtiers and petitioners watched them with tired, drunken eyes and, spotting Cecil, bowed low.

Cecil did not acknowledge them. He knew them well; they all had suits to press on him and he did not wish to hear them. He and Shakespeare marched on towards the Privy Chamber. Two liveried Lifeguards with raised swordpoints stood at the door but moved aside at the sight of Cecil.

Inside, the Queen was playing at cards with three of her gentlewomen beside a hearth of fragrant, slow-burning ash logs. She waved her companions away and they vanished like prodded ants into adjoining chambers.

Shakespeare and Cecil dropped to their knees, hung their heads low and waited. Without haste, Elizabeth approached them, holding out her white-gloved hand to Cecil. He kissed it. 'You are not a nighthawk, cousin,' she said, then touched his shoulder to raise him up.

'Indeed I am not, Your Majesty.'

She held her hand out to her other visitor. 'And you, Mr Shakespeare, we bid you welcome.'

Shakespeare, likewise, kissed her hand and then was raised up by her touch. He bowed again. 'Your memory is as faultless as your beauty, ma'am.'

They had not met in many years, but he knew well enough how she liked to be flattered, even by her most lowly subjects.

She recoiled slightly at the sight of his unkempt appearance.

'You look like a farmer, Mr Shakespeare.'

He bowed yet again. 'Yes, Your Majesty.'

'The hour is late and Sir Robert yearns for his bed, so tell me straightway about Mr Southwell. Is he still set on his course of self-destruction?'

'Yes, ma'am. But he wishes you to know that he honours you and considers himself a true and loyal subject. I believe he intends saying as much at Tyburn in the morning.'

'If he is my loyal subject, why did he come into England secretly, as a traitor?'

'He says he wished to bring comfort to those of his faith and meant no harm to you or your estate.'

Elizabeth tilted her head back, then looked at Cecil. 'What do you say to this, cousin?'

'He calls us heretics, ma'am. He would not defend you against the armies of the Pope. He is a traitor.'

'And yet . . .' She sighed, then looked again at Shakespeare. 'Please continue. I am sure you have more to tell me.'

He had half expected to find her in her nightgown and cap. But though it was late at night, the Queen was immaculate in a gown of gold threads and pearls. Her red wig was fixed as evenly as possible and her face was thick-coated with white powders. She would not let her guard down before any man, be it distinguished statesman or mere intelligencer. He had been expected.

Although he towered over her, he felt stiff and awkward under her falcon gaze. He repeated all that Southwell had told him about Thomasyn Jade. The Queen listened in silence until Shakespeare had ended his tale, then turned once more to Cecil.

'I believe I recall the story of this young woman. Cousin Susan was most distressed when she disappeared. I think we must find the girl. Is that asking too much?'

'No, ma'am. If she is there to be found, we will find her.

Mr Shakespeare will set one of his intelligencers on to the matter.'

'I had thought Mr Southwell had particularly asked for Mr Shakespeare. Should *he* not do the searching rather than some underling?'

'Mr Shakespeare is mighty occupied protecting the realm, ma'am. We have reason to fear conspiracies in the offing.'

A spark of irritation flickered in Elizabeth's bloodshot eye. 'Little man, we have retained the love of our people these thirty-six years of our reign by caring for the smallest and most humble as well as the great. If the people did not rest assured of our special love towards them, they would not readily yield such good obedience. There is none in the realm of greater importance to us at this time than this Thomasyn Jade. Is that plain?'

'It is, ma'am. And we shall keep you informed, as always, of Mr Shakespeare's progress in the matter.'

'And you, Mr Shakespeare. You will go to Tyburn on the morrow and ensure that Mr Southwell does not suffer unduly. You know what that means?'

Shakespeare bowed low. He knew what the Queen meant.

Chapter 4

S HAKESPEARE WAS EXHAUSTED. After leaving the Queen's presence, he rode back to London and slumped into his bed at Dowgate. But, unable to sleep, within two hours he was up and riding out to Tyburn with his assistant, Boltfoot Cooper, to ensure a position close to the scaffold.

The green at the execution site was already crowded long before dawn, which was the time that Robert Southwell would be taken from his cell at Newgate. Outside in the cold air, the horse would be waiting, harnessed to a hurdle of wood, on which the Jesuit would be tied, his head sloping down to the rear so that every jolt of the journey to death would bring agony to his back, neck and head.

And so the procession would begin, watched by crowds all along the way: across the dirty floodwaters of the Fleet, then uphill towards Holborn, through the fields of St Giles and on to the long, muddy highway that travellers took to Oxford. Southwell's journey would stop here, at Paddington Green.

A bellman rang out the hour. Six o'clock. Shakespeare knew that Southwell would not have slept.

'You know what to do, Boltfoot?'

'Yes, master.'

Shakespeare looked at his squat assistant and wondered about his terse, grunted reply. He was uncommonly abrupt this day, but perhaps he had reason to be; he was being asked to perform a task that no man could enjoy. Shakespeare considered explaining himself to Boltfoot, telling him why it would not be politic to do the deed himself, but he held his tongue. Boltfoot understood such things without need of explanation.

Shakespeare put a sixpence in his hand. 'Fetch us possets, Boltfoot. I saw a seller a little way off to the west.'

Boltfoot took the coin and limped off into the crowd to fetch the warming spiced drink of curdled milk and liquor. Anything to keep the chill at bay. Soon, he returned with the possets and they drank in silence. The morning was crisp and fresh. By now, the procession would be on its way.

The wait seemed interminable until, at last, a murmur arose in the crowd. The throng surged forward. Shakespeare sensed danger. There were screams and moans as men and women struggled to maintain their footing in the deadly crush. In the distance, Shakespeare saw the horse dragging Robert Southwell on the hurdle. It halted, unable to pass through the crowds. The sheriff ordered in a squadron of pikemen to clear a path, and the procession of death moved on.

Shakespeare was in the front rank, within a few yards of the scaffold, among the noblemen and city aldermen who had come to witness the traitor's execution. A few yards away, he recognised Lord Mountjoy. The Earl of Southampton was there, too. Shakespeare knew his open secret: like several other nobles, he was a crypto-Catholic. The whole court knew it, but nothing would ever be done about it. Common men and women might die for harbouring priests, but the earl could keep a dozen of them at Southampton House and never once have his peace disturbed by the dread knock of Topcliffe and his pursuivants.

The buzz and roar of the crowd grew louder. Someone

called out a paternoster. Shakespeare knew there would be seminary priests and Jesuits here in this press of bodies, all praying for Southwell's soul and, all the while, hoping to catch a thrown cap or a shred of clothing from the condemned man. The merest drop of spittle or blood could change a man's life. Henry Walpole had told his questioners that he had decided to become a Jesuit missionary after watching the execution in 1581 of Edmund Campion and being splashed with his blood. Now Walpole awaited his fate in the Tower, broken by Topcliffe's torture.

The hangman untied Southwell from the hurdle and hauled him up into the back of a cart. The Jesuit looked around at the ocean of expectant faces. His eyes met Shakespeare's, but then Southwell looked away. Was he searching for some face he knew, perhaps his father or a sister, or a fellow Jesuit?

Without ado, the hangman turned his attention to the condemned man's clothing and began to loosen the ties of his doublet.

'May I speak to the people?' Southwell said in a clear voice.

The hangman stopped his work and stepped back. 'Yes, speak if you will.'

The huge mass of people hushed. A baby cried and a dog barked, but no one said a word. Every eye with a view was trained on Robert Southwell.

A man shouted out: 'Hang him and to hell with him. The devil awaits the foul traitor.'

Shakespeare recognised the voice. It was Richard Topcliffe, standing at the far side of the scaffold by the cauldron into which the condemned man's bowels and heart would be tossed. Beside him stood several of his black-clad pursuivants. When the crowd hushed him, he spat into the ground.

Southwell ignored the interruption and began his speech. He had had many years to prepare these words. He told the crowd that he never intended harm to the Queen and that he had always prayed for her. But his message was not untrammelled, for he made clear that he prayed for her to be brought to the righteous path – the path of the Roman Church.

'And lastly, I commend into the hands of Almighty God my own poor soul. This is my death, my last farewell to this unfortunate life, and yet to me most happy and fortunate . . . I hope that in time to come it will be to my eternal glory.'

Topcliffe's voice raged out again. 'He has not begged pardon of the Queen! He has not begged pardon for his treasonous crimes!'

Southwell rocked back and forth. For a moment, Shakespeare thought he would crumple and faint, but he held firm. In a voice that seemed to say, *I am tired of this life, it is time to go*, he spoke yet again: 'If I have offended the Queen with my coming to England, I humbly desire her to forget it, and I accept this punishment for it most thankfully.'

And then he called on any Catholics present to pray with him, so that he might live and die a Catholic in the presence of members of his faith.

Topcliffe jumped up on to the scaffold and scowled out into the crowd. His hair was as white as the frost, but his eyes were hot with fury, daring any Catholic to defy him. He tapped his silver-tipped blackthorn cane on the wooden deck of the death place, looking for dissenters.

The hangman moved forward and removed Southwell's doublet, then pulled back the collar of his shirt. Without bidding, Southwell put his head into the noose. He called on the Mother of God.

'Blessed Mary, ever a virgin, and all you angels and saints assist me. *In manus tuas, Domine commendo spiritum meum . . .*'

There was no hood. Shakespeare saw no pain in his eyes, only an insistent love and a longing for death.

Topcliffe slapped his stick against the side of the cart and the butchers dragged it forward, leaving Southwell swinging and kicking at air. The only sound was the creaking of the rope and the breeze. Southwell hung there, choking, his neck unbroken. Topcliffe moved towards him, knife in hand to cut the rope and bring him, still alive, to the butchers' platform so that he might be forced to watch his own evisceration. But Boltfoot Cooper and Shakespeare were already there. Boltfoot clasped the dying man's body and clung to it, dragging it down to shorten his suffering by hastening death. Shakespeare stood in Topcliffe's path.

'Get out of my way, God damn you, Shakespeare, or I will slit you with this dagger.'

Now Lord Mountjoy was at Shakespeare's side, then they were joined by more noblemen, all standing firm against Topcliffe. A man from the crowd stepped forward and assisted Boltfoot in his act of mercy, choking the life out of Father Southwell until he hung lifeless in their arms. They let him go and he swung, unresisting, in the cold breeze. Quite dead.

Shakespeare stood back. 'He's all yours now, Topcliffe. He is gone way beyond your cruelty, I pray to a better place.'

He looked at the frothing torturer with incredulity. He knew he was cruel and brutal. What he had not understood was quite how deranged Topcliffe had become by the gallons of blood that had washed through his fingers. *This man should be locked away among the mad and the dangerous.*

Topcliffe cut the dead body from the hanging tree and brought it to the platform, where he attacked it with insane ferocity, slavering as he dragged out the entrails. He snatched the axe from the headsman and began chopping the flesh into quarters.

At last he held up the once-beautiful head and shouted, 'Here is the head of a traitor!'

The crowd was supposed to shout back, 'Traitor! Traitor!' But they remained silent. Only the wondering Lord Mountjoy had anything to say, bringing his mouth close to Shakespeare's ear so that no one else should hear.

'I cannot answer for the Jesuit's religion, Mr Shakespeare, but I wish to God that my soul may be with his.'

Jane Cooper held little John in her arms outside the old stone house in Fylpot Street. The boy was two now, and could walk, but he was sickly and weak. She looked down at him, listless in her arms, and mouthed some words of prayer.

Summoning up all her courage, she banged on the door. Boltfoot had forbidden her to come here, calling it a place of magic and necromancy, and declaring they should have none of it. Well, that was fine for him to say, but he had no ideas of his own how to help their son. Anyway, her friend Ellen Fowler had sworn that Dr Forman, who lived in this house, could cure any ill known to man.

'I don't know how he does it, Jane, honest I don't, but I promise you that he makes things right. *Whatever* ails you. I'd go to him with the pestilence if I had it, and I'd hope to be saved.'

Jane banged on the door again. A boy of about thirteen answered it and glared at her. 'He's busy. You'll have to come back.'

'When? When can he see me?'

The boy ran his nail-bitten fingers through his straggled hair, and then scratched the front of his grubby hose. 'When he's free.' He went to close the door, but Jane pushed forward.

'No. I've come this far. I want you to tell him I'm here. Then *he* can tell me to go away if he wishes.'

The apprentice spat into his hands and slicked the hair back from his forehead. 'Wait here. Don't come in. He don't like to be disturbed when he's about his business.'

Was there something lascivious about the way the boy studied her? She never even considered her looks these days. All her thoughts were for others: little John, of course; getting food to the table for the master and his children; keeping an eye out for the new girl, Ursula Dancer. Anyway, she had no looking glass. Boltfoot Cooper loved her but he would never tell her she was pretty or any such thing.

The apprentice wandered off upstairs, taking his time, glancing back. After a few minutes, he returned.

'He says he'll see you in a quarter-hour, when he's finished with Janey. He says you can come in, wait here in the hall.'

'Thank you.'

'I'm John Braddedge. You can tip me a farthing for my trouble.' He held out his hand.

'Maybe after I've seen Dr Forman. Not before.'

He nodded to a table by the window. 'Go over there then.'

She went and sat down. Baby John began to cry and she rocked him gently.

The Braddedge boy stood and watched. 'Shall I get him a beaker of milk?'

Jane shook her head. 'No, thank you.'

She heard footsteps on the stairs and looked up. A woman about her age was coming down, clutching the railing. Her head was bowed and Jane thought she might be crying. She stood up and went to her and asked if she could help.

The woman looked up; she wasn't crying, but nor did she look happy.

'Jane Cooper, meet Janey,' the apprentice said. He laughed, as though he had made some sort of jest.

Janey glared at him. 'Go and geld yourself with a blunt knife, Braddedge.'

From upstairs, there was a call. 'Boy! Come here!'

Braddedge slunk off up the stairs.

'Never mind him,' said Janey. 'He's as daft as a dawcock. Been with Dr Forman these six months and won't last another six.' She looked at the bundle in Jane's arms. 'You here about the child?'

'Yes . . . and other things.'

'What ails the mite?'

Jane shook her head and felt the prick of tears. She couldn't bear it if anything happened to him. The way things were going, she'd never have another baby.

Janey put an arm around her. She wasn't pretty and she had wary eyes, but Jane saw kindness there.

'I'm frightened, that's all. He won't eat, nor drink more than a thimble-full. He's wasting away. Just lies there, day by day. Boltfoot – that's my husband – says all will be well, but I know that he don't really think that. Dr Forman's my only hope . . .'

Janey peered into little John's face. 'He's a fair little thing, isn't he? Does he take after you or your man?'

Jane laughed. 'Me, God willing. His father looks like the stump of a tree. But, pray tell me, will Dr Forman help us?'

'Most like. He's a good man in his own way, but you be careful with him, Jane Cooper, because you're still a pretty enough lass and if you let him, he'll have his hand up your skirts and his prick out before he's asked you your name.'

Jane was shocked. But then she recalled the curious glint in Ellen Fowler's eye and remembered that what ailed Ellen most was the lack of a man in her bed.

'Mistress Cooper, he'll see you now.' The boy had reappeared on silent feet. He handed a package to Janey. 'And this is your philtre. He says you know all about it.'

Janey ignored the boy's begging palm and smiled at Jane. 'Just tell him to keep his dirty hands to himself and he'll leave you alone. Good fortune with the babe. I'm sure all will be well.'

Simon Forman sat at a table and wrote down the names of Jane, her husband and son, then began to ask her questions. How long had the child languished? Could she still produce milk of her own? When did she last have marital relations with her husband? Did either of them have the pox? Then he wrote down the date and hour of the babe's birth and her own, as far as she knew it.

Jane's hands were shaking. Dr Forman was a thickset, hairy man with a wiry beard that went from yellow to red. She was alarmed to discover that they were in his bedchamber. The canopied four-poster had rumpled sheets as though it had recently been occupied. Her eyes flicked from the strange man to the bed and back again.

And yet despite his alarming appearance, she gradually found herself at ease with him. Soon she was answering the most intimate questions about her monthly flowers and her bedtime activities, with and without Boltfoot, with complete honesty. These were not normally subjects she would discuss with her own mother or sisters, nor any other woman on earth – and certainly not with a man.

'Now hand me the boy.'

John was still whimpering. Jane put him in Simon Forman's hairy arms. He was very gentle, stroking the hair back from the boy's forehead with the tips of his fingers. John's crying subsided a little and he opened his eyes wide, fixing them on the stranger's face.

'Don't fret about the boy, Mistress Cooper. You have come here about another matter, have you not?'

Jane's face reddened. How did he *know* that? She nodded.

'Why not tell me? I may be able to help.'

She hesitated. He waited. At last she nodded and spoke what was on her mind. 'I want another baby, Dr Forman. I am scared I'll lose little John and never have another.'

'You won't lose little John, I promise you. I have often seen children in this poor way and I have never lost one. I shall give you a tincture of herbs for the boy. But it's *you* that I'm most worried for, Jane Cooper. Have you had many shifts?'

She closed her eyes and looked down. 'I have miscarried six,' she said quietly. 'Maybe seven. The last one just three months past.'

'Does your husband know?'

'He knows of the shifts, though not all of them. I cannot truly tell him all my fears. We lost our first at birth and I thought Boltfoot would die of torment. He blames himself, you see, because he is lame with a club-foot. He believes it is his bad blood that damages the unborn babes.'

'So you want me to help you bring a babe to term.' Forman spoke slowly. 'And are you presently with child?'

'No.'

'Well, the first thing I must do is cast your chart. It would help, too, if I could have the date and time and place of your husband's birth so that I may cast his, too.'

Forman smiled and handed the child back to his mother. He walked through to an adjoining room. Through the open door, Jane could see strange objects on shelves. Large glass jars and small vials, like those to be seen at the apothecary's shop. There were other curious things: rolled papers and parchments, books, something that looked like a dead animal or a demon. She averted her eyes. Her heart was rushing like the conduit.

Forman returned and handed her a twist of paper. 'Take this in the evening and again tomorrow morning, then return to me in four days. All will be well, Jane Cooper.'

Chapter 5

John Shakespeare surprised himself. He was hungry. On the way back to London from Tyburn, he and Boltfoot stopped at a busy post inn, sat in a booth and tucked into sirloins of beef that overlapped their trenchers, with half a loaf each of manchet bread. They ate it all and downed quart tankards of strong beer.

They did not talk. What was there to say? Instead, they just ate, drank, pissed in the gutter outside, then remounted and rode for Dowgate. Their morning's work was done. As commanded by the Queen, they had ensured that Robert Southwell had not suffered unduly.

Back at Dowgate, Shakespeare asked whether he had had any visitors, but no one had called. He tried to shrug it off. So Garrick Loake was a time-waster. And yet there had been a quiet desperation about Mr Loake that worried him and he resolved to seek him out when time permitted. For now, he ordered a fresh horse saddled up, then went to his chamber to wash the grime and dust from his face and hands. Perhaps, too, he was trying to wash away the memory of the brutal, unnecessary death of a poet.

He found his daughter, Mary, and his adopted daughter, Grace, in the schoolroom with their tutor. Grace was growing into a fine girl. She was twelve years of age, tall like her brother,

Andrew, but slender. She held little Mary's hand and stroked her hair, as if she were the smaller girl's mother.

Shakespeare gazed on them for a few moments and said a silent prayer of thanks to God for this calm sanity and kindness at the centre of his life. Then he kissed them and left for his meeting with Cecil.

Cecil's mood had not improved. The Queen had kept him with her until the early hours and when, at last, he had been freed to go to bed, he had plainly not slept well. This morning he had risen with the dawn to ride for London.

'You will make the obvious inquiries, John,' he said to Shakespeare, waving him irritably to a chair. They were in the high-ceilinged meeting room of Sir Robert's small mansion in the Strand. 'Talk to the Countess of Kent, find the others who were subjected to these exorcism rituals, find any priests who were at Denham House. Go through it by rote. Take two days, no more. If you have not discovered the fate or where-abouts of this Thomasyn Jade within forty-eight hours, then you will say she is believed dead and the investigation will be forgotten. Dropped like a stone into a well, never to be seen or heard of again. Is that understood?'

Shakespeare nodded.

'And you, Frank.' Cecil turned to Francis Mills, the other senior member of his intelligence staff. 'Take a close look at this.' He slid a paper across the table. 'I do not pretend to understand what this is about, but, in John's absence, you will put your mind to it. Is that understood?'

Mills took the paper. Shakespeare watched the tall, hunched figure as he read the document. Preoccupied by his wife's infidelity, Mills seemed thinner and more haunted than ever. Word had it that his neighbours had taken to jeering at him. Cuckold's horns had been nailed up above his front door; Mills had not even had the energy to tear them down.

'That letter was seized by a searcher at Gravesend,' Cecil said. 'It was among the belongings of a mariner who died of the bloody flux aboard a carrack named *The Ruth*, returned from Bordeaux. No one knows for whom it was intended. The letter was concealed and would not have been found, had the courier not died. You look at it, too, John.'

Shakespeare took the paper from Mills. It was written in English.

'*Be strong in faith, Father. The plan is advanced, and you must only be patient. We will come to you, that between us we may rid England of Satan's seed for ever. With the love and righteous vengeance of God, the demons will be cast down with raging tempests and torrents of rain. Like the flood of old, we shall sweep away the rotten House of Tudor and all that dwell there. Be ready to play your part. Yours, in the love of Christ our only saviour and Gregory, great England's truest friend, this twenty-third day.*'

'It is the hand of Robert Persons,' Shakespeare said without hesitation. 'I have seen enough of *his* letters and writings.'

Suddenly, Cecil was alert. 'Persons? You are certain?'

'Never more so. And the reference to Gregory might suggest Seville, the Jesuit college of St Gregory.' As he spoke, a hot shiver seared into Shakespeare's blood. Garrick Loake had mentioned the College of St Gregory.

'And from what we know, Persons has been in Seville much in recent months,' Cecil continued.

Mills took the paper back and cast his eyes over it again, but Shakespeare was not sure he took in what he saw. The man appeared to have little enough mind left to don doublet and hose of a morning, let alone inquire into important matters of state. This letter should be Shakespeare's task. The Thomasyn Jade affair had arrived at a most inopportune time.

'Frank, are you with us?' Cecil said sharply. 'It is as if you were in another county!'

Mills closed his eyes, then opened them and nodded to his master.

'You understand what the missive is saying?'

'Yes . . . I agree with John that this is the hand of Persons. But the implication is not clear. Perhaps it is encoded.'

'That is possible, of course, but even without encryption, we can see murderous intent: "sweep away the House of Tudor". There is no ambiguity there. Are they talking about another Armada? Is this a call to the Catholic faithful to be ready to rise up when the invasion starts? We know King Philip is preparing a new war fleet. Or is this something else, something more specific and yet more sinister?'

'What could be worse than invasion, Sir Robert?'

'I don't know, Frank. That is for you to discover.'

'We can see that it is intended for a priest,' Shakespeare said. 'It is addressed *Father*.'

'There is Jesuit conspiracy here,' Cecil said abruptly.

Shakespeare grimaced. Cecil's surmise seemed not only possible, but highly probable. 'The number twenty-three, at the end, is interesting. That *could* be code. Why would Persons mark down the date of writing? I think he is revealing a date when something will happen. But which month? As for the mention of Gregory, that is exceedingly interesting. A man came to me last night, one Garrick Loake. He spoke of a plot emanating from the seminaries of Spain and mentioned the Gregory college. This is no coincidence. I will seek him out today.'

'Seek him out? Why is he not in custody?'

'On what charge? He was bringing me information, Sir Robert. He wants money – a great deal of money.'

Cecil rubbed his neck to ease the stiffness of his hunch.

'Well, we must hope and pray that he returns with the information. Promise him what he wants, then when he has told what he knows, give him its worth.'

'Very well.'

'And remember, the Jesuit college in Seville is a very hornets' nest of intrigue. The whole of that coast east of Cadiz is awash with traitors . . . The English trading community in Jerez and Sanlúcar, those men who stayed behind when the war began. Catholics to a man, many married to Spanish women.'

Shakespeare was thinking hard. 'One thing is clear, both from the hints Garrick Loake gave – if we are to believe him – and from the letter: the plan, whatever it is, is already known to somebody in England. This letter is merely to say that it is now confirmed and imminent, and that those involved should be prepared. Perhaps it was intended for Henry Garnett. He is the Jesuit superior in England – and he is still at large.'

'Keep an open mind.' Cecil scowled with exasperation. 'But are we getting ahead of ourselves?' He stabbed the paper with his right index finger. 'Perhaps there *is* some hidden code there. In God's name, John, I wish you had never mentioned the Jade girl to Her Royal Majesty. You must talk with this Garrick Loake before all else.'

Shakespeare said nothing. He had given his word to a condemned man. He would not break such an oath.

Cecil read his thoughts. 'As for giving your word to a Jesuit traitor . . . sometimes, I do wonder whether you are seduced by the devilish nature of these hellhounds. They call themselves the Society of Jesus, clothing themselves in Jesus's name, and yet they carry beneath their cloaks most unholy weapons of murder and treachery. They are all traitors, every one.'

Shakespeare said nothing.

Cecil did not press the point. 'The matter with Southwell is done and, soon, so will be the affair of Thomasyn Jade. In two days' time, John, you will take over the inquiry into *this* letter and follow up any leads that Garrick Loake gives you. Two days. That is the limit I will allow you. In the meantime, Frank, I desire you to make rapid progress. Examine the letter in great detail. Is there secret writing there? A code we cannot see? Do this, but also find out all you can about the dead sailor in whose box the letter was found. Is he linked in any way to Loake? Someone must know who he was. The captain of *The Ruth* is here in my hall, awaiting you. He will escort you downriver to his vessel. The crew has been held aboard. Get someone to help you, if necessary. Robert Poley perhaps – no, Anthony Friday would be better. He knows everyone. Get him into the Catholic cells and houses. Have him listen for whisperings. But no more than two marks a week. Is that understood? And you, John.'

'Yes, Sir Robert.'

Shakespeare hoped Cecil did not hear the wry note in his voice. Poley was untrustworthy and Friday was unreliable. How, he wondered, was it possible for Cecil to have hundreds of informants around the world, as well as two score or more here in London, and yet be unable to find sound assistance when he needed it? The service required more gold to train recruits in the art of intelligencing, as he had been taught by Walsingham.

'I would talk to you privately.' Cecil dismissed Mills with a curt nod.

Head hanging on his long, uneasy frame, Mills shuffled from the room, clutching the intercepted letter. To Shakespeare, he looked a broken man. Cecil closed the door and returned to the table.

'Who do we have in Seville, John?'

'One man inside St Gregory's. Real name Robert Warner. I do not know what name he is using there. Two merchants at Seville, one at Jerez.'

NEATH PORT TALBOT LIBRARIES

'Nothing from them?'

'Nothing unusual from the merchants. We hear of war preparations, the fitting of fleets for the Indies and a new Armada, but you have all those details. Nothing on this specific threat.'

'What of this Robert Warner?'

Shakespeare winced. 'I have not heard from him. In truth, Sir Robert, I have fears for him.'

'You think him turned?'

'I fear the worst.'

'I'm sorry.' Cecil paced to the window and back. 'And Frank Mills . . . what are we to do about him?'

'You know about his wife?'

'Indeed. But the slattern has been spreading her legs for years. What has changed?'

'His neighbours. They know all about it now and have been taunting him most grievously. Even the children in the street call him cuckold and make lewd gestures at him. He is not thinking aright.'

'No, and if it were not for this Thomasyn Jade, I would have him relieved of his duties. Yet for the present I cannot. I had dared hope that the welcome death of Cardinal Allen would give us some respite from these turbulent priests, yet this letter proves otherwise.' The young statesman shook his head in weary frustration. 'John, I have great fears for this year. We have left Brittany to the enemy, for our armies are needed in Ireland, which bubbles up. Tyrone is raging for a fight. Meanwhile our greatest captains-general are either dead or engaged on other matters. Ralegh has set sail on his errand to find the gold of Guiana, though unkind enemies at court whisper that he is hidden away, terrified, in a Devon cove. Drake and Hawkins have been given royal let to fit their fleets for some secret expedition. God's blood, is this a time for such ventures? I would have them confined to home waters, but I suspect Her Majesty sniffs Spanish gold. And she needs it, for I have here the figures spent in these last two years: two hundred thousand crowns on Essex's vain expedition to help Henri of France; forty-seven thousand, two hundred and forty-three on last autumn's foray into Brittany. The coffers are full of nothing but air, John.'

Shakespeare nodded. The only good news was that the King of Scotland had finally ceased vacillating and was levying armies to bolster England's defences against Spain. But when England seemed so vulnerable, it did seem a mighty curious time for Drake and Hawkins to be embarking on foreign ventures.

'I will send messages to all the ports, Sir Robert. We will double and redouble our efforts against the possibility of assassins or others sliding into England. The port searchers will hold anyone about whom they have the slightest doubt.'

'Good. And John, more than ever, I will rely on you and your war of secrets. Deal with this Thomasyn Jade gibberish in short order. We have not a moment to spare on such trivial matters.'

Chapter 6

SHAKESPEARE RETURNED TO Dowgate and remained there several hours, but Garrick Loake did not arrive. He told Boltfoot that if Loake came, he was to detain him, by force if necessary.

Furious with himself for ever letting the man go, he rode hard to the Theatre in Shoreditch, where Loake had claimed to be working. He spoke to his brother, but Will had not seen him, nor knew where he was lodged, and neither did anyone else.

'But fear not, brother, he is reliable enough,' Will said. 'He will come to you.'

'If he arrives here today, hold him at gunpoint and bring him to me.'

Will laughed. 'I do believe you are confusing me with one of your intelligencers.'

Shakespeare smiled. 'Forgive me. These are trying times.'

'For all of us.'

'Will, Garrick Loake told me you suggested he should come to me. What precisely did he say to you?'

'He said he had some intelligence of great importance to the realm. He seemed to believe it would be worth a lot of money.'

'Did he tell what that information was?'

'No. He told me nothing, only that he had it. I thought of you straightway.'

Shakespeare cursed. 'If you hear anything – anything at all – I beg you send word to me.'

'You know I will, brother.'

From Shoreditch, Shakespeare rode back south to London, seeking a once-great house just north of the city wall, in Barbican Street. He found what he was looking for, reined in and gazed up at the old stone mansion. None would have marked the place; it was ugly and neglected. He was not surprised by this, for the house belonged to the ancient Willoughby family and its air of austerity reflected the character of the present Lord Willoughby. Peregrine Bertie was known far and wide as a stern, fearless soldier and a severe Protestant with little time for material show.

Not that the earl was here at present. He was off on his travels, the way he had spent much of his life. Instead, his sister, Susan, the Countess of Kent, lived here and made do as best she could. Widowed by the age of nineteen, she was now married to Peregrine's impoverished brother officer, the equally heroic Sir John Wingfield. It suited her very well to use this great house, even though the hangings were threadbare and repairs remained undone.

A servant asked Shakespeare to wait in an ante-room and soon summoned him to the library, a homely room with tall shelves of books and a warm fire. Lady Susan was with four friends, all women, all close to the hearth. One sat on a settle with cushions, one on the floor, her arms about her knees, drawing on a pipe of tobacco. The other three stood. Shakespeare bowed to them, and then addressed Lady Susan.

'My lady.'

'Mr Shakespeare, what a pleasure to see you.'

'Forgive me for intruding. The footman did not tell me you had company.'

'Oh, take no note of these gossips, Mr Shakespeare. They are all worthless creatures with whom I idle away the hours in inconsequential chatter.'

'Might I have a word alone?'

'Do you have state secrets to impart to me?'

'Not exactly.'

'Then you may discuss whatever you wish in front of these ladies. We have no secrets between us. Husbands, children, affairs of state, philosophy and religion, all are as one in our little debates.'

Shakespeare looked around the gathering. He recognised three of the four women. One was the exquisite black-haired musician Emilia Lanier, the former courtesan of Lord Hunsdon. She was standing close to a yet more striking woman whom Shakespeare knew to be Lady Lucia Trevail, lady-in-waiting to the Queen. The dark-haired and matronly woman on the settle was familiar to him from court as the eminently sensible and witty Countess of Cumberland. The woman on the floor was the only one he did not know. She was younger than the others, probably in her mid-twenties, and sat gazing into the fire from beneath a mass of hair that tumbled across her forehead, all the while smoking her pipe. She seemed quite oblivious to their conversation.

'Come now, Mr Shakespeare. Anything spoken within these four walls is safe with us.' It was Emilia Lanier who spoke. 'Do we look the sort of ladies to spread tittle-tattle?'

Indeed, they did. Shakespeare smiled.

'You know, Mr Shakespeare, you need spare us nothing. We will not swoon at some horror you tell us, nor will our little minds be befuddled by matters of high politics, the sciences or exploration.' Lady Susan looked to her friends for approval.

'Do indulge us, Mr Shakespeare,' Lady Trevail said. 'We gather here to discuss matters of great weight . . . and mutterings of no import whatsoever. It would be such a diversion to hear a little of the world of intelligencing.'

'But you must know I am sworn to secrecy, madam.'

The Countess of Cumberland, on the settle, put a hand to her mouth and made a noise like a chicken clucking, which was evidently laughter. 'Oh, Mr Shakespeare, please,' she said. 'It amuses us to call ourselves the School of Day. Is that not droll?'

Lady Susan took Shakespeare's arm. 'Come, sir, you need have no fear of us. We are as able as any man on the Queen's Council to discuss great matters of state. Why, we were just talking of the succession. Who do *you* think should succeed to the throne when Her Royal Majesty finally succumbs to time's fell hand, as, certain, one day she must?'

'I have no opinion on such matters.'

'Oh, come, come, Mr Shakespeare. No one talks of anything else these days. You must know that this book late out of the Low Countries, Father Persons's *Conference about the Next Succession to the Crown of England*, is spoken of in every great house in London. It is said he favours the Spanish infanta.'

'Well, *I* would favour almost any man or woman above the wormlike little Scotch king,' Lady Trevail said. 'Even the monstrous Arbella Stuart who thinks herself a queen already would be preferable, for she must at least be pliable. Such a shame poor Ferdinando of Derby was not more careful about his venomous diet. He would have made a magnificent king of England, if a little proud.'

'And a little too Romish, perhaps?' Lady Susan said. 'Or what of my lord of Essex? Now *there* is a man with the stomach and bearing of a monarch. Nor must we forget the charming infanta. Father Persons assures us that young Isabella is of John of Gaunt's lineage.'

'And she keeps a dwarf,' the Countess of Cumberland said, adding with mischief, 'just as our own beloved Elizabeth does.'

Shakespeare looked at her sharply and saw the glint in her eye. He was well aware that 'Elizabeth's dwarf' was meant to be Sir Robert Cecil. This was dangerous talk. If it was intended to provoke him to discomfort, they were succeeding in their aim. So he was providing the ladies with their day's mirth, but they would do well to be more circumspect; there were many ears in England. The Queen had never been amused by discussions about her throne and crown, and she especially disliked to hear of the merits of *Spanish* claimants.

'Do you think it wise to talk of such things?' he asked politely.

'Are you afraid of losing your head, Mr Shakespeare?' Lady Trevail said. 'I had heard you were a brave man.'

Their eyes met and held. 'I do believe that courage without caution is foolhardiness.'

Lady Trevail clapped her delicately gloved hands.

'Mr Shakespeare,' Lady Susan said. 'I have no idea why you are here, but you are very welcome. At least take a sip of sack with us, for we would love to prise some secrets from you. Do you know all my friends?'

'Indeed, I have met Mistress Lanier and I recognise the ladies Trevail and Cumberland from court.'

'The young lady by the fire, who seems to be in a tobacco-induced dream, is Miss Beatrice Eastley, my young companion and protégée. Now then, Mr Shakespeare, be good enough to tell us why you are here.'

Shakespeare had little time. If Lady Susan would not see him alone, then so be it.

'Very well, my lady, let me be direct with you. I believe that some years ago, the year 1586 to be precise, you took into your household a young woman named Thomasyn Jade.'

The woman on the floor looked up and removed the pipe as though she would say something. Meanwhile, a frown of puzzlement crossed Lady Susan's brow, then her lips parted in surprise. 'Thomasyn?'

'You recall her?'

'Of course, Mr Shakespeare, how could I not? Do you know where she is?'

Shakespeare shook his head. All eyes were fixed on him as though he were a bear in the ring. 'I am afraid not, my lady. But I am looking for her. I had hoped you might be able to help me in this quest.'

'Thomasyn Jade,' Lady Trevail said, emphasising every syllable. 'Wasn't she the—'

'Yes, Lucia, she was the poor young girl who was subjected to such horrible torments by those egregious priests. The things they did to her were beyond hideous.' Lady Susan turned to Shakespeare. 'But pray tell me, why are you looking for her now? Do you believe her alive? To speak true, I feared that, in her insanity, she had run away with intent to destroy herself.'

'I regret I have no idea whether she is alive or dead.'

'But *why* are you looking for her, Mr Shakespeare?' Lady Trevail said. 'What interest can Sir Robert's chief intelligencer have in her?'

'I cannot say. Did you meet the girl, Lady Trevail?'

'Indeed, I did. And felt deeply for the poor thing.'

His eyes scanned the assembled ladies. 'Do any of you know where she might have gone?'

'I had believed her to come from Buckinghamshire, Sir George Peckham's seat,' Lady Susan said. 'For that was where these rituals took place. But, Mr Shakespeare, this is most unusual and mysterious. Can you not give us a little notion of the reason for this strange visit?'

'No, my lady.'

'But it is clearly important to you and Sir Robert.'

'Indeed, it is.'

The countess sighed. 'I have thought about her often and would dearly love to discover what became of her. Mr Shakespeare, I shall do all I can to help.'

'We will *all* do what we can,' Lady Trevail said, to approving glances and nods from the Countess of Cumberland and Emilia Lanier. Only the girl by the fire, Beatrice, did not respond, nor even seem interested.

Shakespeare bowed again. 'Thank you. In which case, Lady Susan, I would be grateful to hear all that you remember of her. Whom she met, whom she talked with.'

'She was not well, physically or in the mind. I offered her sanctuary, for she needed a safe and loving home to recover from her torments.'

A maidservant came in with a tray bearing wine and a goblet for Shakespeare. He took it with gratitude and sipped the wine, which was sweet and smooth.

'She was with us a week,' Lady Susan continued. 'I did not have her brought here as a servant, but as a pupil, just as I educated my friend Mistress Lanier here in her youth.' She nodded towards Emilia. 'It is the correct way, Mr Shakespeare. Girls need education as much as boys. Is not Elizabeth herself among the greatest scholars in the land?'

'Indeed, my lady, I do not need convincing. My own daughters are taught to a high degree.'

'Thomasyn had endured a great ordeal. But after four or five days, I truly believed that she was settling here and becoming more tranquil and serene. I thought she would fit very well into our household and that we would make a fine young lady of her, for she had wit enough.'

'But something happened?'

The countess gave a sad smile. She was remarkably well kept for her forty years and there was kindness in her eyes.

Shakespeare wondered why Thomasyn Jade had wanted to leave such a welcoming home.

'No, nothing happened. Not that I know of, anyway.'

'She disappeared on a day very like today, Mr Shakespeare,' Lady Trevail said. 'We were all here as usual, talking of poetry and music. Of course most of the talk in those days was of the Babington horrors and the exorcisms. Also the likely fate of Mary Stuart and the possibility of invasion. On any other day, that would have been our bill of fare, but we had too much sensibility to discuss treason and horror in front of the girl. The last thing she wished to hear was talk of executions and conspiracy.'

'How did she seem?'

'Agitated,' Lady Susan said. 'Greatly agitated. She asked to be excused from our presence, hurried from this very room and was gone. That was the last anyone saw of her. No one witnessed her leaving the house. She did not even go to her room to collect her few belongings.'

'None of the servants saw her leave?'

'No.'

'And what belongings did she leave behind?'

'We found her purse with two pennies and a farthing in it, a comb, and the night garments I had given her. That is all. She took nothing but the clothes she wore.'

'Can you describe her to me? Was she tall? Fair? Plump?'

'Mousy red, I would say,' Lady Susan said. 'Not especially pretty, but fair enough. She was thin, but I don't think she had eaten properly for weeks on end. She did not like to meet your eye.'

'She might look very different now,' Shakespeare said, musing aloud.

'Indeed she might, if she has recovered from her madness.'

The woman on the floor said something too. Her voice was

low and rough with smoke, and he could not make out the words. He leant forward. 'Miss Eastley?' he asked, hoping she would repeat her observation, but she did not.

He would have asked them more, might well have enjoyed passing the day with them, but he was learning very little and there was too much to be done elsewhere. He bowed. 'My ladies, I will take up no more of your time, for the present.'

Francis Mills accompanied Captain Roberts in the barge downstream to Gravesend. He asked little and heard almost nothing; his head was filled with crashing waves of noise, like an incoming tide on a pebble beach.

'Who was this dead mariner, Captain?' Mills asked, like a child repeating its numbers by rote.

'His name was Franklin Smith. He was an ordinary seaman. The ship's master, who you will meet on board *The Ruth*, says Smith approached him when we were in Bordeaux. He was looking to work his passage home. From what the master tells me, he was no more than a bilge monkey, useful for loading of goods or hauling of cables but nothing more. Lower than the rats in the scuppers.'

'And what is your cargo?'

'From Bordeaux? Wine, of course, Mr Mills. Well, here we are, sir.' The barge pulled into the quayside near the smoking chimneys and massed masts of Gravesend. Captain Roberts lifted his chin in the direction of a large carrack, at anchor with its sails furled, a little way from shore. 'And there she is, *The Ruth*. The sooner this is all over, the better. The men are becoming restive, penned in like livestock, and we must discharge our cargo. The investors will not allow another day's delay. Mr Mills? Mr Mills . . .'

Francis Mills did not move at first, but then rose from his bench seat and disembarked with Roberts, who hailed a ship's boat. Through the surging roar of his mind, it occurred to Mills that he really should have heeded Sir Robert Cecil's instructions and brought someone with him to help interview the crew of this vessel. Alone, it was a daunting prospect. No, it was impossible. He could not do it this day. He was not thinking aright. Not thinking right at all. He wasn't really here. He was in a bedroom, dank with lust and sweat and skin. There was a blade in his hand and he was wondering how it would slip through flesh.

Suddenly he was caught short of breath. He closed his eyes and grasped the captain's arm.

'Mr Mills, you do not look well, sir.'

He couldn't move. He felt his knees would give way and that he would fall. The rushing in his head was a storm. His breathing was fast and shallow. A pain assailed his heart. He bent forward and clutched at his chest. He was going to die; he knew he was going to die.

'Mr Mills . . .'

Mills turned and stumbled back towards the barge, still holding his chest, fearing his heart would burst from his body. He had to get home; he had to get back to London.

Chapter 7

'HE LOOKS A little better, Jane,' Boltfoot said, staring at his two-year-old son who lay in the small wooden cot he had made for the boy. 'Do you not think he looks more lively?'

'I do so think, Boltfoot. I pray it is so, leastwise.'

'And is he taking more food?'

Jane nodded. 'A little more.'

'Did I not tell you it would be so? We have no need for physicians and apothecaries with their unholy magic and conjuring of spirits.'

He might say such things, but Jane knew her husband worried even more than she did about the boy.

'Boltfoot Cooper, I do sometimes think the years you spent at sea turned your brain to pease pudding.'

Boltfoot smiled at his wife then leant into the cot and kissed the boy. He patted Jane on the small of her back and was about to take his leave of her and go in search of Mr Shakespeare, when she stayed him.

'Why is it that we never celebrate your birthday, Boltfoot? What day were you born?'

'You say my brain is turned to pease pudding, Jane. What of yours, to be asking such daft questions? I don't even know the year I was born, let alone the day.'

Jane let him go. How was she to discover the information Dr Forman needed to cast a chart if Boltfoot did not know it himself?

They were all living in cramped quarters, in the part of the house that had survived the fire of last year. There were still smoke-black marks on timbers, but the structure, close to the Thames at Dowgate, was sound enough. The part of the building that had been utterly destroyed had been cleared away and was already being rebuilt, from the ground up. This time the house would be smaller, with a larger garden and improved stabling.

Shakespeare looked up from his table, where he had been scribbling a note to Cecil, telling him of the meeting with the Countess of Kent and her circle. He would need to speak with Lady Susan again, and preferably without the distractions of her companions. He wished to learn more about her ward, the sullen Beatrice Eastley, too. Something seemed not quite right there. He would also welcome another meeting with Lady Trevail; but that was another matter.

'You summoned me, master?'

'Ah yes, Boltfoot. I take it there is still no word of Mr Garrick Loake?'

'No, master.'

Shakespeare cursed. The man had disappeared like smoke in air. Well, Loake would have to wait. He would add word of this in the letter to Cecil, and urge him to engage Anthony Friday to find the would-be informant. Friday was unreliable, but no one knew the world of players and playhouses better than he did.

Shakespeare turned back to Boltfoot. 'We are riding for Buckinghamshire. Have horses saddled.'

'Yes, master.'

'And Boltfoot . . .'

Boltfoot stopped. It seemed to Shakespeare that he had aged five years in the past few months since the fire. This latest sickness afflicting their child had only made matters worse.

'How does little John fare?'

'Better, master. Better.'

'Good. Well, if he requires remedies or if you wish him to be seen by a physician, I will bear the cost.'

'Thank you, Mr Shakespeare. I am sure we won't need that.'

'As you will, but the offer is there. And send Andrew to me, if you would.'

Shakespeare continued to write his note to Cecil. Within a minute his adopted son, Andrew Woode, appeared in the doorway.

'Andrew.'

'You wanted me, Father?'

'I had meant to talk with you at length this day, Andrew. But I must be away on Queen's business. For the present, I desire you to know that I have been considering your suggestion with great care and I have concluded that you are truly set on a seafaring life. So, yes, you may go with Drake and Hawkins with my blessing, if they will accept you. Mr Hakluyt's book *Principal Navigations* has much to answer for, I fear.'

Andrew beamed. 'Thank you, Father.'

'You should talk with Boltfoot. No man knows the hazards and joys of the sea better than he does.'

Andrew laughed. 'I have already spoken with Boltfoot. He thinks I am mad to even consider going with Drake on his voyage. He says he will rob me and treat me like a dog. Also, that I will die of scurvy if I have not first drowned or been killed by a Spaniard.'

'And you are not deterred? You may have the size and strength of a man, Andrew, and I know how brave you are, but you are still only fourteen years.'

Andrew walked forward and knelt before Shakespeare. He kissed his hand. 'The world is out there, beyond the western sea, and it holds my future. I am more certain of this than anything in my life.'

Shakespeare gazed down fondly at the boy he regarded as his own son. Andrew's short life had not been easy, and Shakespeare knew that he had considered his decision to go to sea with great thoroughness.

'Then God speed you, boy. And learn well. Master the astrolabe and quadrant, the hourglass, the compass and the chart, for then you will be a true mariner and indispensable to your captain. But that is for tomorrow. For today, I have an errand for you.' He folded the letter he had been writing and sealed it, then handed it to Andrew. 'Take this to Sir Robert Cecil for me.'

Regis Roag slid from the saddle in the noisy Plaza de la Magdalena. He had been riding since dawn, but he was still cool and his long, oak-brown hair was unruffled. With sharp, experienced eyes, he glanced around at the bustle of traders, the working men, the women scrubbing stone steps and the promenading señoras in their mantillas. All the time, he looked for the face that might seem out of place. As a hunter of men, he knew how to spot a predator.

There was warmth and the scent of orange in the evening air. Roag breathed deeply. Seville was a fine place. The magnificent buildings, the wide-open squares, the perfume of strange plants and incense, the many religious houses, the workers in gold: all spoke of a town created by God. This was the wealthiest city in the greatest empire in history – a world away from the mud, stench and squalor of lowly London, the city that had spat him out like a stone, and its dirty neighbour Southwark, the place of his birth.

Tethering his horse to the base of a palm tree, he composed a smile and pushed open the door of the four-storey, anonymous house that held the grand title of the College of St Gregory. It was an inadequate building for its purpose, a poor tenement wedged between a bakery with intoxicating aromas and a leather shop that exuded animal stench.

He recoiled at the noxious blend of stinks. This was no place for the training of young men in the disciplines of faith. The boys who came here from England needed to pray and meditate in quiet solitude if they were to return to their homeland as God's soldiers and to die as martyrs. Here, they were closeted together like sheep in a pen. In the high summer, they sweltered, with no relief from the cloying heat and the stale sweat of each other's unwashed bodies.

Even as he stepped inside, he sensed panic in the air. A boy, no more than eleven years of age, was scurrying past. Roag grabbed him by the shoulder. 'Where is Father Persons?'

The boy was wide-eyed. 'He is with Thomas Eaglet.'

'Where?'

'In the sickroom, at the back.'

'Take me there.'

A group of robed men stood around a bed. Roag instantly spotted Father Robert Persons among them. He was standing beside his assistant, Father Joseph Creswell.

Roag touched Persons on the shoulder. Slowly, he turned around and Roag saw that the priest's once-handsome eyes were deep and haggard.

Persons made the sign of the cross. '*Dominus vobiscum*, my son.'

Roag bowed, his mane of hair falling about his glowing face. '*Et cum spiritu tuo*, Father.'

'You have arrived at a most sad time, Mr Roag.'

'So it seems.'

'Thomas Eaglet is close to death.'

Roag looked beyond Persons to the shrunken figure curled up on the cot, laid on his side to minimise the pain. But it seemed Eaglet was already past such worldly cares. His shallow breathing was only just audible.

To Roag, the dying man's body looked like raw flesh on a butcher's counter. He gazed on the loathsome mess of meat with interest, nothing more. No skin was visible save on Eaglet's face and hands.

'How has he come to this state, Father?'

'He scourged himself with a flail. It is *white martyrdom*. That is what we will call it, but it is a waste. It is not true martyrdom. It will be the second such death at St Gregory's this year. Such things unsettle our other young men and boys.'

Roag nodded. More than the unsettling of the boys here, he realised that if news of the event reached England it would not reflect well upon the Society of Jesus. 'I will end his misery.' His hand went to his dagger.

Shock registered on Persons's face. He reached out and restrained Roag's hand. 'Indeed, you will not. God will decide the time.'

Roag removed his slender fingers from the dagger and said nothing more.

Persons shook his head. 'I am told young Eaglet and others have risen every midnight these two weeks past, to scourge themselves with the discipline in front of the Blessed Sacrament. They must be commended for such diligence in the mortification of the flesh, but Eaglet did not know when to stop. *Why* would he not stop? He has lost so much blood.' Persons suddenly steeled himself and touched the dying man's hand, one of the few parts of the body that still looked human. He turned to Father Chamberlain, who was acting as nurse. 'Has extreme unction been given?'

'Yes, Father.'

Persons walked across the room and picked up a heavy iron brace, studded with short spikes designed to dig into the flesh and keep wounds open, however rotten they became.

'He wore this, Mr Roag. The Lord only knows where he obtained it. We must all pray for his soul. He is a very brave young man. You know, when he first came here I doubted his faith, but he has proved me wrong.' Persons made the sign of the cross over the forehead and face of the young man in the cot, then turned away. 'Come, Mr Roag, let us go to my office.'

The room was austere. Nothing but a table, chairs and papers. Its only ornament was a gilded cross on the wall. A shaft of late sunlight lit the thin arm muscles of the crucified Christ.

'Is everything ready?' Persons asked. 'The ships arranged, the money all in place, your men trained?'

Roag had a youthful smile that would win over maidens and emperors with its easy charm. In his forty-third year, he could pass for a man of thirty, exuding warmth and confidence. 'All is in place.' He held up a scroll. 'I have the authorisation of the *casa*.'

The document bore the seal of the *casa de contratación* – the house of trade – whose absolute seat of power rested within the Alcázar royal palace and whose word was law in all matters of shipping and without whose authority no vessel might leave Spain.

Persons nodded. 'Good. Which just leaves the matter of the traitor. He is in the hands of the Holy Office. I shudder to think that we ever trusted him. I fear he will burn in this world and the next.'

A lazy tic fluttered in the parchment-thin skin around Persons's left eye. There was a softness about the priest, but he had a certain aura. His beard was short and neat, his eye clever and wary. He had an intimate manner that turned those he met into either devoted friends or dedicated enemies. Roag knew he was not given to squeamish women's ways, nor subject to doubts in matters of faith. Yet he could see that the prospect of burning live human flesh disturbed him, as though the stench would remain in his nostrils, like bitter wormwood, for all eternity.

'Men such as Warner make life difficult for us here,' Persons continued. 'And yet it were better it did not come to the fire.'

'Then we must make do,' Roag said evenly. 'I will go to the Castillo de Triana from here. I am sure I will have a hearing.'

Joseph Creswell, Persons' loyal assistant, sensed his superior's discomfort. 'Remember, Father, the holy doctor Thomas Aquinas himself concluded that execution by the secular authorities was the proper way to deal with heretics who refuse to be reconciled. First, excommunication from the Church and if, stubbornly, they refuse to recant, then by His law they should be excluded from life itself. The fire is God's hand.'

Persons nodded, but without conviction.

There was silence in the room. From outside came the shouts of Spanish traders and the thump of drums.

'Would you be a king, Mr Roag?' Persons said suddenly.

'Would you have me be a king?'

Father Persons smiled and folded his arms. 'Come, I will hear your confession now, before you embark on your great enterprise.'

Roag did not move. 'No, Father. I will confess when I return to you, for I know I must commit mortal sins in this holy war. I cannot yet cast off my coat of steel.'

'Do not imperil your immortal soul, Mr Roag.'

'No, Father.'

Creswell watched from a first-floor window as Roag untethered his horse and trotted eastwards towards the fish market and the bridge over the Guadalquivir. 'He is cold and mad,' he said, half to himself, half to Robert Persons who sat at the table behind him. 'He has no religion, only resentment.'

'He will carry out the task we wish, in the way we desire it.'

'Will he? Can we trust him that much?'

'Have faith, Joseph, have faith. After all, it is said he is the son of a king.'

'And do you truly believe he has royal blood in his veins?'

Persons shrugged his shoulders but did not reply.

Chapter 8

REGIS ROAG GAZED up at the Castillo de Triana. The stone walls were sand-coloured and warm, yet the overall impression was of dark foreboding. The fortress had been built on a massive scale to dominate the old Moorish town of Seville and to many people it was hell on earth, a huge cavern of pain and horror. Roag was not a sentimental man, but even he was struck by its grim power.

The castle stood on the western bank of the Guadalquivir river in the poorer quarter, where the old mariners and prostitutes, the manumitted slaves and beggars, scraped a living. It was the first sight of Seville to greet ships navigating up the olive-green waters of the river and it never failed to cast a gloom over the mariners' mood. For a hundred and fourteen years now, the building had served as the prison of the city's Inquisition. Countless men and women – mostly Jews, Moors and Lutherans, but also Catholics – had been brought here, accused of heresy and other crimes. Thousands had been tortured and hundreds had been handed over to the civil authorities – *relaxed to the secular arm*, as they called it piously – to be burnt at the stake. Those who repented, the fortunate ones, would be strangled by garrotte before the fire was lit.

Roag glanced back across the river to the fish market and, a little further south, to the splendid Torre del Oro. The tower of gold shimmered with warmth in the evening light, amid a tangle of shipyard masts and rigging. Turning back to the Castillo de Triana, the contrast was palpable. He entered through a great arch, next to the pontoon bridge, then dismounted and led his horse on foot. Roag was well known here and faced only peremptory questions from the guard. Striding across the outer courtyard, he passed a queue of black-clad and cowled men and women. He knew, from their furtive glances and the hiding of their faces, why they were there: they were informers, come to denounce enemies, neighbours, mothers or brothers, for gain or spite.

'She is a fornicator,' one would say in a shameless whisper; 'I have heard him lauding the Luther sect,' another would rasp, venom in her voice; 'I saw her place a crucifix on the ground, then spread her skirts, squat down and piss on it,' a scorned suitor would say, 'what is worse, she is a Jew.' And so those accused would be hauled before the Inquisitor, while the accusers slunk back into the shadows.

The malice here, amid the immense walls and embattled turrets, was almost tangible.

Roag was recognised by the gatekeeper, who showed him where to tether his horse, then admitted him through the heavy iron door. The would-be informers surged forward, but the gatekeeper pushed them back at the point of a pike and told them to wait for the prosecutor or his secretary. They were in Carmona with the Inquisitor-General, he said with a sneer. He did not know whether they would be here this week or the next. If the informers didn't want to wait, they could take their chances with the civil authorities and have their testimony passed on to the assessors.

Roag had enough Spanish to ask to be taken to the gaoler, a magistrate named Enrique Jorge whose serious face betrayed no laughter lines; it did not do to laugh. One woman had found herself incarcerated simply for smiling when the name of the Virgin Mary was mentioned during a sermon. The witness who denounced her called the smile a *sonrisita* – a smirk.

But though he dared not smile, Enrique Jorge was a likeable, well-fed man who clearly enjoyed his mutton, bread and wine. He also enjoyed Roag's company.

'It is pleasant to see you again, Señor Roag,' Jorge said. 'But it always surprises me when you come here. I know of no other man who enters these walls unpaid and of his own volition.'

Roag bowed his head. 'I am here to see Mr Warner. If you would take me to him, Señor Jorge, I would be happy to make a donation of gold to the Holy Office.'

Enrique Jorge shook his head and refused the money. 'That will not be necessary. First drink a little *chocolatl* with me, then we will go to Warner. He is chained and has the *mordaza* about his face, for he is like a brute beast without it, cursing the Inquisitor, the Jesuit college and even you. He uses words that no Christian could repeat.'

Roag and the keeper drank their exquisite beverage, sweetened with sugar and spiced with vanilla, then walked through the echoing halls of the prison.

Enrique Jorge threw open the door to the cell. Roag gazed in with distaste. It was cold, gloomy and damp. Water streamed down the walls and settled in puddles.

Warner, the only prisoner, lay curled on his mattress, a clamp across his mouth. His hands were manacled in front of him, and he was chained to the wall.

Roag turned to the gaoler. 'Would you remove the *mordaza* for me, señor. I must speak with the prisoner.'

'I cannot do that, Mr Roag, for it has been ordered by Don Juan de Saavedra, the Chief Constable of the Inquisition. We require tranquillity within these walls and Mr Warner has been a disturbance to the peace.'

Roag bowed. It would make no difference to him whether the gag stayed or not. He had all the information he needed: under torture, they had extracted his real name – Robert Warner – and he had confessed that he was a spy, sent by the office of Sir Robert Cecil to report back on the College of St Gregory. His fate was sealed.

'I understand. Perhaps, though, you would leave us a little while, for I must try this one last time to reconcile him. If I fail, then nothing is left but to pray for his soul and relax him to the secular arm.'

The gaoler bowed his grave, tonsured head, handed a candle to Roag and left the cell. Roag closed the door, put down the candlestick and went to sit on the mattress beside the prisoner, 'Are you afraid, Mr Warner?' he whispered. 'Do you have demons? Do not be afraid. You will not die in the fire. I will rid you of your demons.'

Warner's eyes were wide open. He struggled to speak, but the iron clamp prevented anything emerging but guttural, animal sounds from the back of his throat. In terror, he scrambled backwards, into the corner, away from Roag.

A needle glinted in the candlelight. Roag held it between the thumb and forefinger of his left hand. It was a long needle, three or four inches, sharp but strong. The sort of needle sail-makers used in their craft, the sort he had used as a child working in his mother's sail-loft in Southwark. Strong enough to pierce the heaviest canvas.

Roag smacked his right hand hard up into Warner's throat, just beneath the iron brace that encased his mouth and lower face. His hand caressed the throat.

'There is a demon in here, Mr Warner. I feel it moving, just beneath the skin. Its claws are fixed tight. It is inside your throat, hooked to you like a bat on a beam.' His voice was quiet, ice in the prisoner's ear.

In a frenzy, Warner tried to push Roag away, but the manacle and chains sapped his strength and he did not have the force to protect himself.

'It is this demon, Mr Warner, that has made you a tool of the heretics. It is this demon that endangers me.' Now Roag had the bright tip of the needle at the side of Warner's throat. 'Here, here is the devil, dug deep into your gullet. I think it is Beelzebub himself. Feel his sharp little claws and his ugly snout. He is here and I will do for him.'

A bead of white saliva flecked the edges of Roag's lips. His right hand smoothed Warner's lank hair. He smiled at him, kissed his forehead. His left hand stroked Warner's throat, at the side, just below the arc of the jawline, identifying and singling out the great vein that throbbed there. He slid the needle in, jerking downward to cause a jagged wound. Warner went rigid with the shock. His blood spurted out, across the mattress and the stone floor.

'Hush, Mr Warner, all is well. I am the seed of a monarch and I will protect you from Lucifer's sting. I have dealt the demon a mortal blow. He will die soon, and then you will be free of him for ever. Be still.'

In his mind, unspoken, words reverberated: *I can smile, and murder while I smile. I can smile, and murder . . .*

Roag went to the cell door and hailed the keeper, ordering him to fetch the gaoler.

The floor was sticky with a deep pool of blood. Roag had blood all over his hands but he had been careful to avoid it spoiling his expensive gold and black doublet. He held up his hands. 'I tried to stem the flow of blood, but the wound he made was too great.'

'Where did he get the needle?'

'You must ask the constable that, or one of your guards.

They should have searched him with greater care. One moment I was talking with him, attempting to reconcile him, the next he had the needle in his manacled hands. Before I could move, he was stabbing at his throat. He knew what he did.'

The gaoler looked at Roag with suspicion. 'What did you say to him? What happened in that cell?'

'I told him he was a disgrace.'

'Why should I believe this story?'

'Why should you not, señor? It is no difficult thing to conceal a needle. Who would not prefer the sudden stab of a needle to the lingering pain of the fire?'

For a few moments, the gaoler's gaze held Roag's, then he gave a brusque nod. 'Well, such things happen from time to time, and the inquisitors have a great deal too much work as it is. These Jews, these *conversos*, these Moriscos. I suppose it is one less for the fire. They can burn Mr Warner in effigy if they so wish.'

'Indeed, señor. Indeed they can.'

Chapter 9

Riding hard, Shakespeare and Boltfoot arrived at Denham House, near Uxbridge, in a little under three hours. The house was down a long track through overgrown woods. It was bleak and shuttered. So this, thought Shakespeare, was where the priests had wrought their evil. A dozen or more of them had found refuge here and had done unspeakable things for months on end in the name of their religion. It was no surprise that Father Southwell had trouble going easy to his death. But what had happened to the Peckhams, the owners of the house? And what had become of the unfortunate souls subjected to the exorcisms? Surely the local people must have known what was going on.

Shakespeare dismounted and approached the front door of the brick-built building. He hammered at it, more in hope than in expectation of a reply. The sound echoed, but no one came. 'Break open the door, Boltfoot.'

Boltfoot slid from his horse and unpacked an iron crowbar from his saddlebag, forced it into a gap near the lock and wrenched. The lock gave and the door flew open.

'The lantern.'

Boltfoot returned the crow to his saddle and unhooked the lantern, struck a light with his tinderbox and handed the lamp to Shakespeare. He pulled out his pipe, tamped in a wedge of tobacco, lit it and drew deeply, then waited by the horses as his master entered the house.

Shakespeare stepped in through the doorway and held the lantern aloft. The hall was large and empty of furnishings. No table, no settles, no hangings. He tried to imagine the exorcism services held there: a table in the centre of the room, with just one girl sitting there, bound, while priests and acolytes swarmed around, chanting their Latin gibberish, describing the demons in detail as they were cast out. Behind them, all the Catholics from the district would be gathered, to watch and wonder. It would have been some display; his own brother, Will, might have been pleased with such powerful theatre.

He walked through the echoing rooms of the shuttered house. There was nothing here but emptiness and a pervasive whiff of damp and rot. Certainly, there was nothing to give a clue to the whereabouts of Thomasyn Jade.

Back in the main hall, he spotted some writing on a wall and held the lantern up to read it. The strange words sounded like the names of demons. Hobberdidance, Modu, Succubus, Mahu and many more. Some scratched in ink, some scrawled in paint. He returned to the front door.

'Come, Boltfoot.'

They mounted up again. 'Did you note the gatehouse, master?' Boltfoot said.

'I did. It seemed as empty as this place.'

'There was a thin spiral of smoke behind it, as though a bonfire had been lit.'

Shakespeare nodded, recalling the scent of burning wood. 'Let us go there.' He handed the lantern to Boltfoot. 'Keep that lit; we may need it.'

They rode back along the track. Night was closing in and soon they would have to find an inn. The gatehouse seemed to be unoccupied but Boltfoot had been right: there was a bonfire, still alight. Shakespeare went to the back of the little house and lifted the latch on the door. It was unlocked and he entered. The gloom was pervasive, but the lantern showed him all he needed to know. There was a home-made coffer containing threadbare linen from another age, a single palliasse instead of a bed. Some bread, dried oats and a leather jug with a meagre mouthful or two of spirit at the bottom; a tallow rushlight, extinguished.

'Someone doesn't wish to be found, master,' said Boltfoot. 'Must have seen us coming and fled into the woods. Perhaps a vagabond or an outlaw.'

'Or a priest.'

Boltfoot stood at the doorway, surveying the woods for movement. They were vulnerable here, especially with the lantern illuminating them. A silent arrow from the trees, a musket-shot . . . they wouldn't even see their killer. Boltfoot unslung his caliver from his back and loaded it.

Shakespeare turned over the palliasse but there was nothing underneath, then he tipped the old linen from the coffer. He was about to put it all back in when he spotted a scrap of paper in the fold of a sheet. He picked it up and held it close to the lantern. It appeared to be a map, showing southern and eastern England. Certain towns were marked with dots: Norwich, Yarmouth, Lincoln, Wisbech, Bury St Edmunds, Canterbury, Sandwich, Winchester, Portsmouth, Weymouth. Beside each town there was a set of initials. He stuffed the paper in his doublet, then returned to the palliasse and felt carefully along its seams, but found nothing.

He looked up at the walls. A small recess caught his eye. On his toes, he could just reach into it. At first he felt nothing but dust, but when he stretched a little higher, his hand went further and touched something else, some sort of small jar or jug, set back deep into the wall. He could not get a grip on it.

'Come here, Boltfoot.'

Reluctantly, Boltfoot left his guard post. Shakespeare locked his fingers into a mounting stirrup to hoist him up. 'There is some kind of jar in there, Boltfoot. Bring it down.'

Boltfoot used his master's hands as a step-up and quickly retrieved the jar.

'There is something in it, master.'

Shakespeare smiled. He had a good idea what it would be. He was correct. It was money – a great deal of money.

'Come, Boltfoot, I think I know what all this is about. Let us take this jar. We will return here soon enough. First, we will go to the village.'

They found a room at the Honest Brew, near the square-towered church in Denham. The inn seemed to be the only place in the village with any warmth, yet there were few drinkers. Shakespeare and Boltfoot settled into a booth near the taproom's well-tended hearth. They would eat and drink and make some inquiries before taking to their beds.

The landlord brought tankards of beer to their table, soon followed by beef puddings and peas.

Shakespeare gestured the landlord to stay and talk, which he seemed happy to do for he was clearly not busy.

'Strangers are always welcome in my house. Times are hard.'

'I am sorry to hear that.' Shakespeare took out a sixpence and put it on the table. 'You might be able to help us,' he said. 'We wish to know of the Denham manor house. Does no one live there these days?'

The landlord stiffened. 'Who are you?'

'My name is John Shakespeare. I am on Queen's business. Does that worry you?'

The landlord laughed, but it seemed to Shakespeare that he was uneasy. With greasy fingers, he took the coin, thrusting it into his apron pocket. 'No, that don't worry me. What would worry me is if you were one of those demon-hunting priests come back to haunt us.'

'So you are not a Catholic?'

'No, that I am not.'

'I am from the office of Sir Robert Cecil and I would like you to tell me all you know of the house and what went on there.'

'Back in eighty-six, you mean? Those were ugly days. But, of course, it all came out at the time. Topcliffe, Justice Young and all the pursuivants moved in and cleared out the vermin. All been told before.'

'But I wasn't here, so tell *me*. Did the people of the village know what was going on at the house?'

The landlord pulled at his wiry beard. At last he nodded. 'I'm not saying I knew what was going on, but most folks knew all right, Protestants as well as Catholics. You understand that I never went to one of the exorcisms. But even if I had known – and, of course, I didn't – who would I have told? It was Sir George Peckham's estate, and he was sheriff of the county!'

'But he isn't there any more?'

'Crown property now, they do say. Lost all his money on one of those New World ventures. Seems he had ideas of setting up a colony for English Catholics there. I think he fell foul of the recusancy laws, too. Twenty pounds a time for non-attendance at the parish church. That'll ruin any man in short order. Peckham went deep into debt and the Queen's lawyers took the house from him. It's been shut up these five years.'

'And the gatehouse?'

'What of it?'

'Who lives there?'

'No one.'

'We have just come from there and found food. Bread no more than two or three days old, and a fire outside.'

'Someone passing through then, a vagabond.'

Shakespeare cut a wedge of pudding with his knife and pushed it into his mouth, all the time looking hard at the landlord. There was no reason to disbelieve him, and yet he did.

'Have I told you all you wish to know, master? I have work to do.'

Shakespeare shook his head and gulped down his mouthful. 'A few more questions, that is all. Did you ever know or hear tell of a girl named Thomasyn Jade?'

The landlord hesitated, averted his gaze, then stared into Shakespeare's eyes a little too long. 'Yes, I knew of Thomasyn. How could I not?'

'So you heard her story?'

'Yes.'

'But did you know her yourself?'

'Mr Shakespeare, this is all a long, long time ago. Should it not all be laid to rest? Must we plough it up like last year's topsoil?'

'What is your name, landlord?'

'Do you need my name?'

'If I am to write my report for the Queen and her Council, yes, I need your name. I need to be certain, too, that what you tell me is the truth, for it would not sit well with you to be discovered in a lie.'

Shakespeare caught Boltfoot's eye as he spoke. Boltfoot had his caliver on the bench at his side; now his hand went to it and stroked the ornate Spanish stock. The landlord saw the movement.

'My name is Swinehead, Augustus Swinehead.' The landlord glanced around the room. A customer was waiting to be served. 'Might we talk of this a little later, Mr Shakespeare? I pledge I will tell you all I know, for I have nothing to hide.'

'No, we will talk now. Sit down, Mr Swinehead.'

Reluctantly, the landlord sat down. Sweat was dripping from his brow. He brushed his hands down his beer-stained apron. Shakespeare noted that they were shaking.

Boltfoot lit his pipe from a candle and passed it to the man. 'Try that, Mr Swinehead. That's fine tobacco. That will soothe you.'

The landlord shook his head. 'I'll tell you who to talk with.' He looked across the room to a large man standing close to the kegs, as though he could not bear to be too far from the source of his ale. 'That's Goliath. He's Thomasyn's brother-in-law. His wife was Thomasyn's elder sister.'

'Thank you, Mr Swinehead.'

With Boltfoot limping behind him, Shakespeare strode across the taproom. The drinkers watched them with a mixture of hostility and fear.

'Mr Goliath?'

The man rose to his full height, his thick stack of hair scraping the beams. 'Who wants me?'

'John Shakespeare. I am from the office of Sir Robert Cecil. I am seeking Thomasyn Jade.'

Goliath was well named. Shakespeare was six feet, but this man was two inches taller, and brawny. He eyed Shakespeare and Boltfoot with disdain and spat into the sawdust. 'And what is *this thing*?' he demanded, indicating Boltfoot.

'Boltfoot Cooper, my assistant. And he does not take kindly to being called a *thing*.'

'Is that so? I could kill both of you before he got off one shot from his little musket.'

The big man looked for support from the other drinkers, but

got none. Despite Goliath's great size, Shakespeare had already reckoned him as all bluster.

'It will go easier with you if you cooperate.'

Goliath wavered, then nodded. 'Buy me a gage of beer, Mr Shakespeare, and I'll tell you what I know.'

'Let us sit down then.'

They went back to their booth. Boltfoot ordered the landlord to bring beer.

'Talk,' Shakespeare said. 'Tell me about Thomasyn Jade. I believe she was your wife's sister.'

'Yes, that is so.' Goliath rocked back and forth. His mouth was turned down at the edges and he seemed a long way away. 'That is so, indeed. My late wife Agatha was the best a man could have, but Thomasyn was always trouble. Got with child unwed and no one knew the name of the father.' He gazed around the taproom. 'Could have been any one of this lot.'

'Where is this child?'

'Thomasyn lost the babe in the sixth month, which was a mercy from God.'

'How did she become involved with the priests?'

'That was her mother's idea. When she heard what was going on up at the manor, she decided Thomasyn must be pos-sessed of demons, too. I heard there were thirteen or fourteen priests up there, and they were doing their demon-chasing through night and day. Like harvest time for the saving of souls, it was. Mother Jade marched the girl to the manor and left her there, prisoner of the popish fiends.'

'What happened?'

'You must have heard it all. They pricked her with needles all over and put relics inside her, God knows where, and gave her herb broths and burning brimstone that made her yet madder than she already was. Tied her to the chair and stuck her like a pig and burnt her with holy water and bones till she cried out in pain. I saw her spit out needles and pins, and I saw devils come crawling from her belly, clasping at her with their talons, like horned cats with no fur.'

The landlord brought the beer, avoiding Goliath as best he could. He was drenched with sweat.

Shakespeare tried to stop him. 'Mr Swinehead?' But the landlord scurried away. Shakespeare let him go. There must be a good few men in these parts who would rather not be reminded of Thomasyn Jade. He turned back to Goliath. 'So you saw these exorcisms?'

'I saw one. The priests let local people attend, mostly relatives of those to be exorcised, for they were after the catching of souls and they wished them to see their kin being saved. They were careful at first because they were worried that spies would come and report back to the Council, but it all came out of their control as more and more people from hereabouts went to gape and gasp. Great Catholic nobles and gentlemen from London and elsewhere, too. Many men – and goodwives – liked the exorcisms better than a hanging. It is to my eternal shame that I went even that once.'

'Why shame, Mr Goliath?'

The man drank half his beer and sat for a few moments, lost in his memories again. Shakespeare waited.

At last Goliath spoke, carefully, in measured tones. 'Though I am a big man, I must tell you that I was scared almost to the point of death by what I saw. You may doubt what I say, but I saw the demon run up her leg, under her skirts, and I saw her shiver with pleasure as it entered her. I tell you, Mr Shakespeare, I never went there again and nor have I missed a Sunday service at St Mary's ever since.'

Shakespeare lowered his voice so that no one beyond the booth could possibly hear him. 'Take me to the house where she lived.'

'There is no point. It's been empty since her mother died. No one will live there, for they believe it haunted.'

'Take me. Finish your beer and we will go.'

'Very well, if I must.'

They rose from the table, Boltfoot, too, but Shakespeare restrained him. 'Stay here, Boltfoot. Get sleep. I will go alone with Mr Goliath.'

Boltfoot nodded. He knew what to do.

Goliath picked up his beer and downed it in one long gulp. Stooping beneath the low ceiling, he trudged to the doorway. Shakespeare demanded a lantern from the landlord and went out on to the street. The track was slippery, making it difficult for them to keep their footing as he and Goliath walked warily past the church.

'Was it *you*, Mr Goliath? Was it you who went to the pursuivants to put an end to the exorcisms?'

Goliath's whole body shook. 'No,' he said. 'But I wish I had done so. It went on for many months. I should have done something sooner while there was still hope for the girl. But I didn't. I was a coward, you see, and a poor Christian.' He stopped before a bank of hovels set against the muddy road. Piles of horse dung clogged the path. 'There it is,' he said.

It was a tiny house, no more than twelve feet wide, and windowless. There was no front door, just a hole. Holding the lantern in front of him, Shakespeare stepped over the threshold. The yellow light threw strange shadows around the single ground-floor room There was nothing except rubble and dirt. It seemed to him that this whole village was composed of lightless empty houses, like a town after the plague had swept through – the echoing emptiness of the Denham manor, the eerie presence of the gatehouse and now this wreck of a hovel.

'What of the father?'

'Tom Jade? Died when Thomasyn was ten. Trampled to death by cattle.'

'They must have other relatives in the village.'

'No more. Look around you, Mr Shakespeare. The very heart has been ripped out of the place by what happened.'

'Someone must know where she is. She must have made contact with someone from Denham.'

'Not to my knowledge. I do not know where she is, which I will promise on the Holy Bible. I believe she has not been seen in Denham since the pursuivants took her away. If you were to ask me my opinion, I must tell you I believe her dead. Most likely by her own hand.'

Shakespeare would not let it go. 'On the way to Denham House, there is a gatehouse. Someone is living there. Could that be Thomasyn? Could she have come back here?'

Goliath creased his mouth down firmly. 'No. If there's anyone there, it must be a vagabond passing through.'

'That's what Mr Swinehead said.'

'Well, it's probably true, that is why.' There was an edge of frustration or anger in his voice.

'And yet I am surprised that the people in such a small village should not notice a new inhabitant with a fire and bread. Has bread been stolen – or has the baker been selling loaves to strangers?'

Goliath said nothing, just stood there, arms wrapped around his chest against the cold.

'So where, then? If Thomasyn is not dead, and she is not in the village, where might she be?'

Goliath sighed heavily. 'Who knows? Not me. But if you asked me to make a guess, then I would say she is probably in a stinking whorehouse, somewhere . . . or in Bedlam Hospital.'

*

Boltfoot bade the landlord goodnight and went to the allotted chamber. He closed the latch, listened a moment, then opened the casement window and clambered out as soundlessly as he could.

Dragging his left foot, he limped halfway around the building to the stableyard, where he hid behind a puncheon cask. He did not have long to wait. Augustus Swinehead emerged from the inn, ordering his customers out into the cold night air and home. A minute or two later, after they had all gone, Swinehead went back inside before re-emerging swathed in a heavy cloak. He looked around furtively before setting off at a brisk walk into farmland at the back of the building.

With no more than a sliver of moon to light his way, Boltfoot followed at a distance, just enough to muffle the sound of his soft-shod feet. But the task was simple enough, for he knew exactly where the landlord was going; ten minutes later, they arrived at the gatehouse to Denham House.

Boltfoot unslung his caliver and crouched in the undergrowth. Quickly, he primed and loaded the weapon. He had a clear view of the open doorway, thanks to the guttering glow of tallow indoors. Swinehead was in the house and there was someone else with him; he could not make out features, only shadows and yellow light. He heard a murmur of voices, though he could not discern words. He rose from his hiding place and walked forward, the butt of his caliver wedged firmly into his chest, the muzzle moving from side to side. Without hesitation, he pushed into the house.

Two pairs of eyes turned on him in shock and alarm.

'Be still, Mr Swinehead.'

Boltfoot's caliver swivelled from one to the other as he assessed the situation. Swinehead was unarmed; he was no threat. His companion was even less dangerous: a small, bent old woman, scarcely as big as a child of eight. Boltfoot lowered his gun.

'Who are you?' he demanded.

'No,' the old woman replied, her voice high but surprisingly firm. 'Who are *you* to come marching into my home?'

'Boltfoot Cooper. My master John Shakespeare has questions for you. And you, Mr Swinehead . . .'

Swinehead's shoulders slumped.

'Come with me,' Boltfoot said. 'Both of you.'

'And if I don't?' The old woman raised her chin in a way that spoke defiance.

She wore a plain black gown and it seemed probable to Boltfoot that she was a member of some religious order. He shrugged. 'Then I shall bind you and leave you here until I return with my master.' He turned to Swinehead. 'You, however, *will* come with me, or I shall shoot you dead.'

'Very well,' the woman said. 'I will come with you, too, though I have nothing to say to you or your master. Nothing at all.'

Chapter 10

SHAKESPEARE WAS SITTING on the bench in the booth, leaning against the wall with his feet on the table. He looked up as Boltfoot ushered Augustus Swinehead and the old woman into the taproom, then rose and walked over to them. He placed a hand on his assistant's shoulder. 'Well, what have you brought me, Boltfoot?'

'She was in the gatehouse. Won't tell me her name. Looks like a nun to me.'

'He is a man of great wit, your little fellow,' the woman said.

'Indeed he is.' Shakespeare stared at her. She was undoubtedly a nun and, from the tuneful timbre of her voice, he imagined that she might be Irish.

'She insists she will say nothing to you, but it occurred to me, master, that she could have been sent here by Rome and that she has entered the country illegally, which is counted high treason.'

'You may well be correct, Boltfoot. *Is* he correct, mistress?'

'I have never entered any country illegally in my life. I was here before this usurper came to the throne and I shall still be here after she has died and gone to hell, God willing.'

'What is your name?'

'And why should I answer your questions? Who are *you* to be inquiring of such things?'

Shakespeare turned to the landlord. The man was terrified. He knew what could become of those who harboured priests or those deemed traitors. 'What is this woman's name, Mr Swinehead?'

'Michael . . . Sister Michael.'

'Tell him nothing, Augustus. There is no crime committed so he has no power over you.'

Augustus Swinehead put his hands to his head and dug his cracked fingernails into his scalp. He could not decide whether to look to the woman or to his interrogator. 'Mr Shakespeare, please—'

'Now I ask you again, Mr Swinehead. Who is this woman and what was she doing in the gatehouse? If you answer honestly, it may go well with you. If you do not . . .' He left the other possibility hanging in the air.

The woman stepped forward and pushed Swinehead away. 'You are a poor sort of man, Swinehead. Will you lack courage like this at the judgment? If so, then I know which way you will be sent. Fetch me brandy and be done with you.' She turned to Shakespeare with a face of stone-hard loathing. 'Very well, I will tell you what you want. Swinehead says you want to know about Thomasyn Jade.'

The landlord produced a small cup of brandy, which the woman took from his quaking hand. She threw the contents down her throat. Shakespeare studied her more closely. Her black habit was crusted in dirt. She wore a common coif that had become as grey as the strands of knotted hair that protruded around her forehead and temples. He estimated her age in the region of sixty but realised he could be ten years out either way.

'Oh, I know all about Thomasyn Jade. When first I saw her there were more dirty, wicked devils in her than a hive has bees. But she was not a fool; she knew she needed our help and came to us willingly to have the demons cast out. Nor did she run away, even when her trials were hard and full of great pain. Six months she was with us and we worked day and night to free her with our prayers and supplications. Father Weston prayed on his knees all night every night. He was racked to the limits of endurance with the agony and his eyesight was failing, yet never did he cease to pray. Those months almost brought the father to his death from pain and exhaustion.'

Shakespeare was having none of it. 'She was brought to you against her will and you held her prisoner, just as you did with all the others. It was all a trick to convert those who witnessed or were subjected to your trickery and foul super-stitious rites.'

'Think what you like, Mr Shakespeare. I know the truth, for I was there. She could have gone at any time, but then she would never have been rid of the evil. She ran from *your* fine friends, though, didn't she? Lady Susan and her damnable coven. She ran from them as soon as she could.'

'How do you know of Lady Susan?'

The old woman laughed with scorn. 'We know everything that goes on in this realm of sin and heresy. We have friends everywhere, in the palaces and the courts of law. Do you think we don't? Do you think this pseudo-religion can survive? It will be cast out as surely as the demons were expelled from Thomasyn Jade.'

'Where is she?'

Sister Michael looked Shakespeare directly in the eye. He saw no fear there, only reproach.

'Perhaps Father Weston will tell you. Why do you not ask him? You must know where he is for you keep him in your dungeons, even though he is frail and sick. As for myself, I have told you all I will say. You have no power over me for I took my vows in the reign of Queen Mary, so I was here in the days before the accession of the usurper and contravene none of your heretical laws.'

At this, she dropped to her knees and began to pray silently. Shakespeare removed the paper he had found from his doublet and held it up. 'You know what this is. I found it in your coffer. This paper could hang you, mistress.'

The nun kept her eyes shut.

'It is a map of routes and safe houses. You are organising the secret transport of young men and women to the seminaries and convents of Europe. This is so, is it not?'

She did not move nor acknowledge his presence.

'These initials are your contacts in these towns. They provide safe lodging for the would-be priests and nuns as they make their way to the coast. And the ones in the coastal ports organise berths upon vessels to France or the Spanish Low Countries. Answer me or face yet greater consequences!'

At this, a quiet smirk seemed to cross the old woman's lips.

'And then there is the matter of the money. Funds from Rome to pay travel expenses, yes?'

At last he got a reaction. Her eyes opened and he detected a glow of such cold revulsion that it almost seemed *she* was the one possessed. Shakespeare tried hard to contain his own fury. He held up the jar of money, which he had counted out to forty-two pounds and a few shillings. 'This will remain as crown property until you can prove ownership. As for questioning, I will not press you further this night. Boltfoot, you will hold this woman under armed guard until morning, when you will escort her to London and have her held in Bridewell.'

Boltfoot lifted his caliver.

'And you, Mr Swinehead, will think very carefully what else you might wish to tell me, unless you, too, desire a journey to the treadmill and whipping post.'

*

Shakespeare slept lightly. In the morning, he found Boltfoot and the nun in the taproom, where he had left them. She was still on her knees, in prayer, her eyes closed. He ignored her, spoke briefly to Boltfoot and gave him money to buy food for himself and the woman, and to hire a horse.

'I will see you in Dowgate this evening.'

Shakespeare rode alone. The road was pitted, but he made good progress and was at Dowgate by late morning. He found Jane still out of sorts and reassured her that Boltfoot would soon be home.

'This came for you last night, master,' Jane said, handing him a letter. He recognised the seal as Cecil's and sliced it open with his dagger.

Mr Mills is sick and frenzied. I can no longer spare you on the matter of Thomasyn Jade. Go to The Ruth *at Gravesend without delay.*

Shakespeare uttered a low curse and threw the letter into the hearth. He wrote a brief reply with news of Denham, then walked at a brisk pace to the Old Swan waterstairs.

'Queen's business!' he called, striding to the front of the mass of people awaiting tilt-boats. A pair of young men dressed in black like lawyers were clambering into a four-oarsmen barge, but Shakespeare ordered them out.

'Damn you, sir, we have business at Greenwich Palace.'

Shakespeare thrust his letters patent from Robert Cecil before their eyes. 'Argue with that if you will.'

Grudgingly, they made way for him and he commanded the oarsmen to row him to Gravesend with all haste. The journey was long and tiresome and when he arrived, he saw that he was too late. *The Ruth* was already being unloaded.

'The investors would not wait another day,' Captain Roberts said, as they sipped wine from Bordeaux in his cabin. 'I had no option in the matter but to let her be discharged and lay off most of the crew.'

'You could have said Sir Robert Cecil ordered the cargo impounded.'

The captain smiled. 'Indeed, I might, but the investors included Sir Robert's own father, Lord Burghley, as well as the Earl of Essex and the Mayor of London. Since this war started, French wine sells at a fine price. Investors want their money in their coffers, not wallowing in casks aboard ship. And after Mr Topcliffe's visit, I had no more cause to delay.'

'Topcliffe was here?'

'Why, yes, not twenty hours since. Sent by Sir Robert Cecil like your good self, sir. And I hope I do not speak out of turn in saying it was a most uncomfortable experience for all concerned.'

'God's wounds, Mr Roberts! Tell me what happened.'

'He lined up the crew, called them papist dogs and threatened them with the rack if they did not speak out and denounce the traitors among them. We were all mighty bewildered.'

'What did he discover?'

'Nothing. He scared all the men into utter silence.'

So with Shakespeare away and Mills incapacitated, Cecil had panicked and brought in Topcliffe. He was the last person to extract information by subtle means.

'However,' Roberts continued, 'all may not be lost. When things had calmed down, I made some inquiries of my own among the crew, and I did find one man who knew the dead mariner, though not as a friend. He begged me not to reveal this information to Topcliffe.'

'Don't worry. His name will not be revealed to Topcliffe by me. Where is this man now?'

'Still with us, grumbling at being kept from the bawdy

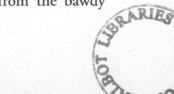

houses and drinking dens. His name is Jed Yorke. He is an ordinary seaman. Wait here and I will have him brought to you.'

'And I would like to see the dead man's box, where the letter was found.'

'Of course. I have it here.'

Roberts called in a midshipman and sent him to get Yorke, then fished under his bed, which was short and narrow, seeming scarce big enough for a child of twelve. He fetched out scraps of wood that had once been the box, a cup, a tin eating vessel and a knife.

'That's it, Mr Shakespeare – or all that remains of it after the the searchers broke it apart.'

Shakespeare examined the objects. They were cheap, everyday things, without markings on them. The box was no more than firewood.

The midshipman returned with Jed Yorke, an unremarkable man with long whiskers and a brow lined by a great many sea-winds. He bowed in deference to the captain and then to Shakespeare, clutching a felt cap tightly.

'Mr Yorke,' Shakespeare said, 'I believe you knew the dead mariner.'

'Yes, master. He called himself Franklin Smith.'

'Did you doubt that was his real name?'

'I doubt it of *all* mariners, sir. Many seafarers have reason to go under aliases. Wives they never wish to see again, justices they wish to escape . . .'

'I understand. Tell me, what did you make of Mr Smith?'

'He was not a seasoned mariner, sir. He did not know the ways of a ship. I would say he could not tell a capstan from a keel.'

'Indeed.' Shakespeare turned to the captain. 'Where is the corpse, Mr Roberts?'

'Fifty fathoms deep, Mr Shakespeare. Stitched in canvas and buried at sea.'

'And his clothes?'

'Dispersed among his crewmates.'

'And his crewmates are all gone. Mr Yorke, did *you* have any of his apparel?'

'Only his cap, master.' He held out the cap. 'This.'

'What is it worth?'

'It is a poor thing, in truth. No more than a groat.'

Shakespeare took the cap and examined it. He slit it open and felt inside the lining for secret messages, but there was nothing. 'Now tell me more. I want to know of all your conversations.'

'He did not talk much, but there was one thing I recall, master.'

'Yes?'

'He asked me where he could get a berth to work his passage from the Thames to the east of England. He wanted to go to Wisbech.'

Wisbech. *A papist fastness in the east.* The words of Garrick Loake came gusting back. He had said the plot 'wafts from the papist fastness of the east, gathers force in the seminaries of Spain, but it will blow into a tempest here. A conspiracy the like of which England has never seen.' Wisbech was certainly a papist fastness, for it was in the castle of that eastern port that the most aggressive of the country's renegade Catholic priests were interned.

'Did he say why, Mr Yorke?'

'He said his home was near there.'

'And what did you tell him?'

'I told him I had no idea, master, for it is the truth. I do not even know quite where Wisbech is, though I believe it to be near the Wash.'

'Did he talk with anyone else about this matter?'

'I do not know.'

'Very well.' He gave the man the remains of the cap, and sixpence compensation for its destruction. 'Thank you, Mr Yorke. That will be all.'

Chapter 11

O N THE RIVER barge back to London, it became clear
to Shakespeare that he must go to Wisbech in
Cambridgeshire. The thought of travelling to that remote outpost of England did not fill him with joy, but Cecil would
demand it of him, and he would be right to do so. It was
almost certain that the letter from Father Persons had been
destined for the castle prison there. One name above all came
to mind as the intended recipient: the zealous Father William
Weston, who sometimes went by the name Edmunds, former
superior of the Jesuit mission to England and still highly influ-
ential among England's Catholics, even though he had been
incarcerated these nine years.

Shakespeare had met him once before and did not like him
much. He would have no qualms about interrogating him hard
to discover the truth about this letter. And while he did so, he
could question him concerning Thomasyn Jade's whereabouts.

Ursula Dancer was pushing her handbarrow across the
courtyard when he arrived at Dowgate. He hailed her. 'A good
day at market, Ursula?'

'Surviving, Mr Shakespeare. Just surviving.'

He laughed out loud. Ursula was eighteen years of age and
though she had been at Dowgate only since the autumn, she was
already part of the family. The children loved her and Jane valued

her assistance. Recently, Shakespeare had given her funds to set up a market stall among the booksellers of St Paul's. He knew some printers and publishers, and had contacts at Stationers' Hall who had agreed, against their better judgment, to help her make a start. Boltfoot had accompanied her on her earliest outings to ensure she did not suffer violence at the hands of her competitors, but it soon became clear she could look after herself very well in the sharp world of street-selling. And she quickly realised that there were more profitable commodities than books.

'How much have you sold today?'

'Every ounce of tobacco I could scour from the ports. And all my pipes.' She swept her arm across the barrow, which was, indeed, almost empty, save for a few books and some curious artefacts from the Indies. 'It's the sotweed that sells, not the books. The lawyers want it and so do the churchmen. I could do the same business twice pigging over, Mr Shakespeare, if only I could find the sotweed to sell!'

'Well done. But you must also attend to your lessons, Ursula, for if you learn to read and write I do believe you will be a great London merchant one day.'

She screwed her pinched, yet strangely beautiful, face into a smile. 'Yes, sir.'

He laughed again, for he knew her well enough. When she said, *Yes, sir*, she really meant, *Lessons? Only after I have gone down to the pigging dockyard taverns and ships to see what I can buy from the homecoming mariners to sell at a great profit at St Paul's.*

'I do believe you will soon be the wealthiest member of this household,' he said. More importantly to both of them, she no longer had to steal for a living. Her days of vagabondage were, he hoped, at an end. He was about to walk on when she stayed him.

'It seems you have a visitor, Mr Shakespeare.'

'Garrick Loake?'

'I don't think so. I have no idea who or what Garrick Loake is, but, I promise you, it's better than that.'

'Indeed?'

'A beautiful lady, looks like a princess. A very goddess to steal away your heart.'

'Thank you, Ursula. I am too busy for this.'

'But you *do* have a pigging visitor. Jane put her in your solar and took her sweetmeats and wine, not half an hour since. And there's another one, too, out by the horses. A dismal pigging cow that one, won't say a word.'

Shakespeare strode on and found Jane in the kitchen with baby John. 'Is Boltfoot back yet?'

'He is, master. But I have put him to bed. It seems he had no sleep last night.'

'Let him sleep a while longer. Ursula tells me I have visitors.'

'A lady named Trevail. I told her I did not know when you would return, but she said she was happy to wait.'

'Thank you, Jane. Please inform her that I will be with her presently.'

So, Lucia Trevail was here. Why, he wondered, did that seem to brighten this grey day?

'And there was another young lady with her, but she has stayed at the stables with their horses. And good luck to her with her sullen way and her sotweed smoke.'

He bowed to Lucia Trevail. 'My lady, this is a most delightful surprise. You are well served with refreshment, I hope?'

'Your servant has treated me most hospitably. And I must say that the pleasure is all mine, Mr Shakespeare. We were all most intrigued by your visit to Susan's house. None of us could quite understand why the whereabouts of poor Thomasyn Jade should suddenly be of such interest to an esteemed government officer.'

'I can understand your puzzlement and I would tell you more. But I am not at liberty—'

She put up a hand, encased in a delicate white-kid glove. 'Please,' she said, 'I am not here to question you on the matter. Rather, it occurred to me that I might be of some little assistance to you. You asked what Thomasyn looked like. Well, I now recall that she had a distinguishing mark – a faint red blemish above her right eyebrow, in the shape of a crescent moon. I found it quite intriguing and beautiful.'

'Thank you. That may well be of use to me.'

'It is not much, I know. But I wish to help. We all feel some guilt in the matter. Perhaps we were too beguiled by her story, which made us seem a little unkind, though that was not our intent. We peppered her with all manner of questions . . .'

Shakespeare nodded. Thomasyn had been an object of wonder during the exorcisms. She must have wished for a quiet life and, instead, found herself stared at all the more.

He found himself wondering why Lucia Trevail was here. She could as easily have told him of the crescent mark in a letter. He wondered, too, why she was not at court, for the Queen did not like her ladies-in-waiting to take leave of absence, especially not a Gentlewoman of the Privy Chamber.

She answered his unspoken question. 'Mr Shakespeare, I have been given time away from court to attend my properties in Cornwall, where I must go to deal with some legal matters. On my return, I would dearly like to help you in your quest to find Thomasyn, if you have not already discovered her fate.'

She had a crisp tongue that did justice to her sharp mind. He could well understand why Elizabeth valued her company. Her attire was well cut from the finest cloths, neither modest nor brazen in the manner of most court ladies. Nor did she wear powder or paint on her clear-skinned face. She was beautiful, but he guessed that she was too clever to try to outshine the sun queen by donning glittering apparel and great pearls as others did, often to their cost.

What else did he know of her? Only that, like Lady Susan, she had been widowed before her twentieth birthday and left wealthy. He guessed her age now at late twenties or thirty.

'Mr Shakespeare, you are looking at me most intently.'

He averted his gaze quickly and thanked her for her offer. He had been looking in her eyes, where the fire was reflected.

'Mr Shakespeare?'

'Forgive me. My thoughts drifted.' *To the fire, where many a man had followed and fallen.*

'Well, I just hope that in helping poor Thomasyn, we might right a wrong – and discomfit the papist traitors who treated her so ill.'

'I am told you have a companion here with you.'

'That is Miss Eastley, whom you met at Susan's house. She is to accompany me to Cornwall where she has distant relatives. Susan asked if I would take her.'

Shakespeare nodded. 'Does she ever talk?'

'Very little, particularly not with men.' Lucia lowered her voice. 'In truth I think her a little mad. However, I am delighted to have her with me, and to help her with her studies, as Susan has done. She is young, Mr Shakespeare, and we both hope to set her on the correct path of life. I am afraid she is not always easy with others. As I said, it is the company of men she avoids. She has reason enough, I think.'

Shakespeare dared look closely again at Lady Trevail's exquisite face, not quite sure what he hoped to divine. Humour, certainly, and more besides. He was about to travel one hundred miles to the north and she was heading two hundred or three hundred miles south and west. It was bad timing.

*

Shakespeare's meeting with Sir Robert Cecil was curt and direct. 'You must indeed go to Wisbech, John. I can hardly spare you here, but I have no one else to send.'

There was someone, but Shakespeare would not say his name: Topcliffe. He would be delighted to go and wreak torment among the Catholic priests.

'I know what you are thinking, John,' Cecil continued. 'And no, I shall not be sending Mr Topcliffe, delighted as both you and my lord Puckering would doubtless be to have him out of the way.'

Shakespeare smiled at the reference to the Lord Keeper, Sir John Puckering. He was at present trying a long-winded Chancery case involving Topcliffe, and word had it that he was not enjoying the experience.

'I have no desire for yet more martyr priests,' Cecil went on. 'I desire no torture, no executions. I am sure I do not need to impress that upon you.'

'Indeed not.'

'Then go, discover what you can – and return in haste. In the meantime, I shall set Mr Anthony Friday to work.'

'He will not like it.'

'Fear not. I have a hold over Mr Friday. A stranglehold.'

When Boltfoot awoke, Shakespeare summoned him and asked about the old nun, Sister Michael. 'Did she maintain her silence all the way to Bridewell?'

His assistant looked uneasy. 'She did, master . . .'

'Boltfoot?'

'Master, it is not my place to say such things, but I believe I must speak plain. I could not but be troubled by the woman, sir. I wondered what she had done to merit confinement in Bridewell, for I would not put a dead cat in that place.'

Shakespeare nodded. It had been preying on his own mind

and he wondered about his motives for sending her there. He did not like locking people away simply for the supposed crime of helping others to seek religious freedom in another country. Perhaps he wanted her imprisoned simply for refusing to answer his questions. Or was there more to it than that? Had it been purely because he disliked her? He felt uncomfortable at the thought.

'You are right, Boltfoot,' he said finally. 'Go to the keeper and authorise her release. Bring her to the Swan Inn, give the landlord money for her keep, and tell her she must stay there or be damned as an outlaw. I will speak with her on our return.'

Chapter 12

THE GOING WAS easy enough until Cambridge, but Shakespeare knew it could not last. Soon they would be entering the strange, boggy flatlands of the fens and the rain was coming hard. They stayed the night at the Dolphin Inn, hoping the rain would stop, but in the morning he looked from the leaded window of their chamber and saw that it was worse. The downpour was cold and relentless. Instinct told him to wait here in comfort until it let up, but duty told him they must press on regardless. Duty won.

Progress became desperately slow. Six hours later, at two o'clock, they had managed only a little over five miles along a drenched causeway that, at times, became completely submerged beneath the flood. They found themselves crossing between islands of mud until they made landfall at the village of Waterbeach. They stopped at a tavern, ate and drank without talking, then travelled on. Two hours later, Shakespeare's worst fears were confirmed as they reined in their horses, up to the fetlocks in thick, peaty earth, and surveyed the way ahead.

'Should have come by sea, master,' Boltfoot grunted testily.

The causeway sloped down at a gentle gradient and simply disappeared into water. They were looking across the desolate spectacle of a lake that seemed to stretch for ever in front of them until black water melded into sky in a dismal haze. A few hundred yards offshore they could see a small island with a few trees, no more than a spinney. There was no other sign of land. Somewhere in the distance, the lonely clang of a church bell revealed that there was life.

'Is that so, Boltfoot?' Shakespeare replied, his tone as tart and impatient as his assistant's. 'Well, it seems we have a sea to cross now, so let us find a way.'

Shakespeare hunched into his bear cloak. Though the fur was soaked flat, the skin should have kept him dry. Except that the cold rain slid from his hat down inside the back of his collar.

'Over there,' Boltfoot said with a nod of his head. 'I do believe I make out a church spire. That's the only way across the fens when they flood. Follow the line of churches, for they are all on higher ground. That is why they ring their bells.'

Shakespeare sighed. They were hopelessly equipped for a journey across such a waterscape. If they could not see the line of the causeway, horses would be useless. Even if the water was only a couple of feet deep in most places, they would never know when they came to a river or other decline until they were on it and the horses lost their footing in the black depths.

Beneath his breath, he cursed Sir Robert Cecil for insisting they ride to Wisbech rather than go by ship. 'If the winds are against you in the North Sea, you could take weeks over such a journey. God's blood, John, the land route might be hard, but you should be there within three days, or four at the outside.'

Well, they had come *the land route* and now they were faced with what looked like a vast inland sea.

During the ride here he had been thinking of Lucia Trevail. She stirred him mightily, but he was enough the man of the world to be aware that something was not right. There had been matters unspoken when they met in his solar; questions unasked and unanswered. He had mentioned her visit to Cecil.

The young statesman had uttered an uncharacteristically lewd laugh.

'Beware, John. Your prick has led you to trouble before, like a bull pulled by the nose to slaughter. There can be no greater peril for a man than to lure away a lady of the Privy Chamber. Mark the fate of Ralegh when he married Bess Throckmorton! You would do better to meet a thousand furies in combat than cross Her Majesty by bedding one of her favourites.'

Shakespeare became defensive, shocked by Cecil's bawdiness. Very rarely did he engage in such low tittle-tattle. 'Sir Robert, I merely mentioned that Lady Trevail had come to Dowgate with information, that is all.'

'Indeed, John. Well, I shall take your word for it. Mind you, Lucia is a fine woman, one of us.'

By which he meant, Shakespeare deduced, that she was a hard Protestant in the Cecilian mould. He would find out more about her when he returned from this mission. Whenever that might be.

'We'll have to stable the horses and find a boatman to carry us. Come, Boltfoot, let us return to that tavern in Waterbeach.'

Even as he said the words, he recalled the repast they had taken there. It had been cheery enough with good ale and a blazing hearth, but the laughter of the other drinkers and the landlord had made him uneasy. Now he realised why they were so merry: they were laughing at the two horsemen who thought they could ride to Wisbech . . .

'They will cheat us there, master. I wouldn't trust one of the villains to take us across the Thames in a tilt-boat, let alone carry us across this ocean.'

Boltfoot was right. Shakespeare wheeled his horse's head and shook the reins. Slowly, they began to retrace their steps while he contemplated their position. Ahead of them, a lone rider was approaching. Shakespeare hailed him.

The rider halted. Shakespeare recognised him from the night before at the Dolphin in Cambridge. He was a traveller, like them.

'There is no way ahead,' Shakespeare said.

The man grinned beneath his rain-sodden hat. 'Not for a horseman, no. But I have other means. Where are you headed?'

'Wisbech.'

'Then travel with me. My name is Paul Hooft.'

Shakespeare noted that he had a very slight Dutch accent; his name obviously emanated from the Low Countries.

'John Shakespeare. I am on Queen's business. This is my assistant, Mr Cooper.'

'Then you are well met, sir.' Hooft reached back and took a chart from his packsaddle. The map was on vellum and waxed against the weather. He held it out to Shakespeare and stabbed his finger at an inked cross on the word *Abbey*. 'This is my property, Mr Shakespeare, it is a little way east along the high banking. We can stay the night there, then travel on in the morning, for I have business in Wisbech myself.' He stowed the map.

Shakespeare hesitated. 'What is your business in Wisbech, Mr Hooft?'

'I export farm produce to the Low Countries, for they have much need of food and wool during these endless wars. That is where my family hails from.'

'We saw you at the Dolphin in Cambridge. Do you have business there, too?'

'Indeed, sir, yes. And I believe I saw you there also.'

They rode a mile along the raised gravel bank at the edge of the flood. A little way off, on slightly higher ground, Shakespeare made out the buildings of what had clearly been one of the great religious houses of the fens. From the preponderance of livestock and agricultural implements in the vicinity, it now looked very much like a farm – if a rather grand farm.

A dairymaid carrying pails on a yoke across her shoulders bowed her soaking head to Hooft as they rode past. He nodded back to her and they continued on to the flint priory, which seemed to have survived the Dissolution almost intact. They reined in to a halt before the front porch.

'This is my home,' Hooft said with a sweep of his arm. 'You are most welcome. Please, a groom will see to your horses. Come inside. This is no weather for travel.'

Paul Hooft was a fair-haired young man with a short, neat beard but no moustache. With his heavy riding cape removed, Shakespeare saw that he wore the plain broadcloth and falling band of a Puritan.

'You are on Queen's business? Then I am doubly bound to help you, sir,' Hooft said. 'Over meat and drink we will discuss how to get you to Wisbech from here.' He summoned a servant and ordered beds to be prepared, then turned back to his guest.

'Thank you, Mr Hooft.'

'It is my pleasure as well as my duty, sir, for your country has given my family refuge from the wars. I am delighted to have the opportunity to help.'

'That is good to hear, Mr Hooft.' Shakespeare was polite but circumspect. Hooft seemed genuine, but it did not mean, however, that he was to be trusted without question.

Their host was warming to his subject, his blue eyes shining in the firelight. 'I am a man of many parts, Mr Shakespeare. I am a trader, a farmer and an engineer, and I do all this work for the furtherance of God's glory. It is honest toil that reaps rewards. Man must not simply wait for the Lord to provide. He has given us this world to cultivate and cherish so that we may bring forth riches.'

'It is a point of view,' Shakespeare said. *A rather Calvinist point of view, perhaps.* Mr Hooft was a most curious young man.

'In northern Holland, I believe the land under cultivation has increased by a third in just fifty years. Once the fens here are drained, this land will have the richest soil in all England. I tell you, the pasture here will put beef on the table of every family in your country.'

Shakespeare nodded, indulging his host. 'That would be most welcome.'

'Forgive me if I press my case hard, but the evidence is there for all to see. I go to many markets in this country and nowhere do I find a cow that weighs above a thousand pounds, yet in Holland and Friesland you may commonly find cattle of sixteen hundred pounds. God helps those who help themselves, which is something the papists will never understand.'

As Hooft spoke, Shakespeare could see the glow of visionary zeal. But he saw, too, that he was a hard and practical man who might well have his way.

'I would be most grateful, Mr Shakespeare, for your assistance in this. I must have the patronage of wealthy men for my notions to be transformed into great works. I have sent letters to members of the Council before, but received no reply. Would you carry word from me to Sir Robert Cecil? Truly, he could enrich himself and the crown with this work.'

'I will carry letters for you, Mr Hooft, but I can promise nothing on Sir Robert's behalf.'

'Thank you, sir.'

It was becoming clear to Shakespeare why Hooft was so helpful and welcoming to two rain-sodden strangers. Their arrival had been like a piece of driftwood to a drowning man. He saw them as the pathway to men of influence.

The Dutchman told them that his great-uncle had bought

the old abbey and lands in the 1560s; on his death in the late 1570s it had passed to Paul Hooft's father, Cornelius.

'My great-uncle saved this house and farm from ruin, but my father had little taste for it. He was more interested in making war on the Spanish tyrants and died fighting. He had already sent my mother here to run the farm for him and I came with her.'

'Is she here?'

'She went to God last year.'

Shakespeare studied Paul Hooft closely. There was something unsettling about the man. Was it the casual denunciation of papists, or merely the gleam in his eye that seemed slightly unwholesome?

Hooft brought out a chart and showed Shakespeare the route they would take on the morrow.

'We will go by boat across to the Isle of Ely, and from there onwards to the isles of Chatteris and March before the final crossing to Wisbech.'

'What of the causeways? My own map shows a path from Cottenham to Rampton, then Haven Drove, Belsars Hill and Aldreth Bridge.'

'All under water save the bridge itself. We must go by boat. The bargemen who are certain of their paths might trust the heavy horses to wade along the courses, but I am not so certain. I will not take my horses into that flood. We must move you stage by stage, but I cannot promise you that it will be an easy journey.'

Shakespeare thought wryly of the decision to imprison the priests in Wisbech Castle. That had been the work of the late Mr Secretary, Sir Francis Walsingham, back in the 1580s. The wily old fox had chosen well, for it would surely be easier to escape from the Tower of London than get away from such a remote and desolate place.

The guests ate well in ill-fitting attire lent them by Hooft while their own clothes dried at the hearth. Shakespeare dismissed his initial doubts about his host's zealotry and began to see that his ambition could, indeed, bring great wealth to this part of England. There might be something barnacle-like in the way he had fixed himself upon his guests, but then the truth struck Shakespeare: the man was simply lonely. Shakespeare found himself speaking his mind.

'Do you not think you might be a little happier here if you were to take a wife?'

The sadness in Hooft's eyes told the story. 'There was someone, Mr Shakespeare, but it did not end well. I do not like to talk about it . . .'

'Forgive me, Mr Hooft. I should not talk in such a way on first acquaintance.'

Hooft tried to laugh. 'Well, I am sure we will be better acquainted by the time we reach Wisbech. But you are right, it will never be easy for me living here. Though I speak English as a native and have lived here most of my life, yet I am still a stranger. People are not welcoming, unless they are one in religion. And many of those here have little or no faith. You did well to find me, for they will not help *you* either. They are a breed apart, living mostly by fowling, fishing of eels and common thievery. They think no more of traversing the floodwaters than you or I would think of walking along a city road. They resent all strangers and see them but as prey to be robbed.'

Shakespeare turned to Boltfoot, who had remained silent. 'I think Mr Hooft is telling you to keep your cutlass honed and your powder dry.'

Boltfoot grunted dismissively. When had he *not* been prepared for a fight?

After supper, they sat before the fire with cups of wine while Hooft read them some verses he had composed; Shakespeare thought them rustic but fair and thanked him, then they retired to their beds.

Before sleep took him, he wondered again about Lucia Trevail, but her face vanished and was replaced by the grim visage of the old Marian nun, Sister Michael. He had worried that he was wrong to imprison her; now he was concerned that he might have made a worse error of judgment in having her freed. He had made a similar mistake in letting Loake go away instead of extracting his secret first. Two errors, both of them bad. Was he losing his way?

At last, he descended into a dreamless sleep.

The morning was crisp and chilly. On the bank of the Thames at Richmond, Annis Farrier was walking her dog. This morning, like every other, she threw sticks for the mongrel. It was the time of day she liked above all others, for she would slip out of the house and let the children fend for themselves; they were old enough now and she needed a little peace for herself. The remainder of her day would be given over to backbreaking work in the palace laundry.

One of the sticks landed in the river. The dog jumped in to fetch it, but instead of bringing it ashore, he began tugging at something caught in the roots of a tree. Annis called the animal to come out, but it would not. Edging carefully down the muddy incline she saw that the dog was pulling at something pink with blue, spidery veins. She recoiled in horror. It was flesh that she saw, something very much like a hand, with rings on all the fingers. She gasped. It *was* a hand, and it was attached to a body . . .

LIBRARIES NEATH PORT TALBOT

Chapter 13

JANE COOPER WALKED to the Stone House in Fylpot Street with hope and fear in her heart. Her son John was already over the worst of the sickness and was up and about again. She had left him with Ursula so that she could come here alone.

The serving boy John Braddedge opened the door, looked at her and said, 'Oh it's you.' He held out his hand for money.

'You had a farthing before. I'll tell Dr Forman you have been demanding money.'

Braddedge snorted. 'Why should I care what old Hairy Balls thinks? He can't sack me – I know enough of his little secrets. He was up the skirts of a bishop's wife yesterday, and you won't be the first one he's swived *this* day, mistress.'

Jane wanted to slap the boy for his lewd impertinence, but simply pushed past him into the hallway. Braddedge shrugged indifferently and closed the door. With ill grace, he trudged up the stairway to his master's rooms, then reappeared a minute later.

'You can go up. He's waiting for you.'

Jane was relieved to find Forman looking businesslike. He was fully dressed and the bed was unruffled.

'Good morrow, Mistress Cooper,' he said cheerily. 'Have

you not brought the little one? How does he fare? Sit down, sit down.'

Jane took a seat. 'He is a great deal better, thank you, Dr Forman. He has his vitality back.'

Forman smiled. 'I knew all would be well with the boy. It is good. But, pray tell me, what of you and your husband? Have you increased the frequency of your congress?'

She shook her head hurriedly. 'He is away at the moment.'

In truth, she was pleased he was absent, for she had dreaded making some excuse to come out today to see Dr Forman. Above all else, she could not bear to think of betraying Boltfoot by deceitful dealings, even in a good cause.

'Well, when he returns, mistress, make sure he couples with you each day, for it is certain that the more a man occupies his wife, the more potent is his seed. Wait here if you will, for I have cast your horoscope and that of little John.'

He went through to the next room and returned with charts, full of circles, lines and astrological symbols that Jane did not understand. He laid them out carefully on the floor-boards.

'You see here,' he prodded an area of the paper with his stained yellow finger. 'This tells me that you will experience new life, which I believe to mean a healthy baby.' He smiled at her briefly, then pointed again at the chart and his eyes betrayed concern. 'But there is death also, someone close to you.'

'A death?'

'Not a child. More than that I cannot say. I am certain of this because I have your son's chart here.' He indicated the second paper. 'It shows a healthy line and prosperity. The heavens say he will live to a good age and bring you great pride.'

'Who then?'

'I cannot say, Mistress Cooper. I am sorry.' He hesitated a

moment too long. 'Did you bring me Mr Cooper's time and place of birth?'

'He does not know it. Do you think *he* is the one in danger?'

'No, no, mistress, I did not say that. Now tell me, did your month arrive?'

'Yes, two days since.'

'Then you must engage in congress four days from the last day of flux. Do not fail in this.'

'But I do not know if Mr Cooper will be returned by then.'

He jabbed his finger once more at the chart. 'It is not my rule; this is merely what the stars tell me, Mistress Cooper.' He shrugged. 'Next Tuesday at noon. It must be done if you would get great with child and come to term.'

Jane averted her eyes. She could not bear the way he looked at her, nor the unwanted churning she felt inside as he spoke. She rose from her seat. 'I must pay you,' she said, still looking away. 'How much do I owe you, Dr Forman?'

'We will talk of that anon.' He handed her a ring, a twist of metal in which were trapped fragments of coral. 'This is a sigil that I have made for you, with symbols of fecundity from the warmer regions of the earth. Wear it close to your wedding band. Return to me next week and we will discuss money then. I can see that you are not wealthy, mistress, so I shall ask a pittance from you, nothing more.'

Jane hunched her head into her shoulders and scuttled to the door, clutching the ring tight in her fist. She hurried down the stairs, horribly aware that the boy Braddedge was leering at her. She did not wait for him to open the front door, but bolted past him into the street, as though she were escaping from the abyss.

Simon Forman watched the woman go, with interest. He closed the door after her, then picked up the charts, rolled them neatly and took them into the adjoining room, where he kept his immense collection of books and cures. Here was his life's work. It was here that he had divined his cure for the plague and it was here that he wrote the encoded diary of his work. He knew that men derided him, particularly those fools from the College of Physicians, but he knew, too, that he was in the right. He was the true man of science and none of them understood the significance of the stars as well as he did.

He put down the charts on a bench with dozens of others. They told men whether or not to propose marriage, whether to invest in a voyage and whether they would live to old age. They told women how to find love, what name to give their new-born son for good fortune, and whether they would be found out if they went to bed with a handsome servant.

Beside the charts, there were many more papers and books. There were, too, glass vials small and large, and earthenware pots, copper pans for heating substances and glass jars for examining them, and the curious dead bodies and foetuses of animals from the Africas, the Indies and the Russias.

There was, too, a woman in the room. He gazed at her thoughtfully and scratched his beard.

'Well?' she said.

'I say she is genuine.'

'But you say, too, that she is a servant at Shakespeare's house.'

'That is by the by. You have nothing to worry about.'

'I am not so certain. Indeed, I am not certain at all.'

At the front of Ovid Sloth's ancient farmhouse, his grooms assisted the two moneylenders to mount their horses. They were sober-looking, dressed in black and dark brown, with no evidence on display of their vast wealth. Their retinue of twenty-two armed men waited motionless on their mounts. Sloth stood before the great door and watched them. Their meeting had not been easy, but he was relieved that he had bought some time.

The quieter of the two creditors settled himself into the saddle, clutched the reins of his steed and leant towards Sloth. 'Remember, Señor Sloth,' he said, without anger or any other emotion in his voice, 'if you do not repay at least half of the twenty thousand ducats by summer's end, all your goods and properties will be seized. Everything you possess in Spain.' He nodded towards his expensive attire. 'Even the clothes you wear.'

Sloth nodded in acquiescence and his immense bulk shook. 'You will have your gold.'

'If we do not, then there will be yet worse,' the other moneylender said. 'We will have not only your vineyards and houses, but your eyes.'

Sloth smiled at them. They gazed back at him for a moment, without expression, then wheeled their horses' heads and kicked the animals into a trot with their retinue around them. He watched them go, along the dusty path to the nearby port town of Sanlúcar de Barrameda, from whence they would take the river ferry to Seville. At last, his shoulders slumped.

The meeting had been deeply unpleasant. He had promised them everything they asked, and more. He had boasted of his new ventures with expansive optimism, but they had not been mollified.

Their words were spoken in soft voices, but Sloth knew that the moneylenders meant what they said. They would, indeed, pluck out his eyes. Now, like a top-heavy galleon, he turned away and waddled on splayed feet through the courtyard of his palatial farmhouse. It was built in the Moorish style, with light walls, a large square patio with cool cloisters on three sides. All this and more would be lost to him if trade did not improve, and soon.

He stopped beneath a mature olive tree and supported himself against the trunk while he caught his breath. He had a thirst that ate at his soul. A breeze blew the leaves above him; nearby, a fig and an oleander swayed. A central fountain sparkled in the sunlight.

The crack of a musket-shot broke the still air. A vein in Sloth's neck bulged, but with an effort he moved on across the courtyard and out through the arched entranceway. Before him stood a large outhouse with white walls, thick and strong to keep the interior temperature as constant as possible throughout the year. Through the dark doorway he could just see the immense barrels of manzanilla ranged before him, comfortingly dark, rich and timeless.

Sloth shambled into the bodega with a ponderous, awkward gait. The cellarman stiffened and bowed low at his approach, but Sloth ignored him. He ran his white bulbous fingers along the staves of a fine oak cask. This, above all, was his love. He breathed deep, separating the scents he knew so well into their constituent parts, imbibing the intoxicating aromas of fermented grape and salt from the sea. It was said he could tell the quality of wine by sniffing the air in the cellar, while the wine was still in the cask. He signalled to the servant with a curt tilt of the chin. The servant knew what was required of him and instantly produced a long-handled ladle, dipping it through the bunghole of one of the casks. With a flourish, he proffered the cup to his master. Sloth gulped down the wine, then gasped and wiped his sleeve across his dribbling lip and his beardless chin. He ran his hand across his glistening bald head.

The conversation with the creditors spun through his mind. 'Go and live in England with your own kind, señor,' the smaller of the two had said with a sneer. 'Leave all this for us.'

'I am Spanish, damn you.'

'Your mother may have been Spanish, but you are English, like your father before you.'

'You will be paid. In full.'

'Time is running out.'

He could not believe that England had not fallen yet. When it did, his coffers would fill again like the incoming tide. It should have fallen in eighty-eight, the year he had borrowed so much, certain that Medina-Sidonia's Armada would triumph. He could not possibly go to live in England; his debts there were, if anything, deeper even than they were here and his business interests, such as his investment in the playhouses, were simply inadequate to cope.

Like a dripping tap, every day that passed without resolution emptied his coffers a little more, brought his affairs closer to ruin. His family had been trading wines from Sanlúcar to England for more than a century. These last eight years of open warfare had brought an embargo and put an end to legal trading. Sloth needed this war to end. He needed Spain and Catholicism to gain power over England. He needed the trade routes to London and the west country to reopen – and fast.

A second musket-shot split the peace of the morning. Sloth swore, then threw the long-stemmed cup to the floor. He waddled out of the bodega and stood in the cool air. The last miles of the Guadalquivir river stretched before him, flowing from right to left to spew into the Atlantic. They were just east of Bonanza, the riverside docks from which both Magellan and Columbus had once departed on momentous voyages.

Sloth glared into the bright morning light. Hugh Fitzgerald, one of the pretty brothers he had found at the Irish College in Salamanca, was engaged in swordplay with three Spanish soldiers in armour. He was working with his short sword, cutting at the left side of the neck of the first man, then back into the right side of the neck for the second, before bringing the blade forward again for a thrust into the belly of the third. His skill was impressive. The clang of metal blade on metal armour rang across the plain. The whole sequence – step forward, cut, cut again, thrust – took less than four seconds. Had the three Spaniards not been heavily protected by chain mail and steel, they would be dead by now.

Hugh Fitzgerald's brother, Seamus, was working with knives. He stood, arms outstretched, a knife in each hand. Opposing him was a Spanish soldier with a short sword. Seamus was weaving and thrusting, evading the Spanish sword and jabbing with his own blade, like a prizefighter. Nearby, the diminutive Dick Winnow was powdering his wheel-lock, preparing to take another shot at the waterfowl that lived on the river and in the wetlands beyond.

'No more, God damn you!' Sloth shouted. 'It is like a circle of hell! You disturb my morning peace.'

The Irishmen stopped their training and looked across at him, then made a face at each other. Seeing this, Winnow approached them with his pistol and, though they were a head taller than he was, pushed them hard in their chests with the butt. 'Move away,' he said, an edge to his voice. 'If he says stop, then do so. Do not rile him for he is a boiling kettle.'

The Spanish soldiers retreated towards their encampment. But the Irish brothers and Dick Winnow stayed. Winnow was no more than five feet tall, yet he was afraid of no man, least of all these two callow Irish gentlemen with their jewelled swords and knives, their gentry airs and their tutored swordplay. He gazed at Ovid Sloth and wished to God that Roag would return soon. Surely they could wait no longer.

'Come on, move away,' Winnow repeated, pushing Hugh and Seamus Fitzgerald out of Sloth's line of vision.

'Why should we pay heed to the slimy fat sodomite?' Hugh said. 'What can he do to us?'

Winnow grasped Hugh Fitzgerald's balls in his left hand and with his right thrust the muzzle of his gun up into his jaw. 'Because without him, none of this will work, Mr Fitzgerald. Make it easy. Come away.' He squeezed the balls. Hard. 'He is indispensable. You may not be.'

Hugh Fitzgerald let out a small howl. His brother pulled him away, laughing.

Winnow released his grip. 'Go to the other side of the farmhouse and rehearse your moves there. You will need them, sure enough. Just as you may need your balls one day.'

Just then, Seamus Fitzgerald held up his hand. In the distance they heard the sound of horse's hoofs on the hard, dusty earth. Dick Winnow and Hugh looked towards the east and there was a palpable easing of tension. Roag had returned.

Roag reined in to a walk. He did not dismount, but rode right up to Ovid Sloth. Leaning from the high-pommelled saddle, he clasped Sloth's naked head between his dusty hands and kissed his brow.

'*Pax vobiscum*,' Roag said. 'I just saw some friends of yours on the road.'

'Those dirty moneylenders are no friends of mine, Mr Roag.'

'Well, I bring fair news. We sail.' He brought out the *casa de contratación* authorisation document, waved it in the air and then replaced it in his doublet. 'Let us load up our weapons. We will have a mass said, then sail on the tide.'

Sloth heaved a great sigh that seemed to shake his whole body in ripples. He took Roag's hands and clasped them between his own. 'Thanks be to God,' he said.

Roag removed his hands from Sloth's and gazed around the vineyard. 'Where are Ratbane and Paget?'

'Drinking, whoring . . . who knows?' Sloth said. 'Can they even read?'

Roag laughed. 'Well enough for our needs.'

'And the spy?' Winnow said quietly.

'He is no longer a threat, Dick. No word will ever pass his lips again.'

Roag put his head on one side and regarded Winnow. Warner may have been caught, but there would be others. Could one of *these* men be a spy, too?

Chapter 14

RAIN AND WIND swept across the inland sea. Paul Hooft pushed the large punt away from the muddy shore with his quant – a long, heavy pole with a prong at the end to prevent it sticking in the mud. They were watched by a sullen crowd of fishers, preparing their osier eel hives and sharp, three-tined glaives. Within a few moments they had disappeared into the rain. Paul Hooft stood at the back of the punt, poling, while Shakespeare and Boltfoot sat on the benches, gazing into an endless vista of grey sky and black floodwaters.

'Would a rowing boat not get us across faster, Mr Hooft?' Shakespeare demanded, worried by the prospect of a long, tortuous journey. 'Perhaps a sailing skiff would make more haste.'

'This will suffice, sir. Its bottom is flat and will skim over areas of reed, sedge and thatch. You will see.'

A narrow barge, heavy laden with corn or grain and six sodden sheep, emerged from the north and drifted past them going south. She was being drawn by two heavy horses, up to their withers as they waded through the shallows. The two men steering her gazed across at the punt without a word or even nod of greeting and were gone as suddenly as they had appeared.

Within minutes, three men carrying rods and nets strode

past them through the flood, as though walking on the water. Shakespeare and Boltfoot looked at them in astonishment.

'Stilts,' Hooft said. 'They are walking on stilts, like the clowns you must have seen at Bartholomew Fair. Many men use these in the fens.'

Occasionally, they passed islands of higher ground where they saw men with eel hives. Sometimes they spied men with muskets for fowling and Boltfoot fingered the trigger of his caliver, which lay in his lap, wondering whether any of his powder was still dry in this world of eternal damp.

The minutes wore on into hours, and it was impossible for Shakespeare to tell what progress they were making, though Hooft continually insisted they would be in Ely by dark, and would find an inn there. A church steeple loomed out of the grey. The water lapped at its very base. As they glided past, they made out old gravestones protruding from the flood, ghostly and ominous.

Then, at last, long into the afternoon as the sky was darkening, they saw the immense tower of Ely Cathedral emerge into view, as welcome a sight as any sailor ever saw when spying land.

The taproom was thick with a heady blend of woodsmoke and the aroma of beer. Over a supper of roasted eels, they considered their situation. Shakespeare was grateful to Hooft for bringing them thus far in safety, but he was anxious to get to Wisbech and felt certain there must be a faster way to travel. When they landed on the isle, he had noted the various ferrymen and bargees shouting prices for their services.

Now, as they wiped up the last of the fish juices with dense slabs of bread, Shakespeare announced that he intended talking to the ferrymen to discover their opinion of the best way ahead.

'They will rob you, Mr Shakespeare.'

Hooft paused as a serving girl came over. Her hair was long and uncovered and her dress was low-cut, showing off her inviting breasts.

Hooft stood up from his stool. 'Cover yourself, mistress!'

The girl looked shocked and put a hand to her chest. Shakespeare smiled at her. 'Ask the landlord or one of his men to come over and serve us,' he said softly. He touched the Dutchman's sleeve. 'Sit down, Mr Hooft. It has been a long day.'

Hooft watched the girl back away, then sat down slowly. 'Why do they employ whores to serve us? Is there no modesty here?'

Shakespeare tried to calm him. 'It was ever thus in England, Mr Hooft. You are not the first newcomer to be surprised by the freedoms enjoyed by our womenfolk.'

Hooft bowed his head. 'Forgive me, Mr Shakespeare. I do indeed sometimes feel a stranger to this country, even though I have spent a great deal of my life here. I was brought up by my mother to expect modesty and domesticity from women and girls. But you are right, I spoke out of place.'

'We are all tired. Let us retire to sleep and be on our way at dawn.'

When they awoke, Paul Hooft had gone.

He had left a few coins – his portion of the reckoning – but the promised letter for Cecil was not there. After breaking their fast with bread and eggs, they walked in the shadow of the great cathedral down to the water's edge. The rain had stopped, but the sky was still grey and lowering. They discovered that Hooft's punt was also gone.

'I think we offended him, Boltfoot.'

'Well, master, that is his choice.'

There were two ferries. One already had two passengers but there was room for two more.

'Where are you headed?' Shakespeare demanded.

'Where are you going?' retorted the ferryman, a slight man of fifty years or so.

'Wisbech.'

The ferryman looked them up and down. 'Clamber in. It'll be three shillings for both of you.'

Shakespeare gazed at the man, who looked like a water-rat, slick-haired and pinched about the mouth. He glanced at Boltfoot, who shrugged.

'You'll find none quicker, master,' the ferryman continued. 'We'll be there in six hours, which will include an hour's stop for our midday repast at Chatteris.'

The ferry was a large rowing skiff with four oarsmen. Soon they were out on the broad flooded plain, with Ely Cathedral receding behind them.

It was then that Shakespeare really took note of the rowers and the other two passengers. They *all* looked like water-rats. A whole family of them, throwing sly glances at each other. Shakespeare sighed and looked sideways at Boltfoot. He, too, had seen the connection between the men. And they were out-numbered seven to two. They would be robbed; it was simply a matter of when.

'Well, Boltfoot, this is going to be an interesting journey.'

'Indeed, master.'

Visibility was better than the previous day. Now they really did feel as if they were on an ocean. Save for a few spots of land and distant pinpricks, which they knew to be church spires, all they could see was black water, in all directions.

'Where you from, stranger?' the ferryman asked Shakespeare.

'London.'

'That's like Fenland only different, so I'm told.'

The ferryman was clearly the father of the family. He stood at the rear of the boat, directing the course and urging the rowers on.

The attack came with terrifying suddenness. They were half an hour out, near a small island, and there were no other boats in the vicinity, no witnesses, and no help.

Shakespeare noticed that the rowers were slowing. His hand went to the poniard in his belt. Boltfoot drew his cutlass.

'Now,' said the ferryman.

The four rowers dropped their oars and the two fake passengers were up in an instant. The boat rocked violently and Shakespeare was nearly thrown into the water. He dropped his poniard and gripped the side to steady himself, only to find three men surrounding him, all with weapons out and ready to kill. The sharp edge of a blade hovered at his throat. Daggers prodded at his belly. He was utterly at the mercy of the assailants.

Boltfoot had somehow edged himself into a better position. He was at bay, cutlass held out before him as he crouched at the side of the boat. Three heavily armed men were closing on him.

'No need for unpleasantness, masters,' the ferryman said in a quiet, well-mannered voice. He was still standing at the rear of the skiff, hands on hips and unconcerned, as though this were his daily business to be attended to. 'It is time for the collection of fares. Hand over your purses and your weapons and we will set you down safely upon that island there. If you resist, you will discover that my sons are as adept at filleting a man as they are at drawing the entrails from plover, swan or bittern.'

Shakespeare brushed the blade away from his throat with the back of his hand. 'I must tell you that I am on Queen's business. If you rob me or harm me, you will all hang.'

The ferryman smiled. 'You are mistaken, Mr Traveller, for if we decide to slit your throats, then you will sink into these waters as food for pike, and none will ever know that you are there.'

Boltfoot reached out with his left hand and gripped Shakespeare's arm. 'Give him your purse, master. It is not worth dying for.'

Shakespeare looked at his assistant with surprise. Boltfoot never shied away from a fight.

'Listen to your serving man, Mr Traveller. He is a man of wisdom.'

The ferryman nodded to his accomplices, who all stood back in the boat to give their victims room to hand over their possessions. Again, the shallow-keeled vessel swayed alarmingly, but this was home territory for the attackers and they kept their footing with ease.

Shakespeare pulled open his bear cloak and removed his kidskin purse from his belt. He also picked up his poniard and handed it over, hilt first, although it hurt him greatly to do so.

'And your sword, master.'

Shakespeare shook his head. 'I keep the sword, and it will stay sheathed until you are gone.'

The ferryman ignored him and turned to Boltfoot.

Boltfoot did not loosen the grip on his cutlass. 'No, I will *not* give up my weapons.' His voice was hard, stubborn, unbending. 'I travelled the world to take this cutlass and this caliver from Spaniards, and I will not surrender them to an English rogue.'

'Then it is simple. You will die.'

'And you will, too, Mr Ferryman. For whatever else happens, I will make certain of your death, even as I go to mine.'

The ferryman hesitated. The eyes of his men were on him, waiting to see which way he would turn, waiting to plunge their blades into Boltfoot at their master's word. 'Travelled the world, you say?'

'Aye, with Drake. Across all the oceans. And this –' he indicated the floods – 'is naught but a puddle of piss to me.'

The ferryman laughed. 'Very well,' he said. 'I like your spirit. That gun across your back would not do for fowling anyway. But hand me your powder, shot and purse – and I will consider the bargain struck.'

Boltfoot took his purse from his thick hide jerkin; there was little enough money in it. He tossed it to the ferryman, followed by his powder horn and bag of balls.

The ferryman poured the contents of the two purses into his slender hand. His eyes widened at the gold coins Shakespeare had given him. 'Well, indeed,' he said. 'This is a good day. This will pay for your lives and you may even keep your weapons.'

'Put us on the island,' Shakespeare demanded.

'Take yourselves there, masters. If you will step from my craft, you will find the water no more than three feet deep. And so I bid you God speed – and I will thank you to pay my respects to the Queen, and inform her that she will always be welcome in the fens.'

Chapter 15

BEHIND CLOSED DOORS at the upper end of Westminster Hall, the court of Chancery was in session. No members of the public were admitted. The Queen and Council had commanded that this case be heard in secret.

The case of Richard Topcliffe, Queen's servant, priest-hunter and official torturer, against Thomas Fitzherbert, commonly known as Tom, had been a long, drawn-out affair with constant adjournments, but it was about to take a dramatic turn.

Topcliffe was suing Fitzherbert for non-payment of a contract for five thousand pounds. The money had supposedly been promised to Topcliffe if he would persecute to death Tom Fitzherbert's papist father John Fitzherbert, so that Tom could inherit his estates.

The case was dragging on because no one, least of all the Queen of England, wanted to be on record as allowing a contract to murder to be sanctioned. It would be a gift to her many enemies at home and abroad.

Lord Keeper Sir John Puckering, resplendent in his ermine and scarlet robe, lounged back in his great throne of a chair as Topcliffe, incoherent in his rage, repeatedly berated Tom Fitzherbert and his advisers for their bad faith.

'Do you think you can agree this sum, to be paid on John

Fitzherbert's death, and then, when he dies, not pay?' Topcliffe's voice was a mastiff growl.

Puckering yawned and his eyes turned upwards to the heavens. This had been told and retold a hundred times. He just wanted them all to give up and go back to their wives and whores.

Fitzherbert rose to his feet. 'But, I repeat, your honour, my father died of natural causes, so why should I pay?'

Topcliffe slammed his fist on to the table in fury. 'Yes, but he was in the Tower – where *I* put him and tormented him! He died of natural causes because *my* racking weakened him to the point of death!'

Puckering had had enough. His gout ailed him and he had other matters on his mind, particularly the forthcoming visit of Her Majesty to his home in Kew. He knew that he must entertain her lavishly if he was to be sure of her continuing favour, so every detail must be attended to. He had a good mind to call another adjournment to this never-ending case. Hopefully by summer's end either Topcliffe or Fitzherbert or both of them might be dead, and then the case could be shuffled away. Quietly.

Topcliffe stormed towards Fitzherbert, brandishing his silver-tipped blackthorn stick.

Puckering was suddenly alarmed. He wanted no blood spilt here. 'Mr Topcliffe, you will halt where you are! Sit down, sir, sit down. This is a court of law, not an alehouse or your foul dungeon.'

The old white-haired torturer looked at Puckering with loathing. His stick hovered with menace. 'He is a dog, Mr Puckering, and he must be beaten like one. You must order him to give me my money!'

'Sit down, Mr Topcliffe.'

Grudgingly, Topcliffe lowered his heavy cane and slunk back towards his seat.

Puckering sighed. He had felt it prudent not to make comment on the merits or otherwise of the case. But he was mightily tired of this pair.

'Thank you, Mr Topcliffe, and in future you will address me as your honour or as Lord Keeper Puckering. You will not call me *mister* in this court. Is that clear?'

Topcliffe looked away sullenly.

'It is incumbent upon me to say a few words at this juncture,' Puckering said. 'I have listened to your plea with restraint these many months, but it is time now for me to speak. And I must tell you that whatever the claim you have in law, you have no *moral* right to make such a contract, nor demand it be honoured.'

Topcliffe turned back and glared. 'So the law means nothing in this court. A contract is to be torn up because of your finer feelings, *Mr* Puckering.'

'It cannot be right to accept five thousand pounds for murder, Topcliffe.'

Topcliffe smirked, looked around the assembled lawyers in their black robes, then pointed his blackthorn at the judge. 'And is it right, therefore, for Judge Puckering to accept ten thousand pounds in a bribe? For I know he has done so. Why should I not accept five thousand, when he takes ten?'

Puckering blanched, then the blood rose to his face. He turned to his fellow judge, Sir Thomas Egerton, Master of the Rolls and sometime friend of Topcliffe. Even he had had his fill and he shook his head slowly. Puckering brought his fist down on the table with a resounding thud.

'Enough. Topcliffe, you have gone too far.' He leant over the table to his side. 'Mr Clerk, you will have the guards take Topcliffe into custody for contempt of court. Have him taken in manacles to the Marshalsea to await our pleasure.' He hammered his fist again. 'Court adjourned!'

*

Frank Mills shuffled into the office of Sir Robert Cecil. His head was low and, though he had made some effort to brush his hair, he did not look well.

Cecil recoiled. His assistant secretary was unwashed and stank. 'Sit down, Frank,' he said, indicating the far side of the table; as far away as possible.

'Thank you, Sir Robert.' He took the seat.

Cecil remained standing. In front of him, on the table, were a book and a sheet of paper. He squared the edges so that they were both aligned and neat, like his own immaculate black attire and his trimmed little beard.

'Anthony Friday will be here shortly. First, I must talk with you, Frank. In truth, I can no longer do without your services. You must stiffen your resolve and return to your duties. Do you understand?'

'Yes, Sir Robert.'

'For, by God's faith, you seem absent even when you are with us. However, I shall allow you to stay at your desk. You will deal with the intercepts and reports from abroad. I am hoping that Mr Friday will agree to be at your service, for while John is away in the east, you will need assistance.'

'Thank you.'

'Good man.' Cecil produced a paper. 'For instance, there is this report. It tells us that four companies of General del Águila's most effective Spanish troops are engaged in intense training at Port-Louis, in Brittany. You have a mind for such things, Frank. What does it signify?'

Mills read the letter quickly. 'It might suggest that they intend returning to the Crozon peninsula, to rebuild the fortress.'

Cecil shook his small head. 'I don't think so. Henri of France will not allow it. Since Norreys and Frobisher took the fortress in November, the Spanish have looked vulnerable. It suits

Henri that they stay down. He will fight such a move, and Águila knows it.'

'Ireland then?'

'My thoughts, too. So put your mind to it, Frank. And call in reports from Brittany and elsewhere to discover what they are about. I do not like such unexplained manoeuvres.'

There was a knock at the door. Clarkson appeared.

'Mr Friday is here, Sir Robert.'

'Show him in.'

Anthony Friday strode into the room. With a sweep of his right arm, he bowed so low that his long fair hair almost brushed the wooden floorboards. He then drew himself up to his full height, which was not great, and bowed again to Cecil, though it might have been taken as merely an exaggerated nod of the head.

'Good morrow, Mr Friday. Be seated beside Mr Mills, whom I believe you know.'

'Indeed, Sir Robert, and good morrow to you.' He smiled at Mills in acknowledgment, took the seat reserved for him and reeled at the waft of bodily odours.

Cecil clapped his hands. 'Well, gentlemen, this must be like old times with Mr Secretary Walsingham. You worked together then, I believe, and I am sure it will be well for you to work side by side once again, for Queen and country.'

Friday shifted uneasily, but said nothing.

'We have a problem,' Cecil continued. 'A shortage of man-power, to be precise. Mr Topcliffe, as I am sure the whole of London knows, is sweating in the Marshalsea, scratching pleading letters to Her Majesty, so he is of no use to us. Mr Shakespeare, meanwhile, is away, engaged on other matters. To be plain, Mr Friday, I would have you return to service for me, if only for a short while.'

Friday spread his palms extravagantly. 'You know, of course, that I would do anything for you and for Her Majesty, but I am exceeding busy. The playhouse owners are impatient and I must produce plays for them. I also have a private commission of great value to me.'

This was about money. If Friday was going to work for him, he expected a good deal of gold. Cecil was having none of it.

'I recall when you were busy priest-hunting with Topcliffe, Mr Friday. I recall the days when you put your quill to use to denounce the Pope, the Jesuits and all their diabolical works. And while you did so, you were given leeway for your less salubrious writing. A translation of the lewd works of Aretino . . . that was yours, was it not? Now, if that had been brought to the attention of the Master of the Revels or Stationers' Hall, how would you have fared? Why, you would have been a guest of Mr Topcliffe's dungeon, not his comrade-at-arms. Has so much changed now? Do you think *all* your present writings would pass muster?'

If he was worried, Friday strove not to show it. He was a player as well as a playmaker. 'I have a wife; I have children. A man has needs, and so I must write. I am contracted to the Rose and have commissions from the Theatre. My playhouse masters are hard men and will allow me no respite. And, as you may know, the world of the intelligencer is fraught with dangers and erratic rewards.'

'And this?' Cecil pushed the book across the table to him. 'Why, only this week this work crossed my desk. *The Pleasures of the Flesh*, it is called. Do you recognise it, Mr Friday?'

He shook his head. 'Sir Robert, I have never seen this book.'

'Here, let me show you.' Cecil leant over the table and opened the pages. There were drawings of men and women engaged in all manner of couplings, with erotic verses to accompany the pictures. 'What do you think, Mr Friday? How would Stationers' Hall react to this?'

'This is a calumny, Sir Robert! This is not my work. Look, my name is nowhere to be seen. I am not the coter. By no means, no, sir.'

Cecil smiled. '*The Pleasures of the Flesh*. The printer Christopher Bynneman tells me it has sold well and made a fine purse. I believe he is not as circumspect as his late father was in the books he chooses to publish. He tells me *you* wrote it, Mr Friday. Now, who am I to believe?'

Friday shifted uneasily. 'Why would you believe that flea-arsed dog Bynneman?'

'Because he has shown me the contract between you.'

'I'll geld him, God shrivel his balls!'

'I think it fair to say that he was under some duress when he admitted as much to me. I think it also must be said that a word of this, from me to Stationers' Hall, and you will likely lose fingers, if not a hand or two.'

'How much will you pay me?'

'Two marks a week, Mr Friday. But I expect results. The main problem I have is the death of a man named Garrick Loake, fished out of the Thames at Richmond. Does the name mean anything to you?'

Friday suddenly showed interest. 'Garrick Loake dead? How?'

'We are still trying to determine that. It was only the etching of his name on all his rings – and it seems he had a lot of them – that enabled him to be identified at all.'

'I am sorry to hear of this, but Garrick is – *was* – of no importance to any man other than his creditors. Why is the government interested in his death?'

'Because he came to Mr Shakespeare offering secrets for sale and then disappeared. A tale of a plot fomented in Spain, which we might not have taken seriously, except that we have corroboration. I rather suspect he was murdered because the plotters feared they were about to be betrayed.'

'Plenty of men might have wished him dead. He owed money to usurers. Debts he could not pay. That is reason enough to hurl a man to his doom in this town.'

'Find out which usurers, then. Talk to anyone who might know anything. His body is now with the Searcher of the Dead, Mr Peace.'

Anthony Friday, visibly disconsolate, stood up as if to go.

'Sit down, Mr Friday. I have not finished with you yet. I want you to do more. I want you to revisit your old haunts. In the past, you have posed as a papist. I wish you to do so again, and listen carefully to all that is said. There is a plot out there and I want it uncovered, and fast. You will go to every mass and meeting of priests in London, and you will discover what is going on. And you, Mr Mills, you will decode every scrap of paper that comes our way at double speed. You will bring every sliver of information to my attention. Something is happening; a snake of insurrection is rearing its head, and its sting is deadly. It comes from Seville and it may involve the army of General Águila. Someone in England, some traitor, knows what it is about. I am as certain of this as anything in my life. It may be that Mr Shakespeare will cut this serpent off at the head, but we cannot take that for granted. Until he returns, gentlemen, I am relying on you.'

The two men looked at their master with reluctant obedience. There was no doubt who held the power in this room.

'And Frank,' Cecil continued, 'in God's name, bathe. Whatever troubles afflict you in your home life, you must deal with them like a man. Go bravely, sir, go bravely.'

Shakespeare gazed out across the bleak landscape. His nether-stocks, hose and half his cloak were soaked through. He and Boltfoot stood by the reeds at the water's edge on an island of no more than acre.

'By God's faith, Boltfoot, we are in the middle of a sub-merged field! This is nowhere near the route to any town. No passing boats will see us. Should we try to wade through the flood? If so, which direction should we take? There are not even any church bells to show us the way.'

Boltfoot shook his head. 'We'd stumble and drown walking any great distance through that.'

Whereas if we stay here, Shakespeare thought wryly, we could just starve.

Boltfoot suddenly laughed and pointed into the distance. 'Look, master.'

A quarter of a mile to the south, there was the clear outline of a craft in the water, coming in their direction.

'I do believe Mr Hooft is coming to fetch us to safety.'

Chapter 16

THEY STOPPED AT the town of March for the night. Paul Hooft paid for the inn and their food, and refrained from excessive gloating.

'I knew they were thieves, Mr Shakespeare, so I followed at a distance. Mostly, they like to rob the Catholics who flock like crows to Wisbech to receive blessings from Father Weston and others. But they are not always as precise as they might be in their choice of victim.'

'So you know about Weston?'

'He is famous in these parts. The papist idolaters come from great distances to see him.'

In the morning, they inspected the Fen Causeway, but it had vanished into the floods, so they continued by punt. By midday, Hooft's little vessel drew up at the long coastal bank on which the port of Wisbech stood. It was a strange town, looking one way to the Wash of the North Sea, the other across an inland sea of floodwater.

'Even in long spells of dry summer weather, it is stranded between the river Nene to the west and the marshy estuary of the Ouse to the east,' Hooft told them.

Behind the town stood the castle. The old fortress had long since been destroyed and replaced with this building, commissioned by Archbishop Morton when he was Bishop of Ely a hundred years ago or more. He was, said Hooft, an enlightened man for a papist and he applauded his early efforts to drain part of the fens.

Shakespeare examined the building. It had a high outer wall, but it had obviously been built as a comfortable bishop's palace rather than a fort and it still held much of the lustre of past glory, a pleasant surprise in this bleak waterland. He was, however, alarmed by its vulnerability; it was practically defenceless. Its crenellated towers were constructed for show rather than effect. Anyway, how could a brick-built structure with no cannon be defended? It could not even keep out the water, for the waves lapped against the lower portions of the outer walls and washed over the drawbridge.

The keeper, William Medley, greeted Shakespeare warmly, but when he turned to Hooft and Boltfoot his body stiffened and he frowned, as if in recognition of something he disliked. He did not acknowledge them and addressed Shakespeare alone.

'In truth, sir, I am mighty amazed you have made it here, for no one recalls worse floods than these. Our cellars are flooded and we have lost much from our victual stores.'

Shakespeare was brisk. 'Mr Medley, I am here on urgent business from the office of Sir Robert Cecil. I would be grateful if we could confer privately. In the meantime, perhaps you could find lodgings and food for my assistant, Mr Cooper. And you, Mr Hooft?'

'I usually lodge at the inn, Mr Shakespeare.'

'Well, this time stay here at the castle. I am sure there will be a berth somewhere.'

Shakespeare stood in front of a blazing hearth in the keeper's office, which was sumptuously appointed.

Medley apologised for the lack of wine. 'It is all under water and ruined, I fear. But we have ale or beer.'

'English ale will suit me well enough.' Shakespeare removed the letter he carried from inside his doublet, where he had kept it protected in a waxed packet. 'Look at this, Mr Medley. It was discovered in the box of a mariner who died of some sickness aboard a vessel named *The Ruth*, out of Bordeaux. We have no exact knowledge of its intended recipient, but we do know that the courier had asked about a ship to carry him to Wisbech, claiming it was his home. That is an obvious lie. He was ordered to bring the letter here. I am certain the intended recipient was a priest.'

Medley laughed. 'There is no shortage of those. Take your pick: we have thirty-two of them.'

Shakespeare studied Medley. On the surface, the prison governor was smooth, confident and urbane. But underneath the bluff exterior he seemed nervous. Was he worried by the intelligencer's presence?

'Indeed, I know you have a veritable snake pit of priests,' Shakespeare replied, 'yet I think it most likely the priest is no ordinary seminary man, but a Jesuit—'

'Then it must be William Weston, though some say that Thomas Pound has taken Jesuit orders in secret.'

'My instinct and all I know tells me it is Weston.'

What Shakespeare knew was that Weston had always been a stern, unbending enemy of Elizabeth and her government, and a close friend of Robert Persons, the Jesuit author of the letter. There were many who believed Weston should have gone to the scaffold as a conspirator in the Babington plot, but nothing had ever been proved. For some reason, Lord Burghley and Walsingham had seen fit to let him live and rot in gaol.

'What do *you* make of the man, Mr Medley?'

'William Weston? He divides people. The stricter priests – eighteen of them at last count – revere him as though he were a martyr and a saint. He organises their studies and devotional practices, distributes the alms sent them and generally keeps order. The other thirteen cannot abide him. They are led by one Christopher Bagshawe, who nurtures a deep loathing of all Jesuits and Weston in particular. I honestly believe that he would happily see him cast into eternal hellfire. Things are so bad between the two factions that they eat apart and barrack each other across the halls. One of Bagshawe's men was put in solitary confinement after trying to club a Weston follower to death with a stone mug. None of this is pleasant to see, even for one not of their faith.'

'Well, I shall need to talk with Weston as soon as possible. I will see Bagshawe, too, and perhaps others if I deem it necessary. Please ensure that I have access to them as and when I desire.'

'Very well. But I can tell you that they are not locked away. Conditions have been relaxed considerably since the unfortunate death of my predecessor, Mr Gray. Those were my express orders from the Privy Council.'

'Is that so? Well, not too lax, I trust.'

'No, indeed not . . .' The prison keeper paused, looking even more ill at ease.

'Mr Medley, was there something else I should know?'

'It is nothing.'

'No? Well, be so good as to tell me what this *nothing* is.'

'It is merely . . . well, I could not help notice that you arrived with Hooft, the Dutchman.'

'Do you know him?'

Medley nodded. 'I hope I do not speak out of order, for he seemed to be a companion of yours.'

'He helped us make our way here, that is all. Say what you wish about the man.'

Medley drew a deep breath, then exhaled. 'Very well, I must confess that I find him an irritant. A *great* irritant, and not just to me but to the peace and well-being of my prison.'

'I know nothing of him, except that he has been of assistance. A little zealous in his enthusiasms, perhaps, but that need not be a bad thing. Tell me more.'

'He is a Calvinist hedge-priest. He comes here all the time. Every Sunday, he gathers all of the more righteous Puritans of the county and leads them in prayer, either on a patch of land inside the castle, or sometimes, when the land is dry, on the roadway and green outside. I must tell you, Mr Shakespeare, that even in this time of flooding, the numbers he summons are growing. I do believe there were a thousand or more men and women here last Sunday. He foments Bedlam, sir.'

'How long has this been going on?'

'Since before I arrived just over two years ago. You must know that my predecessor, Gray, was a most upright Puritan who welcomed these hordes. The Puritans hold their services in loud voices so that the Catholic priests might see and hear them from their cells. It is done to provoke them, for the Puritans know how despised they are by the priests, and the feeling is mutual. There is much disputation and odium within the ranks of the Puritans, too. They even strike each other with fists over the meaning of certain passages in the scriptures.'

This was preposterous. Shakespeare's voice sharpened. 'Well, why do you not get your guards to clear them away? Pull up the drawbridge, call in the constable and townsmen?'

'It is not so easy. The Puritans evoke much sympathy among the townspeople, and among my watchers. Four local justices are meant to maintain discipline, but they, too, are of a Puritan bent. I feel outnumbered and powerless, Mr Shakespeare.'

Shakespeare suddenly realised that the keeper, for all his airs, was out of his depth. He was not fit to run a Southwark stew, let alone a prison of such importance to the realm.

'God's blood, Mr Medley, this is intolerable!' He clenched his fist, hard.

So Hooft was a hedge-priest as well as a would-be engineer. He wondered, briefly, about their meeting at Waterbeach. He could not quite shake off a vision of a spider in its web, waiting for flies to buzz into its net unawares. He wondered, too, about the security of this castle. Why, if things got out of hand, there could be a massacre. He would have to bring order to this place, and quickly. The most pressing matter, however, was the Jesuit.

Suddenly, from somewhere within the castle, they heard a cacophony of shouts and banging.

'What is that noise, Mr Medley?'

'I fear it is disputatious priests.'

'Take me to them.'

They found the clerics in the dining hall. A short, box-shaped man with red hair and beard was being restrained by two of his friends. He was struggling to free himself and yelling.

'You are a foul corruption and a fraud, Weston! You steal from us by the day. I say you are more wicked than the devils you purport to expel!'

Shakespeare saw that the priest was not fighting hard against the restraint of his fellows. He had no desire to enjoin physical battle.

At the other end of the room, four or five men were making their exit. At their centre, Shakespeare noted the unmistakable, short-cropped grey hair of William Weston. He did not look back but allowed himself to be smuggled away to safety.

'What is this, Dr Bagshawe?' Medley demanded of the man being restrained.

'God forgive me, I wish to kill him. He is a viper. He has been trying to bring his unspeakable ways into this place. He insists young Master Potter has been infected by a succubus and has told him he will exorcise the devil from his loins. It is heresy.'

Medley shook his head. 'You know, Dr Bagshawe, I cannot tolerate this behaviour. If you wish to have the freedom of the castle, you must live in harmony.'

'Tell that to Weston.'

Shakespeare had heard enough. 'Take this man to his cell,' he ordered the two guards restraining Bagshawe. 'Lock him there until I come.' As the guards removed Bagshawe, Shakespeare turned again to Medley. 'Is this true that there are exorcisms here?'

Medley's face reddened, betraying his dismay and pain at being spoken to in such sharp terms by his guest. 'Not to my knowledge, Mr Shakespeare. Indeed not.'

'Nor will there be. Come, sir, take me to Weston.'

William Weston was in his forty-fifth year, but looked to Shakespeare like an old man of sixty. It was still possible to see how his features had once been remarkably handsome and admired by women, but his hair was dry and brittle, his skin sallow and tired. His robe was a rag, held together by much darning. He knelt, motionless, praying at the side of his rolled blanket, for he would have no bed.

'Get up, Father, you have questions to answer.'

Slowly, Weston turned his body, the movement clearly causing him pain in the joints. Shakespeare bent forward and offered his hand to raise him to his feet. The priest's eyes were dull and distant.

'My name is John Shakespeare. You may recall that we met in the year eighty-six, shortly after you were arrested. I was with the clerk of the Privy Council at your interrogation. Do you remember?'

Weston reached out and took Shakespeare's hand. The Jesuit's own was shaking, but there was strength left in it and he was able to pull himself to his feet.

'You may sit if you wish.'

'I will stand.' The priest moved his face closer to Shakespeare's, trying to make out his features. 'I cannot see you clearly, but I recollect your name and your voice. Why are you here? Are you to take me to the scaffold for my martyrdom?'

'No. You will stay alive for the present. But you will answer my questions.'

'Ask your questions. But I may decline to answer.'

'Why was Dr Bagshawe angry? What did you do to him?'

'I do nothing to Bagshawe. He does it all himself – drunkenness, womanising, thieving. Ask him about Mistress Wentworth who visits him behind his bolted cell door, if you will. Worse, though, he is a traitor to God and his faith, as you must know, Mr Shakespeare, for is he not one of *your* spies?'

Shakespeare ignored the question; it was more than likely that Bagshawe had once worked for Walsingham. Instead, he held up the letter, too far away for Weston's half-blind eyes to read.

'This is a letter, sent by Robert Persons at St Gregory's in Seville. I believe it is intended for you.'

A glimmer of light brightened the priest's eyes. 'Father Robert has written to me?'

'I believe so.'

'Give me the letter, please.' He reached out to take it, but Shakespeare held it away from his clutching hand.

'He urges you to be strong in your faith.'

'If it is for me, then place it in my hands. My spectacle-glasses are lost and I cannot see, save close to my eyes.'

'No, it is evidence. I will hold on to it.'

'What else, then, does Father Robert say? You cannot imagine the joy, Mr Shakespeare. This letter is like water at the lips of a dying man.'

'There is no joy in this letter. He threatens England and the

Queen in most violent language. What do you know of this? And think well before you reply, for I will not be taken for a fool by you.'

Shakespeare looked around the room. The cell was austere. All Weston had was a picture of saints on the wall, his blanket, a three-legged stool, and a table that seemed to serve as an altar, for it held a Latin Bible, two candles and a crucifix. There was, too, a reliquary, which Shakespeare opened, to reveal a small golden cross, a bone and a string of ivory beads.

'Campion's finger?' Shakespeare demanded, holding up the bone.

Weston's face was a mask of ice. 'I will have you know that certain of Blessed Father Campion's bones burn the devil most wonderfully. But I would not expect a heretic to understand such things.'

'Or a chicken bone, perhaps . . .'

Weston looked to the door. A serving boy of about eleven years stood there. He moved towards his master, but Weston shook his head and the boy held back.

Shakespeare returned the bone to its box and turned once more to the matter of the letter. 'Persons says you must be ready to play your part. He says the plan is advanced and will bring down the House of Tudor. This is prima facie evidence. You are party to treason, Father Weston.'

'What can you do to me? How can you frighten me with threats of sending my body to its tomb when this cell is already sepulchre to my soul? You think you can scare me with your talk?'

'This is not just you. It is all the other priests here. You will not be executed, but others will, and you will be responsible for it. Would you have that mortal sin on your conscience?'

Shakespeare was lying, for there was nothing in this letter to say who the intended recipient might be and nothing that might convict any man.

'Mortal sin? How little you heretics understand us! Every martyrdom is but a rung on the ladder to God's kingdom.'

Shakespeare pulled back his fist. Weston did not flinch. Shakespeare's hand quivered in fury, then fell. The secret was here, in this prison; he was certain of it. But he was equally sure that giving Weston a bloody nose was not the way to discover it.

He thrust the letter back into his doublet. He remembered now why he had so disliked Weston at that first meeting. It was the lack of doubt, the utter certainty that he was right and that anyone who disagreed with him was wrong and was destined for damnation. It was, too, the man's utter contempt for human life, his own and everyone else's, that riled him. He and the clerk had got nowhere with their questioning nine years ago; the chances now seemed equally slender. This priest had grown old in austerity and defiance.

For the moment, Shakespeare would take another tack. He calmed himself, tried to soften the ire in his voice.

'We will move on then,' he said. 'There is another matter. Among the many young men and women you tormented with your exorcisms, there was one named Thomasyn Jade. Do you recall her?'

If Weston was surprised by the question, he did not show it. 'Yes, I recall her well. She imbibed the light of Divine grace. We saved her for Christ.'

'You left her broken, in spirit and body. She has been missing ever since then. Is she alive or dead? Mad or sane? I want to know where she is.'

'I cannot help you.'

'It was Father Southwell's dying wish that she be found and cared for.'

The priest's palsied shaking suddenly intensified. His knees seemed to be giving way. Shakespeare put a hand to his elbow and helped him to sit down on the stool.

'Father Southwell is dead?'

'Executed at Tyburn a few days since. He died well. The crowd refused to denounce him.'

'And you spoke with him before his death?'

'In his last hours. He called me to his cell and asked me this favour, to find Thomasyn, for he was sore troubled by her fate. He did not agree with you that she had been saved. Quite the opposite, I would say.'

Weston closed his dull, opaque eyes. 'It is true. We did not concur on the best way to rid the body of demons ...' Suddenly, he clutched Shakespeare's hand. 'Please, I beg you, tell me more of Father Southwell and his martyrdom.'

'No one who saw him die was unmoved. I am not of your faith, Father Weston, but I would say he died in holiness.'

The Jesuit crossed himself. 'We must sing mass for him, this very day. This day, and every day hereafter. I must proclaim the news—'

Shakespeare pulled his hand free. 'You will have time enough for that. First, I ask again: do you know where Thomasyn Jade is? If you do, then you owe it to your brother in Christ to tell me.'

The priest shook his head. 'I know little about her, Mr Shakespeare. All I recall is that she was haunted by lustful thoughts and imaginings and would have gone to hell without us. I recall that many demons were in her. We cast them all out with Campion's bone, holy pins and vapour of brimstone. They fled with great screaming and beating of wings into the dark night.'

'Did she come with friends, family? Who else might know where she is?'

'I cannot help you. I am sorry, for if this is Father Southwell's wish, then I would indeed give my assistance.'

'There must be something you recall.'

The priest hesitated.

'Yes?'

'There was one to whom she seemed close. An old nun . . . one who is beyond your reach, for she was here at the time of good Queen Mary. I am sure she must be with God by now.'

'Sister Michael?'

'Yes, yes. How did you know?'

Shakespeare cursed silently. He should have let the old hag rot in Bridewell. Now, she would be long gone.

Chapter 17

CHRISTOPHER BAGSHAWE WAS a very different man to Weston, but Shakespeare was drawn to him no more than he had been to the Jesuit.

'I believe you and Father Weston do not agree on much, Dr Bagshawe.'

'He would corrupt our faith. Weston and Persons – all of them from the so-called Society of Jesus. They design their morals to suit their needs. They bring man's politicking into a world of heavenly spirituality. He thinks to rule us here, but I will not have it.'

'Did you strike him?'

'No, I have never done that. *Would* never do that . . .'

'And yet you had to be restrained.'

'They could not have held me back had I wished to attack the man.'

'He accuses you of licentiousness.'

'I accuse him of tyranny, like all Jesuits. He would rule here like a very king.'

They were in Bagshawe's cell, which stood in remarkable contrast to the plainness of Weston's, for it was cluttered with books, half-burnt candles, a comfortable but tangled bed, boxes with clothing. There were more boxes with food spilling out. Two wine flagons, one on its side and empty, the other stoppered. Bagshawe's countenance oozed cunning.

'You hear a great deal, Dr Bagshawe. I need you to help me, for I am trying to solve a puzzle.'

'The only puzzle is why you do not hang the egregious worm. Why does the Council send the saintly Campion to the gallows and leave Weston alive? We had morris dancers, card-playing, feasting and hobby-horses at Christmas in times gone by, but he forbids them with his rules and insists, instead, on solemn high mass and spiritual exercises. I cannot abide him. What gives him the right to rule over ordained priests who are not of his order?'

Shakespeare had no interest in the dispute between Bagshawe and Weston. He went straight to the point. 'In times past, too, I know you supplied intelligence to Walsingham and my associate Mr Mills. What is the price these days for information about conspiracies?'

'There are conspiracies here by the cartload. How much will you pay? When they instituted the daily recitation of the lit-anies after dinner, it was nothing but a device to cover the hatching of plots. They beg God's mercy on England, all the while planning schemes to bring her under the Spanish king's sword.'

'I am interested in one specific plot. It involves your old friend Robert Persons.' Shakespeare paused and smiled.

'That treacherous earwig is no friend of mine.'

'No, I know your history. You are old enemies from Balliol College, Oxford, I believe.'

'I have nothing but contempt for the man. So he and Weston have a conspiracy? Well, that does not surprise me. They both make me wish to puke up my bread and meat, for they do Catholicism more harm than ever Topcliffe did. Catholic and Protestant could live side by side peacefully in

England were it not for Persons, Weston and their ilk. Every day is a plot for them. Weston was in with Babington and the others, right up to the collar of his fetid hairshirt. He should have been hanged and bowelled.'

'So tell me what you know.'

Bagshawe's mouth creased as though he had broken open a rotten egg. 'Do you think they would tell *me* of their dirty dealings? If you want to know anything, talk to that whimpering catamite of his.'

'His servant boy?'

'No. Caldor. Gavin Caldor. He is no Jesuit yet, but he fervently wishes to be one. He's always around Weston, like a flesh-fly around an ulcer. See how he cringes and wrings his sinful hands.'

'I shall talk to him.'

'Ask him about the many visitors Weston has received these past two years since we were allowed the freedom of the castle.'

'Do you know these visitors?'

Bagshawe laughed without mirth. 'They are too sly for that. None of them come under their own names. I have seen one or two and have been suspicious of their fervent eyes, but I could not tell you their true names. And then .... .e the boys who come as servants, as though they were Wisbech lads looking to earn a penny. In truth, they are the sons of great families sent in to study under Weston, as though this place were a seminary, not a gaol.'

'Is that how Caldor came here?'

'No, but he will tell you all you wish to know. Show him the rack: that will open his mouth wide enough to satisfy any effeminate boy-priest.'

'That is not the way I work, Dr Bagshawe.'

'No, indeed, I know it is not. We may be almost at the

other end of the world here, but we hear enough. I know a little about you, Mr Shakespeare. There are those who call you a crypto-Catholic.'

'You should not listen to gossip, Dr Bagshawe. You should work for me. There will be gold for you, perhaps freedom. Bring me true intelligence as you once did for Mr Secretary Walsingham.'

'We shall see. In the meantime, I wish you well in your quest. I shall sing high mass myself if you can bring Weston to the noose.'

Shakespeare ordered the keeper, Medley, to have Gavin Caldor brought to the office. Caldor was to come in chains, his hands manacled, guarded by two men.

Medley looked slightly bewildered. 'Caldor is a lamb, no threat to anyone and the least likely of all the prisoners to try to escape. Why, I think he would jump from his skin if I clapped my hands behind his back. There is no need for such stern measures.'

'I will decide what is necessary, Mr Medley.'

Medley bowed without conviction. 'As you will.'

'And, Mr Medley, when was the last search of all the cells carried out?'

'As I recall, it was Michaelmas.'

'That is half a year and more! Have all the cells examined this day. The prisoners will be removed to the dining hall and held there under guard while the search is carried out. And make it thorough. I want all writings and letters brought to me, bundled up and unread by you or the guards. All, Mr Medley. None are to be discounted as unimportant. Every scrap of paper. Do you understand?'

'Yes, Mr Shakespeare.'

'Now leave me.'

Medley bowed nervously. 'There is also the matter of Mr Hooft . . .'

'We will discuss that later.'

'Yes, sir.' Medley bowed again, even lower, then backed from the room, all swagger gone.

When Caldor arrived, flanked by guards, Shakespeare was lounging on a settle, his feet up and his hands behind his head. He watched the prisoner out of the corner of his eye without moving. He let him wait a few minutes, then languidly rose to his feet and walked over to the prisoner so that their faces were little more than a foot apart.

'So you are Mr Caldor. What are you: priest? Jesuit? Conspirator?'

Caldor's eyes were wide and grew even larger in horror at the accusation. 'I am a lay brother, sir,' he stuttered. 'I have served the Society of Jesus and others in certain ways.'

Shakespeare saw that the young man was drenched in sweat. He walked across to the fire and turned his back on him. Moments passed. A faint aroma of urine wafted across the room from the prisoner. Shakespeare shook his head as though in despair, then turned back to him.

'Helping to build hiding holes, I do believe. You are fortunate to have your head. Have you been brought to trial?'

'No, sir.'

Shakespeare tried to estimate Caldor's age. He could not be much over twenty and looked younger.

'Well, that can be arranged, if I deem it necessary.'

The young man shook uncontrollably. His slender body slumped and had to be held up by the guards at either side of him.

'I have a few questions for you, Mr Caldor. Direct, honest answers will serve you well.'

A dark stain of urine had spread down across the front of the young man's hose. Shakespeare suddenly felt a stab of shame for using him thus. But better to be questioned in this way than have his body crippled for ever by Topcliffe's rack.

'Tell me more about yourself, Mr Caldor. Are you carpenter or stonemason?'

'I was a carpenter, of sorts.'

'And where did you learn this skill?'

'In the playhouses, sir. I built props and scenery.'

'And then you turned your hand to hidey-holes. Did you work alone on them?'

'Please, sir, do not ask that of me.'

'Where did you work?'

'Great houses. I beg you, do not ask me which ones. You must know the one where I was caught.'

'You do not answer my questions, Mr Caldor. Do you have no care for your life? I tell you what I will do for you: I will put those matters aside for the moment. Whether or not I return to them depends very much on how you answer my next questions. It has been suggested to me that you are Father Weston's catamite. Is this true?'

Caldor's sweating brow knitted in confusion. 'Catamite?'

'His partner in sodomy.'

The horror on the young man's face was evidence enough. 'In God's name, no, sir.'

'Why should I believe you?'

'Because I speak the truth. I am a chaste man, sir. I would never engage in such things, nor, I am certain, would Father Weston.'

'You are close to him, though. Does he confide in you?'

'We talk much. We pray a great deal together and meditate on the holy scriptures. He instructs me in my studies and teaches me Hebrew. Sir, I consider Father Weston my best teacher and mentor. I revere him.'

'What are his secrets?'

'He has none. He is what he seems, a man of God.'

'Your cell is about to be searched, Mr Caldor. Tell me precisely what will be found there. Letters? Secret codes? Correspondence from Father Persons in Seville?'

The prisoner shook his head with vigour. Beads of sweat splashed on to the rush-matted floor.

Shakespeare fished the Seville letter from his doublet. He handed it to the young man and watched his eyes as he read it, looking for a reaction. All he saw was fear.

'What does that letter mean to you?'

'Nothing, sir. It seems like treason, but I have no knowledge of it, neither who wrote it, nor for whom it is intended.'

Shakespeare took back the letter and tilted his head to the guards. 'Remove the manacles and chains.'

One of the men, surly and heavy-set, unlocked the heavy iron bands.

'You may sit down, Mr Caldor. Take the stool by the table.'

'Thank you, sir.' Caldor sat down, leaning forward in the vain hope of concealing his pissed-upon hose.

'Now, I repeat, what will be found in your cell?'

'A cross, sir, a Latin Bible, a rosary, letters from my mother in Ripon, a mattress and blanket, some conserved greengage. That is all. No, forgive me, there is also my comb, some quills, an inkhorn—'

'The letters from your mother, what do they say?'

'She asks after my health, gives me news of home and prays that I may stay strong in the love of God.'

'And with whom is she in contact? Does she receive letters from Seville? Should I, perhaps, send pursuivants to search her house?'

'Please, sir, no. My mother is very sick with a canker. I confess she is true to the Roman faith, but surely that is no crime. I promise you, there are no secrets there.'

'What does the name Loake mean to you?'

'Loake?'

'Garrick Loake.'

'Nothing, sir, I do not know the name.'

Did he hesitate? Was his voice a note higher as he gave his answer? He was so nervous, his sweating so profuse, that it was difficult to discern a reaction.

'Let us return to Father Weston. I believe he has had a number of visitors during the past two years since the prison regime was relaxed. Which of those would interest me most, Mr Caldor?'

'I cannot think that any of them would interest you—'

'Have there been any Jesuit priests?'

Caldor averted his eyes.

Shakespeare seized on this. 'Well?'

'Father Walley has been here.'

'Walley?' The name struck home like an arrow. 'You mean Henry Garnett?'

This was serious news, if true. Henry Garnett was superior of the Jesuit mission to England. He had held the position since the incarceration of Weston and Southwell. He was the most wanted man in the country.

The young Catholic prisoner closed his eyes with shame at having revealed such important information. 'I did not know he was Father Garnett.' His voice was a whisper. 'I knew him only as Walley.'

'When was this?'

'Fifteen months since.'

Shakespeare felt his stomach tighten. Yes, that fitted. Garnett had been using the name Walley at that time. He had probably changed it again since then. But his alias was not the important thing here; the vital matter was what had transpired between Garnett and Weston when they were alone together. What had they plotted here in the supposedly secure confines of this castle while Keeper Medley looked the other way? What plans did they hatch and what messages did they agree to send to Seville?

Shakespeare drew his sword from its scabbard and brought the shining tip to rest on the prisoner's bare throat.

'So tell me, Mr Caldor, what did they discuss? Did they plan to kill the Queen with poison, blade, powder, pistol?'

Caldor could scarce breathe for fear. He put his hands to his throat and tried to fend off the sword, drawing blood from his fingers along the edge of the unmoving blade.

'I am running short of patience.'

'Please, sir, nothing,' he gasped. 'I heard nothing. They sang solemn high mass and they spoke of the imprisoned men's studies, nothing more.'

'Were you with them all the time, then?'

'No, sir. They spent time together alone, but I am certain it was a meeting of joy. It was not a secret meeting of conspiracy. That is not Father Weston's way. In the name of God, I beg you to believe me.'

One thing was certain: Garnett and Weston would not have had a meeting without conspiring to further the cause of Rome and the Society of Jesus by whatever means they considered effective, either criminal or otherwise. It would not have been in the nature of either man to pass up such an opportunity.

Shakespeare withdrew his sword-tip from the prisoner's throat, but did not replace it in its scabbard. 'Very well,' he said at last. 'But let us return to your background. You said you learnt your trade in the playhouses. Which ones?'

'The Theatre and the Curtain in Shoreditch.'

Garrick Loake had worked at the Theatre. Did he have any link to Wisbech? To Caldor? Shakespeare thought back to Loake's warning: *There is a most foul conspiracy unfolding. It wafts from the papist fastness of eastern England* . . .

'I ask again, did you have dealings with a man called Garrick Loake?'

'No, sir, I do not think I know him. Is he a player?'

'You understand the consequences if you lie to me?'

'Yes, sir. Every word I have said to you is true, though it has caused me great distress. I feel as though I have betrayed Father Weston.'

Shakespeare looked at Caldor, trying to see beyond the man's fear. He could not make up his mind about him. His terror might suggest guilt, but equally he could just be afraid. Shakespeare had come across enough innocent men and women who quaked with fear at the name Topcliffe. He would have to find other ways to discover the truth.

'There is something else. I believe there have been converts while the priests have been here. Men and women who have gone over to your faith, yes?'

'There have been many.'

'And have any gone away to the seminaries? In particular, have any spoken of becoming Jesuits? Have you heard of any going to the seminaries of Spain?'

'It is possible . . . I do not know for certain.'

'Some young man, perhaps, so inspired by Father Weston's teachings that he enrolled in the College of St Gregory at Seville?'

'I cannot say, sir. If that happened, then I was not party to it. Yet I can tell you that many have come here heretics and been reconciled to the true Church.'

One of the guards cleared his throat. Not the sullen one

with the keys but his companion. Shakespeare had almost forgotten they were there, but now he turned his attention to the man.

'Did you wish to say something, turnkey?'

'Forgive me for speaking out of order, master, but there was the Gray girl. She had her head turned by Weston and went away. There are those that said she went to Rome or France, sir, perhaps to become a nun.'

'Gray?'

'The daughter of Thomas Gray, the former keeper of Wisbech. Mr Gray is no longer with us sadly, drowned in the Nene. He was a strict Puritan gentleman, much respected in these parts for his stern dealings with the prisoners. The coroner found that he took his own life, distraught at the loss of his daughter to the papists. At one time, it is said, he ran at her with a knife as though he would kill her. Her name was Sorrow. Sorrow Gray. She is long gone from here. It was a scandalous event at the time. I hope that I am not doing anyone a disservice, master, but I am sure Mr Medley could give you the complete tale, if you wished to hear it.'

'Thank you, guard. It is something I shall look into.' Shakespeare turned back to Gavin Caldor. He had one last question. 'Did you know this woman, this Sorrow Gray?'

'To say good day to, yes, sir. But I could not say I knew her well.'

'What sort of young woman was she?'

'I cannot say. She was a Puritan and then a Catholic. That is all I know.'

Shakespeare looked at him long and hard. Gavin Caldor was close to collapse. 'If I find you have kept information from me, I shall return to this place and take you to the Tower. You know what that means?'

Caldor nodded frantically.

'Go now.' Shakespeare dismissed him with a flick of the hand. 'Take the prisoner to clean himself up,' he ordered the guards, 'then put him in the dining room where the others are to be mustered. Keep him apart from Weston. I do not want them talking. And have Mr Medley sent to me.'

Shakespeare watched the departing back of Gavin Caldor. He had had his fill of papist priests and their acolytes this day.

Chapter 18

MEDLEY NODDED HIS head gravely 'So you have heard some of the tale of Sorrow Gray,' he said. 'Tell me what you know and I shall endeavour to fill in the spaces.'

'All I know is that she was converted by Weston and has gone to be a nun.'

'Converted? I would say *perverted*. As to whether she became a nun, no one knows, but it is certainly possible.'

'Start at the beginning.'

Medley was trying to regain his composure having felt the sting of humiliation, but it was all too clear that, while he was here, Shakespeare was the master of the castle.

'Indeed, from the beginning,' Medley said. 'As you must know, my predecessor as keeper, Thomas Gray, had no truck with the ways of the papists. He kept them locked in their cells save for an hour a day of exercise. And when they dined, he would sit at the table with his deputy and with his wife to monitor all that was said.'

'He had a daughter, Sorrow, yes?'

'He had three daughters – Sorrow, Comfort and Endurance. They were raised in the Puritan way and went modestly at all times. From what I have heard, I would say they were as devout as their father, particularly Sorrow, who was considered a prophetess in these parts, for she had visions. She begged her father to allow her to dispute with the priests, that she might through argument and sermonising demonstrate to them that they were in error.'

Shakespeare laughed grimly. 'But the old serpent Weston lured her to *his* way instead.'

'Yes. At first, she kept her conversion secret. She found excuses not to join the Puritan meetings and Bible readings. But she could not keep living this lie and confessed all. Her father was aflame with rage. He tried everything to turn her away from her foolishness, but she would not listen. He tried locking her away, depriving her of food. In the end he ran at her with a knife, but she managed to escape.'

'There must have been a hue and cry.'

'Indeed. But there was no sign of her and she has not been seen since. Most men assume that she had learnt of some safe Catholic house in the neighbourhood and that she went from there to the Carthusian nunnery at Louvain. Some say her father found her and killed her, sinking her body into the mere. Whatever her fate, her father was a broken man. I think the shame was too great for him. He drank a great deal of brandy and threw himself into the torrent.'

Shakespeare was thinking hard. There could be many possibilities other than those suggested by Medley. Perhaps she had travelled to Seville, not Louvain. It was not impossible that she had taken messages from Weston to Garnett and then onwards to Robert Persons. She would not be the first woman involved in subversion.

'And then, there is the matter of Paul Hooft,' Medley continued.

'What has he to do with all this?'

'That is what I have been trying to tell you, Mr Shakespeare. He was to have married Sorrow. Their wedding day was settled. It would have been the grandest event of the year in Wisbech.'

'Hooft was engaged to this woman?' What in God's name had been going on in this outpost?

'He was left at the altar, so to speak. But his reaction was very different from that of her father. He did not sink into melancholia, nor did he rage against her. What he did do was to become yet more zealous in his Calvinist faith. He spent all his time preaching, winning converts as though it were a contest between him and Weston as to who could gain the most souls. Nor was that enough for him. He brought more and more of his Puritan followers here to the prison, to taunt and threaten the priests with hellfire.'

'You do not like him.' It was a statement, not a question.

'I fear there is darkness in so firm a faith. Hooft and Weston are two halves of the same form, cast from the same mould. They may seem like opposites yet they share much in common. Neither will allow any doubt that they are right, and neither would balk at the killing of a man they see as a heretic or idolater. I do believe they would each take pleasure in the other's death. That is why I was concerned when you gave Mr Hooft access to the inner castle, sir.'

The smell of baking bread in the kitchens was balm to Shakespeare's senses. He found Boltfoot sitting at a small table, with a trencher laden with half a loaf of steaming manchet and a rapidly disappearing roasted waterfowl.

'Where is Mr Hooft, Boltfoot?'

'He said he had some business, master.'

'Inside the castle, or without?'

'He did not say.'

Suddenly there was a din of shouting from elsewhere. Shakespeare felt a chill. 'Come with me, Boltfoot.'

*

The dining hall was in uproar. Paul Hooft was standing on a square table in the centre of the room, clutching his Bible in both hands, facing down the two groups of priests: Weston and his cohort at one end of the room; Bagshawe and his followers at the other.

'You are all steeped in venery, superstition and wickedness!' Hooft bellowed. 'Before God, you stand condemned. Your way is total depravity!'

One of the priests from Weston's crowd pushed forward, like a bull daring to advance from the herd. '*You* are the sinner, Hooft. *You* are the heretic!'

Hooft pointed past the priest at Weston. 'You, Weston, are the Antichrist, the archdemon, the lewd acolyte of Satan! I say you are an abomination in the sight of God.'

Weston crossed himself but did not respond. Shakespeare watched the scene, aghast at the image of chaos and disorder, then clapped his hands for silence.

The hubbub died down to a murmur as the priests and Hooft turned towards the two newcomers. The three guards, who had been enjoying the spectacle of traded insults and rhetoric, looked sheepish at the sight of Shakespeare and began trying to shepherd the priests back into lines.

'Get down, Mr Hooft,' Shakespeare commanded. 'Guards, make the prisoners sit on the floor. They are to observe absolute silence until they are free to return to their cells. Any spoken word is to be recorded and will be punished by a week's solitary confinement with short commons.'

Hooft did not move. Shakespeare nodded to Boltfoot, who stepped forward and dragged the man down from the table.

'Take him to Mr Medley's room, Boltfoot.'

Boltfoot thrust his powerful arms under Hooft's shoulders and began to haul him across the floor.

*

Hooft showed no repentance for his action and met Shakespeare's fury with a defiant glare.

'Any more interventions like that and you will be clapped in irons, Mr Hooft.'

'Why should I not talk to them thus? They are all traitors and idolaters, every man of them. You know this yourself.'

'Indeed, there are traitors among them, but I am on Queen's business here and I will be impeded by no man. Now, a matter has come to my attention. The affair of you and Sorrow Gray. Why did you not mention her?'

'Why do you think? Would you wish to tell the world of the bride who betrayed you?'

'But you knew of my interest in the events at this place. Tell me your story, Mr Hooft.'

'Very well. We were betrothed before witnesses; she had no right in law to turn aside from me. I would sue for breach of contract if she could be found. As for her apostasy, she has ruined many lives.'

'I wish to know more about her. Could she be involved in conspiracy?'

There is no man, nor woman, more intense and dangerous than a convert, Walsingham had once told him.

'Sorrow Gray is capable of any deceit or evil. Beyond that, I cannot help you for I can scarce utter the words. If you wish to know more of her, speak to her mother or sisters. They live within half a furlong of here, by the market square.'

'Take me there.'

'As you wish.'

'It must have been hard for you, Mr Hooft.'

Hooft laughed without humour. 'I had thought that we would conquer the world for God, Sorrow and I. Truly, I did believe we would transform this landscape, both physically and spiritually, draining the fens and spreading the word.

But Satan proved too strong for her. I never knew she was so frail . . .'

'Thank you, Mr Hooft.' Shakespeare's voice softened. Hooft was a man scorned in the most brutal fashion. 'And, please, write your letters to Sir Robert Cecil on the Fenland drainage. I will happily convey your message to him.'

The house in Wisbech was constructed of knapped Norfolk flint and was well kept. Thorny rose briers neatly enveloped the front.

Hooft knocked at the door, then pushed it open. 'Mistress Gray,' he called out. 'It is I, Paul Hooft.'

A woman bustled through into the hallway, brushing her flour-dusty hands on her apron, and then adjusting her plain white coif. She was slender, of middle years and good-looking. She smiled at Hooft. 'It is good to see you, Paul. Are you well?'

'Yes, I am well.'

'Then you should come to see us more often. You are still as welcome here as you always were.'

'Thank you, mistress. Perhaps I will come more when the land is dry again.'

The woman's gaze turned to the newcomer.

'This is Mr Shakespeare,' Hooft said. 'He wishes to speak with you.'

'I am Mary Gray. How may I help you, sir?'

Where had he seen that face before? No, not that face, but one a little like it. Something in the eyes . . .

'He wishes to hear about Sorrow. He is here at the castle on Queen's business.'

The woman's eyes flicked from Hooft to Shakespeare, unsure of herself.

'You have nothing to fear from me. This may not have any

bearing on your daughter,' he said, 'but at the risk of opening old wounds, I would ask for your cooperation.'

'Very well, sir. We have naught to hide in this house. You know a little of the story, do you? Well, when we called her Sorrow, I fear we did not know how well named she would turn out to be. My husband insisted on the name, for he said we must always remember that this world is not given to us solely to experience joy. At the end, he rued his choice.'

There was a movement behind Mistress Gray and another, younger, woman entered the room. Shakespeare gazed on her face with utter astonishment.

Beatrice Eastley stood before him. Beatrice Eastley, the brooding, pipe-smoking companion of Lady Susan Bertie, Countess of Kent.

'This is my daughter, Mistress Adamson,' Mary Gray said by way of introduction. 'She is twin sister to Sorrow, but unlike her in all but looks, thank the Lord.'

'Your name is Adamson?' Shakespeare asked, the incredulity clear in his voice. 'What is your first name?'

'Comfort, sir. Comfort Adamson. I am wife to Shipwright Adamson, an alderman of this town.'

'Your name is not Beatrice Eastley?'

She laughed. 'No, sir.'

'Does the name mean anything to you?'

'Indeed it does not, sir.'

'And would I be correct in thinking that you are identical to your sister Sorrow?'

'In looks, she may be,' Hooft put in. 'But not in other ways. Sorrow has a hollow heart.'

So Beatrice Eastley was none other than Sorrow Gray. It had to be thus. There was no other explanation. Sorrow Gray had not gone off to be a nun, but instead had become a lady's companion in one of the great Protestant houses of England.

For a few moments, he gathered his thoughts. *A strange move for a devout Catholic convert.* That was the first thought, and then, *What plot is hatching here – and what is Lady Susan Bertie's role in it? Is she an innocent dupe, or what?*

A sudden fear struck him: Beatrice Eastley was now with Lucia Trevail on her journey to Cornwall. A dozen questions spun through his mind, all at once. He sensed terrible danger.

He turned again to Mary Gray. 'Have you heard anything of your daughter? Has she written or contacted you in any way?'

'No, sir. I know not whether she be alive or dead. When she left, she cursed us and swore that God would unleash raging tempests upon the land. She died for us on the day my husband took his life in the flood.'

Raging tempests. The words were familiar. Had not the letter found aboard *The Ruth* vowed to bring down raging tempests and torrents upon the House of Tudor?

'I must ask you again, for this is mighty important: you are certain that you know of no woman named Beatrice Eastley? You have no close cousin of that name?'

Mother and daughter both looked blank. 'No, indeed not, sir.'

'Or Lady Susan Bertie, Countess of Kent? Do you know of her? Has she had any contact with this family?'

Mother and daughter shook their heads. 'No, sir.'

Hooft put up his hand like a schoolboy in class. 'If I may be permitted to say something, Mr Shakespeare?'

'Go on.'

'It is none of my business, you might think. But I believe that William Weston turned her mind with his rites of exorcism. He told her she had demons within and she believed him. I saw the pinpricks where he stuck her with needles. I believe she was sent mad by the Catholic slurry that he heaped on her . . .'

'What are you suggesting?'

'Would it not be the correct thing to do to take Weston back to London for questioning in the Tower? There is a rack there, I believe. That will make him talk. If there is some conspiracy, he will know it all.'

Shakespeare stared at Hooft. 'You are right,' he said at last. 'It *is* none of your business.'

Apart from his own distaste for torture, Shakespeare had not forgotten Cecil's command: there was to be no more martyrdom. The other thought in his mind was the strange coincidence that he was now looking for *two* young women who had undergone exorcism: Thomasyn Jade and Sorrow Gray. Mere coincidence? Mr Secretary Walsingham would not have believed it so, and neither did he.

He turned back towards the mother. 'If you ever hear word of your daughter, you are to send messages to me. Is that understood? Mr Medley at the castle will know how to contact me.'

He returned to the Dutchman, with some reluctance. 'Mr Hooft, I will have to make haste from this place. I would be grateful to have your assistance once again in crossing the flood. Please be ready at dawn to escort me back to Waterbeach.'

He bowed to the two women. 'Good day to you both.'

Chapter 19

WILLIAM WESTON WAS brought to Shakespeare in Medley's office. The old Jesuit's face was set hard.

'I believe you entertained a visitor in recent months, one Henry Garnett, Jesuit superior in the England mission.'

'Garnett? Is he in England? I recall him from Rome, of course, Mr Shakespeare. A Christian with saintly virtues.'

'So you are talking. That is a start. Garnett, as you well know, has been in England since the year eighty-six. He came over that summer with Father Southwell, and you met them both shortly before your capture. When he came here to Wisbech, he went by the name of Walley. You spoke to him alone and conspiratorially.'

'Ah yes, I remember Mr Walley. Another fine gentleman who wished to be reconciled to the Sacraments of Rome. But I thought you mentioned Father Garnett? Do you have news of him?'

'Is this your damnable practice of equivocation? We know all about it now, thanks to Father Southwell's trial. You may think yourself full of wit with such clever answers, but they are lies, and you are guilty of mortal sin by uttering them.'

The priest's face remained blank. Neither amused nor angry.

'This will end badly, Weston. You must know it. Some of

you Jesuits think you can meddle in affairs of state, but the Bible tells us what happens when a man sows the wind.'

'You have had your say, Mr Shakespeare, and I have listened. It is late. If that is all, then I would like to return to my cell, which is my oratory. It is time for compline.'

'No, that is not all. You mentioned to me that Sister Michael was close to Thomasyn Jade. Write me a letter to take to her, instructing her to assist me, for so far she is of no help. I promise you that no harm will come to the girl, or to Sister Michael. Do this for your friend Father Southwell.'

Who was a better man than you, Weston, or any of the stubborn, disputatious priests in this forsaken castle of despair.

'Very well.'

'Here.' Shakespeare handed him a quill, inkhorn and paper. 'Do it now.'

Weston took the writing implements and wrote a brief letter in Latin, greeting Sister Michael in Christ, and telling her to trust and assist Shakespeare in any matter concerning Thomasyn Jade, but in no other way. He signed the paper, sliced off the edges with the quill-knife so that no extra words could be added by forgery, then folded it and handed it back to Shakespeare.

'Thank you. Now let us talk of Sorrow Gray.'

At last Weston showed some emotion. He smiled. 'Sorrow? Was ever a child so ill named. I tell you, Mr Shakespeare, the casting out of her demons and her conversion to the true faith brought me more happiness than any other event in my life.'

'So you *did* practise your foul rite of exorcism on her?'

'I saved her from the devil and baptised her anew.'

'And so you learnt nothing from your disgraceful treatment of Thomasyn Jade. You bring one girl to madness, then another. Is this your true religion, Father? Is this what God desires of you?'

'You know nothing of it, Mr Shakespeare. You live in error, ignorance and heresy, and you will burn in the fire with no hope of salvation.'

Hellfire. Shakespeare understood. Weston had given the girl her new name: Beatrice, the woman who guided Dante out of purgatory to heaven.

'Beatrice Eastley,' he said, and looked for a reaction. He saw it, a mere flicker of shock in Weston's eyes, then back to the face of stone. 'I know exactly where she is, Father Weston. Whatever is plotted by you, it is in your power to end it here and now, with a few words to me, for I would not wish the alternative on any man or woman. Help me, otherwise I fear Sorrow Gray will reap the whirlwind you have sown.'

'I have nothing more to say. Do your heretic worst. Take me to the Tower and give my bones to Topcliffe. I will do what I must.'

By the light of a solitary candle, Francis Mills gazed down at the two bodies with a curious lack of passion. He had longed for the day when he would see his wife and her lover lying naked, bespattered with blood, their throats torn open. But this was not how he had imagined it in his tortured dreams.

Anne Mills no longer looked pretty, no longer looked like his wife. Her fair hair was thick with gore; her eyes were open, staring in horror. Her hands were bound before her with twine and so were her ankles. Blood was spread in jagged smears across her pale pink neck and breasts. Her lover, the grocer, was also naked, also tied up. His eyes were closed, but his mouth was open in an endless scream.

It was their fault. They should not have been here, together, naked like this, for this was Mills's marriage bed. How could they expect to survive when they indulged in their glistening obscenities in another man's marriage bed?

Mills had a knife in his hand. It was clean and shiny and hung loose from his fingers. Suddenly he dropped it. He looked around the bedchamber he knew so well. The candle stood on a coffer by the window, guttering in the draught and throwing strange shadows across the walls and ceilings. He walked over to the coffer, put the candle on the floor, then opened the lid of the ancient box. Inside were blankets and linen. Stooping down, he took out a large woollen blanket. It had come to them from Anne's father, with the marriage bond. Now it would make a shroud for the harlot. He grimaced at the word. No man should speak ill of the dead, however much their death was merited.

With exquisite gentleness, he spread the blanket over her and turned away, his tall thin body hunched into his black doublet and hose like a pecking crow. Even in death, he loved her. He averted his eyes from the grocer's screaming mouth. It disturbed him. For some reason he picked up the knife again. He wasn't thinking clearly. He walked to the chamber door-way and just stood there for a few moments. The stairway in front of him led down to the hall. His neighbour, Barnaby, was there, at the foot of the stairs, holding a lantern.

'We heard the screams, Mr Mills. What is it?'

Mills held up the knife, as if by way of explanation. 'They are dead, Barnaby. Anne and the grocer. They are in here.'

'You had better come downstairs, Frank. The constable is with me. Come on, drop the knife and come down.'

Mills placed the knife on the flat-topped newel post, then nodded his head in silent acquiescence and began walking down the stairs, slowly, as though they were his last steps to the gallows.

Shakespeare prepared to set off from Wisbech Castle with Paul Hooft in the grey chill of dawn.

LIBRARIES NEATH PORT TALBOT

'Is it too late to persuade you to bring Weston with us? I do believe most powerfully that he should be brought away from this place and be held in the Tower. This castle is not safe—'

'Mr Hooft, you have suffered greatly by the loss of the woman you were to have married, but I do not wish to hear another word on this subject of William Weston.' He looked the Dutchman in the eye and saw sullen resentment. 'Come, load the boat. I want all the castle inmates' correspondence kept safe and dry.'

Shakespeare turned away and bade farewell to Boltfoot.

'I have told Mr Medley that you will be overseeing the security of the prison. He tells me Wisbech has a trainband of townsmen, smiths and traders. They are mostly Puritans. Bring them in, explain that I fear some trouble and have them mount watches, day and night. At least six men, in addition to the guards. Is that clear?'

'Yes, master,' Botfoot said without enthusiasm.

'From what I understand, some of the priests have even been allowed to make visits to the market. That will cease unless the Privy Council orders otherwise. If there are any visitors, you will sit in on the meetings with a clerk supplied by Medley, who will take a note of all that is said. These notes, as well as all letters going in or out, will be retained and brought to me. You may let the priests know that this is intended as a temporary measure until I am certain that all threat has passed. Is that clear?'

Boltfoot nodded. His face told the whole story: he was mighty disconsolate.

'It should not be for long,' Shakespeare reassured him. 'A squadron of soldiers will be despatched here as soon as that can be organised. All being well, you will be able to follow me home in a week. If I am not there, I will leave instructions with Jane.'

He did not like leaving Boltfoot here like this, but Cecil and the Privy Council had to know about the way things were at this prison. The priests' letters and papers had to be gone through in fine detail, for there could be clues in them. Most importantly of all, he needed to track down Lucia Trevail and her new companion, Beatrice Eastley. The young woman had many questions to answer.

Shakespeare clasped Boltfoot's hand in his, then turned away and stepped into the punt, where Hooft was stowing a large pack of letters, all bundled up in waxed cloth. Hooft stood up from his task and took his position in the back of the craft, holding his long wooden quant. With a smooth practised movement, he pushed away and the punt slid off into the flood.

The day was fair. Progress should be swift, God willing. Shakespeare's heart quickened. The thought of meeting Lucia Trevail again stirred him with pleasant apprehension.

John Shakespeare retrieved his horse and took his leave of Paul Hooft at his farm near Waterbeach. After that, he rode hard, sleeping at the roadside when necessary, and eating and drinking only while his horse was being fed and watered. By the time he reached London and was ushered into Sir Robert Cecil's office at his mansion on the Strand, his clothes were ragged and his face haggard with exhaustion.

He bowed to the Privy Councillor and placed his bundle of papers on the table. 'Sir Robert.'

Cecil was brisk and to the point. 'Before you say anything, I must acquaint you with grave news. Frank Mills has been arrested on a charge of murdering his wife and her paramour, a grocer named Heartsease. Frank is now held at Newgate.'

Shakespeare was about to take a seat at the table, but he remained upright, his body stiffened with shock, all aches suddenly forgotten. 'Christ's blood! Is this certain?'

'Their throats were slit and he had the knife in his hand when a neighbour and the constable went to the house. They had heard a scream.'

'Has he said anything?'

'Nothing of sense. He has been taken by madness.'

Shakespeare drew a deep breath. This was the worst news. There had been an occasion when he had had cause to despise Frank Mills, but in recent times they had worked together well enough. He should not be surprised by the crime; Frank had been threatening to do for his wife and her lover for the best part of two years now. And yet Shakespeare had never really believed he would do it.

'It seems he found them in the marital bed,' Cecil continued. 'I have ordered the bodies removed to the Searcher of the Dead at St Paul's, though I cannot think he will discover anything of interest. The sheriff says it is a clear case of murder by a cuckold. A story as old as human life itself. The fact that Mills holds a position as assistant secretary in this office will not save him from the noose.'

'I must go to him.'

'Indeed, do that. And go to the Searcher, too, for I have other news. Garrick Loake has been found dead. You may visit the corpses together. Now then, John, let me hear your report.'

Loake dead? Shakespeare slumped into the chair. How had he let him slip through his fingers? There would be time enough to reproach himself later; for now he had to reveal all he had discovered at Wisbech Castle. Cecil listened carefully.

'The stink of conspiracy emanating from that foul dungeon is as high as a jakes in summer,' Shakespeare concluded. 'I suspect Weston knows the truth of it. Perhaps this woman Sorrow Gray, too. There is another I'm not certain of, a young carpenter named Caldor. He is close to Weston, and afraid.'

'You haven't brought Weston with you, please God.'

'No. I think I understood your instructions quite well, Sir Robert.'

Cecil smiled. 'He would never have broken under torture anyway.'

'Indeed not, Sir Robert. He relishes pain. He has a hairshirt, he kneels most of the night at prayer and, when he sleeps, he reclines on the hard stone. Pain is very ecstasy to him. He would happily embrace martyrdom, and still you would not get a word from him.'

'Then he is better consigned to obscurity. That is why Wisbech is so useful. If only . . .' Cecil trailed off.

Shakespeare knew what words he withheld: *if only Father Southwell had been sent there rather than to Tyburn, where he had won an undoubted victory for the Pope.*

'But you are sure there is a plot?' Cecil continued. 'In God's faith, it is like chasing air.'

'The letter is real enough. So is the death of Garrick Loake. And so is the strange departure of Sorrow Gray, a Catholic convert, and her reappearance as Beatrice Eastley, posing as a loyal member of the English Church.'

'Indeed. But what are they up to? Every sinew in my body tells me that we are under attack. But what is the nature of the assault? Where will it come?'

'The history of these past few years tells us they will try to assassinate Her Majesty. It has been tried often enough.'

'I agree, John. But let us not discount the alternatives.'

'As I see it, there are four other possibilities. Firstly, it could be an attempt to assassinate someone else of importance. They tried to kill Drake before. Whom might they target this time?' Shakespeare looked at Cecil; he would certainly be a prize for Spain and Rome. 'Secondly, it could be yet another invasion plan, but that would not involve priests at Wisbech. Thirdly, it might involve the smuggling of books or the setting up of an illegal press. Fourthly, there is the possibility of an attack on some vital target. Something that requires the assistance of spies and traitors already in England: shipping comes to mind.'

'Plymouth? Drake and Hawkins are fitting their fleets there . . .' Cecil produced a paper from his shelf. 'I have this flimsy report from Trott. He says there is an unconfirmed report of Spanish shipping around the western coasts. Like most reports from Trott, I treat it with scepticism. I am sure, however, that Drake will have his own preparations against attack.'

'Again, if that is the target, then what is the link to Wisbech?'

Cecil looked at the bundle that Shakespeare had deposited on the table. 'Perhaps the secret lies there. Those papers and letters must be gone through in fine detail.'

'In other days, it would have been a task for Frank.'

'Well, that is not an option. I shall have to call in favours. I want Thomas Phelippes to look through them.'

Phelippes? Shakespeare frowned. Phelippes was England's greatest codebreaker. In the old days, working for Sir Francis Walsingham, he had deciphered the letters that had brought Mary, Queen of Scots to the headsman's axe. But now he worked for the Earl of Essex, most bitter rival of the Cecil faction.

'I know what you are thinking, John, but I know enough of the earl's dirty secrets to hang him ten times over.' Cecil's thin lips turned down with distaste. 'I think I can secure the services of Mr Phelippes. Leave that to me. Turn *your* thoughts to Susan Bertie's companion. I know Susan well enough and I find it hard – nay, impossible – to believe that she would do anything against England. Do you agree?'

'I scarcely know her. Anyway, the girl is now with Lady Trevail and gone to her Cornish estates.'

'Then you will have to go to her. Something of a holiday

after Wisbech, I imagine,' Cecil continued drily. 'I cannot accept that any of the women in Susan Bertie's circle would be involved in popish plots, but we cannot take that for granted – nor can we assume that there is no danger to them from this renegade companion of theirs. Find this she-serpent Sorrow Gray, bring her in. See if she is party to conspiracy.'

Shakespeare nodded.

'Before you go, I want you to talk with Anthony Friday. I have employed him to insinuate himself into the Catholic circles he knows so well, to see what he can discover. I have been expecting him to report to me, but there has been no word. See what is going on. He knew Garrick Loake and those of his circle. If anyone can discover the truth about Loake's secret – and his death – I am certain it is Friday.'

Shakespeare kept to himself his feelings about Anthony Friday; the man was a ferocious anti-Catholic attack dog who had often ridden with Topcliffe in pursuit of priests and those harbouring them. Would any Catholic now trust him?

Cecil continued his theme. 'In the meantime, I shall send a squadron of eight men to Wisbech to ensure the prisoners are held secure and that the castle is properly defended.'

'It would help to send a clerk, too. Someone to read and censor all incoming and outgoing letters.'

'A good thought. Weston and company can pay for it them-selves. They have been living too high, so their diet will be reduced.' Cecil sat back in his seat. 'And, John, let me just add that all is not bad with the world. You will likely be pleased to know that Richard Topcliffe languishes in Marshalsea gaol, condemned for contempt of court. He is reduced to writing anguished letters to the Queen, begging her to intercede. But for the present, she will not.'

Shakespeare wanted to laugh out loud, but there was noth-ing remotely amusing about the murder, rape and torture that had been committed unchecked for so long by Richard Topcliffe.

Cecil held up a paper. 'The man has the wit of a flea-infested mongrel. This is one of his letters to Her Majesty. He writes, "I have helped more traitors to Tyburn than all the noblemen and gentlemen of the court, your counsellors excepted. In all prisons rejoicings; it is like that the fresh dead bones of Father Southwell at Tyburn and Father Walpole at York, executed both since Shrovetide, will dance for joy."'

'What make of man would brag of hunting other men to their deaths? He is where he belongs.'

'However,' Cecil said, 'whatever we think of Mr Topcliffe, he did work for us. Now that he is in gaol, we are another man down. So it is imperative that you stoke the fires of the idle Anthony Friday and make him earn his two marks!'

Chapter 20

FROM THE STRAND, Shakespeare repaired straightway to his home in Dowgate, where a letter awaited him. He shook his head in dismay at the writing, which was the scrawl of an idiot infant: Topcliffe. His inclination was to hurl it into the fire unread, but he cut it open nonetheless.

'*You may think yourself free of me, but do not. I am your master in the Marshalsea as ever I was on the outer side, for you must know I have men everywhere, men who love God and England. Have you brought the traitor Weston to London for godly racking? If not, then send for him now, for the Queen Her Majesty will not abide any man that lets the dirty Jesuit go untormented and his secrets so undiscovered. Do this or I will wreak such storms on your head that you will wish yourself dead, and your spawn likewise.*'

Shakespeare crumpled the letter into a ball and lit it from a candle. It burned bright and fell in black ashes to the ground, where he stamped on its embers.

Jane served him rabbit and capon pie with a goblet of good wine. After that, he bathed, then slept.

In the morning, he ate breakfast with his family. The table was busy and noisy. Andrew was talking enthusiastically about his new-found knowledge of navigation and sailing.

'Are you still set on this course?'

'More than ever, Father. I wish to join Drake at the soonest opportunity.'

'But you do not even know where he is planning to sail! No one does except Drake himself, Hawkins and the Privy Council. Even I have not been made party to this secret.'

In truth, though he would not say it, Shakespeare did know that the intended destination was Panama, where the Spanish treasure fleets gathered. But that was not to be spoken, either in this room or anywhere else.

'I would not care if the voyage was to the moon. I know this to be my destiny.'

Shakespeare smiled at the boy; Andrew had seen enough in his fourteen years not to have a romantic notion of what he faced. 'Very well. I am going westward and will escort you to Plymouth, where we can talk with Drake himself.'

Shakespeare had no doubt the admiral would take him. It was difficult enough to find crew for such a voyage at the best of times. A lad like Andrew would be a godsend.

'Thank you, Father.'

Shakespeare clasped Andrew to his breast. The sea brought perils but also the potential for adventure and riches. It was the boy's own choice.

Their discussion was interrupted by a fit of girlish giggling. Mary and Grace were deep in some secret conversation that was causing them enormous mirth.

'What is it, Mary?' Shakespeare asked his daughter.

'Ursula's got a swain,' Mary said without hesitation.

'She told us not to tell anyone!' Grace looked at her younger sister with mock fury.

'Well, she has. Ask her yourself.'

'Mary, if Ursula has a swain, then that is her business. And if she asked you to keep it a secret, then you should abide by her wishes. Do you understand?'

'But he is very handsome. He walked her home from the market last night and we saw him kiss her. She said he has a stall selling salad vegetables from the Dutch gardens in Islington.'

Ursula could not hear this betrayal of her new romance for she was already out buying produce for her stall. Shakespeare felt content. It was, he reflected, the way life should be: a family laughing, being indiscreet and squabbling as they planned their day; a welcome refuge from the unwholesome tribulations of Wisbech and conspiracy.

His only worry was Jane. She had seemed miserable as she served fresh bread and eggs for them all. Clearly, she was unhappy that Boltfoot was still away, but Shakespeare had known her long enough to see that something else was wrong. She could barely meet his eyes when he greeted her with news of her husband.

After breakfast, he took her aside. 'Jane, if you are anxious about something, you must know that you can always confide in me, whatever it is. You are family to me.'

'I know that, master.' She looked down at her feet as she spoke.

Shakespeare saw that she had lost weight. Her normally ample bosom was shrunken and there was a gauntness in her cheeks. He saw, too, that she had a new ring on a finger of her left hand and could not stop twisting it.

'I do not mean to pry, you understand. But neither can I stand by and say nothing when I see you in such anguish, especially with Boltfoot away. Can I ask you, Jane, is this something to do with the sickness that lately afflicted little John? I had thought him better than he was. He eats well and seems full of life.'

'Oh, master, if I were to speak to you, would you really not go to Boltfoot with what I say?'

Shakespeare had no intention of coming between a wife and husband, but neither could he fail to help Jane if she needed him. He nodded. She seemed on the edge of tears. 'You can trust me, Jane.'

There was silence between them, then Jane spoke so quietly that he could only just hear her. 'I have disobeyed my husband.'

Shakespeare frowned. Had she been unfaithful to Boltfoot? He could not believe it of her. 'Tell me more.'

'I went to Dr Forman. Boltfoot had said he was a conjuror and forbade me to go, but other wives told me he really could cure ills. I went to him secretly and he told me little John would be well, and he was.'

'Did he give you that ring to wear?'

She reddened furiously and hid her hand.

'Then all is well. Say nothing to Boltfoot and think no more of it. But do not let him see the ring.'

'I am racked with guilt for my disobedience, for there is another matter . . .'

'Yes?'

'I cannot speak of it.'

'Are you worried that Dr Forman will reveal your secret?'

'I – I don't know. He is a most strange man. I talk to him in a way I could not talk with my own mother or sisters. And then when I am gone from him I worry about the things I have revealed. Private things: things that no wife should say to any man other than her husband.'

Shakespeare knew Forman well enough, having had cause to deal with him on official matters in the past. He was a lewd, bawdy man, but clever and honest. He doubted that he would betray one of those who came to see him. But that opinion of his character was not going to put Jane's mind at rest.

'I will go to him, Jane. I have power over him, for I know

certain secrets about him. I will extract a promise from him that he will never speak of your visit. Would that help?'

Jane looked frightened. 'There was something else, master.' Her voice was barely audible. 'He asked for details of my birth and John's and Boltfoot's to make charts for us. I fear he is a necromancer and I might be hanged for consorting with him.'

Shakespeare put an arm around the terrified woman's shoulders. 'No one is going to be hanged, Jane, least of all you. Simon Forman's practices might earn him a few weeks in the Clink, but nothing more. You are safe, believe me.'

The tears were streaming down her cheeks now. A sob escaped from deep within her. She nodded, and buried her head in his chest.

'I will see him before I leave London, Jane. Consider it done.'

As Shakespeare reined in close by the Theatre in Shoreditch, three boys raced forward, offering to hold his horse for a farthing. He slid from the saddle and handed the lead rein to the fastest of the three. The boy tipped his hat and offered to have the nag fed and watered for a farthing more.

Shakespeare agreed to the deal and said he would pay him when he departed, not before.

It was a few minutes before three o'clock in the afternoon. The pennant was raised atop the playhouse mast and a trumpet blared to show that the play was about to begin. Shakespeare glanced at the bills posted on all available spaces. *Romeo and Juliet*, they pronounced in bold letters. If he had the time to spare, he would view it, for the play was already the talk of London. But first he had work to do.

He strode up to the entrance. Four whores pushed their wares in his direction, offering use of their bodies in exchange for admission to the play and a bottle of ale. He declined their soliciting politely.

At the door, a large woman with the muscles of a man barred his way. 'It's full. Every inch of space is taken.'

'I am here on Queen's business. I must go to the back of the stage to speak with a member of this company.'

'Who do you want?'

'Mr Shakespeare. Will Shakespeare.'

'He's a very busy man,' the woman said, thrusting her grimy hand forward for a bribe. 'A very important man. The whole world wishes to speak with him.'

'He is my brother.'

The woman's begging hand shot back. 'That's different.' She stood aside. 'Go on through. Do you know the way?'

'Indeed.'

The noise inside the playhouse was deafening. Shakespeare could see that the ground space, where the poorer sort stood for a penny, was packed as tight as the doorkeeper had said. Men, women and children were crowded together in an unwashed mass, stinking of ale and sweat. The galleries in the upper two tiers, where the wealthier patrons sat for tuppence with a cushion for an extra penny, were equally full. Sellers jostled and pushed their way through the noisy, excited throngs, shouting out their offerings.

'Filberts and oranges here.'

'Saffron cakes! Four for a halfpenny.'

'Strong beer!'

He found his brother behind the scenes in the tiring-house, making last-minute adjustments to the costume of a fresh-faced boy who was about to play the part of Juliet.

'Good day to you, Will.'

Will tugged at the stays on the boy's elaborate gown, gave them a last twist to tighten them, then pushed him away with a pat on the shoulder and turned to greet his brother. 'John, well met.'

The brothers embraced. Will pulled back apologetically.

'I am afraid the play is about to begin. You have caught me at the worst of times.'

'Forgive me, I had no option.' Shakespeare looked his younger brother up and down and noted his rich costume.

'Is anything amiss?'

'No, you look splendid. Like a king.'

Will laughed. 'Not a king, a noble gentleman of Verona. Montague. And I am Chorus, too, so I must make haste, for I am first on. Briefly, John, how may I help you?'

'I am looking into the death of Garrick Loake. I need to go over the same questions I asked you before. There must be some clue here. Whom was he close to among your company?'

'He was good with needles and threads and worked mostly in the wardrobe. In truth I would happily murder him myself, were he not already killed, for he took a mighty expensive costume with him to his death. But I cannot say that he was especially close to anyone. Not to my knowledge, leastwise.'

'It was at this playhouse that he learnt the secret that probably led to his death. What I need to know is from whom he learnt it. Was it overheard – or did someone confide in him?'

'As you say, I have told you all I know. And these are the selfsame matters that Anthony Friday put to me. He is working for you now, is he not?'

'Is he here?'

'Why, yes. He is in the sharers' room. You will find him there with the company manager. Together, they are making amendments to some works that we are thinking of putting on this summer.'

'Then I had better go to him.'

'Can you not watch the play first?'

'Another day.'

The trumpet blared again. 'That's it,' Will said. 'I must go into the lions' den and play my part.'

The sharers' room did not offer much respite from the audience's roars, cheers, shouts and gasps. The company manager was not in evidence. Only Anthony Friday was there, sitting at a table chewing at the end of a quill, staring down at a much scrawled-upon sheet of paper. His hands were covered in ink stains, as was the table and the floor around him. He did not look up as the door opened.

Shakespeare walked over to him and grasped his long fair hair in his fist, dragging him to his feet.

Friday recoiled from the assault, and then recognised his assailant. 'Mr Shakespeare!'

'Is this what Sir Robert Cecil pays you two marks a week for?'

Friday tried to twist free, but Shakespeare's grip was too strong, and he was six inches taller. Suddenly, he released him and pushed him back down on to the stool.

'What in God's name is going on, Friday? You know better than this.'

'I must finish this work, whatever Cecil says. One play is too long, another is too short. Both are horse-shit. Besides, I have reached a stone wall in my questions regarding Garrick Loake.'

'You have spoken to everyone here who worked with him?'

'Yes, and I have been to his lodgings. There is nothing. And before you ask, he lived alone. No wife, no mistress, no boy. None in evidence, leastwise.'

'You told Sir Robert that Loake owed money. Why did he borrow the money – and who was the moneylender? How much was due?'

'Cutting Ball lent him the money. A hundred and fifty

pounds, I am told, at usurer's rates. Loake was behind with his payments and was told to produce twenty sovereigns or he would be gelded like a pig.'

'Have you found Ball?'

'No, nor would I wish to. Anyway, Shakespeare, you know Ball did not kill Loake. What use is a dead man to a money-lender?'

Shakespeare nodded. The only relevance of the debt to this inquiry was that it explained why Loake had his heart set on the specific sum of twenty sovereigns. This death was linked to a conspiracy stretching from Wisbech Castle to the College of St Gregory in Seville. But why would a lowly playhouse factotum hear about such a plot?

'What of a young man named Caldor? Gavin Caldor? Have you heard of him?'

Friday thought a moment, then shook his head. 'No.'

'He used to work here building sets and props.'

'What of him?'

'He is in Wisbech Castle now.'

'Well, I'll ask around for you. Your brother should know him if he worked here.'

'What of your orders to infiltrate the Catholic netherworld?'

Friday ran a hand through his hair where it had been tugged and tousled. 'God knows, I told Sir Robert I had work to do, but he insisted. A man must make a living. I am also writing a play for Henslowe at the the Rose. Am I supposed to let these people down? This is my livelihood.' He sighed. 'I have been trying to fit in some inquiries for Cecil, though.'

'You are trying to *fit in* some inquiries?' Shakespeare was incredulous. 'Would you like to go now to Cecil and tell him that?'

For the first time, Friday looked ill at ease. He shook his head.

'You will leave this work and go about the business to which Sir Robert Cecil has contracted you. I shall square it with my brother and Mr Burbage. Do you understand? You will go to the gaols and to the inns where the known Catholic agitators gather. You will bring every titbit you hear to me.'

Friday shook his head more violently, so that his long fair locks swung like barleycorn in the wind. 'They know me too well, Mr Shakespeare! I have had occasion to search many of their pox-ridden houses when riding with Mr Topcliffe. Now, they slam their cell doors in my face when I go to the gaols. The lackeys will not let me past the gateways to the great Catholic houses. And when I try to overhear them in their drinking dens, they shy away and vanish.'

'Then you had better get yourself a new costume here in this playhouse and find yourself a fine disguise. That is daily bread for players like you, is it not? And when you have done that, you will prepare a report of everything you have told me and all other details you have not said, and bring it to my house at Dowgate by nightfall. Get you gone, Mr Friday. Do what you are best at – or I will have you whipped at the cart's arse!'

Chapter 21

SHAKESPEARE LOOKED ACROSS at the players. He was standing close to the Theatre exit. His brother was on stage, declaiming about an *envious worm*. He needed to talk with him again.

His gaze wandered around the assembled throng and his eyes lifted to the second and third galleries. Did anyone here know the secret of Garrick Loake and his death? Suddenly his eyes alighted upon a booth on the third tier. There were two faces he recognised, peering intently at the stage: Lady Susan Bertie, the Countess of Kent, and one of the young gentlewomen he had met at her house in Barbican Street, Emilia Lanier. Shakespeare smiled to himself. Very convenient.

Lady Susan caught his eye and nudged her companion. They both waved to him.

He tilted his chin in acknowledgment, then ducked down into the outer passage and found the wooden steps that led up to the gallery where they were seated. In the gallery, the crowd was so dense it had spilt beyond the seating into the aisles, and he had to elbow his way to the front to reach the women. He bowed to them.

A voice boomed from behind. 'Get out of the way, you outsized maggot!'

Shakespeare turned and apologised to the irate spectator, then sank to his knees at Lady Susan's side.

'Forgive me for interrupting the performance, my lady,' he said as quietly as possible. 'I had wished to talk with you.'

'It is quite perfect to see you, Mr Shakespeare. But why should I be surprised? Of course you are here; it is your brother's play. We are great admirers of Will Shakespeare.' She turned to her companion. 'Are we not, Emilia?'

'Hush, for pity's sake!' Another angry voice from the row behind.

'I think now might not be a good time to talk.' Lady Susan's voice lowered to a discreet whisper. 'Why do we not meet directly afterwards, if we can find each other in the throng?'

'Thank you, my lady. I shall be behind the scenes.'

Two hours later, Shakespeare found Will in the tiring-house and complimented him on his play, then apologised as he explained that Anthony Friday would have to be removed from work on the other dramas.

'In truth, I am not worried,' Will said. 'The plays he was working on are poor things that have been submitted to us by members of the company. We merely wondered whether Friday could salvage something from them, for he is a fair writer. There is no hurry.'

'There was another thing I meant to ask you. Do you recall a scene-builder named Gavin Caldor?'

'Yes, I do. Why?'

'Did he have any connection to Garrick Loake?'

'Not to my knowledge.' He shook his head. 'No, he could not have done. Loake did not work here in those days. Again, I ask, why do you wish to know? What happened to young Caldor? Always rather indiscreet in his papism, I recall.'

'It's led him to gaol.'

Lady Susan, Countess of Kent, and her companion swept regally into the tiring-house and seemed not at all alarmed to find themselves in the company of a dozen or more men in various stages of undress. The brothers turned at their approach.

Lady Susan beamed a beguiling smile and proffered her hand to be kissed. Will obliged with a flourish.

'Well, well, Emilia, *two* Mr Shakespeares. What more could any lady ask? You amuse yourself with one, while I talk to the other.'

Shakespeare did not like this public place. 'My lady, perhaps we might go to the sharers' room to talk in private.'

'As you wish, Mr Shakespeare. This is all exceeding mysterious.'

'I hope your brother is safe with Emilia, Mr Shakespeare. She is a very naughty girl, you know.'

'I am sure Will can look after himself, my lady. However, I am here to ask you about Beatrice Eastley. How did you meet her?'

The countess was wandering around the room, picking up papers and examining them in an idle fashion. She cast a glance over her shoulder. 'Very naughty indeed. You must know that Hunsdon, the Lord Chamberlain, is father to her whelp.'

'It is generally known. But back to the point—'

'Why would you wish to know how I met Beatrice?'

'Because she is not the person she seems to be.'

'Is that so? Tell me more and perhaps I will tell you what I know.'

'Her real name is not Beatrice Eastley, but Sorrow Gray. She is the daughter of the late keeper of Wisbech Castle gaol.'

'How very interesting. But then, are *any* of us what we seem?'

'She was an evangelist Puritan, and she was converted to Catholicism by William Weston, the notorious Jesuit. From what I am told she has become a very devout, unyielding Catholic. Those who knew her rather imagined that she had gone off to Louvain to be a nun.'

Lady Susan stopped her perambulation. 'Now that *does* surprise me. I think her a little too worldly to be cloistered away in a nunnery. But nuns are all mad, are they not, and Beatrice has always struck me as not quite of this world.'

'Before her change of heart, she was to have been married to a most correct Calvinist gentleman named Paul Hooft, but she ran away from him and from her family, so successful was Weston in seducing the young woman from her original faith. So you must see, my lady, why I am intrigued to know how she came to be in the company of a group such as yours.'

'Yes, I do see that.'

'I cannot speak for your other friends, but I am given to believe that you and Lady Lucia Trevail conform powerfully to the established English Church.'

'That is true, but I am not so precise in religion. For all I care, Beatrice could be a pagan or a Mussulman, so long as she is amusing company. You see, I took her in because I believed that with education and guidance she might become someone of note. It is what happened with Emilia, who had her education in my household and is now a most remarkable poet. We must give young women a chance, Mr Shakespeare . . .'

'I must tell you that I fear this is a matter of conspiracy against Queen and country.'

'Mr Shakespeare, what are you saying?'

He weighed his words delicately. How much could he trust this charming, beautiful, good-humoured and very aristocratic woman? He decided there was nothing to be lost by being direct and honest with her.

'What I say to you must not go beyond these walls. We fear a great conspiracy coming out of Wisbech. I have no evidence against Miss Gray, or Miss Eastley if you prefer, but we must pursue every possibility. That is why I wish to know how she came to be in your company. Nothing about her makes sense to me.'

The countess stood facing Shakespeare. She hesitated a moment, then sighed. 'You seem worthy of trust, so I shall tell you all I know, which is little enough. It may surprise you to discover that it was through this very playhouse that I came to know of Beatrice, as I must still call her. We are all great devotees of the players' art. It is through this closeness to the playhouses, and your brother's poetic works in particular, that we came to know Beatrice. At one time she was living with a player, who treated her ill, beat her without mercy and then simply disappeared, taking all her few possessions and what little money she had. When I met her, she was destitute, and so I took her in.'

'Who told you of her?'

'Why, your own dear brother did, Mr Shakespeare. Well, in truth, he first mentioned her plight to Emilia Lanier, who is a good friend to both of us. Emilia came to me with the tale and my heart was touched. How could I resist such a challenge? I consider the schooling of women my life's work, you see. Emilia was my first. I tried to do the same for Thomasyn Jade, as you well know. There have been others, too, and I am proud of every one of them. I do not ask them their religion, nor do I ask for thanks. My only failure has been poor Thomasyn. Does that answer your question, sir?'

'Who was the man, the player who mistreated Beatrice?'

'You will have to ask Will.'

Shakespeare pressed Lady Susan for all she knew of Beatrice, but the answers did not help him.

'I fear I did not interrogate her before taking her in, Mr Shakespeare. How terribly remiss of me.'

He saw that she was mocking him and bowed to her curtly before going off to seek out his brother again.

Will recalled the girl instantly. 'Why, yes, John, of course I recall Beatrice. A strange beauty. Intense and troubling. The sort that any man should learn to avoid before they have reached manhood.'

'In what way?'

'Nothing obvious, but those who know to look for the signs might see the touch of madness. An inability to meet the eye, a strange sweetness of tongue for some, long silences with others, and then, on occasion, ferocity in argument, particularly in matters of religion, which I took to be most unwholesome.'

'Papist?'

'Probably. It was difficult to discern. A puritanical papism if that makes any sense. And beneath the surface, something crawls, not quite visible. It is the unspoken threat of violence that jars with the softness of the skin and the paleness of the breast.'

'You seem to know her well.'

'She came to this place frequently and would watch as we rehearsed. That was how she met Emilia, who was here directing the musicians for me.'

'And so Emilia and Beatrice became close.'

'Too close. I thought it unwise of Emilia to befriend such a woman, but I could say nothing. It was none of my business.'

'And the man who beat her? Lady Susan says he was a player and that he attacked her with great force, then disappeared.'

Will shook his head slowly. 'I know nothing of such matters, John. That is the story Beatrice told Emilia, but I do not have any knowledge of such a man, and she has given no name to him. Players come and go, for in some plays we need a great cast and our company is small, but I have no idea who this man might be. If he existed at all.'

'You doubt even that?'

'I doubt *everything* about Beatrice Eastley. In truth, I was delighted when the countess took her in, for that meant she stopped coming here.'

'What of the beating she had? Was she badly injured?'

'Cuts and bruises about the face. She could have walked into a wall for all I know. Emilia might have more to say on the matter. Perhaps she even knows the name of the player who supposedly loved her and left her.'

Shakespeare drew a deep breath. 'Then let us talk with Emilia,' he said.

He found Emilia with some of the players, all of whom clearly knew and liked her. It was with some difficulty that he prised her away from them and managed to ask about Beatrice.

'I wish I could help you,' she said. 'But I fear I know no more than Lady Susan. I became quite friendly with Beatrice, but she never confided in me. Then one day she came to me in a bad state, saying she had been beaten by her lover, who was one of the players. She did not tell me his name and I did not ask. All I know is that he treated her badly and we rescued her. Is she in some sort of trouble?'

Shakespeare did not answer the question, but pressed on with his own. 'What is her character? Do you trust her?'

'I would not say a word against her. You have not seen the best of her; perhaps none of us has, for I believe her to have hidden qualities.'

A large spider crawled up Francis Mills's leg. By the thin light of a small barred hatch set high in the ceiling of the pit, he watched it without moving. It crawled on up his hose to his doublet, which was stained with his own vomit and his wife's blood. At another time, he might have squashed the creature in his hand, but he had neither the inclination nor the energy to kill it.

The cell walls dripped. One of the other prisoners suddenly screamed and rattled his chains against the stone flags, then fell silent as quickly as he had erupted.

Shakespeare stood and gazed on the scene with pity but no astonishment. He had been inside gaols often enough to know how low the prisoners could be brought. Some pissed themselves and eased their bowels without moving from where they sat, for they did not have the strength nor the care to drag their chains and their skeletal bodies to the corner where the stinking, ordure-thick straw was banked up.

Shakespeare carried a blackjack of ale and a box of bread and meats. He crouched down at Mills's side and showed him the box, then held the leather jug of ale to his lips. Mills sipped at it without enthusiasm, then looked up and his dead eyes met Shakespeare's.

'I am sorry it has come to this, Frank.'

'She is dead, isn't she? I must have killed her.'

'Do you not recall it?'

'No. All I remember is looking at their bodies, the dagger in my hand. I have dreams . . .'

Shakespeare put down the blackjack, broke a piece of bread and spread it with butter. He applied a slice of cold beef to it and handed it to Mills, who shook his head. 'I cannot eat in this place.'

'You have to.'

Mills laughed. 'So that I am alive for the hangman?'

'So that you can plead intolerable provocation. There must be hope of a pardon for you have done much service on behalf of the crown.'

'I care not for my life.'

Mills's back was bent and the notches of his spine at his bare neck were like stepping stones. He was a carrion crow on an icy midwinter day, sitting alone, waiting for whatever fate might bring him.

'Tell me about your dreams, Frank.'

'I have dreamt of this for two years, slitting both their throats in a great cataract of blood. Now, in this place, I have a new dream. I dream that the house was deathly silent and I was scared. I drew my dagger, mounted the stairs and stepped into that room, and found the bodies there. But that cannot be so . . .'

Another man might have held a kerchief or pomander to his nose in this place, but Shakespeare merely endured the stench. The prisoners had no option in the matter, so he would join them in their discomfort.

'No,' he said, 'that cannot be so, Frank.'

'And yet I cannot recall killing them.'

'You were found with knife in hand and blood on your apparel. It must have been you.'

'She was ugly, lying there, naked and covered in gore. I had to cover her.'

'You must write letters. One to Her Majesty, one to old Burghley and another to Cecil. I will send a lawyer to you to help compose them. They are your best hope.'

'And if I am pardoned, will I not just die here in depravity? A hanging is a quick end to all misery.'

'I will send a lawyer anyway. Tell him everything. Mention your dreams. I will send you a churchman, too, if you wish.'

'No.'

'Frank, much has happened since you have been in this place. Were you aware that the letter found in the box aboard *The Ruth* was bound for Wisbech Castle, to the Jesuit Weston?'

Mills's long, crooked frame quaked with what Shakespeare took to be laughter. 'So the old fraud is at his tricks again. He should have gone to the gallows long before Southwell ever did.'

'What could they be plotting? Garrick Loake is dead, too. His fate and the letter to Weston both lead back to Seville and the College of St Gregory. And yet my man there sends no word. Is he alive – or is he dead? I admit, I fear the worst.'

'Perhaps it is nothing. Loake knew dangerous men. Cutting Ball is not a man to borrow money from if you care for your health.'

'It wasn't him. Loake died for the secret he offered to sell to me.'

In a quiet voice, Shakespeare then disclosed all he had uncovered at Wisbech and the truth about Beatrice Eastley.

Mills appeared to listen, drank a little more ale and picked at some of the food.

'John,' he said at last, 'I cannot help. My hours here are spent weeping and dreaming. I would put my mind to your puzzle, but I cannot. All I can do is wait until the day I dance my jig at Tyburn.'

Chapter 22

SHAKESPEARE LEFT MONEY with the Newgate keeper in return for a promise to ensure fresh food and ale for Mills, then walked the few yards to St Paul's. He found Joshua Peace in the crypt where he carried out his duties as Searcher of the Dead. Peace immediately wiped his hands on his apron and shook his visitor by the hand.

'Welcome, old friend.'

'It is good to see you looking so hale, Joshua.'

'Do not mock me, John. I know I look like one of my corpses.'

Shakespeare held on to Peace's hand. 'Let me look at you then.' He affected to study him in minute detail. 'Yes, the hair is a little thinner. Completely bald on top, but a few strands decorate the edges, like a monk. There is an extra wrinkle at the side of each eye, a touch of pallor about the cheeks. And from the chill of your hand, I would estimate you had been dead for two days at least.'

Peace roared with laughter. 'Any man's hand would be cold here in this crypt! Just don't examine me any further, you might not like what you find.'

'You know why I am here.'

'You wish to know what I have discovered about three bodies that were entrusted to my care.'

Here in the old crypt it was, indeed, as cold as the grave. In the middle of the room stood a pair of trestle tables with small wheels at the end of their legs to make them movable. Two bodies were stretched out on them on their backs, staring up at the stone ceiling with lifeless eyes.

'Yes, that's Mills's wife,' Peace said. 'And I am told the other one is called Heartsease and made his living as a grocer.'

'What have you discovered?'

'That the time of death was about an hour before the constable arrived. Certainly no more than that. Cause of death was massive blood loss due to throat wounds. They had copulated a short while before their deaths. When they were found, they were both naked and bound, so it is possible to imagine that they were surprised in the act and threatened in some way to submit to their bindings. A pistol comes to mind; otherwise why would a strong, healthy man like Heartsease allow himself to be tied up? But that is merely my speculation.'

'I do not think any pistol was found.'

'Then it is up to you to discover how they were subdued, John. But don't get me involved in your investigations, please. They are too dangerous.'

Shakespeare walked over to take a closer look at the bodies. He was well aware why Joshua Peace would wish to avoid further involvement. He had been involved once before, a few months since, and had got in so deep that his very life had been imperilled. Such ventures were not in Peace's nature.

Gazing down at the still, bloodied corpses, it was hard for Shakespeare to imagine them ever having been imbued with life and passion. He had met Anne Mills only twice and had thought her unremarkable, mousy even, but he was aware how much she had meant to Mills. It was almost as though she had possessed him, like some evil spirit. What a thing was the human heart, that one man should give his life and soul for a woman that another man would not even grace with a second glance. Shakespeare touched the woman's face gently, with his knuckles.

'The interesting thing for me is that Mills remembers being in the room with the bodies, but does not remember the killing itself.'

'Are you saying you have doubts about his guilt?'

Shakespeare shrugged. 'I would merely like to be certain that he has a fair trial. His brain has become addled and I have worked with him too long to see him go to his death if there is any chance that he is innocent.'

'Well, I have already looked at the bodies closely, but I will examine them again. I do not expect to find anything of note, though.'

'Thank you, Joshua. I would ask you to get word to the lawyer Cornelius Bligh at Lincoln's Inn. He is a good man. Ask him to visit Mr Mills and represent him as best he can. I shall pay his fees.'

'I will do that today.'

'And what of the remains of Garrick Loake, the body from the river?'

Peace nodded towards the doorway into the other room. 'He's in there. Would you like to see him?'

Shakespeare had no desire to see or smell the putrid carcass; he knew what a few days in the Thames could do to a dead body. But he had to show willing. 'Very well.'

The corpse was every bit as repulsive as he had expected, so bloated and mutilated that only the distinctive, over-large nose could tell you that the man was Loake. The skin was slimy and mottled, like a dead goose that had been hung far too long before roasting. There were cuts in many places, particularly on the head and face.

'It was tangled in branches, pulled this way and that by the currents. What was left of his clothing, part of a doublet and his breeches, were in tatters. What I cannot establish yet is whether the skin tears and the deeper wounds were the result of buffeting against logs and banks, and feeding by predators, or whether the injuries were caused before immersion.'

'So you do not know the cause of death?'

'I am as certain as I can be that it was not drowning. No water emerged when I pressed down hard on his ribs, which suggests to me that he was dead when he entered the river. He could have been murdered elsewhere and thrown in. He was found upstream of the tideway close to Richmond, therefore he could not have entered the water anywhere downstream of there. The body is washed clean of blood, so I am still trying to determine the location of the death wound. It is not obvious, I am afraid, but I will not give up.'

'Do you not even have any possibilities?'

'There are wounds of different shapes and sizes. I need to look at them all individually to see if any are likely to have been caused by a dagger. The head injuries are more difficult. Cracks in the skull would indicate battering by a heavy object. This is not a simple task, John.'

He picked up a basin from a shelf. From it he took a number of rings and a thin chain with a cross at the end.

'The rings were on his fingers. You will see his name carved on each of them. The cross was in the pocket of his breeches. It is possible it means something to you.'

Shakespeare turned the silver chain and cross in his hands. The only thing it meant to him was that, perhaps, Garrick Loake had been a Catholic. There were plenty of such men and women in England: people who clung to the old faith in secret but found it made their life more tenable to pretend otherwise. Perhaps the most interesting thing about Garrick Loake was his connection to the Theatre – a connection he shared in common with Beatrice Eastley, late of Wisbech. If both were Catholic, then the circle seemed complete. Had Loake perhaps heard his lethal secret from Beatrice, or someone close to her? Had she, in fact, tried to recruit him to conspiracy?

He handed the object back to Peace. 'Keep it safe.'

'As always.'

'And keep me informed, Joshua. Will you share a flagon of Gascon wine at the Three Tuns before I leave you? I am certain I promised you as much.'

Peace shook Shakespeare by the hand again. 'Another day, John. For the present, I must force some more work out of my decrepit limbs and brain.'

Shakespeare found Ursula at her market stall among the booksellers. Three books lay on her table, but they were there for show. It was the leaves of tobacco that caught the attention.

'Another good day, Ursula?'

'Like stealing from babies. The pigging lawyers are the best. They'll pay anything to get their hands on an ounce or two of verinshe sotweed. Brown gold, they call it, and they're not far wrong.'

'Well, I was merely passing, visiting an old friend, and I thought I would see how you were faring.'

He looked at her fondly. She was well fed now, but her pinched mouth and cheeks would always betray the truth: that she had been ill nourished as a child.

Ursula's transformation was amazing. She had been born to the wild, staying alive by cheating and thieving as part of one of the feared vagabond bands. She had done a good deed for Shakespeare and his family, and in return he had taken her in, promising her an education and a home if she would help with the younger children, Grace and Mary.

'Got something for you, Mr Shakespeare. Here.' She handed him a paper, folded over like a letter.

He took it. His name was written in bold lettering on the front. 'Where did this come from?'

'A little brat brought it, said it was for you, then ran away, so I couldn't question him. Read it and see.'

Shakespeare cut open the letter, read the words and recoiled. The letter was unsigned and was written in a brownish-red ink. It said, *Exorcise your own demons, lest they claw away all you hold dear*. There were two names, in capital letters: GRACE at the top; MARY at the foot of the page. The whole effect was of a cross. And then Shakespeare realised what the ink was: it was blood. He shuddered.

'What does it say, Mr Shakespeare?'

It was a warning. *Cease your delving or your family will pay a terrible price. A blood price.* But whilst he might discount threats from Topcliffe while he remained in gaol, this one could not be ignored.

'I must go.' He looked at the girl and knew that she could see the fear in his eyes. 'You must take care, Ursula. Come home before dark. Have your young man accompany you, for the sake of safety.'

'You're pigging worrying me now.'

'There is nothing for you to fear. I just want you to be safe. Do you understand?'

She nodded. She wasn't going to argue with him about this; she had seen enough misery and death to know terror when she saw it.

Shakespeare ran the half-mile home through crowded streets thick with horse-dung and piles of waste, pushing carters and apprentices out of his way. At the house in Dowgate, out of breath, he shouted for Jane, who came hurrying and tried to hush him as he demanded to know where the girls were. She took him to the schoolroom and pointed to them.

'There, master, see. They are safe.'

They were sitting at a table, working very seriously together. Without thinking, he swept them both up in his arms and hugged them.

'What is it, master?' Jane said. She stood in the doorway, her face creased with confusion and anxiety.

He shook his head, unable to express what he knew and feared. All he could do was try to think how he could protect the girls. He had to go away soon, that was set, but first he had to find somewhere safe for his family.

Of a sudden it came to him. If Sir Robert Cecil wished him to do this work, he could protect his family. There was space enough at his mansion on the Strand, and guards aplenty.

'Jane, we are all leaving this place. This very hour. The girls can collect their most favoured possessions and clothes, and then we go.'

When Cecil read the blood letter, he nodded. 'Yes, John, of course they must stay here. The girls can join classes with our own tutors. They will be well cared for. Your servant, Jane Cooper, is welcome, too, with her son.'

'Thank you, Sir Robert. My mind is greatly eased. Someone does not wish me to continue my inquiries.'

'But from the death of Loake, we can assume the conspirators are utterly ruthless and relentless. Would such people send threats, or go straight for the kill?'

Shakespeare shrugged. 'I do not know. But the threat seems serious enough.'

'Indeed. And now you must go westward at speed. Find Beatrice Eastley and bring her in. Logic tells me that she is the key to everything and instinct tells me that she is dangerous. I do not like the thought of her being in company with Lucia Trevail, for Lucia has access to the Queen.'

Jane, the two girls and little John Cooper were waiting in an ante-room with their bags of possessions. Other clothes and belongings had been packed up at home, waiting to be fetched by Cecil's servants. But where was Ursula Dancer? She could not stay at Dowgate alone. Shakespeare decided to send a message to her with money; she might be safer at an inn, or perhaps her swain's parents might find room for her.

Cecil held up the blood letter again. He seemed as troubled by it as Shakespeare himself. 'Who wrote this foul missive, John?'

'I wish I knew.'

'And you think it written in blood?'

'I do.'

'John, something very bad is happening. Take your leave of your daughters and go. You can rest at ease knowing that they will be safe here. An assassin would need a company of arquebusiers to get past my guards.'

The next morning, Shakespeare rode out from Dowgate with Andrew at his side. He had left messages with the stablehands for Boltfoot, informing him of the whereabouts of Jane and the children. He had also left orders for Boltfoot with Cecil's servant Clarkson; Boltfoot was to follow Shakespeare and Andrew down to the west country.

'I have one last task before we leave London,' Shakespeare told Andrew. 'Come, we must take a detour to Fylpot Street.'

He kicked on into a trot and they rode a little way northwards, up through the early morning streets.

Shakespeare reined in outside the old stone house. It was a place he knew well. Dr Simon Forman had had cause to regret crossing Shakespeare's path before.

The door was unlocked and he pushed his way in. A surly youth stepped forward, but Shakespeare ignored him and strode up the staircase to Forman's chamber.

The doctor was in bed, but not alone. There was not much bedding in evidence. His heavy testicles and notorious prick hung flaccidly along his hairy leg. A woman was snoring softly at his side, her ripe breasts uncovered and pointing in opposite directions. Her hair was a mess. She was not pretty but she was endowed with an air of raw lust.

Shakespeare stood and looked at them for a moment, then jabbed Forman in the ribs with his index finger. 'Get up and put on some clothes.'

Forman stirred. His eyes opened, bleary and full of sleep. He saw his uninvited guest and suddenly he was wide awake. He scrabbled to pull some bedclothes about his person.

'Don't bother about that, get up, Forman.'

The doctor jumped from the bed, then shook the arm of the sleeping woman. 'Wake up, Janey. We have a visitor.'

As she stirred, he scuttled around the floor, picking up his shirt and hose, putting them on as best he could. The woman, meanwhile, sat up in bed, not in the least shamed by her nakedness.

'Who's this then?' she said.

'This is Mr Shakespeare, Janey.'

She looked at him with inquiring eyes. 'Is it now? And who's he?'

Shakespeare looked back at her. Her expression had changed; his name meant something to her. He was sure of it.

'Mr Shakespeare, Janey. Sir Robert Cecil's officer . . .'

'I don't know the name. Have you mentioned him to me?' She smiled with warm lasciviousness. 'Nice looking, isn't he?'

'I don't have time for this. Forman, come downstairs with me. I want to talk with you alone.'

Shakespeare led the way from the chamber down the stairs to the hall. He pushed the protesting servant boy from the room, out of the back of the house into the yard, and slammed the door after him.

Forman was still adjusting his attire when Shakespeare returned. 'Now, Dr Forman, my servant Jane Cooper has been here to consult you in recent days.'

'Yes, I do recall Mistress Cooper. A very pleasant young lady.'

'Never mind that. You have worried her with your charts and potions, and I do not like her to be worried. She is terrified that her husband will discover she has been here.'

Forman stopped shaking. 'Yes, Mr Shakespeare, I know she was worried about that. But tell her she must fear nothing. I would not tell a soul that she has been here under my roof, though I believe I could help her.'

'Good, Dr Forman.' Shakespeare's stern tones mellowed. 'That is exactly what I wanted to hear. And I wished to remind you that I know enough about you to have you consigned to Newgate for the rest of your life, which would not be very long. I know that you have devised a life chart for a certain great lady, a crime that would be construed as treason.'

'You do not need to remind me, sir.'

'Very well. Then we are as one on this matter. Jane Cooper's husband will never hear of her visit.'

'No.'

Shakespeare believed him. He put out his hand and Forman took it tentatively, and they shook on the deal. Shakespeare tilted his head towards the stairway. 'Who is the young lady?'

'Janey? She is no one, a trull of no importance.'

'Does she live here with you?'

'No, she is a drab at a clergyman's house.'

'Which clergyman would that be?'

'Mr Shakespeare, please, is the young lady not to be allowed a little courtesy? She has been found by you in most unfortunate circumstances. She has her reputation . . .'

Shakespeare laughed. 'Reputation? A moment ago you called her trull and drab! And as for being found in unfortunate circumstances, she showed not the slightest degree of modesty.'

Forman sighed. 'Very well.' He lowered his voice. 'She is lady's maid to Alice Blague, the wife of the Dean of Rochester over at Lambeth. She is supposed to be visiting her sister. She would be thrown out of her job and home if Mistress Blague or her husband were to hear of her assignation with me.'

'Why did she affect not to have heard of me when it was clear that she had?'

'Perhaps she was scared of you, Mr Shakespeare. Many people are, you know.'

Chapter 23

THEY STOOD ON the shore at Plymouth, gazing out at the jagged horizon of masts and rigging. Dozens of great ships blotted the skyline with their tangle of spars and sheets. Some rode high in the water, waiting to be loaded with provisions; others wallowed under the weight of guns and balls, ballast and enormous kegs of victuals.

The ride here from London had been long and arduous. Shakespeare clapped an arm around Andrew's shoulder as they took in the magnitude of the great fleet.

'Your new life lies there. No change of heart?'

'None, Father. I cannot wait to board and set sail.'

'Come on, let us seek out Drake.'

They found him aboard the *Defiance*, a royal ship of five hundred tons, heavily armoured with forty-six guns and bearing a lion as its figurehead. Drake was in his cabin, directing operations and complaining loudly about the lack of money and provisions.

'In God's faith, I shall go and find ale and salt pork myself!' he thundered. He turned and recognised Shakespeare. 'Ah, Mr Shakespeare, do you bring word from Sir Robert of beef, munitions and ale?'

Shakespeare bowed, and then looked up at the old mariner. Drake was beginning to show his age. His barrelled chest seemed to have shrunk and his bold head was hunched lower, so that his once-proud beard resembled the tail of a cowed dog.

'I fear not, Sir Francis, but it is a pleasure and an honour to find you in good health.'

Drake sighed deeply. 'Not so good, Mr Shakespeare. But nothing that will not be healed by taking Spanish gold and silver. And what is this?' He nodded towards Andrew.

'My son by adoption, Andrew Woode. He has been studying navigation and wishes now to learn how to use these skills at sea under your command that one day he may aspire to be a ship's master.'

'He looks strong enough. Do you have the stomach to kill Spaniards, boy?'

Andrew met his father's eye. Shakespeare nodded. 'There can be no doubt about that, Sir Francis.'

Drake examined the boy more closely. Realisation dawned, some memory of news heard some months ago. 'Ah yes, now I recall something of the tale. Was he not at the taking of the Spanish fort at Brest, alongside that pirate Frobisher, whom no man mourns?'

'He was indeed.'

'Good. But that does not make him a seafarer. We shall find space for him here on the *Defiance*, starting at the bottom as page to one of the officers. He will turn the hourglass and have an education, but there will be no pay and he will have no favours from me.' Drake looked about, as if searching for a face. 'I am pleased to see you have not brought that misbegotten cripple Mr Cooper with you.'

'Indeed not, Admiral, but I am hoping he will follow soon.'

'Then keep him out of my sight.' Drake poured brandy from a flask into silver goblets and handed them to Shakespeare and Andrew. 'Now then, sir, you have arrived at an opportune time. Spanish shipping has been spotted around these coasts. A fishing boat was seized off St Keverne and the men taken over to Brittany. I suspect they wished to discover the plans of my fleet, but they must think us fools if they imagine we would entrust such intelligence to fishers. I suspect, too, that they might have hopes to attack us here and destroy our fleet in harbour as I did to them in Cadiz. I have ordered five vessels out to sea to stay to windward and watch our backs. I know that Trott has already sent word to Cecil, but I will supply you with all the details as we have them, and you can go to the Council and demand more money for our cause.'

Shakespeare sipped the brandy. 'Forgive me, I am here on other matters. I must visit the Lady Trevail, who has estates in Cornwall.'

'Lucia Trevail? Then your journey is far from done. Trevail Hall is a good deal west of here, abutting Francis Godolphin's estates. I saw her recently. She broke her journey, staying with Lady Drake and myself at Buckland.'

'Who was with her?'

'A retinue of servants, I think. I paid them no heed.'

'Was there one called Beatrice Eastley?'

'Not that I met.'

'Are you certain, Sir Francis? Forgive me for pressing you, but this is mighty important.'

'I was there the whole time. Lucia was at Buckland Abbey only one night and she dined with us alone. There was no one else. Why? What is this about?'

'Nothing that I can reveal.'

Drake laughed loud. 'You were always one for dark dealings, Mr Shakespeare. As I recall, you are an admirer of beauty, too. Lucia is a perfect delicate example of her sex, I think. A gentle summer flower . . .'

Shakespeare did not need Sir Francis Drake to remind him.

'As for this boy of yours, he shall stay aboard ship with me and start his work this very day.'

The Shakespeare house in Dowgate was dark when Boltfoot Cooper reined in at the courtyard close to midnight. That was no surprise to him at such an ungodly hour, but something about the place chilled him.

He lifted the latch on the door and tried to push it open, but it was locked. He was instantly alert, for this door was never locked when people were at home. Suddenly he felt the touch of a crab-like hand on his arm and he pulled back, his own hand going to his dagger with the speed of an adder's jaws.

'They're not here. They are hiding.'

It was the old woman, the nun from Denham. But even as he realised this, the point of Boltfoot's dagger was at her chest and his other hand was clutching her throat. He immediately relaxed his grip and drew back the dagger.

'Why are you here?'

'I am staying just along the road at the Swan Inn as you ordered, Mr Cooper. I gave my word, did I not? And just now, I saw you passing.'

'You say my family is not here?'

'Gone to young Cecil's great house on the Strand. I watched them go. Gone to hide themselves away like molewarps in a tunnel.'

'And my master, John Shakespeare? Is he with them?'

'You had best go and see.'

'I ask again: why are *you* here?'

'Because I may have some matter for your master. I have heard something of the reason for his questioning, and I now believe the Lord God would wish me to help him.'

*

Shakespeare walked through the back streets of Plymouth searching for a house. He had been here once before, in 1587, soon after Sir Francis Walsingham, the late principal secretary, commanded the place to be set up to watch the movements of foreign spies in this most vital of ports.

As the man with complete responsibility for the security of the realm, Walsingham had considered it prudent to have a permanent intelligence outpost in the town. He had spies and correspondents of varying degrees in all the major cities of Europe and beyond, and in all the great houses of England. But he valued this man in Plymouth above all, for it was infested with spies from Spain and the Low Countries. And with the threat of an Armada invasion looming, as it had been then, he knew how dearly King Philip of Spain would love to cripple Drake and his fleets before they ever set sail.

Shakespeare banged at the door with his knuckles. Three times, a pause, and then once. No one came. He tried again, louder, to no effect.

An old fishwife with a basket shuffled down the street past him, then stopped and turned. 'You'll find no one there today, master.'

'Where is he?'

'Haven't seen him in a week.'

'Do you know who he is?'

'Agent of the Queen, it is said. I know he has dealings with Drake and the sea captains, and also with the mayor and merchants. I do not know his name, but he is friendly enough and touches his cap. Many messengers come and go, as does the man himself. It is no strangeness for him to be away in such days.'

Shakespeare tried the door. It was locked solid. The woman was waddling away.

'Wait,' Shakespeare said. 'What do you mean?'

'I mean with the fleets being fitted. Drake and Hawkins off on another great venture, and now the news from Cornwall that the pestilential Spaniards are circling like sharks around a fishnet.'

Shakespeare walked around to the rear of the house, which stood at the centre of a terrace. There was a high wall but the gate in it was open. He walked through the backyard to a door. It was locked, but it was not strong, and he broke it open with his shoulder. Inside, he came across a pantry, which was no more than a store cupboard with plate and jug and a keg of ale.

He pushed on through into the main room. It contained a table and a straight-backed chair, some books, quills, ink, unused papers, a belt and a threadbare hat. No dead bodies, no scene of mayhem. Only a fireplace with the blackened ashes of burnt papers. Good: that meant he was diligent about destroying all messages sent him from London.

A ladder led up from the room to a hatch, which gave way to a loft. Shakespeare climbed up. The upper room was dark and at first glance he thought it empty, but then he heard a sound, like a pig at its feed. He peered more closely into the gloom and spied the mound of a body beneath blankets. Shakespeare prodded it with his foot. It groaned and turned.

'Wake up, Mr Trott.'

The man emitted a long, drawn-out snore and turned again. Shakespeare bent down and pulled the man up by his shirt, noting the overpowering stench of liquor. He slapped him hard across the face.

Trott grunted with shock and recoiled, scrabbling against the wall.

Shakespeare withdrew his poniard and thrust it against the man's throat. 'If I were your enemy, Mr Trott, you would be dead now. Is this what we pay you for?'

Trott went rigid at the touch of the poniard's point against his skin. Shakespeare pulled the weapon away and thrust it back in his belt. 'Get up, man. You are a disgrace.'

Trott stumbled to his feet, shivering and shaking. Shakespeare estimated his age as fifty. He had been in the service of Walsingham throughout the eighties and had passed into Sir Robert Cecil's employ on the principal secretary's death in 1590. Shakespeare had met him only once before, eight years ago, when he had looked a great deal sharper. He would have to be replaced. But for the moment, Trott was needed.

'Forgive me . . . the ague.'

'The ague be damned. You have been drinking too much strong beer.'

The man could not stop his shaking. He bowed his head.

'Now, Mr Trott, collect your thoughts. There is work to be done. First, I need you to collate detailed and to-the-minute reports of these Spanish shipping manoeuvres and send them post to Sir Robert Cecil before day's end. Go to Drake and local captains for this. Then you are to inquire into the whereabouts of a woman named Beatrice Eastley, also known as Sorrow Gray. I believe her to be in the train of Lady Lucia Trevail of Cornwall and I will be continuing westward in search of her. But there is a possibility the young woman has not made it that far. Lady Trevail stayed at Buckland Abbey and Sir Francis Drake does not recall meeting Miss Eastley there. So perhaps she has broken away from the retinue near here, for it is said she has relatives in the west country. And, though I doubt this, I cannot ignore the possibility that it is true. I can tell you that she affects to smoke a pipe and has a curious, rasping voice. If you find her, detain her in the town gaol until I return. If you fall down on this, if I find you drunk, I shall have you arraigned on a felony charge of misuse of crown monies and you will be hanged. Is this clear?'

'Yes, Mr Shakespeare. Please do not tell Sir Robert.'

'That is in your hands. Find the woman and you may be given another chance.'

Chapter 24

Two days later, Shakespeare arrived at Trevail Hall. He found the old building bathed in late evening sunshine. Its grey stone walls nestled into warm folds of woodland as though it had always been there, placed by God rather than man. It seemed to Shakespeare the most perfectly proportioned house he had ever set eyes on.

He trotted his horse up to an arched gateway, which led into a pleasant courtyard. A groom appeared and took the reins while he dismounted. The groom summoned a serving man, who informed Shakespeare that Lady Trevail was visiting the Godolphins for a few days. It was only a short ride away, or there was an inn close by if he so desired. The hour was late and it would be dark soon, but Shakespeare accepted directions from the footman and rode on.

Godolphin House was only two miles further on and the sun had just dipped below the horizon as Shakespeare made his entrance. It was built around a courtyard, with stables near by. Like Trevail Hall, it was made of granite, but it was larger and more splendid, as befitted the deputy Lord Lieutenant of the county, Sir Francis Godolphin.

He heard music. The leaded windows were lit by the flames of many candles. Shakespeare handed his horse into the care of the stableman and went in search of a servant. A pair of pikemen barred his way and made him wait outside while one of them went to fetch a more senior officer. After a few minutes a grey-haired man appeared in black clothes and a crisp white ruff, inquired after the nature of Shakespeare's business, then asked him to wait in an ante-room.

'Sir Francis might be a few minutes. He is entertaining guests.'

Shakespeare turned away and examined his surroundings. The room was richly appointed with linenfold panelling. Indeed, the whole house reeked of the great wealth that the Godolphin family had accrued from the mining of copper and tin. He swung round at the sound of footsteps. A man of military bearing with a ruddy face and a good-humoured aspect stood before him.

'May I inquire who you are, sir?'

Shakespeare gathered that this must be Sir Francis Godolphin and bowed to him. 'John Shakespeare. I am from the office of Sir Robert Cecil.'

'Good evening to you, Mr Shakespeare. You are welcome.' He took his guest by the hand. 'And you will be pleased to know that you are arrived in good time for the dancing. Come, sir, join the revels for you have come a damnable long way and must need stretch your legs and take wine and food.'

'If I might just explain why I am here.'

'Well, I *hope* you are here because of the hostile Spanish shipping in these waters. I would like it all the more if you could tell me that you have brought a company of fighting men with you, but I fear from your face that you have not.'

'Have there been more sightings?'

'Spanish ships-of-war have taken an English merchantman in the Channel and it is possible they have captured more fishers, six men of Newlyn, whose craft has not returned to safe harbour. The Spanish galleys have also been spotted off the north shore of Cornwall, past St Ives and close by St Eval. That was three days ago. I am informed that Grenville raised a militia, armed them with calivers and manned the beach; the Spanish did not attempt to land. Of course I have sent messengers with all this to my lord of Essex and to Cecil, but it would be well if a voice such as yours were to press our case to the Council, Mr Shakespeare.'

'I will take back your reports and recommendations to Sir Robert. But I am also here to talk with a guest of yours, Lady Trevail. A private matter, Sir Francis, but one of most potent concern to the realm.'

'Sir, it is not my way to inquire into other men's secrets, so I will not ask you to explain yourself. All I will say is that Lucia is among my oldest friends, and I would wish you to treat her with courtesy and respect, whatever your business with her. Do I make myself clear?'

Shakespeare bowed again. 'Indeed.'

'Good man, then come and join the merry-making. We will talk more of hostile Spaniards on the morrow.'

Lucia Trevail had shrugged off her modest court attire and replaced it with a dazzling gown of gold and silver threads that caught the light and made her the centre of attention for every man and woman in the room. In the light of the candle flames, Shakespeare thought her sublime.

There were about fifty guests in the hall, talking and drinking in little groups to the sound of viols and lutes. Shakespeare stood at the entrance as Godolphin clapped his hands for silence. The music ceased, and all eyes turned to him.

'Lords, ladies and gentlemen, we have an unexpected guest, Mr John Shakespeare. Please do me the courtesy of extending him a warm Cornish welcome.'

The guests all nodded their heads in acknowledgment, but

Shakespeare's own eyes were fixed on Lucia. She smiled and left her group to step towards him.

'Mr Shakespeare, what a marvellous surprise.'

He took her small gloved hand and kissed her fingers. 'My lady . . .'

'Am I so irresistible that you travelled this far to see me?'

He laughed. 'I would, of course, traverse the Straits of Magellan and swim the Pacific Ocean for the honour of kissing your hand.'

'I should hope you would, for such bounty is bestowed on few and is as precious as nutmeg. Now then, sir, why are you here? Yet again, you are most mysterious.'

He scanned the room. There was no sign of Beatrice Eastley.

'Are you looking for something, Mr Shakespeare?'

'Could we repair elsewhere to talk? I have questions to ask.'

'Why, yes. Let us take the night air. And I should be pleased to have a few answers myself.'

Outside in the gardens, the air was warm. With their way lit by burning cressets of pitch, they wandered through arbours, across a lawn to a bank of yew, where they were well away from eyes and ears.

'It is about Lady Susan's companion, Beatrice Eastley,' Shakespeare said. 'Is she still with you?'

'No, indeed she is not. Why?'

'I had expected her to be here with you.'

'So had I, Mr Shakespeare, so had I, for we left London together. Along the way, she decided she did not like me or my company, though I am still puzzled as to what exactly happened. I do not lie when I tell you that I have never been spoken to in my life the way that hussy addressed me.'

'What happened?'

She began walking again, slowly, into the darkness where only the moon and stars lit her path.

'We were at an inn, just before the leg of the journey towards Buckland Abbey. I was expecting to go to see Elizabeth Drake and from there we would take a little detour to the relatives of whom Beatrice spoke. At the inn, we were in our room and somehow the talk came around to matters of religion. I do not know why, but I had always assumed she was of the same persuasion as me, but it appears I was wrong. In my bags, I had a small copy of sections from Foxe's *Book of Martyrs*, telling the horrific yet chastening tales of our brave English men and women who died in the fires of Bloody Mary's inquisition. Have you read it, Mr Shakespeare?'

'Indeed.'

'Well, Beatrice suddenly turned into a wildcat. She snatched the book from my travelling bag and tore out the pages, one by one, and threw them on the fire. "Let their memory turn to ashes," she said, "for they were all heretics and will burn in hell for all time." I was shocked to my soul and perhaps did not react as quickly as I might. She picked up a cup, threw it at me and called me a heretic whore and worse. Despicable words that I cannot repeat. I shied away from her, for I suddenly wondered whether she might have a dagger, but she merely stood her ground and laughed at me. My fear turned to anger and I told her to get out. She made an obscene gesture, Mr Shakespeare, then spat at the ground by my feet and was gone. I have not seen her since, and I thank God for it.'

'I need to find her. Exactly where did you part?'

'A village called Bickleigh, by the bridge over the Exe. Mr Shakespeare, I cannot tell you how distraught I was. Though I did not count Beatrice a friend, yet I had always thought she must have the makings of a gentlewoman, otherwise why would Susan have taken her on as she had? And, certainly,

Emilia always thought well of her.' Lucia Trevail stopped beneath the spreading branches of a cedar. The music from the hall had faded to a distant hum. 'I find myself agitated to think of it still.'

Shakespeare touched her arm and his fingers lingered a moment.

Her hand clutched his and held it. They were a quarter-mile from the house and the light cressets.

'Now *you* must talk to me, Mr Shakespeare. What exactly is your interest in Beatrice and why have you come so far in quest of her? The last time we met you were engaged on a hunt for Thomasyn Jade. Now it seems you have switched your attention to my erstwhile companion. I believe you owe me some explanation.'

'Very well. Beatrice Eastley is not her real name. She is Sorrow Gray, the daughter of the late keeper of Wisbech Castle.'

Shakespeare told her all he knew about her conversion and the suspicions now raised against her.

'Sir Robert Cecil and I had great fears for *you*, Lady Trevail, for you are close to the Queen.'

'Are you suggesting you suspected *me* of something?'

'I did not say that, but you were in the company of an impostor. We need to be certain: did she insinuate her way into your acquaintance, or was she welcomed?'

She removed her hand from his, sharply. 'You seem to be calling me a traitor.'

'You have access to Her Royal Majesty. It is my job to be suspicious.'

'What exactly do you suspect me of doing?'

'I am simply being cautious. I must find out what Beatrice Eastley is scheming.'

'I feel rather insulted, sir.'

'My intention is merely to clear your name from this difficult inquiry.'

For a moment there was silence. Then Lucia Trevail shivered and smiled. 'Come, you are right to have suspicions. It is indeed your job, sir.'

The night air was cooling. He moved towards her, but she stepped lightly aside.

'Mr Shakespeare, we are in danger of straying too far.' She took his hand in hers once again. 'Take me back to the hall and let us join the dance.'

Chapter 25

HE DRANK A good deal too much brandy and danced late into the night. The dancing, which had started sedately with the pavane, progressed to a vigorous volta and a riotous galliard. Lucia was like a feather in his arms when he lifted her and held her. They danced with abandon.

He had not drunk this much in many years. It was the headiness of the night, the long ride here – and his desire for her. He could not go to his chamber while she still danced, and so he stayed. Yet each time that he felt he could carry her away, she kissed his cheek and fluttered off like a butterfly, to the company of others. Then, as he consoled himself with one more silver goblet of brandy or wine, she was there again.

At last, some time in the early hours, the music stopped. Sir Francis Godolphin clapped his arm across Shakespeare's back.

'You, sir, will be the worse for drink, come morning. But, damn me, I say you hold it well, for you have downed enough to drown a horse.'

Shakespeare couldn't speak.

Godolphin laughed. 'Come, I will have a bluecoat show you to your chamber and fling you on to the bed.'

Shakespeare looked around through a fog of liquor. Where was Lucia? He groaned as he tried to find her in the crowd of dispersing guests.

Godolphin was at his side again. 'She has gone to her chamber, Mr Shakespeare,' he said quietly. 'Alone.'

He woke late in the morning. Sun streamed through open shutters. He rose from the bed and wondered what had come over him. He could not recall a time when he had been so drunk. It was not his way. Now his head hurt and he felt in great need of a bath to cleanse the dust of the road from his face and body. There was a knock at the chamber door.

'Enter.'

A servant came in and bowed. 'Sir Francis's compliments, sir. He has urgent business at Penzance and would like you to accompany him. He leaves within the hour.'

'What business?'

The footman hesitated, but then decided it was safe enough to talk. 'It is said that Spanish men-at-arms have landed in Mount's Bay, Mr Shakespeare. The whole house is in turmoil.'

Shakespeare looked at the man as though he had not quite heard him properly. 'What did you just say?'

'The Armada has come, master. We are being invaded.'

'Bring me water to wash, and some milk, bread and meats to wake me. Quickly, man. And tell Sir Francis I will be down very soon.'

'Yes, sir.' The servant bowed and backed out of the room.

Shakespeare sat down on the bed and held his head in his hands and, through the cup-shotten stupor that passed for a brain, tried to make some sense of what he had just been told.

Two dozen men were already mounted in the stableyard when Shakespeare arrived. He had scrubbed himself in haste, and had thrown food and milk down his throat.

Sir Francis Godolphin was just mounting up. 'Ah, good man,' he said. 'Have you been told what has happened?'

'A servant suggested Spanish soldiers had landed. Is this true?'

'It seems so. That is what I intend to find out.'

Shakespeare looked around the motley group Godolphin had thrown together. Some were faces he recognised from the dancing; others, from their rather more lowly manner of dress, were retainers. Three of them had white hair and, though they sat bravely, they did not look as though they would be of great help in a fight. All were armed in one way or another. He made out three old matchlock arquebuses, and a pair of ornate pistols thrust into Godolphin's belt. Swords and daggers, of course, and crossbows. A horse-drawn wagon was loaded up with bills, pikes, halberds and half a dozen muskets; also some powder, shot and various pieces of armour, shields and helmets.

Shakespeare gripped the saddle of his own horse and a groom made a cup of his hands for his boot, to help him up.

'Now, gentlemen,' Godolphin said in a firm voice, 'we will ride from here to Penzance. I have sent a pair of scouts ahead to order the trainband, and all fishers and townsmen, to gather arms and to meet on the western green. I have also sent messengers to Drake and Hawkins at Plymouth to consider what is to be done for their own safety and our defence. Orders have gone to Captain Hannibal Vyvyan at St Mawes fort to send all available men.' He pulled his shoulders back and lifted his chin. 'Only the Lord knows what this day holds for us, but let us acquit ourselves with dignity and courage, as Cornishmen and true subjects of Her Royal Majesty. God be with you all.'

Towards the south, plumes of dense black smoke were visible for many miles around. Sir Francis Godolphin raised his hand to call a halt to his troop. They looked down from the higher ground above Penzance, and saw four galleys at anchor, close to the shoreline on the south-western coast of Mount's Bay.

'In God's name, that's the village of Mousehole ablaze,' the deputy Lord Lieutenant said, horror in his voice. 'So it is true.'

At his side, Shakespeare's hand went to his sword hilt. All along the coastal path, he could see streams of people hurrying away from the fires, northwards in the direction of Penzance. He could see no Spanish soldiers, but he could hear explosions as they mined houses with gunpowder.

Suddenly he realised the date. It was the twenty-third day of July. The letter found aboard *The Ruth* had mentioned the twenty-third, though there had been no month. *Yours, in the love of Christ our only saviour and Gregory, great England's truest friend, this twenty-third day.* Was this the start? Was the long-feared invasion to start this day?

The commander summoned his two closest lieutenants. 'Ride ahead, ensure that men are gathering at the green. There must be no panic, no retreating. Tell them there are only four galleys. There cannot be that many enemy soldiers; surely no more than seventy or eighty. Instil courage in our men. Tell them they will be reinforced soon, by sea and by land.'

The lieutenants kicked on.

Shakespeare had doubts. His main fear was that there could be many more troops than Godolphin estimated. Large galleys, such as the ones in the bay, equipped with both sails and oars – galleasses – could hold a hundred soldiers each with room to spare.

Worse than that was the knowledge that the Spanish already had a beachhead. The only point at which this ragtag force of Godolphin's could have stopped seasoned fighting men in their tracks was when they were wading ashore, burdened with armour and arms. Now, it was too late. And who knew how many other ships were stood out to sea, protecting the galleys should Drake's fleet arrive. Indeed, the horrible thought struck home that this could all be a trap, a means to lure the ships at Plymouth out of their safe harbour.

The scene on the greensward to the west of Penzance was one of utter chaos. Men in fishermen's smocks and hats were clutching any weapon that came to hand. Some had mooring rods from their boats; others had old billhooks and bows and arrows.

They surged forward as Godolphin's wagon of weapons and armour arrived. His men tried to bring order to the throng. 'What skill have you? Have you used pike or halberd? Are you well trained in bowmanship?' Each man was handed a weapon dependent upon his answer.

Women and children milled around among their menfolk. Some carried packs of hastily snatched belongings and food. Godolphin drew one of his pistols from his belt and fired it in the air. Some people began to scatter, thinking they were under attack, but their din of clattering arms and wild talking died down enough for Godolphin's booming voice to be heard.

'I will have order! Line up in ranks, from west to east. The chief man of each village is to come to me.' He nodded to the men who had accompanied him from Godolphin Hall. 'Line them into squadrons of a dozen men. Anyone between the ages of twelve and sixty. None are to move away on pain of death. Women and younger children to carry on without their men and seek refuge where they may, in Penzance or beyond.'

Two men trudged towards him.

'Who are you?' Godolphin demanded of the older of the two, a thickset fisher with little hair and hands like frying pans.

'Jacob Keigwin of Mousehole.'

'Tell me what happened.'

'They came out of the morning mist. We did not see them until they were upon us. They drove ashore in shallops, which are still on the beach. Three hundred or more soldiers, mostly with hagbuts and pikes, all in heavy armour. They strode into Mousehole as if they owned the place. Turned us out of our houses and began to fire them with pitch and powder.'

'Did they kill villagers?'

'My brother Jenken. He would not let them take his house, so they shot him dead where he stood. We had nothing to fight them with and came away, thinking to raise the trainband at Penzance.'

Shakespeare listened with dismay. If this was happening here, were there simultaneous attacks elsewhere along the coast? And where did this group of raiders plan to go next? Would they march eastwards towards the heart of England?

'I am sorry to hear about your brother,' Shakespeare said, 'but I must ask you, where are the Spaniards now?'

Another man stepped forward. 'Some of them marched up to Paul village and set fire to the church, which is the most ungodly act I ever heard of.'

'How many of them? What are their arms?' Godolphin pressed.

'I would say a thousand. They are like men built of steel with guns the manner of which I have not seen.'

'Well, return to your squadrons and help keep them in good order. I am relying on men such as you. Stout men with hearts of Cornwall and England.'

Godolphin looked at Shakespeare. They were not going to get an accurate view of the Spanish invaders from these villagers. The two men shuffled off, back to their friends.

'We need sound intelligence,' said Shakespeare. 'A scout to bring back definite numbers, movements and armaments of the enemy. I will go.'

Chapter 26

H E TOOK TWO wheel-lock pistols, both primed with
powder and loaded with shot, and a map drawn by
Godolphin, and rode towards the little fishing village of
Newlyn. There he tethered the horse and began the long steep
climb inland on foot.

A black dog loped past him downhill. Otherwise the dusty
path was deserted and the fishers' houses were empty. Acrid
fumes from the burning dwellings in the nearby villages of
Mousehole and Paul blew across the sky in a black cloud. At
the top of the hill, he stopped in the shade of a windblown tree
and consulted his sketchy chart. He could see Paul less than
half a mile away, ablaze, the flames leaping and roaring. As he
got closer, the smoke thinned and he ducked down behind
a grass-covered knoll. He could see Spanish soldiers on the
northern fringe of the village. Some were lined up in order,
defensively. Others sat and smoked pipes or drank from clay
jugs, refreshing themselves from the hot work of destroying
other men's homes and possessions. None looked in his
direction.

Shakespeare moved in short bursts, from cover to cover,
behind hedgerows and trees, going around the village's western
margins. Finally, as he came closer to open ground, he dropped

to his belly and crawled. He spotted a sentry, some two hundred yards from the village, standing nonchalantly, his pike resting over his shoulder. Shakespeare pulled out his dagger and wondered about taking him, but he was too close to the village. He let him live, and skirted around him.

On the south-western edge of the village, he came across two men, standing by a cottage some distance from the rest of the troops. One wore the clothes of a workman: hide jerkin and hose. The other looked like a senior Spanish officer. Shakespeare moved on through the woods, keeping them in view. When he was close enough, he dashed at a crouch to the shelter of a wagon, laden with crates of fish, not more than twenty yards from the two men. Above them, the roof of the house crackled and burnt, but they paid it no heed.

Looking out from between the wheels of the heavy oak cart, Shakespeare strained to hear what the two men were saying. Suddenly, they both laughed, and the officer slapped the workman on the back. As the man turned, Shakespeare got a good view of his features. The jerkin might be that of a labourer or a blacksmith, but the smooth, tanned skin, the handsome face and the long, well-kept brown hair were those of a gentleman. The officer said something in Spanish, which Shakespeare could not quite catch, and his companion drew his sword from its scabbard. He ran his finger along the razor-sharp edge and drew blood.

'See how my sword weeps . . .'

Shakespeare froze. He had spoken in perfect English.

The man licked the blood from his finger and grinned at the Spanish officer, then they turned and walked back into the village.

For the next hour, Shakespeare hid in undergrowth and in whatever cover he could find, watching the soldiers' movements, counting their strength and assessing their armaments. Finally, when he had learnt as much as he could, he began to descend the hill towards Mousehole, keeping to the woods that shrouded the steep, narrow pathway.

From a vantage point just above the little fishing port, he saw that thirty shallops – longboats for transporting men ashore from large vessels – were beached, just as Jacob Keigwin had indicated. He concealed himself in undergrowth where he could watch and wait. Spanish soldiers were everywhere – above and below him – destroying everything they found.

In the middle of the afternoon, the soldiers in Paul suddenly began to move. They were lined up by their officers and marched downhill to Mousehole. They passed within twenty yards of his hiding place, their arms shouldered. He counted them: three hundred in all. And he reckoned a hundred more had stayed at Mousehole to protect the boats. That meant a total strength of four hundred.

Within half an hour, they had embarked on the shallops. And then they were gone, leaving only fire and ashes in their wake.

As the longboat rowers hauled across the still seas of Mount's Bay to the galleys, Shakespeare watched them from the shade of a tree on the hillside. In the distance, across the bay, stood the fortress of St Michael's Mount, its heavy cannon too far away to attack the vessels. He could not see the green where Godolphin was attempting to raise a defence force. Would it be needed, though? Had the Spaniards gone for good, or was this return to their vessel merely the prelude to another attack, somewhere further along the coast? Was this all a test of defences? Or was it, as he had already wondered, something more: a ruse to lure Drake's ships from safe harbour at Plymouth, or even the first shots in an invasion?

He turned and strode downhill between the burning,

blackened ruins of family homes and outhouses. At the harbour shore all the fishing boats had been coated in pitch and set ablaze. In a scene of desolation, only one house remained unburnt. A man's body was sprawled, half in, half out of the doorway, surrounded by a dark stain of blood in the dust. Shakespeare turned him over. This must be Jenken Keigwin, who had refused to leave his house to the fire. Shakespeare felt sick; if he had ever doubted the rightness of the war of secrets that he and Sir Robert Cecil fought, those qualms had gone for ever.

Shakespeare looked out to sea once more and realised with dismay that the longboats were not returning to the galleasses after all, but were heading north towards Newlyn and Penzance. And in their wake came the main ships, their ranks of slave oarsmen rowing hard, their big guns already rolled out. For Godolphin's band of defenders it would be a deadly onslaught.

Encumbered by his sword and pistols, Shakespeare ran along the cliff path until his lungs burnt from exertion and the choking smoke.

He reached Newlyn in about ten minutes, to find his horse still there. He pulled himself up into the saddle just as the first of the longboats reached the shore. The galleasses, meanwhile, had moved on north towards the green where the defenders were preparing to make their stand. As he kicked on, he saw that the four vessels were stopping, ready to stand off, no more than a hundred yards from the English militia.

The first bombardment came as he rode towards the green. A shattering blast of powder, the guns belching fire and smoke as they hurled their iron balls and stones at human flesh.

And then he spotted Lucia Trevail. She sat astride her horse like a man, at the side of Sir Francis Godolphin. She had a pistol in her hand. It was pointing out to sea, towards the galleys. She pulled the trigger, the steel wheel spun, the spark lit the touchpowder. Smoke and fire spewed forth and the shot was hurled harmlessly into the water.

She looked across at him with a curious smile. 'Ah, Mr Shakespeare, I thought you had run away.'

He rode forward and came alongside her. 'What in the name of God are you doing here, my lady?'

'Shooting at Spaniards. What else should I be doing? How many would you like me to kill to prove that I am no traitor to England?'

'You must return to the safety of Trevail Hall.' He turned to Godolphin. 'Sir Francis—'

Godolphin shrugged his shoulders helplessly. 'She is beyond my reckoning, Mr Shakespeare. Always has been.'

'My lady, this is no place for you. Hundreds of heavily armed enemy soldiers are presently coming ashore no more than half a mile from here. They are in murderous mood.'

'Mr Shakespeare, did you learn nothing when you came to our little gathering at Susan's house in Barbican Street? Do you think the ladies you met there are fainthearts who would be ruled by men or would miss the spectacle of a Spanish invasion? Anyway, I have brought three of my retainers. They will soon learn to be fighting men if they wish to remain in my employ.'

She tilted her head in the direction of three serving men standing beside packhorses. They bowed at her gaze and, thought Shakespeare, looked mighty disconsolate.

'You are not practised in the art of war. Look around you at the damage being wrought. At least one man has already been killed. Others are fleeing for their lives.'

'I know how to shoot a pistol as well as any man. And you must know that when I return to court, the first thing Her Royal Majesty will demand of me is a full account of this day's events. How, I beseech you, will I provide her with the detail she requires, unless I witness whatever befalls? I would not miss it, sir. Come, allow me some courage. Does not Elizabeth herself have the heart of a king?'

Shakespeare sighed. He looked to Godolphin for support, but he was preoccupied with sending messengers to collect arms and men. Well, so be it. For the moment, he had other things to do, the first of which was to move the English militia to a better defensive position. He rode to Godolphin's side and interrupted him.

'We have little time, Sir Francis. The Spanish army will soon be upon us and we will be overwhelmed. We must make a tactical retreat, for we have no hope of defending this flat green against insuperable odds.'

'How many men do they have?'

'Four hundred, as Mr Keigwin suggested. Possibly more than that, and they are true soldiers whereas your men—'

'—are a rabble. Yes, I know that, Mr Shakespeare.'

'I merely meant to say that they are untried in battle.'

A cannonball ripped into the earth just a few feet from them. Shakespeare's horse reared up and nearly threw him. Godolphin reached over and grabbed the reins to steady him. 'Be careful, Mr Shakespeare. We need you alive.'

Shakespeare patted the spooked animal down the neck to soothe it.

'Come, let us head for the market square in Penzance,' Godolphin said. 'It is higher ground and we will have cover among the houses. Give the order, sir.'

As Shakespeare looked around the green, it became clear that an orderly retreat was already out of the question; the men were deserting eastwards like a stampede of terrified cattle. And then he realised why: Newlyn was on fire and the Spanish troops were advancing from the west.

*

By the time they reached the market square, Godolphin's force was reduced to twenty men – mostly his own retainers and colleagues – and Lady Lucia Trevail. For half an hour, they fought a battle of musketfire. Shakespeare's arquebus became so hot with firing that he feared it would explode.

A Spaniard raced forward, a pistol in hand, his head encased in a steel morion. Shakespeare took aim and shot him in the apex of the collarbone. The man crumpled, blood shooting before him into the dusty road.

It was a small victory, for there were hundreds of Spaniards behind him, all heavily armed and advancing steadily.

'This is hopeless, Mr Shakespeare,' Godolphin said. 'We cannot defend this position. We must retreat to Marazion and the fortress of St Michael's Mount.'

Shakespeare well understood why the commander's expression was so grim. 'We must hope reinforcements arrive very soon or I fear the worst.'

He knew that if the enemy was not thrown back from the beaches in short order, they would entrench and set up defensive works of their own. If that happened, they could use Mount's Bay as a haven for their fleets, while landing troops at will for a full-scale invasion.

Godolphin gave the order. 'Collect up your arms and follow me. I want a fighting retreat.'

The trek to Marazion was dogged every step by the Spanish advance guard. At the causeway to St Michael's Mount, the tide was encroaching, but they managed to cross before the path was lost to the waves. Exhausted, they climbed the steep, rocky footpath to the ramparts of the fort that topped the Mount.

Godolphin shook his head in something akin to despair. 'Cowardly dogs,' he muttered to no one in particular, though

Shakespeare understood that it was not the Spaniards he was talking about, but his own countrymen.

Across the bay, Penzance had been taken and was in flames. The evening was darkening and the fires lit the sky with a hellish red glow all around the shoreline. The boom and crack of cannon fire and gunshot filled the air over the fishing town.

Godolphin summoned a castle servant and ordered brandy. The only thing that gave him any hope was that small boats had begun pulling into the harbour at the base of the Mount, discharging men from villages and towns throughout the south-west. Many were armed with ancient weapons; all were volunteering to fight.

There was news, too, from a messenger who had arrived after a gruelling ride from St Mawes fort, at the entrance to Falmouth Harbour. He blurted out his message before catching his breath.

'I bring word from Captain Hannibal Vyvyan, sir. He has sent a company of men. He believes they will be here by morning.'

'Good man. But be pleased to tell Mr Vyvyan that one company is not likely to be enough.'

'Word has gone post to Drake and Hawkins at Plymouth. They have been asked to send ships-of-war, sir, and soldiers by land.'

Shakespeare stood at Lucia Trevail's side. Night had almost come, but her face and eyes were alive with the reflected light of the fires.

'Have you seen enough of war now, my lady?'

'Why, it is like a display of fireworks, Mr Shakespeare.'

'It is not so pretty for those who have lost their homes, livelihoods or lives.'

'Indeed not. I had not meant to make light of their misery.'

She moved closer to him, so that he could smell her soft scent, mingled strangely with the smoke of gunpowder.

'Sir Francis tells me you were quite the hero today. That you scouted the enemy positions on your own. Will you not tell me about it?'

'There is little to tell. I managed to make an estimate of their numbers and armaments, and I saw the body of a man who had had the temerity to resist them.'

'And that is all?'

Yes, except that I also saw an Englishman among their number; but I will keep that information to myself until I see Sir Robert Cecil.

'That is all, my lady.'

She looked deeper into his eyes, as though searching for something. 'You are a strange, mysterious man, Mr Shakespeare. I think you keep much to yourself. Do you trust *anyone*?'

'Experience has taught me caution.'

She kissed him quickly. It was a chaste kiss, the sort of kiss that men and women at court gave to each other in greeting. And yet it wasn't chaste at all.

'War and death, Mr Shakespeare. Whatever your misgivings, you must own that they stir the passions. They do something to a man, do they not?'

He looked out at the distant flames. He knew that what she said was true. He knew, too, that the same effect could be wrought in a woman at war.

'Do you think me forward, sir? I seek no pardon for that, for I do not have time to wait on wooing. I tell you, the Queen's Privy Chamber is a very nunnery of virgins, so I have not time enough nor do I care for the good opinion of the world when I am away from her presence. Come to me tonight, Mr Shakespeare.'

Lucia looped her arm into Shakespeare's. Her fingers touched his side like a feather.

Inside the fortress hall, more than a hundred candles blazed on the orders of Godolphin.

'We shall light up the night as well as they,' he said, as they entered.

This island, rising so dramatically from the sea, had once housed a Benedictine monastery. Now it was home to a Cornish family called Morston and, though ill defended, it dominated the bay. Shakespeare hoped its presence would make the Spaniards think hard about the wisdom of moving against it.

A castle servant approached and bowed low. 'There is a man to see you, sir.'

'Indeed. And who is he?'

The servant grimaced as though he had put something foul-tasting in his mouth. 'He says he is Boltfoot Cooper and that he is known to you.'

Shakespeare smiled. 'Thank God.' He turned to Lucia. 'My lady, Mr Cooper is my manservant. Forgive me. I must go to him.'

Lucia released her grip on his arm. 'Mr Shakespeare, you do not escape from me that easily. I shall reserve a place for you, next to mine.'

Chapter 27

SHAKESPEARE CLASPED BOLTFOOT to his breast, then stood back and looked him up and down. He looked like some nameless creature that had crawled out of the Fenland mud and slime.

'Good God, Boltfoot. It is a fine thing to see you. Is Wisbech secured?'

'I believe so, master. The squadron arrived and straightway set about bringing military order to the prison. I was less happy about leaving London, though, sir.'

'You found Jane at Sir Robert Cecil's residence?'

'Yes. But I am most fearful about this threat that has been laid against your girls. I wished to protect them myself, but Sir Robert said that all would be well in his house and that I was to follow you.'

'You did the correct thing. We need every man we can lay hands on. But first, have you eaten? You must need sleep.'

Boltfoot took out his pipe from his mud-encrusted jerkin pocket. 'This will do me for the present, master.' He knocked it against the wall and dirt and ashes fell to the floor. He tamped in the last few strands of his tobacco and lit it from a candle, sucked deeply, then exhaled smoke. 'But I do bring other news. You recall the old nun, Sister Michael?'

'I could not forget the hag.'

'She came to Dowgate, looking for you.'

'Now that *is* interesting. What did she have to say for herself?'

'She said she had information for you, that word had reached her that you should be trusted in the matter of Thomasyn Jade.'

And how did she learn that, when he had not yet managed to pass on to her Father Weston's letter? He recalled what the old nun had said when they were at Denham: *We know every-thing that goes on in this realm of sin and heresy. We have friends everywhere, in the palaces and the courts of law.* It was a disturb-ing thought, but maybe she spoke true; she had clearly learnt somehow of his meeting with Weston.

'Did she tell you what the intelligence was?'

'No, master.'

'Is she in safe keeping for me on my return?'

'She is still at the Swan Inn. I think she will stay there and come to you. She asked me to thank you for ordering her release from Bridewell, which she said had surprised her greatly.'

Shakespeare sighed. The whole matter of Thomasyn Jade and the exorcisms seemed unimportant in present circumstances.

'Master,' Boltfoot said tentatively, 'there is something we might do this night. It was something Drake planned once, when we were off the coast of Peru back in the days of our voyage around the world.'

'Yes?'

'There are many boats hereabouts, and many fishers. They must know all the shoals and rocks in this bay as though it were their own backyard, and so are able to traverse the waters by night, unseen. I do believe that sometime between midnight and dawn, on the middle watch when most aboard the galleys sleep, we might approach them in silence, by cockboat or skiff, and shoot arrows of fire into them.'

'Did this work for Drake?'

Boltfoot's mouth creased. 'I had hoped you would not ask me that, master, for in the end he decided not to attempt it. And yet he did lay plans of this nature and I could see no reason then why it would not have worked. Nor can I see any reason not to try it now.'

Shakespeare computed the possible gains and risks. Everything would depend on utter silence and surprise. The fishing boats would be vulnerable to counter-attack, for it would not take long for the galleasses to turn their guns on them. Oar-driven vessels could lift anchor and mount an attack very quickly. For the plan to work and the men to survive, they would have to launch dozens of fire arrows in a minute or so and then row like the devil for shore.

Finally, he nodded. 'Come, Boltfoot, let us put your scheme to Sir Francis Godolphin. I will speak for it.'

For the first time that day, Godolphin's florid face lightened a shade. 'Yes, let us do it. I shall order it organised straightway. Thank you, Mr Shakespeare, and please convey my gratitude to your man for devising the plan.'

'Let us pray something comes of it.'

Godolphin waved his finger like a stern minister in the pulpit. 'Nothing can be worse than has already occurred, sir. I tell you, this has been the most shameful day in the proud history of Cornwall. Never did I expect to see Cornishmen turn tail in the face of an enemy, however great their numbers. All honour is lost. We can but hope that this attack upon their ships will enable us to atone in some small way for the disgrace of our men's cowardice.'

'Sir Francis, I shall go on this foray.'

Godolphin shook his head. 'No, sir. You are no seafarer and you have done quite enough with your scouting. I will not allow you to hazard your life. I need men with your experience at my side. You are a vital member of my council of war.'

'Sir Francis—'

'I say again, no. This mission requires seamen and archers, not intelligencers. You would be a hindrance, not a help, sir. I would, however, desire your Mr Cooper to command the expedition. As a former Drake man, he has experienced sea warfare, has he not.'

'He has.'

'Good. Then he is the man.'

Two boats slipped their moorings and slid away on the still water, each containing six men. Two per boat would row on the way out; all would row on the way back. As the boats had to remain silent, the oars were dipped in the water with exquisite care to avoid splashing. They had to remain invisible, too, so there were no lanterns.

The only light was a burning match, held beneath a canvas so its glow could not be seen. The light of the moon came and went with the swirls of the mist.

'God go with you.'

Shakespeare mouthed the words rather than spoke them, watching from the rocky shore on St Michael's Mount. After a few minutes the boats had vanished into the sea fret. He could see nothing, hear nothing. Just as it should be. The mist had come as a blessing. There was no light from shore, for the blazing houses of Penzance and the other villages had been reduced to blackened, lightless husks.

Somehow, the boats carrying the archers had to get almost within touching distance of the enemy ships. Though the killing range of a longbow might be two hundred yards or more, these arrows would be shot from an insecure platform, the rocking belly of a small rowing boat, at the mercy of the sea's swell and the archers' own unsteadiness. They would have to be as close as fifty yards if they were to hit their targets. But was fifty yards also far enough away for them to have a chance of escape?

Every sinew in Shakespeare's body was stretched taut and his teeth were clenched so tightly he feared they could crack. He turned and made his way back up the long climb of rocky steps to the fortress at the top of the Mount; there would be no rest this night until Boltfoot and his eleven companions were back safe.

Boltfoot was gratified by the skill of the oarsmen, but their care meant that the going was extremely slow, especially as they were moving against the incoming tide. They had timed the assault thus, so that the currents would add speed to their escape.

The galleass lights glimmered in the distance, through the thin mist. The vessels were far out where the bay met the open sea and where the water would not be so calm. At this rate, Boltfoot reckoned it would take them half an hour to get there. The question was: how quickly would they able to return to shore afterwards?

Lucia Trevail was garbed in a long gown of white silk that shimmered in the whispery breeze at the top of the Mount. 'I thought I might find you here, Mr Shakespeare.'

Shakespeare was gazing into the shifting fog. He had lost track of how long he had spent here, on the battlements, wait-ing. Sometimes the mist lifted and then he could see the Spanish vessels clearly, sparkling with a mass of lanterns like four golden carriages. And then the mist came down again, as a theatre curtain closes, shutting out all but the faintest glow. How close were the fishers with their puny boats and their arrows of wood?

He turned and gazed at her.

'You are shivering, my lady.'

'I could not sleep. A strange bed. And I was thinking of you. Our paths have crossed in a rare fashion, sir. War and death . . .'

Shakespeare was unsettled by her in more ways than he cared to admit. He pulled her to him. She was slender and warm against him. He kissed her and she responded with soft, sweet lips. He held her closer, and his fingers slid through her tumbling hair.

In her eye, he saw a sudden reflected light. Gently, he pulled back from her and held her in his arm as, together, they looked across the sea into a rain of fire.

Boltfoot was manning the flaming taper and the half-keg of pitch. The archers dipped their arrowheads into the black tar, touched them to the flame, then drew back their longbows of yew and shot. One every ten seconds. Ten archers in all – five per boat with one man holding the fire and pitch.

They were attacking just one of the four Spanish vessels. Some of the arrows hit their target, but more fell woefully short, hissing into the waves. They weren't close enough and there was too much movement in the boats. Within a few seconds, there was shouting aboard the galleass. Then came the first retaliatory musketfire.

'Two more arrows each!' Boltfoot shouted. 'Then we go.'

Half a dozen fires had started aboard the galleass, but it was already clear to him that they would easily be put out.

More arrows flew through the night, but more fire was now coming back their way. And then Boltfoot saw the saker cannon being rolled out. He gave the order to man the oars. 'Row for your lives, boys! Row for your lives!'

Shot from muskets peppered the water around them. The man beside Boltfoot gasped in pain and shock, and fell back into the water. Boltfoot leant over the side and grasped the shoulder of his woollen smock. 'Help me, lads.'

Two of the other men dropped their oars and assisted Boltfoot to drag the wounded man aboard while the remaining two continued to row. The injured fisher clutched his shattered left arm but did not groan. Boltfoot tossed the pitch keg overboard, extinguished the flame and laid the injured man down as gently as he could in the floor of the boat. He cursed beneath his breath; one man less to row.

Without a word, he returned to his own oar and joined the other six in heaving and hauling with all his considerable strength.

Time was running short. Boltfoot saw that men were already clambering down ropes at the side of the galley to get into the longboats. The saker boomed, and a ball crashed into the water fifteen feet to starboard and a little way ahead.

'Speed men, speed. They'll be on us.'

He dropped his own oar and picked up his caliver, which was already primed and loaded. Resting it carefully in his arms, the stock wedged against his heart, he squinted along the barrel and pulled the trigger. The gun recoiled against him like a rock. There was a scream and one of those climbing from the galleass clutched helplessly at the rope before plummeting into the dark water. *That should slow your enthusiasm for a few moments.* Boltfoot reloaded, fired again without hitting anything, then put down his weapon and returned to the rowing.

Their only hope of escape lay in the darkness of the sea and their superior knowledge of these waters, for the longboats from the galleys were better manned, faster and more powerfully armed. The cannon boomed again. Its shot fell just six feet from the stern, throwing a tower of water into the air and down on the fishers' boat. It rocked violently.

And then it drifted back. The merciful mist . . .

In the candlelight, Shakespeare looked at Lucia's perfect skin without emotion, only hunger. What was she? Whore or lover? Why did he not trust her?

When their lust was sated, he slept without dream and without shame.

He awoke alone in Lucia Trevail's bed. By the light streaming in through the leaded window, he estimated the time at about eight o'clock. There was a note for him. It said simply, *Until we meet again, Mr Shakespeare*. He smiled. Quickly, he dressed and walked out into the hall.

He spotted one of her servants. 'Where is your mistress?' he demanded.

'She is riding for Trevail Hall, master, and then straightway on to London. I am to collect the last of her accoutrements when you have vacated the chamber, and offer my services to Sir Francis Godolphin.'

If the man was at all embarrassed by the knowledge that his mistress had shared her bed with a man, he did not show it. Perhaps this was not such an unusual occurrence in the life of Lady Lucia Trevail.

'You may collect her things.'

'Thank you, sir.'

He found Godolphin on the battlements. The mist had gone and it was a clear morning. 'What news, Sir Francis?'

'You see those specks on the horizon? Those are the Spanish ships-of-war, Mr Shakespeare. They have departed in this last half-hour.'

'Well, that must be good. Perhaps the fire arrows proved some deterrent to them.'

'Perhaps. But where will they land next? From their direction, I confess I fear they might head for the Scilly Isles.'

'How strong is the garrison there?'

'A hundred and fifty men. Strong enough, I pray.'

Shakespeare gazed towards Penzance. It was a desolate mass of charred wood, ash, fallen stones and spiralling black smoke. A line of ants, as it seemed, marched forth from the ruins in the direction of Marazion and this fortress.

'Before you ask, Mr Shakespeare, those are Englishmen released by the Spanish. Some are fishermen taken in the Channel; others are captives from a merchantman or various other prisoners of the wars in Brittany. They were found there this morning, cowering together. I have ordered them brought here for questioning.'

Well, well. That was most interesting. Perhaps they might reveal something about the Englishman he saw talking with the Spanish officer in the village of Paul.

'With your permission, Sir Francis, I will interrogate them. I think we might discover some secrets.'

Chapter 28

SHAKESPEARE WALKED UP and down the great hall like a muster master, inspecting the freed captives. There were more than a hundred of them and they were a bedraggled lot, though pleased to be home with their lives. They knew all too well the fate of other prisoners of Spanish troops. Summary execution was commonplace.

Calling them to order, Shakespeare told them they would be fed and given ale from the castle store-rooms, after which they would be required to answer some straightforward questions. The clearer their answers, the sooner they would be allowed to find passage home to their families.

'Is this all of them?' he asked Godolphin's adjutant, Thomas Chiverton.

'All but one, who ails and is being seen by a physician.'

'Was he wounded?'

'I do not know, Mr Shakespeare. All I can tell you is that the physician is attending to him.'

He left the prisoners in the hall to await their victuals and went to find Boltfoot, who was just waking. Shakespeare had bought some tobacco from one of Godolphin's junior officers and now handed it to his assistant.

'Well done,' he said.

'It amounted to nothing, master.' Boltfoot took the few

ounces of tobacco and thrust them in his jerkin pocket. 'The Spaniards doused the fires as fast as we could start them.'

'Perhaps it meant nothing in military terms, but it was good for English morale. You let the Spaniards know we were here and that we were not to be played with at will. More than that, you showed the Cornishmen that they could fight back.'

Shakespeare had requisitioned an office from the castle steward. After they had eaten, the freed captives began trooping into his presence one by one. He took down each man's name, his port of origin, where he was captured and what experiences he had endured. Many of them spoke of a renegade English pilot aboard the lead galleass, and one man, Barnaby Loe of Ipswich, knew him of old.

'Aye, it was Captain Burley. Richard Burley, most treacherous papist that ever sailed the narrow sea. I saw him close-coupled with the Spaniards, showing them the way through English rock shoals and currents.'

'How do you know him?'

'I sailed with him ten or twelve years ago before he turned coat. He sailed out of Falmouth, but other ports, too. Mostly carrying tin and copper. It pains me to say it, master, but he was a fine pilot. He knew all the waters well, from the Germanies and Low Countries all the way to Spain and beyond. But these were the waters he knew best of all.'

'Describe him.'

'Strong man. Long hair. Bull chest. What more do you want?'

Could this be the Englishman at Paul? It made sense.

'I can tell you, too, that he hails from Weymouth originally. He had a wife and some children, whom he took away when he threw in his lot with Spain. He has a beard down to his breeches.'

Well, that did *not* sound like the man Shakespeare had seen, for he had no more than a short, well-trimmed beard.

'Would you call him handsome or plain-featured?'

'Handsome? The man looks like a pig's arsehole, which you might think mighty disrespectful to pigs' arseholes. When I caught his eye, he summoned me over and did sneer most menacingly, saying that the King of Spain was so rich that he would lay waste to this whole coast, this summer and the next, and every year thereafter.'

'Did he say anything more about their plans?'

'No. I cursed him and he told me to watch my mouth or he would have me put to the oars as a galley slave. By God's faith, master, I did believe him and shut my mouth, for that is a fate I would not wish on any man save a traitor such as Burley himself.'

'Thank you, Mr Loe. And to your knowledge were there any other Englishmen aboard?'

'Only us captives. But we were split between two of the galleys, so I can account only for the one I was in.'

By evening, Shakespeare had not interrogated more than a third of the men. He was becoming tired and realised that he might miss something if he continued his questioning too late into the night. He ordered a platter of meats and some wine to ease him through the last two hours, then found himself a mattress and slept.

At daylight, the questioning began again. The first man brought in said his name was Ambrose Rowse, fisher from Fowey.

Shakespeare went through the questions by rote. 'And were there any Englishmen apart from the prisoners?' he asked finally.

'I recall one Englishman,' Rowse said. 'Never heard his name, though. Saw him deep in conversation with a Spaniard and some other men. That was soon before the attack upon Mousehole.'

'How do you know he was English?'

'I heard him speak, didn't I? He was talking Spanish, I think, but then he said something in English. And from the manner of his speaking, he sounded like a native-born Englishman, not a Spaniard. I recall what he said, too, for I did think it a mighty odd thing for an Englishman to be saying. *The gates are open. Let us enter.* That's what he said, then laughed. I took it to mean that he was in on the attack by enemies of his own country. A traitor, no less.'

'What was his appearance?'

'That's easy. He was a fine-looking man. Looks of a king, I would say. The sort of gentleman a common man would bow to.'

'His beard?'

'Short, well kept.'

The Englishman at Paul. This was not Burley.

'How did you come to see him and hear him?'

'I had been sent to fetch water for the other prisoners. That was the way the guard made me go . . . the devil take his dirty soul.' He pulled open his shirt and turned his bare back to Shakespeare. It was striped with lash-marks. 'That's what he did to me, for nothing. As to the Englishman, it was purest chance that I saw and heard him.'

'What else did he say?'

'Nothing in English, only Spanish. I used to speak a little in the old days, but it's all gone now, so I did not understand it.'

'And did you see the man again?'

'No, sir.'

'Did you mention this man to any of your fellow prisoners?'

'No, sir.'

'Then do not. On the pain of your life you are to say nothing to anyone. This is Queen's business.'

The man shifted uneasily, seemingly fearful of what he had got himself into. 'I will not say a word, sir. I will pledge it on the Holy Bible, if you so desire. May I go now, back to Fowey? I have a wife and six children would wish to see me.'

Shakespeare smiled grimly. 'I fear I must keep you here a while longer, Mr Rowse, but I shall recompense you for your time, and I am sure one of your shipmates will take messages to say you are safe.'

The questioning ran on into a third day. Shakespeare questioned Ambrose Rowse once more about the Englishman, and he spoke with Barnaby Loe about his recollections of Burley, but learnt nothing new of value. He was just about to give up when he recalled the man who had been taken ill. Wearily, he picked up his sword belt from the table where he had laid it, buckled it to his waist and stepped out into the castle hall.

There were many soldiers about now; they had arrived from St Mawes and from towns and villages all around. Although too late for the fight, they would form a basis for Godolphin to shore up his defences. From the battlements, Shakespeare could see six ships, the flotilla that had been asked of Drake. They were at anchor, and bristled with gunports. A comforting sight after the experience of seeing Spanish galleys in control of the bay.

He found Godolphin's officer, Chiverton, and asked him to take him to the sick man who was being housed near the kitchens.

The room contained a bed and the personal possessions of the cook. A large man was on the bed, snoring. He looked nothing like the other captives who were, to a man, lean and wiry seafarers of one sort or another. This man was flabby and looked as though he had not done a day's manual labour in his life.

Shakespeare touched his shoulder. The man grunted and turned over. He shook his shoulder a little more firmly. 'Sir, I must speak with you.'

Suddenly the man was awake. He glared at Shakespeare as he struggled to adjust his immense bulk so that he sat upright against the wall.

'I am John Shakespeare, an officer of Sir Robert Cecil. I am questioning all those set free from the Spanish galleys. I am told you have some ailment, but I must ask you to identify yourself.'

The man stared at Shakespeare for a few moments, as though weighing up his options, then emitted a gurgling noise from somewhere in his gullet. His chins and his chest quivered and his breathing was laboured. 'I am sick. Bring me brandy . . .'

Shakespeare nodded to Chiverton.

'Can you at least tell me your name?'

'Sloth. Ovid Sloth of London. Is that what you wish of me? The brandy, if you please, lest you want a corpse on your hands.'

'I have heard of you.'

The brandy arrived and Shakespeare put the goblet to Sloth's lips. He drank greedily, then coughed, and at last sank back against the cushions.

'Is that better, Mr Sloth?'

'Indeed, yes. Indeed. Now, what is it you require of me?'

'You are a merchant, are you not?'

'Yes, yes.'

'Where were you captured?'

'Brittany. And I would thank you to find me passage to London as soon as possible. I am a busy man. I have wasted enough of my precious time in a Spanish gaol and upon their stinking galleass. I cannot spend yet more time in this foul dungeon.'

'This is not a dungeon, Mr Sloth. This is a perfectly good bedchamber, which has been vacated for you at the expense of its regular incumbent. Why were you in Brittany?'

Sloth struggled to rise. 'First help me up from this filthy midden of a bed. There is a miasma of contagion here, I know it.'

Shakespeare grasped him under the arms and helped raise his enormous bulk from the bed. 'Now then, Mr Sloth, I asked why you were in Brittany.'

Sloth breathed deeply, his chest heaving and juddering. 'Use your wit. Why do you think I was in Brittany?'

'You tell me. And talk to me in a civil manner or you will find me a most unpleasant interrogator.'

'To buy wine. What else would I get from that benighted, war-torn finger of land? Talk to the master at Vintners' Hall if you wish to know more, for you will discover I am an assistant of the vintners' court.'

Shakespeare ignored his bluster. 'And did it not occur to you that you might fall foul of the Spanish armies there?'

'Mr Shakespeare, do you enjoy a goblet a wine? How do you think it is come by? Do you think merchants cease trading simply because there is a war on? Anyway, I had not heard of any embargo on French goods. Is Henri of France not our friend? Indeed, I had thought Brittany liberated from the Spanish yoke last autumn when Frobisher and Norreys took the fort of El Léon. It seems I was mistaken for Norreys has now abandoned Brittany and gone to Ireland. What I demand of you is this: how is a man to make an honest guinea if he cannot trade in safety? Ask this of young Cecil, if you would, for it is the brave English merchants that supply the treasury.

Why does he abandon us to the dirty Spaniard? We must be protected!'

'Did you travel to Brittany alone, Mr Sloth?'

'No, I did not. But they kept my clerks and servants. I am to send them gold if I want them returned, which will not happen. Why should I pay gold for them when I can find men aplenty in London?'

'I am told you are sick.'

'It is true I am not in good health. I am not a young man and these weeks of privation have done me much harm. I must get home to recoup my strength. I am exhausted.'

Shakespeare, too, was tired. He would have liked to postpone further questioning until morning when he might think more clearly, but he pressed on. 'Tell me about the ship you were on. Did you communicate with other Englishmen?'

'Those fish-stinking peasants taken prisoner from their boats? What might I have to say to them, do you think?'

'I was thinking of the English pilot.'

'You mean the damnable traitor Richard Burley. Yes I encountered him, and I spat on his shoes.'

'Did you talk with him?'

'No, Mr Shakespeare, though he tried to engage me in conversation.' Suddenly Sloth slumped on to the bed, clutching at his chest.

'Shall I send for the physician?'

Sloth shook his head as he panted. Finally he spoke, his words coming out in short, harsh bursts.

'In God's name . . . find me a ship . . . out of here . . . to London . . . I will pay you well . . . ten pounds in English gold, sir. If I do not get home, I know I shall die . . .'

Oh I will get you home, Shakespeare thought. *Though you may not like the mode of transport I have planned for you, nor your travelling companion.*

'Answer me one more question, then you may sleep and so may I. Was there another Englishman aboard the galley, a man close-coupled with the Spanish officers? Not Burley, in whom I have little interest, but one with long hair and a short beard and the bearing of a man of breeding?'

Sloth's brow creased and it seemed to Shakespeare that he seemed a little alarmed.

'Does the question disturb you? Do you know of such a man?'

'No . . . I know nothing of such a man.' Sloth fell back into the cushions. 'Get me that physician, sir . . . before my heart gives out . . .'

Regis Roag held Beatrice in his arms. They were spread naked across the covers of a bed, a large, ornately carved oak bed with four posts and an embroidered canopy above and all around them, enclosing them. Beatrice drew slowly on her pipe, opened her lips and watched the smoke rise, and dissipate into the canopy. She was used to the name Beatrice now; could no longer bear to think of the heretic name her father and mother had given her. *Sorrow Gray.* Was that a name or a sentence of despair?

She sighed, rolled over and laid the pipe under the bed-curtain on the floor. With the sinuous movement of a cat, she crawled across to Regis and stroked his chest with kisses.

'Beatrice?'

'Yes?'

'I prayed for this every day.'

'As did I.'

He looked in her eyes and saw the madness there. He knew well that she was insane, as crazed as a fox bitch on heat. He had always known it; he could not resist it. But that was because he could control her demons and bend them to *his* will.

'Do you harbour doubts?'

Her fingers tightened like little talons on his skin. 'Do you?'

He laughed. 'Even Christ had doubts. And yet I am here, am I not, back from fair Seville? And I have the men. In all, six of us. Enough. Good men, perfectly fitted for the task, as long as all else is in place. Do *you* have doubts?'

She sat astride him and held his arms down, her short, boyish hair flopping about her face as she gazed down at him intently.

'No. Never. Not one. A tidal surge of blood would not sway me from my purpose. I will rejoice when the blessed Mary's holy Inquisition is returned to these shores and when the ungodly are consigned to the fires of hell in the market squares, to cleanse our land. This is His word. How could I doubt it, when we have sold our souls to God?'

His hands ranged down her slender frame, his fingers playing from her small breasts to her delicate ribs. He kissed a nipple, then held her face between his well-tended hands and admired his handsome reflection in her eyes.

'But what of Sloth?' she said.

'We *had* to leave him. There was no other way. The journey from Spain to Brittany and onward to England has left him sick and exhausted. We had to move from Mount's Bay at great speed. He could not ride, nor could we carry him here. He would have threatened us all if we had tried to bring him.'

'Will they not torture him and discover all he knows? He will betray us—'

'Fear not, sweet serpent, he knows his part and we will retrieve him. As soon as word comes through.'

'And do the other men all know their parts? The little one, the Irish ones, the two hard-bitten ones? In truth I would not trust those last two to tether a horse.'

'I will take them and Winnow. You take the Irish boys,

Seamus and Hugh. Do what you have to do and then we will meet again at the appointed place.'

'Are they strong enough in will as well as arm? Will they really help us rid England of the beast for ever?'

'Trust me, Beatrice. I can smile—'

'—and murder while you smile?' She bit his neck and felt him rise beneath her thighs. 'I will trust your sail-needle and your God-given prick, my king of men, for I know what they both can do.'

Chapter 29

Shakespeare went to Ovid Sloth again and woke him roughly.

'Lucifer take you, can a man not rest!'

'I am here to offer you passage to London, Mr Sloth. My man Cooper will accompany you on one of Drake's ships. You will disembark at Falmouth and, from there, Mr Cooper will find a vessel bound for Gravesend or elsewhere in the Thames.'

'I do not wish to go with your serving man.'

'This is not an option for you, Mr Sloth. It is what you will do whether you desire it or not. And in London, you will be detained in your house until I have asked you more questions, possibly in the presence of Sir Robert Cecil. I am not happy with the story of your venture to Brittany, nor the manner in which you have returned. Do you understand?'

'No, sir, I do not! I am a free-born Englishman, a freeman of the City of London and an assistant of one the greatest of livery companies. I have endured monstrous privations at the hand of the Spaniard. Am I now to be ill treated by my own countrymen? I will *not* be escorted like a common felon!'

Shakespeare looked at him coldly. 'I am afraid you will, at the point of sword and pistol if necessary. Good day, Mr Sloth. Be ready at noon, for that is when your ship sails, and you will be on it. I wish you a pleasant voyage.'

He left Sloth and found Boltfoot, who was not happy at the prospect of taking Ovid Sloth to London, and even less so at the thought of making even part of the journey on one of Drake's galleons.

'You will have assistance, Boltfoot. I am sending another of the freed prisoners with you, a Mr Ambrose Rowse. Require of him what help you need, for I will recompense him.'

Shakespeare wanted Rowse in London, for he was the only other man who had seen and heard the unidentified Englishman.

As he strode through the castle, seeking Godolphin, he thought over the events of these past days. Was it mere coincidence that Beatrice Eastley had been heading west when the Spanish attack came? Instinctively he felt there was a link and that it somehow connected back to events in London and Wisbech: the death of Garrick Loake; the letter to the Jesuit William Weston in Wisbech Castle. Could this Spanish strike, like a bolt of lightning, be the true meaning of the letter found aboard *The Ruth*?

The possibilities remained jumbled in his mind like the stones of a fallen house. Somehow, he knew, they all made a whole, but for the moment they looked like nothing but rubble. The thing that made the least sense was this attack on Cornwall. Why would Spain authorise such a raid and then vanish into the haze? Yes, it had been a blow to English morale, yet was it worth risking ships and fighting men just for that? England had suffered no material loss to its military machine, And it was likely to serve as an alarm to the Privy Council that defences along the south coast must be strengthened. How would that help Spain?

Shakespeare put these points to Godolphin, who agreed that he too was puzzled by the Spanish action.

'Do they have more ships? Is there still a full Armada waiting to strike? Or do they plan to attack Drake and Hawkins in Plymouth Sound? I have had reports of sixty vessels in the Manacles off the Lizard. Another speaks of forty vessels to seaward of Mount's Bay. And yet I have not seen them. Did you discover anything from your interrogations, Mr Shakespeare?'

'Only that there were four hundred fighting men aboard, from the ranks of General del Águila's regiments, and that their pilot was an English renegade named Richard Burley.'

'I know of him. He is notorious along this coast for his treachery. We cannot take chances, so I will build our defences here, and send word to St Mawes and to the Scillies to prepare likewise. If the Spanish do attack again, however, we may still be found wanting. We need new levies and more powerful shot and armour. It would be best if you return to Cecil straightway and request assistance.'

Shakespeare nodded. That was his plan. What he did not mention to Godolphin was the presence of the unknown Englishman; that intelligence was for Sir Robert Cecil's ears alone. First, however, he had business to attend to, here in the west.

Shakespeare tethered his horse deep in the woods and moved slowly towards his goal. Every few steps, he stopped and listened. His searching gaze swept the rich, ancient woodland of oak and ash and chestnut. He moved on until he could see Trevail Hall, then he stopped and nestled into a bed of leaves to wait until nightfall.

He could hear the yelping of a pack of hounds in their kennels and the whinnying of horses. From his hide, he saw men in workman's attire going about their business. One man in the dark apparel of a steward or a lawyer walked to the stables where a groom waited with his grey mare, saddled up. He mounted and rode away along the tree-lined drive.

A little later he saw the serving man who had given him directions to the Godolphin estate a few days earlier. He was deep in conversation with another man, who patted him on the back before departing into the house.

Trevail Hall had the look of a house that was being shut up for the winter, leaving only a few members of staff to care for it. What had he expected to find here? Lucia Trevail with Beatrice Eastley and the mysterious Englishman, perhaps? He had come here like a dog; a sleuth-hound with the scent of gore in its nose, following a trail without ever asking why.

Had it been pure coincidence that Lucia had come to the west country with Beatrice Eastley, and at the same time as a Spanish landing? John Shakespeare did not like coincidences.

When darkness fell, he moved from his hide and came close to the house, skirted the stable-block and sought rooms with light coming through windows. He found the kitchen, where a matronly woman and a young drudge sat and talked, then the dining hall, where a serving man polished silver. He came too close to the kennels and set the hounds about their infernal barking. Men came from the house and looked about. He shrank back into the woods and watched as discussion sparked among them: had there been an intruder? Should they send out the hounds? Eventually, the dogs fell silent and the men returned to their quarters.

Shakespeare continued to watch until the early hours, then made his way back into the forest to find his horse. He had not seen Lucia, nor Beatrice, nor the Englishman. All he had got for his pains was a night without sleep and a painful neck.

The next day, he rode on eastward, up the great foot of land that encompasses Cornwall and Devon. At Plymouth, he went straight to the intelligencer's house. Once more it was locked.

As before, he went to the back and pushed his way in. He knew immediately that something was wrong; he could smell it.

In the pantry, he stopped.

'Trott?' he called.

There was no reply. He went on through into the front room. Trott was sitting at the table, with his head slumped forward. Dead. Flies buzzed around him, lazily; others settled in his eyes and on his throat, feeding on his blood and laying their spawn.

Shakespeare examined the corpse dispassionately. Trott's arms were bound behind his back and a loop secured him to the straight back of the chair. In front of him was a small dish of some yellow substance, half charred and blackened. Shakespeare sniffed at it and recoiled. Sulphur, otherwise known as brimstone.

Trott was naked from the waist up. His body was stuck with pins, dozens of them, making him seem as prickled as a hedgehog. His chest, abdomen and breeches were drenched in his blood. Shakespeare grasped him by the hair and pulled back his head. The flies buzzed away but quickly resettled.

He gazed with distaste at Trott's throat. There were several holes, and he could see the weapon that had inflicted the wounds, for it was still there, thrust into the side, through the man's jugular. Some sort of heavy needle, perhaps one used for sewing leather or hide. He pulled out the needle, wiped it on his fingers, then secreted it in his own doublet.

So Trott had not found Beatrice Eastley; someone had found him instead.

Shakespeare rode harder than he had ever ridden before, switching horses at every inn he came to, grabbing bread and meats on the run, not sleeping more than two hours at a time and then, at the roadside, using his pack as a pillow.

He reached London within forty hours and went straight to Cecil's mansion on the Strand. Although the secretary was not there, Jane and the children were safely ensconced in the house. Shakespeare was able to reassure them that all was well with Boltfoot, before leaving immediately to take the tilt-boat downstream to the court at Greenwich.

Sir Robert Cecil was in his apartment, sifting through a pile of letters.

'Never, John, has one event generated so much paper as this little invasion in Cornwall. I believe I have had fifty differing accounts of the tale. Some say there were a hundred Spanish ships and ten thousand troops landed. Others put it at fifty men and three galleys. What in God's name is the truth?'

Shakespeare told him all he knew of the attack, then put the sailmaker on the young statesman's table.

'A needle?'

'It was used to kill Trott, our man in Plymouth. That needle was pushed through his jugular several times. The rest of his body was a pincushion and he had been forced to inhale brimstone. It had the flavour of exorcism.'

'Who did it?'

'I cannot rule out Beatrice Eastley. We know she somehow insinuated herself into the company of ladies close to the Queen. We know that she, herself, had undergone exorcism. What is more, I had set Trott the task of finding her, for she had broken away from Lady Trevail. There is some diabolical madness here.'

'Another man down . . .'

'But if it was her, I find it hard to believe she could have acted alone. Trott was a drunk, but he was strong enough in the arm.'

Cecil turned the needle in his hands and studied it closely, then he rubbed three fingers across his throat as though he could feel the point thrusting in. 'You must find out, and quickly. There is more. One of my lord of Essex's intelligencers, the codebreaker Phelippes, has been the subject of an attempted abduction close by Essex House. And all since I gave him the Wisbech letter to study. But perhaps we no longer need his services; the letter's meaning is surely clear now. This attack came on the twenty-third day of the month, as the letter pledged.'

'But is that the sum of their plans, Sir Robert? I think it was but the beginning. They wish to break our intelligencing networks. But to what end?'

Cecil nodded. 'Because we have stopped every plot conceived against the realm by King Philip and his hirelings and, even before that, by Mary of Scots. There have been conspiracies aplenty, but all have failed because *we* discovered them. I sometimes wonder whether Her Royal Majesty ever understood the debt she owed to Mr Secretary Walsingham for his diligence in this regard.'

Shakespeare thought probably not, for Walsingham had died so poor that he had to be buried in secret, at night. And yet this memory of Mr Secretary made him think yet deeper about the meaning of the letter. Walsingham would never have allowed complacency to set in. He recalled his words: *Look for the plot behind the plot, John. And when you have discovered that, look yet again.*

Cecil went to the door and summoned a servant, then stepped back into the room. 'John, when did you last sleep?'

Shakespeare shook his head dismissively. He was beyond the need for sleep.

'If you do not sleep, you will not think straight. You will make errors and miss the obvious. Take an hour to eat and refresh yourself. I will have a lodging set aside for you here in the palace. In the morning, get about your business with urgency. Talk to Anthony Friday. Surely he must have discovered something of value. But first do as I say – and sleep!'

Shakespeare knew that Cecil was right: he was not thinking straight. He was working on instinct, not logic.

'Very well, but I must tell you this: in addition to the prisoners freed by the Spanish, there was an Englishman with their soldiers. I went behind their lines and saw him at the village of Paul.'

'Was he this pilot I have heard of, the renegade Burley?'

'No. This man was nothing like him. He wore workman's attire but affected the air of an officer or a gentleman. Apart from that I know nothing save what I heard him say, which was little enough, a mere jest, something about his sword weeping.'

'Do you think he returned to the galleys?'

Shakespeare shrugged. 'I have no way of knowing, but it would be unsafe to assume that he did.'

'We will talk later. I think we must have a meeting with Essex and his men. Her Royal Majesty insists we work together on this. And she will desire a full and true report from you on everything that has happened in Cornwall. It will not be an easy encounter for you, I fear. She is in a rage that any Spaniard dared set foot on her soil, and in a greater fury yet that any man of her subjects allowed it to happen.'

'There was one more thing. Among the freed prisoners was a man named Ovid Sloth, a merchant vintner trading in wines in Brittany. I have ordered him brought here by ship, escorted by my man Cooper. He is, in effect, under arrest, for I am not certain about him.'

Cecil laughed. 'I know of fat Sloth. Men call him Cardinal Quick, for he is not at all quick, but he is very Romish in his ways. Yes, he is a vintner. His father was English, his mother a well-born Spanish lady and he owns manzanilla vineyards at

Sanlúcar de Barrameda. He produces very fine wines, though they are exceeding hard to come by since the embargo. I can understand why you might be suspicious, but I would be amazed if he were a threat to anyone but himself.'

'He did not mention his Spanish connection to me. That in itself arouses my interest. And, as you know, Sanlúcar is very close to Seville and the College of St Gregory.'

'It is hardly surprising that he did not mention any connection to Spain. These days, a man is likely to be hanged by the mob for admitting as much. Nor does it surprise me that he was seeking wines in France, for his Spanish trade is at a standstill. But there is more to him than this . . .'

Shakespeare waited.

'He has worked for me and my father in the past. Anthony Standen recommended him to my father, for he can travel in Spain at will, as easily as in England or France. He feeds us information. Nothing of great import, but he keeps his eye on the likes of Persons. I am told Sloth was once ordained but discovered the life of a priest unsuitable. In truth, I think it was his superiors who found some of his more venal habits unsuitable.'

'I did not trust him, Sir Robert.'

'You are not alone in that. In Spain, Sloth complains that he is suspected of heresy and spying for England, while in England he is mistrusted for his continued dealings with Spain. He cannot win! But you have my authority to find out more. You know how dearly I value your judgment in these matters. Perhaps you should talk with your brother about Cardinal Quick, for he must know him; when not producing and importing wines, he invests in the playhouses. In the meantime, sleep. That is an order.'

Chapter 30

For the first three days after arriving at Falmouth by ship, Boltfoot could not get passage for London.

'No one's leaving port,' one skipper explained. 'They think there's a Spanish fleet out there, just waiting to attack them and plunder their cargoes.'

It was a fair enough point, but deeply frustrating for Boltfoot. He was holed up in a dockside inn with a complaining invalid named Sloth and a fisherman named Ambrose Rowse who seemed to have no idea why he was being taken on this journey and why he could not simply travel home to his family in Fowey.

This day had started in equally despondent fashion. By evening, Sloth had lost all hope.

'Still no ship, Cooper?' he said, a dribble of wine slipping from his lips as Boltfoot came back from the dockside, dripping wet from the constant rain. 'You are a worthless cripple.'

'And you are as fat and ugly as a tithe-pig, Mr Sloth. But we are stuck with what we are and with each other, so there it is.' Boltfoot shook the water from his felt hat.

'Your master shall pay for this imposition!'

'He is most probably enduring sleepless nights over your plight even now. In the meantime, I am pleased to tell you that, after searching all day, I have at last found us a berth. A tin carrier is on its way to Amsterdam by way of Gravesend. You may be required to scrub the decks and hoist the mainsail, however.' Boltfoot turned to the third member of their party and grinned. 'That would be a fine thing to behold, would it not, Mr Rowse?'

Rowse smiled.

Sloth scowled and looked away. These men had no idea with whom they dealt.

'So if you will move your great arse, Mr Sloth, it is time to be on our way. For the tide is right and the skipper will not wait. You know what these Dutchmen are like.'

'You expect me to go now? Good God, Cooper, it is evening and I want my supper and my bed.'

'Tonight, you will dine on ship's biscuit and sleep on a rolling wave. Now move before Mr Rowse and I move you.'

Sloth looked from one man to the other and saw no sympathy, only humour at his discomfort; it would be a pleasure to see them done for. Painfully, he pushed down on to the table, struggled to his feet and began waddling towards the door.

The inn was five hundred yards from the dock where the cargo ships were moored. Despite the rain, the evening was still light. Slowly, they made their way along the muddy path, through streams of stinking ordure and fish offal. Whores clustered miserably in doorways, holding guttering lanterns to light their soggy offerings.

Boltfoot allowed Ambrose Rowse to take the lead, while he stayed a few paces behind Ovid Sloth. All the while he watched the crowds of mariners, fish traders and drunks, keeping an eye open for possible assailants. When they came, he saw them well enough, but his cutlass was only half out of his belt by the time they bludgeoned him to the ground.

He slithered and slipped in the mud and waste, desperately trying to get a foothold or a handhold to raise him back to his feet. How many attackers were there? Three? No, four. A kick to the face sent him sprawling backwards. A gunshot cracked the air. For a moment, Boltfoot wondered if he had been shot, but then found himself on his hands and knees, crawling, trying to see in the rain and confusion. Where was Sloth, in God's name? In the gloom ahead, he made out a cart. Sloth was being hauled on to the back of it. He turned and sneered at Boltfoot.

To his side, he saw Ambrose Rowse. He was lying on the ground. His hands moved in circular motions, as though he were paddling or swimming. The rain washed down his back, diluting the blood that poured from his dying body.

Boltfoot turned the other way and realised a man was standing over him, sword in hand. Suddenly the man's boot was on his back, pushing him into the stinking filth. He tried to twist away, but could not. The man bent down, grabbed Boltfoot by the hair and rasped in his ear, 'Down, down to hell; and say I sent thee thither.'

His hair was released and his head fell back, his jaw thudding with teeth-fracturing force. He sensed rather than saw the short killing sword being raised above him, like a windmill's sail at its zenith, ready to plunge back down. One thrust would do it. Through hide jerkin, skin, flesh and bone, into his vital organs, with a cut that would tear the very life from his body.

Thomasyn Jane Jade closed the door and walked down the Lambeth road towards the Thames. On her right was the great Lambeth Palace, official home to archbishops, but she did not look at it. She kept her head straight ahead, and wore a close-fitting pynner about her hair and ears so that much of her face was shielded from view. She always walked out this way, and yet it did not suit her to go unremarked. She enjoyed the attention of men too much for that; and much pain and distress it had caused her.

The house she had left was the home of the Dean of Rochester, Thomas Blague. Thomasyn worked there as maid to the dean's young wife, Alice. It was a pleasant enough life for she was not worked hard. Lambeth was an agreeable village. The dean's house was large and brick-built and, though dominated by the nearby palace of the Archbishop of Canterbury, was more than adequate for their needs.

Dean Blague still harboured hopes that he might one day inhabit Lambeth Palace himself and, as chaplain-in-ordinary to the Queen with the patronage of Lord Treasurer Burghley, his optimism was not entirely without reason. But at the age of fifty, events were already conspiring against him. Even his chances of becoming a bishop seemed to be ebbing away. The problem was his wife, who was fifteen years his junior and gaining an unfortunate reputation for licentiousness, taking lovers wherever she could find them, including her husband's clerical colleagues. Others in the church and at court disapproved and spoke of Dean Blague behind his back, averring that he should deal with his wife more firmly. A good beating with a birch-rod was generally agreed to be the correct remedy for an errant wife.

Alice's dalliances placed Thomasyn in a difficult position, for she liked both husband and wife each in their own way. Dean Blague was much too kindly for his own good and as for Alice, she reminded Thomasyn of herself: young in spirit and happily abandoned to temporal pleasures.

The situation between Alice and her husband sometimes amused Thomasyn and sometimes worried her; she did not like anything that drew attention to her own person or to those near her. She had succeeded in living this quiet life for nine years and she wished to continue, undisturbed and unmolested. But she was worried that the edifice of safety she had built for herself was about to crumble. For the truth was that she lived every day in terror of exposure. She knew too much, and there were those who would not hesitate to kill her. These inquiries by this John Shakespeare were deeply disturbing.

By the river, she turned right at the horse ferry and walked along the bank road to the stile before the Stangate waterstairs. There she hailed a tilt-boat, then stood patiently and waited. Across the river, the city of Westminster rose up in majesty. On a day when she was less preoccupied, she might have looked across and picked out the towers and spires of the great abbey, of parliament, of Westminster Hall, and of St Margaret's church, then, slightly further afield, the chaotic mass of buildings that made up the Palace of Whitehall. The houses at this point came right down to the water's edge so that the river lapped at the very stonework. She wondered whether a man might dive from his bedchamber window into the churning depths.

Lambeth was very different to the scene across the river. Here it was still rural, with fields and farmyards just beyond the village boundary; here, away from the teeming streets of the twin cities, she felt as safe as it was possible for her to feel.

The tilt-boat drew up at the waterstairs where two black-clad clerics paid and disembarked. Thomasyn stepped into the boat, which rocked gently, and asked to be taken downriver to the Old Swan stairs, just before the bridge.

The oarsmen gazed at her appreciatively. 'Shouldn't cover your hair like that, mistress,' said one of them. 'Don't want to go hiding your bushel.'

She smiled at him. He was handsome and cheerful, a combination she could never resist in a man. 'Very well,' she said. She untied the straps of her crisp white pynner and pulled it off, then shook out her hair. 'Is that better?'

The talkative oarsman grinned. 'A great deal so, mistress.'

'And was there anything else you would like me to remove?'

'Take it all off, my lady, every last thread of it.'

She laughed out loud. 'You will be desiring me to take control of your oar soon. Is it as hard as some say to pull at it?'

She began to replace her pynner with great care. She felt warm, all the way through. *You still have the devil in you. That old familiar devil.*

'My oar is, indeed, a hard and magnificent instrument. It can get any lady to the place she desires quicker than any other waterman's oar. Is that not so, Josiah?'

The quieter of the two merely maintained his inane grin, staring at Thomasyn with a boyish leer, but saying nothing.

The journey to London continued in this vein. They were travelling with the tide, so made good speed and Thomasyn finally prepared to disembark at the Old Swan.

'How much is that, Mr waterman?'

'Pay me in kind, next time you see me, Your Highness. It has been my pleasure to convey a lady of such breeding and bosom.'

She kissed both men on the cheek, then stepped out into the throng and waved them goodbye as they took on a trio of stern-looking courtiers for the trip to Greenwich. Thomasyn walked northwards through the busy streets of London until she came to Simon Forman's stone house in the narrow lane of Fylpot Street.

The boy Braddedge answered the door, but she pushed past him and climbed the stairs.

'He's not alone, mistress,' Braddedge called after her. Thomasyn continued upwards. 'It's your own fine lady, the grubby Alice Blague, if you want to know.'

At the top of the stairs, Thomasyn pushed open the door to Forman's chamber and walked in. Forman was alone.

'Your boy said you had company, Dr Forman.'

'He thinks himself a jester. I shall put him in a stall at St Bartholomew's Fair and see how much merriment he can rouse when pelted with rotten eggs. We might make a penny or two from him.'

'Even better, put him in the pillory.'

'Indeed, Janey, and how do you fare this fine day?'

Thomasyn proffered her cheek to be kissed, then walked over to the bed and sat on the edge, looking about the room. 'Your boy said my lady Alice was here.'

Forman was rolling up a chart. 'Not today.'

'But she comes other days?'

'You know she does.'

'Have you tupped my lady Blague?'

Forman stopped what he was doing. 'I had not thought you one given over to jealousy, Janey. But as you ask, no, I haven't.' He lied effortlessly, as always.

'How do I know you're telling the truth?'

'Have I ever given you reason not to trust me? But you can rest assured of this: even if I were swiving your mistress, Janey, I would never tell a soul. And no more would I tell the world your secrets. All ladies' secrets are safe with Simon Forman.'

Thomasyn was not sure why she had even asked, for she knew exactly what Forman was like – and she knew as much about Mistress Blague. There was, however, another matter on her mind.

'No more sign of that Cooper woman, I hope? The one that works for John Shakespeare?'

'No, Janey, there hasn't been. Not likely to come here either, is she?'

'I pray not.'

'I think you have done rather more than pray, have you not? And much to your discredit, may I add.'

Thomasyn feigned puzzlement.

'Don't give me that look, mistress. You know very well what I mean. She's scared witless. So's the whole family. I think you have something to confess to me, Janey. Something that could get both of us into a great deal of trouble . . .'

On his way to St Paul's, Shakespeare began to sense that he was being followed. He looked around constantly at the milling crowds, but could not pick out his pursuer. It was an unnerving experience, because he was well trained in the business of spotting the man or woman who would rather not be seen.

As soon as he arrived at the crypt, he handed the needle to Joshua Peace.

'Where did you get this, John?' Peace turned it over in his hand. 'I would guess it is a sailmaker – a needle used by sail seamsters. It is a little like a leather needle, but the triangular point is more tapered. I have seen such things before.'

'That makes sense. It is also a nasty weapon. I found it in Plymouth, thrust through a man's jugular.'

'Now that *is* interesting. Come with me.'

They went through to the room adjoining the crypt, where Peace kept his implements and the bodies awaiting examination.

Shakespeare reeled from the stench.

'Forgive me, John. The odour is not good. I am afraid I have not sent your Mr Loake away for burial as yet.'

He pulled back the winding sheet from Garrick Loake's bloated remains, then held the sail-needle to the side of the corpse's throat. It went into a hole the size of a pinprick and passed straight through, like the pin of a brooch.

'There. I do believe we have discovered the cause of Mr Loake's death.'

'So two men, two hundred miles apart, are killed in exactly the same fashion.'

'Possibly with the same needle.' Peace withdrew the instrument and dropped it into the basin where Loake's cross and chain were held. 'Shall I look after this for you?'

'Thank you.'

'And does this bring you any closer to identifying the killer?'

'No, though I have suspicions. Very grave suspicions. My problem is that I have no idea where she is, nor who her confederates are . . .'

'Well, good fortune to you, John.'

Chapter 31

'M IGHT I ASK, Mr Roag,' Hugh Fitzgerald said, an edge of uncertainty in his voice, 'about the mission?'

Regis Roag smiled. This was why they were so tense. They had been blooded like soldiers but now they wanted to know what more was expected of them. How would they react when the cascade of death was laid out before them?

The band had set up an encampment by the road a little way west of London. They had been here for several days, following their rendezvous and the long trek from the west. Eschewing inns, they had pitched camps in the woods and on the heaths, like any travelling company of players, scarcely noted as they passed. Roag had not been with them all the time, for he had business ahead, in London.

Now that they were settled and rested, it was time for them to learn what they must do and the parts each must play.

He studied them closely.

Hugh and Seamus Fitzgerald were the most easygoing of the band, yet even they were feeling the strain. Ovid Sloth had found them in the Irish College at Salamanca, where they were training for the priesthood. They had absolute belief in the rightness of the Catholic cause against Elizabeth and would do Roag's bidding to the death. Their father, a cousin of the Earl of Desmond and of a rebellious nature, was a wealthy trader in good horses. After his death, the boys' mother sent them to England for an education in the house of a northern gentleman, hoping to wean them off their father's ways. But they had already inherited too much of his untamed spirit. In desperation, she ordered them to Spain for the priesthood. Sloth noted their potential the moment he saw them. Not only did they speak with English accents, they wanted nothing more than to fight and kill.

The deadliest ones were Ratbane and Paget. They were lower than dogs, dredged up by the Spanish from the barrel of the renegade English regiment of the Low Countries. They had gone with Roag on his little forays into London, as lethal as foxes in a covey of partridges. Two of a kind, they could kill to order without compunction. They would do what they were told and would not blink in the face of enemy fire.

And then there was Winnow. The cleverest of the lot, and the one that worried him the most.

Roag clapped his hands and summoned them to him. 'Hugh has asked me the mission,' he said. 'Very well. I will tell you.'

Later, Dick Winnow sat apart, watching the others talk quietly around the campfire, seeing their tension. He put a quart pot of strong ale to his lips and drank it dry, then rose. The liquor gave him courage but did not dull his senses. He went over to Roag.

'What is it, Dick?'

'You know what it is, Mr Roag.'

'Tell me anyway.'

'This plan. It cannot work.'

Roag put his arm around Winnow's shoulder. Winnow stiffened at the touch, but did not move away.

'It will work, Dick. You have my word.'

'But we will not survive—'

Roag hesitated. 'Fear not. All will be well.'

But Winnow knew. 'You remember I told you how my father died?'

'I understand, Dick. We have *all* suffered grievously for our faith. That is why we are here and why we must be prepared to hazard our lives for God.'

Sacrifice our lives for God. That was what he meant.

Winnow had no wish to die. He wanted to kill.

'Trust me.'

He did not look at Roag. He could not bear to see the lie in his eyes. 'If I am to die for God, I want to prepare myself properly. All I require is the truth, Mr Roag.'

The truth? That, Roag knew, was the one thing none of them needed to hear, even though they might suspect it.

'I have told you the truth, Dick. It is all carefully planned. God willing, we will all survive.'

Winnow turned at last to stare at Roag through the ale-gauze of his eyes. The liquor brought steadiness and revealed all. 'Thank you, Mr Roag.' He nodded with deference. 'You have set my mind at rest.'

Except that he hadn't, and they both knew it.

Roag might smile, but inside was only the icy darkness of hell. Winnow realised he had two choices: he must either kill, or escape. It was the only way to stay alive. Neither option would be easily accomplished.

A letter awaited Shakespeare when he awoke from a long sleep at Cecil's mansion in the Strand. He recognised the hand immediately as that of his brother Will.

Come to me as soon as you may, brother. I have intelligence for you concerning Mr Friday. Written in haste, the Theatre, Shoreditch.

As he was pulling on his boots, the door opened, and a footman entered and bowed. 'Mr Cooper is here for you, sir.'

Boltfoot back? Thank the Lord for that. 'Please show him through to the hall, and tell Mistress Cooper that he has arrived.'

'Yes, sir.'

Boltfoot presented a grim sight. He stood in the hall, seemingly more dead than alive. His shoulders were slumped, his face blue and yellow with bruising. He had rough, dirty bandages about his head. A long scab coated his cheek. His clothes were filthy, and not just from the journey back to London. Jane appeared from the interior of the house, and immediately gasped and put a hand to her mouth in horror.

'Jane . . .'

He limped over to her and they embraced awkwardly.

Shakespeare left them a few moments and then intervened. 'I have seen you in a bad way before, Boltfoot Cooper,' he said, ushering him through into a smaller, more comfortable room. 'But never have I witnessed a more dismal spectre than you present this day.'

Boltfoot could barely meet Shakespeare's eye. 'I have lost Ovid Sloth, master,' he said quietly.

'Well, for the moment I care more about *you*. Come in, refresh yourself and we shall talk of this anon. Jane, if you would clean your husband's wounds, I shall meet him in an hour's time.'

Will would have to wait a while. Shakespeare went in search of his girls, who were having lessons from one of the Cecil tutors. He watched them so intently that they began to giggle. He was encouraged by how quickly they had settled here in this safe place, and hoped that Ursula Dancer was equally secure. He did not worry for her; she had had a lifetime of looking out for herself.

When Boltfoot returned, cleaned up, Shakespeare took him through to Cecil's library.

'What happened, Boltfoot?'

'I was hammered to the ground, kicked in the face and trodden on, master. But I fear Mr Rowse fared worse.'

'Sit down. You had better tell me everything.'

Boltfoot lowered himself gently on to a settle. Shakespeare thought him horribly shrunken.

'We were in Falmouth three days before I could secure a berth. At last I found a ship carrying tin and we all walked down to embark. That was when the attack came. I saw them, but we were overpowered. There were four of them, I think. They killed Mr Rowse with a pistol shot and clubbed me to the ground. I was about to be despatched myself when two seamen coming from an ordinary pushed my assailant away from me. I thought he would come back to finish me off, but a mob was gathering and he made good his getaway instead.'

'What of Ovid Sloth?'

'He was carried away on a cart.'

'Do you believe him abducted or rescued by these men?'

'From his smirk, I would say he was complicit, master.'

Shakespeare nodded. It had been his immediate thought. He wondered how these men had known that Boltfoot would be in Falmouth with Sloth. It was a troubling question, which made Shakespeare worry that there was a traitor inside Godolphin's camp.

'What manner of man was your assailant?'

'He had a cowl against the weather, which was as stinking wet as a bilge, but I saw his face and eyes. He had a short beard. A woman might call him a handsome man. Perhaps my age, though he may have been a little younger.'

'Did he say anything?'

'Aye, he told me to go to hell. *Down, down to hell*, he said. *And tell them I sent you there*. That's what he said.'

The words jangled somewhere in Shakespeare's brain, as if

he had somehow heard them before. But where could he have heard such a thing said?

'Was there anything more? Did he say anything else?'

'No, master. And nor did I wait around, for I knew I had to come to you straightway. I did not even wait for the constable or his men, I just picked myself off the ground, saw that Rowse was dead and ran from that place as fast as my foot would carry me. I took passage on the vessel that awaited me. The mariners dressed my wounds after a fashion.'

'You look a great deal more presentable, thanks to Jane's efforts.'

Boltfoot nodded. 'Fortunately, we had a fair wind. Did I do wrong? Should I have searched Falmouth to find Sloth and the killers? I confess I have not thought clearly these past hours and days and I have worried greatly that I have failed you in everything I have done.'

Shakespeare put his arm around his servant. 'You have failed me in nothing, Boltfoot. I suspect Mr Sloth did not wait in Falmouth. Indeed, I would not be surprised if he were not already here in London.'

Chapter 32

SHAKESPEARE TOOK TWO wheel-lock pistols with him to the Theatre. The attack on Boltfoot and the deaths of Trott and Loake could not be ignored. He pulled his brother out of the rehearsal and came straight to the point. 'What is this about Anthony Friday?'

'He came here to see me. Said he had to get word to you.'

'Why did he not bring a message direct to me?'

'Is this the Inquisition, brother? What is going on here?' Will eyed the two pistol butts protruding from Shakespeare's belt. 'Perhaps you would like to take me to the rack-room at the Tower—'

'Forgive me. It is just that my man Boltfoot has suffered grievously, another man has been killed – and Anthony Friday is proving as worthless as a capon in a hen-coop.'

'Come, I understand your impatience, but at least let us take wine together.'

They went to the sharers' room, where Will fetched a flagon of wine hidden behind some old books, poured out two cups and handed one to his brother.

'Anthony Friday tried to find you at Dowgate, but was directed from there to Sir Robert Cecil's home on the Strand. At that he panicked for he had no intention of going anywhere near the Cecils.'

That was understandable enough, given the pressure Cecil had applied to the man.

'Anyway, that is why he came to me and asked me to bring you to him. He's in hiding and he's scared. I believe he was working on a play and has gone to finish it. But before you curse and threaten me with your pistols, he's not far from here, at an old farmhouse in the market gardens to the east of Shoreditch.'

'But why is he in hiding? Why is he scared?'

'I don't know, John. But somebody or something has put him in terror, which I suspect is what he wishes to see you about. I will take you to him once you have finished your drink.'

Shakespeare sipped the sweetened Gascon wine and thought of the fat vintner at St Michael's Mount. 'Sir Robert Cecil suggested you might have had dealings with a man named Ovid Sloth.'

'Cardinal Quick? Of course I know him. Everyone does in my world. He likes to think himself a patron, but I haven't seen him in months. What is your interest in him?'

Shakespeare had no intention of talking about Ovid Sloth within the confines of a playhouse, where there were too many ears and too many loose lips. Had that not been Garrick Loake's downfall?

'For the moment, nothing. I will tell you later. But I would ask you one more thing. Do the words *down, down to hell* mean anything to you?'

'Why, yes, possibly. Is there more?'

'*And tell the devil I sent you there* – or some such.'

'*And say I sent thee thither.*' Will chuckled. 'Richard of Gloucester in the third part of my *Henry VI*. Crookback Richard is killing King Henry. Let me find the lines for you.'

He went over to a shelf and rifled through a pile of papers

bound in string, then pulled out one bundle, cut the string and thumbed through the pages.

'Here we are, Act V. Gloucester is doing his dirty work.'

He put the page in front of his brother and pointed out the lines with his inky forefinger.

See how my sword weeps for the poor king's death!
O! may such purple tears be always shed
From those that wish the downfall of our house.
If any spark of life be yet remaining,
Down, down to hell; and say I sent thee thither.

Shakespeare clutched his brother's wrist. '*See how my sword weeps.* Those are *your* words? I heard another man speak them amid the fires of Cornwall.'

'John, what is this about? You are scaring *me.*'

'Who played the part for you?'

'Richard of Gloucester? Well, it has shown on various occasions, first with my late Lord Strange's Men at the Rose three years since. But the most recent player was Regis Roag when we staged it here at the Theatre. He was well cast.'

'In what way?'

'Beneath the charm, there is a touch of darkness in him, a shimmering of violence under the skin that threatens to erupt at any moment. The cold violence of Gloucester . . . *I can smile and murder while I smile.*'

'Was he the player involved with Beatrice Eastley?'

'What a curious thing to ask. I do not see the connection.'

'Just tell me, is it possible? Were they associated with the Theatre at the same time?'

Will stroked his beard and thought. 'I suppose they were,' he said at last. 'It was certainly about the time he played Gloucester. If there was something between them, however, I didn't know about it. I could ask some of the players, if you wish.'

'No, say nothing. I am not sure that it would be good for your health or theirs to ask questions. Come now, take me to Anthony Friday. Let us hear what he has to say.'

The path was nothing but a farm track between rows of salad vegetables: lettuces one side, radishes the other. Men were at work, harvesting the crop for sale in the London markets. They paid the Shakespeare brothers no heed. Half a mile away stood a low cottage with thatching almost to the ground.

'That's the place, John.'

'Whose is it?'

'I have no idea. But Friday told me it was safe and begged me to tell no one else but you that he would be there. He seemed to think me trustworthy.'

As they came upon the house, Shakespeare took out his pistols. He felt the same dread he had sensed at Plymouth just before discovering Trott bound and dead.

This was different. Friday's body was not in the house. The main room was a scene of utter chaos, a battlefield of blood splashes and debris. The trail of chaos and blood led them out through a back door.

Shakespeare had his pistols clasped in his hands, pointing ahead like a galleon with twin prows. 'You may wish to go now, brother. Fetch the constable.'

'I will stay with you, John.'

'Then draw your dagger.'

Chickens dispersed, clucking, at their approach. They found Friday at the far side of the backyard. His half-naked body was slumped forward over the low wall of a sty. Two pigs sniffed at the corpse with interest.

Will Shakespeare turned away, his hand to his mouth in horror.

His elder brother felt the body. It was still warm. He did not have to be the Searcher of the Dead to know that this killing had taken place within the past hour, perhaps a great deal more recently than that. Nor did he have any doubts about the cause of his death; he had been shot in the back.

He touched his brother's arm. 'Be wary, Will. We may yet have company.'

The playwright nodded and took his hand away from his mouth as he fought to regain his composure.

'This is your Richard of Gloucester at work, Will. Help me move the body.'

'Death and murder are not so squalid on stage.'

'No.'

Together, they pulled the corpse away from the wall and laid it on the ground. There was a single hole in Friday's back where the ball had entered. One of his wrists was bound with rope, the other was raw where he had clearly fought to free himself. There were marks on his face.

'John, I really do not like the world you inhabit.'

'It cannot always be contained. It has a habit of intruding into real lives. Yet this is the threat our sovereign has faced every day of her reign, and faces still today. Imagine *her* fortitude if you will. Come, I must look around. Do you have the stomach for this?'

Will nodded and followed his brother back towards the house. Something shone in the mud. He bent down and picked it up. 'Look at this,' he said, holding it between his fingers.

Shakespeare recognised it instantly. 'A sailmaker.'

'Does this mean something to you?'

'It does. It has been used as a weapon in two murders, one of them Garrick Loake's. It seems Mr Friday did not afford his killers the pleasure of using their ungodly implement.'

The house amounted to one room and a pantry. In one corner of the room lay a mattress with ruffled blankets. A table was on its side, surrounded by pieces of paper. Shakespeare picked them up. They were all blank. An inkhorn had spilt its contents across the sawdust floor and there were several quills scattered about, as well as a book. A chair with upright back had been smashed. Pieces of rope were tied to it, similar to the fragment knotted to Anthony Friday's wrist.

'He had much talent, brother,' Will said. 'But like others of our profession before him – Marlowe, Kyd, Munday – he could not resist the lure of danger.'

'What was he writing? You mentioned he was working on a play – was it for you?'

'No. Probably Henslowe. He has worked for him before now. All he told me was that it was a paean to Her Royal Majesty. *This golden ray, this English goddess, this nonsuch of our hearts* . . . or some such flummery. A good idea if he could pull it off without incurring the censorial wrath of the Master of Revels. That is as much as I know on that score. Do you think it has some relevance?'

'I must go down all roads, however narrow.' He held up one of the blank papers. 'Friday did not seem to be progressing well in his work.'

'He would have delivered it sheet by sheet. Have a word with Henslowe.'

Shakespeare knew Philip Henslowe well enough. The money man behind the Rose playhouse in Southwark was his brother's great rival. He examined the blood on the floor. Idly, he picked up a blood-stained sheet of paper that he had missed. Three words were written there, scratched in what looked like a hurried hand.

They are cousins.

That was all it said. What did that mean? Who were cousins? Half of London were cousins with the other half. Certainly everyone at court was cousin to everyone else.

He thrust the paper into his doublet and ground his teeth together irritably. Whenever he made any move towards solving this puzzle, his way was immediately blocked.

'Is Regis Roag behind this? What more do you know of him, Will?'

'I know that he was much given to bragging and considered himself above the common herd of man. One of his claims was that he was once in the employ of the Earl of Essex, but perhaps his greatest boast was his preposterous conceit that he was born to be a king.'

'What do you mean?'

'He believed he was the son of King Edward VI. He tells this to everyone and anyone who will listen, and to plenty of others who won't. No one took Roag seriously, which made him yet more resentful. That was why he fitted the part of Gloucester so well: that sense of rage that others had what he considered rightfully his. I would say his whole life is a play, a drama.'

The great door of the Marshalsea gaol in Southwark creaked open. Richard Topcliffe shook hands with the keeper, thanked him for the excellent food and comfort of his cell, and stepped out into the fresh air. In his hand he had his silver-tipped blackthorn stick, which he twirled.

A pair of goodwives with their children spotted his shock of white hair and crossed the road to avoid him. He was well known in these parts, and feared. Two men were waiting for him, one of them his assistant Nicholas Jones, the other a man well known to John Shakespeare. A man named Paul Hooft.

'Good day, gentlemen,' Topcliffe said, smacking his stick into the palm of his left hand. 'Has Shakespeare found the papist bitch yet?'

Both men shook their heads.

'Are you certain?'

Both men nodded.

'Then we must find her ourselves. We have work to do: a conspiracy to foil and Romish blood to spill, so that I may be raised once more to the intimate affection of my beloved sovereign lady. Let us make haste to Westminster.'

Behind Topcliffe, the keeper closed the door, glad at last to be rid of his celebrated inmate.

These had been fraught days in the Marshalsea. The keeper had striven to walk a thin line between gaoler and tavern host, for he knew it wise to treat Mr Topcliffe more as a guest than a prisoner. With his back to the heavy oak door, he let out a long sigh of relief, then bent forward and picked up a great handful of sawdust from the floor. He rubbed it hard between his fingers, as though somehow he might scour away the evil infection of Topcliffe's touch.

Chapter 33

SHAKESPEARE ESCORTED HIS brother back to the Theatre and told him to stay among friends. There was no reason to believe him in danger, but no one seemed safe at the moment; it was better not to take unnecessary risks.

He summoned the Shoreditch constable and the watch, and ordered them to inform the sheriff and convey the body of Anthony Friday from the farmyard to the crypt of St Paul's for the attention of Joshua Peace. There was a great deal of grumbling from the constable.

'St Paul's is in London. We don't have no jurisdiction there, and they've got none over us.'

Shakespeare did not have the time or the patience to argue. 'Do it or suffer the consequences, Constable. This is Queen's business. And while you are about it, raise a hue and cry. Search the area around the farm without delay. Anything you find out of the ordinary – anything – is to be brought to me at Sir Robert Cecil's house in the Strand, just west of the city wall.'

On the ride back south from Shoreditch towards Bishopsgate and the city, Shakespeare felt the same sensation he had had when walking from the Strand to the Searcher of the Dead in St Paul's. He was being followed. The road was busy with carts and riders heading in both directions. He looked around with great care, seeking the rider who stopped or slowed when he did, on the lookout for the horseman who wore a cowl despite the warmth of the day. But he could not spot the watcher. Was it the killer of Anthony Friday? He clenched a hand around one of the pistol stocks.

At Cecil's mansion, he had a visitor.

'A ragged old woman, Mr Shakespeare,' the footman said, ill concealing his distaste.

He had her brought to him in one of Cecil's quieter rooms, a small office towards the rear of the house where the Privy Councillor did much of his work when he was not at court.

The old nun walked in slowly with short steps.

'Sister Michael,' Shakespeare said, offering her his hand. 'Thank you for coming. I apologise if I did not treat you well before.'

She did not take his hand, nor did she accept the seat that he proffered. 'I am not here to converse with you, Mr Shakespeare, but to tell you that I now understand that I should trust you in the matter of Thomasyn Jade.'

'I have a letter from Father Weston in this house if you would like to see it.'

'I am not interested in letters. Letters can be forged as blessed Mary of Scots found to the cost of her sainted head. I am here only to try to bring Thomasyn to you. Is that not what you want?'

'Where is she?'

'If I bring her to you, what will you do with her?'

'I just wish to make sure she is well and that she is safe. If she needs any assistance, she will be well looked after. You need have no fear. There will be no religious pressure put upon her and she will be well cared for all her life. I have the names of friends and relatives of Father Southwell who made this pledge to him before he died at Tyburn. I know they have monies set aside that will be hers to achieve a degree of comfort and tranquillity.'

'Perhaps she does not need their assistance. Perhaps she is already happy in her life.'

'I pray that it is so, but the essence of the matter is that I promised Father Southwell I would do my utmost to find her, to set all minds at ease, most particularly his. He worried greatly for her.'

Sister Michael clasped her knuckles together at her breast and closed her sharp eyes, as though in pain. 'It is true, we did not treat her well . . . There were errors. I must beg God's forgiveness in this.'

Shakespeare looked at her in surprise. How much effort must it have taken for the old nun to say that the exorcism was misguided – and to a Protestant, too?

'Sister,' he said, 'will you not sit down? Might I have some refreshment brought to you?'

She uncurled her bony fingers and looked at him with utter disdain. 'Do you think I need heretic victuals to survive? Do you have no idea how many of the true faith there still are in this land? Your pseudo-bishops may have the churches, but we still have the hearts, Mr Shakespeare. Forget that at your peril.'

He smiled, bemused by the sudden squalls of her temperament. 'I merely offered you food and drink, in the same spirit as the Samaritan in the scriptures, one human reaching out to another across the divide.'

'I will never take your victuals, sir. But I find it in my heart to trust you, so I will do what I can to bring Thomasyn forth, if that is her desire. She already knows you are looking for her and is in great fear. I will now go to her and tell her you can be relied upon. The rest is up to her.'

*

'It seems I am to die in the morning, John.'

Shakespeare stepped forward and clasped the broken, man-acled frame of Francis Mills. They were in Limbo, the lowest hole of Newgate, where the Jesuit priest Father Robert Southwell had spent his last night not long since. Shakespeare stood back, still holding Mills by his bone-thin arms.

'I wish there were something I could say.'

'That you are sorry? Why should you be sorry? The evidence against me could not be denied. I must have killed them.'

'I have my doubts.'

Mills picked grubs from his hair, one by one, and crushed them between his fingers. 'Please, John, do not make it worse for me. Unless you bring a royal pardon, you can have no words to ease my night.'

'Has the lawyer Cornelius Bligh been to see you?'

'Yes. He thinks my case hopeless but said he would do his best. It seems his best was not good enough.'

'What of Cecil? Has he been here?'

Mills smiled with unutterable sadness. 'No.'

'He should have done so.'

Shakespeare could not help sniffing the putrid air, nor could he ignore the scuttling of the rats that sometimes lunged and bit at Mills's sores. Was this noisome hellishness the reason Cecil refrained from coming?

'I hoped he would. I gave him fair service for little reward.'

Holding up the tallow candle, which he had bought from the keeper and which was the only source of light in this evil place, Shakespeare looked around at their surroundings. The cell stank of ordure. Mills was not alone; he shared the dun-geon with three other condemned men. It would be a merry morning on the morrow.

'Do you want a priest?'

'No. What I want is to know why you have come here. You

did not come to say farewell, because you did not know I was to die this soon.'

Shakespeare managed a smile. 'As sharp as ever. You will be missed.'

'What is it? Something to do with the letter from *The Ruth*?'

'Yes.'

Shakespeare told him of the trail to Wisbech Castle and Cornwall, and of the quest for Beatrice Eastley.

'And so we come to a man named Regis Roag.'

'Roag, did you say?'

'Do you know him? It seems he claimed to have worked for the Earl of Essex, which is why I have come to you.'

'Yes, we used him when I was at Essex House. Have nothing to do with him, John. He is strange and evil. Oh, yes, I know Regis Roag. He is a killer.'

'Then how has he escaped hanging?'

'Because he was the earl's private assassin.'

Shakespeare took a few seconds to let this information soak in. If Roag was Essex's man, what was going on? Was Essex trying to destroy Cecil's intelligence operation? It was possible, for the earl harboured great loathing for the Cecils and all who took their side. But if that was the case, what role did Ovid Sloth and Beatrice Eastley play in the conspiracy? And how did such a road lead back to St Gregory's College in Seville or to the Spanish raid on Cornwall? Nothing made sense. It was like trying to snatch eels from the river with your bare hands.

'Frank, forgive me. I must ask you more questions. Do you believe Roag is still working for Essex?'

'God's blood, no. They had a bad falling-out over money. That was two years ago, about the time I left Essex House. I thought Roag had been making a living in the playhouses.'

'I was told he has a bee in his head that he is the son of King Edward.'

Mills laughed and immediately began to choke.

'That was always his story, with various embellishments. It seems his mother worked as a seamstress in the royal household and was thrown out when she came great with child. She must have told Roag that the boy king was his father, which seems preposterous enough, given Edward's tender years, his puritanical leanings and fragile health. But the story gave Roag the feeling that he was destined for greatness – and my lord of Essex played on that. He promised him that he would be raised up and that his birthright would be recognised, if only he did certain tasks for him. It afforded my lord much mirth.'

'So he used Roag for his dark deeds, promising him nobility in return.'

'Yes, but what difference would it make even if the boy king *was* his father? He would still be a bastard with no claim to the throne, any more than the bastard sons of Henry VIII had a claim. Roag was vain, but not stupid, however. When he realised how ill he was being used, he walked away from us.'

'Is Roag's mother alive? Where does she live?'

'I have no knowledge. All I know is that she married a sail seamster and that they ran a sail-loft in Southwark, downriver of the bridge. But remember this as you go after him: Roag is a man with a grievance.'

Shakespeare had taken Boltfoot with him to Newgate. Now, as he left Mills to his fate and emerged from the depths of the gaol, he found his assistant waiting for him just inside the forbidding entranceway. He had his caliver, unslung from his back. It rested across his arms, primed with powder and loaded.

'We are being watched, Boltfoot. Why have we not *seen* him?'

'Because he – or she – is mighty good at their work.'

Shakespeare nodded. This was a pursuer as skilled in the art as any of Walsingham's agents. Such men were rare.

'Well, we must take care. You wanted a mission, Boltfoot. I have two for you: find me Ovid Sloth and find me the home of a man named Regis Roag. You may discover them both by going to your dockland haunts.'

'Master?'

'Sloth is a wine merchant. Go to his house by Aldersgate to see if there is any sign of him. If you find Sloth, apprehend him. If he is not there, go to the Vintry by Three Cranes Wharf. He has a counting house there. Ask about. They will know him and he may have been seen. Offer them a few shillings. I must go to Greenwich.'

'And the other mission, Mr Shakespeare?'

'Regis Roag is a most dangerous killer. He is most likely the man who tried to do for you in Falmouth. All I know of his possible whereabouts is that his mother was married to a sail seamster in Southwark; they have a loft there. I do not know her name nor even if she is alive, so I am not expecting a great deal. But we can but try. And Boltfoot . . .'

'Yes, master?'

'Do not let your guard drop for a moment.'

Chapter 34

THE PALACE OF Placentia at Greenwich was abuzz with activity. The royal progress would be under way the following day and there was a huge amount of work to be done. Few understood quite what Her Majesty's annual tour of the great houses of southern England involved. The organisation was terrifying, enough to break any man. More than two thousand men and women on the move, by river barge and horse. Four hundred wagons, two and a half thousand horses. And though the Vice-Chamberlain had effective day-to-day responsibility for the minute detail of the great movement, no one doubted that it was Sir Robert Cecil who carried the burden of overall control, along with his other mass of duties.

Shakespeare was escorted straight to Cecil's apartments, where he found him handing out orders to half a dozen administrative clerks. Cecil shooed them away with a wave, then summoned his man Clarkson.

'Have the Lord Chamberlain and the Lord Steward meet me here in an hour.'

Clarkson bowed and departed. Cecil at last turned to Shakespeare.

'Good, you're here, John.'

'I have a great deal to report.'

'We are going to see Her Majesty. Say your piece then. Be

prepared, for it will not be pleasant. She desires to know everything. Do not try to spare her feelings; hold nothing back or she will know and you will feel the tempest of her fury.'

'Very well.'

'At least you look presentable today. Come, leave your pistols here. She will not have them in her presence.'

Shakespeare removed the pistols from his belt and placed them on Cecil's table. The two men walked briskly through the rooms of the palace until they came to the oak-panelled presence chamber where Sir Thomas Heneage greeted them with a weak nod. Shakespeare was struck by how gaunt and ill the Queen's oldest friend appeared. He bowed to Heneage graciously, though he would never take his hand; he was a man he admired in many ways, but could never respect.

'Sir Robert, Mr Shakespeare, it is a pleasure to see you both, even in such fraught circumstances.'

To his left, Shakespeare noted another small group: the Earl of Essex with three of his senior men – the brothers Francis and Anthony Bacon, and the renowned codebreaker Thomas Phelippes.

Cecil bowed to Essex and the earl raised his hand in dismissive acknowledgment. This was the way the hierarchy worked. Cecil might have the political power as de facto Principal Secretary, but Essex was the nobleman. It was no secret that they loathed each other and were engaged in a life-and-death struggle for influence.

Cecil turned to Shakespeare. 'Wait here, I will see if she is ready for us.'

Shakespeare felt a touch on his shoulder and turned around. Lucia Trevail stood before him in her modest court clothes. She proffered her gloved hand. He took it and kissed it.

'It seems I cannot get away from you, Mr Shakespeare. You really do follow me everywhere.'

He laughed. 'You departed very suddenly. I did not have a chance to say farewell.'

'And now as soon as we meet again, *you* are going to desert *me* for Her Majesty's royal charms, are you not?'

'I have an audience with the Queen . . . but I would see you again.'

She moved closer to him and looked up into his eyes. 'When you have done with your meeting, do not run away. I have information for you.'

'Indeed? Tell me now.'

She fluttered her fingers towards the entrance to the Privy Chamber. 'Go, go, you are being summoned.' Briefly she held his hand and squeezed a small scrap of paper into his palm.

Cecil was at the doorway, signalling Shakespeare and Essex's group to approach. Shakespeare hesitated, but Lucia Trevail was already disappearing through a side door.

Essex immediately pushed forward. He towered over Cecil and elbowed him aside so that he might enter the royal presence first. Cecil deferred to him without complaint, and to Heneage, but to no one else.

The Queen was already in the small, intimate room, seated on a tall-backed throne with bright-red cushions and a red footstool supporting her exquisite silver shoes. She wore a gown of white silk, bordered with giant pearls. A heavy necklace of rubies and diamonds hung down her breast. Armed Lifeguards stood either side of her. Cecil and the other courtiers and intelligencers immediately dropped to their knees and bowed their heads low. All except Essex; he merely bowed his head momentarily and did not kneel. Instead, he stood with an insolent air at the front, in the centre, with Heneage to his right and Cecil to his left. Behind them were the Bacon brothers, along with Phelippes and Shakespeare.

The Queen did not like the smell of sweat, so all save

Shakespeare had doused themselves with perfumes. The air was heavy with the ill-matched combination of their scents, from marjoram to lavender, from rosewater to musk and civet. Shakespeare thought he might gag from the fumes; together they were no more fragrant than a hog's fart.

Her Majesty looked at Essex with displeasure and waited. Essex did not move. Suddenly, she rose from her cushions, stepped forward, fist raised, and hit out towards the side of his head. He raised his own hand as if to fend her off. Her Lifeguards, resplendent in their coats of red, faced in black velvet and the Queen's silver gilt escutcheon on the back, moved forward, swords drawn. Essex managed to avert his head from her blow without touching her, then slowly and with great reluctance, sank to one knee. The Lifeguards did not back off.

'We greet you, cousins,' the Queen said, studiously ad-dressing all but Essex.

She stepped towards Heneage, and raised him up with a touch of her hand to his shoulder. He struggled to his feet, obviously in great pain. She moved on to Cecil, then the Bacons, Shakespeare and Phelippes, raising each of them up with a gentle word of recognition and the lightest of touches. Finally she stood before Essex, who looked as if he would explode with anger. She touched his shoulder and he rose to his full and considerable height.

'There, cousin,' she said. 'That was not so difficult, was it?'

Essex scowled and turned his head away.

The Queen was old and fragile. She moved back to her throne and slumped on to her cushions. Above her extravagant starched ruff, her face was coated in white paint of ceruse that clung to her age-lines like marl in the furrows of a field. Her nose was hooked like a hawk's beak, her lips thin. Shakespeare could not but note that her red wig was the slightest margin askew. And yet her black eyes had lost none of their vigour or perspicacity. When she spoke, her voice was not as firm as once it had been, perhaps afflicted by her reluctance to open wide her mouth and reveal the blackness of her teeth. And yet she demanded attention and even the proud and scornful Essex could not escape the force of her words.

'We do not recall such days as these,' she said. 'Even when Parma and Medina Sidonia threatened our very existence, we suffered no Spaniard on our beaches.'

Her courtiers remained silent. There was nothing to say.

'Were I a man, I would not have moved from that Cornish beach though I were alone, standing against an army one hundred thousand strong that had sailed in from the sea with all the world's cannon and shot. And yet, we are told, our Cornishmen fled before a mere four galleys and four hundred soldiers. It is a stain on their county for all eternity, and shames England. What men were these to surrender our realm without laying down their lives? Call them not men, but craven pups who roll over and expose their soft underbellies to their Spanish masters.'

Her voice had risen in the intensity of its fury, but it was not loud, which somehow made it the more terrifying.

'Mr Shakespeare.' Suddenly she turned to him. 'You were there. Why did *you* not give your life for your sovereign and your country on that beach?'

Shakespeare caught Cecil's eye and the barely discernible shake of the head. *Don't try to defend yourself,* he was saying, *ride the storm.*

'I humbly beg your forgiveness, Your Majesty.'

'Have you nothing to say in your defence?'

'No, ma'am. All I can tell you is what happened. I cannot say we were right. We fought, but we were greatly outnumbered and outgunned. Sir Francis Godolphin believed a tactical retreat would serve England the better and I agreed with him, for we were a dozen and they were four hundred. We battled our way back to St Michael's Mount. If Your Majesty believes we were in the wrong, then I cannot disagree.'

'God's blood! Now they know what mettle our men are made of – and it is base, sir, base! What now will deter them from launching waves of invasion along our southern coasts, safe in the knowledge that the defenders will flee at the sight of them? This was cowardice, Mr Shakespeare. My father would have had your head for this.'

Shakespeare felt the breath of fury and rather wished he was back on the beach at Penzance, being shot at. He hung his head.

'Your Majesty—' Cecil began.

'Do you interrupt me, little man?'

'Forgive me, ma'am, but I would speak in Mr Shakespeare's defence, for I know he will not do so himself.'

'Defence! What defence is there for cowardice?'

'I know that Mr Shakespeare hazarded his life in a most perilous mission that may yet prove invaluable to the safety of your realm.'

'Mr Shakespeare, what was this mission?'

Shakespeare looked at Cecil, who nodded. He drew a breath and began his tale.

'I scouted the enemy positions, ma'am. I counted their strength and spied out their armaments and formations. Perhaps most vitally, I saw an Englishman with the Spanish commander.'

'Is this the pilot Burley, the traitor I have heard of in letters from Godolphin and others?'

'No, this was another man and, from descriptions I have, I believe I know his name. I believe, also, that he is still in the country and that he is among a group of enemy mercenaries and assassins who have been wreaking havoc and death among our own. I fear they threaten your secret networks, ma'am, and perhaps the very future of England.'

'Who is this man?'

'I believe his name is Regis Roag.'

As he spoke, he saw the Earl of Essex stiffen.

'Continue.'

'Mr Mills, who is presently in Newgate awaiting sentence of death to be carried out, tells me he has been known to certain intelligencing circles for some years. Until now, however, he has worked on our side. It seems he is a turncoat and a cold, ruthless killer. He is also a man who feels deeply aggrieved, believing himself of the blood royal.'

The Queen, for a moment, seemed lost for words.

'Let me explain, ma'am,' Shakespeare continued. 'Mr Roag is so deluded that he thinks himself the son of your late brother, King Edward. He believes he was begotten by him of a young serving maid. No one takes these claims seriously, of course, but it is said he clings to them as a terrier holds a fox in its lair. It is possible he seeks revenge on England for a perceived slight. I think he or his confederates killed a man of ours in Plymouth, one Trott, and tried to kill my man Mr Cooper. It is possible, too, that he is responsible for the murder of Anthony Friday, the playmaker and intelligencer.'

Elizabeth turned to Essex. 'Have you heard of this man Roag, cousin?'

'No.'

Shakespeare looked at Essex in astonishment. Why was he lying? He read, too, the subtle smile of Robert Cecil. *Go for the kill, Mr Shakespeare. Do your worst, for you have nothing to lose.* Indeed, he did have nothing to lose. He had crossed the Earl of Essex before and knew that he would be an enemy to death. Nothing he could say would make matters worse between them.

'Forgive me for speaking out of turn, ma'am, but it does seem strange to me that Regis Roag is unknown to his lordship, for Mr Mills told me he was for a time in the earl's service at Essex House. I understand that the earl is an exceeding busy man and has many retainers, so perhaps he was not acquainted with Mr Roag. Perhaps Mr Phelippes knows more than I do.'

Thomas Phelippes pushed nervously at the nosepiece of his metal-framed glasses. He was as brutishly ugly as ever, yet Shakespeare knew that his pock-marked face and lank yellow hair were but the external trappings of the man, and that his head housed a brain as fine as a pearl concealed within the rough husk of an oyster.

The codebreaker nodded hurriedly, avoiding his master's merciless gaze, then spoke with extreme caution.

'There was such a man, ma'am – for a while. I took it upon myself to employ him and there was no reason for the earl ever to have met him or to have known of his existence. He seemed useful, for he inhabited the world of the playhouses where treacherous men such as Marlowe and Kyd plied their trade. But I dispensed with his services when it became obvious that he was insane and dangerous.'

'Did he tell you this story of being our brother's son?'

'Constantly, ma'am. I believed it my duty to make some inquiries. What I discovered was that his mother had, indeed, been a drab in the household of the late king, but she had been dismissed for incontinent lewdness with one of the guards. This tale of your brother being Roag's father is egregious nonsense. But there are many such claims made, as I am sure you are aware. If such tittle-tattle were to be believed, you would have a hundred or more half-brothers and -sisters. But these stories are scurrilous, ma'am, all of them – and no one believes them.'

The Queen turned to Anthony Bacon. 'Cousin, you are in

command of the earl's intelligence network. Do you have knowledge of Roag?'

Bacon shifted uneasily. He was unhealthy-looking, his face pasty and wan. Finally he nodded, so suddenly and sharply that it might have been a tic rather than a signal of affirmation. 'I agree with everything Mr Phelippes has said, Your Majesty.'

It seemed to Shakespeare that these men were like children before a stern parent. The Queen surveyed them with her all-seeing eye, then turned to the most difficult son, Essex, the sullen, defiant one whom she loved but could not control.

'And you say you knew nothing of this man, cousin? We are surprised that you were kept in the dark so. Do you not require reports from Mr Phelippes and Mr Bacon?'

'I have more important matters than the wild imaginings of some lowly intelligencer. That is why I employ Messrs Bacon and Phelippes. And if our men are dying, I think we should look where our enemies are gaining their knowledge.' He pointed with menace at Shakespeare, then Cecil. 'I say there is a traitor in *their* midst, ma'am. Look there to find the enemy within, I say. Ask Mr Shakespeare why he let Garrick Loake die. Ask him why he did not bring the treacherous Jesuit Weston to the Tower for questioning under torture.'

It was a common tactic to deflect criticism. Simply move the attack on to someone else. It mattered not that the attack was unjustified; for men such as Robert Devereux, second Earl of Essex, all was fair in court politics. Shakespeare understood this, and yet the words stung, for there was an element of truth in them; he should not have let Garrick Loake die without learning his secret.

Cecil stepped in again, showing no anger. 'Your Majesty, this is all getting away from the true matter, which is that England is under attack from within.'

'What say you, Thomas?' Elizabeth addressed Heneage.

'Your Majesty, it seems to me that Sir Robert is correct. We are under attack. To defend ourselves, we must join forces, not bicker like children.'

'Our thoughts, too,' the Queen said. 'Mr Bacon, what do you say?' She gazed at Francis Bacon, brother of Anthony and a failed contender for high office.

Bacon looked slightly taken aback, as though unprepared for such a question. 'I would agree, Your Majesty, that we are under most grievous attack.'

'But what do they hope to gain?'

'The destruction of our secret army. Like the late Sir Francis Walsingham, they are learning that knowledge is power, so they wish to do away with our intelligence-gathering capability.'

'Good. You speak well, cousin. So now that we know the enemy, you can all slay him together. Spare us the detail of your investigations but work out between you your strategy to protect our realm, for we believe you must have brains enough.' She turned to Essex. 'And we tell you this, cousin, you will cooperate fully with Sir Robert Cecil and Sir Thomas Heneage. Your men will all work with one another and share intelligence. I will tolerate no politicking among you.'

The men all bowed. The Queen rose.

Shakespeare found himself stepping forward. 'Your Majesty—' he began.

'Mr Shakespeare, sir, do not try our patience. We have heard what you have said and we accept that you have shown some valour, but this audience is now over.'

'Forgive me, but I would crave your indulgence on one other matter.'

'Very well. Are you going to tell us that you have found Thomasyn Jade as we commanded?'

'No, ma'am, I am afraid not.'

'Then why do you think we would be interested in what you have to say? You are a man of remarkable contradictions, Mr Shakespeare. One moment, you seem a fine defender of our realm, the next you are running from the beach or failing in a simple mission.'

Shakespeare refused to be daunted. 'It is the case of my colleague Mr Mills, ma'am. He faces the hangman in a matter of hours, and yet he has done great service to the realm and, more to the point, I have grave doubts as to his guilt.'

'What was his crime?'

'He was convicted of killing his wife and her lover.'

'And was there evidence enough to hang him?'

'I fear there was, ma'am.'

'Then he must hang.' And with those words, she swept from the chamber.

Six men sat around a table in the Earl of Essex's sumptuous apartment. On one side, stiff and serious, Sir Robert Cecil held his position beside his chief intelligencer, John Shakespeare. Ranged against them were the Bacon brothers and Phelippes. The Earl of Essex took the head of the table, as if by right of seniority, his tall figure dominant even though sitting. Heneage had remained behind with the Queen.

'Well, gentlemen, it seems you are to work with me,' Essex said, looking at Cecil pointedly, then at Shakespeare with distaste.

From the way he said 'work with me', it was clear to Shakespeare that he meant 'work *for* me'. It was clear, too, that Cecil would have none of it.

'We know who they are,' Essex continued. 'This man Roag, the slithery fat serpent Ovid Sloth, the woman Sorrow Gray or whatever she calls herself, and various others unknown, conveniently allowed into England by Mr Shakespeare and the craven trainbands of Cornwall. What we do not know is their plan. What say you, Francis?'

It was clear to Shakespeare that Essex's intelligence team had not been sleeping. When he had called in Phelippes to help with the documents and letters seized from the priests, Cecil had told them about the Wisbech situation and Sorrow Gray. Essex would certainly have had letters from Godolphin concerning Ovid Sloth; but had Cecil told him about his disappearance?

He wondered, too, about Topcliffe. The white dog was out of gaol now. He would most certainly wish to help Essex if it could do Shakespeare damage.

'It must be an attack on the Queen's person. It is what Spain and that scarlet whore the Pope have attempted time upon time these past thirty-seven years.'

Essex slammed his fist on the table. 'God's wounds, Shakespeare, you bear responsibility for this. You saw Roag when he landed. Why did you not kill him then? You let him go, sir! Thanks to your negligence, they will now have a small army of assassins landed in England. Nay, a *large* army! They did their utmost to abduct and kill Mr Phelippes here.'

Shakespeare looked across at Phelippes. 'You seem remarkably healthy for one who escaped narrowly from such a heinous foe. What did they do, Mr Phelippes, hit you with their toy rattles?'

'I was saved by the quickness of my lord's guards. Do you doubt my word?'

Shakespeare smiled and raised a sly eyebrow. 'Indeed not. Never have I met a less devious man than you, Mr Phelippes.'

'Enough!' Essex ordered. 'Anthony, have your say.'

Anthony Bacon, more sickly and more studious than his brother, sipped at a cordial of herbs prescribed by his apothecary for one or other of the dozen chronic complaints that assailed him. 'What I would like to know, my lord, is the true nature of all this nonsense from Wisbech. Why were we not kept informed while Mr Shakespeare delved there? And why did he not bring the stinking Jesuit Weston to the Tower for more stringent questioning?'

Shakespeare was not listening. He had much to do this night. He still had in his hand the note from Lucia Trevail. It told him the position of a room in the depths of the palace. She would meet him there.

'Have you found the Gray girl yet?'

'I may be about to make some progress,' Shakespeare said. 'When I have found her, she will be presented to you and the Council for questioning.'

Essex was not satisfied. 'What is this *progress*?'

'That I cannot say as yet.'

'God in heaven, Shakespeare, you always were a treacherous cur, but this is beyond treason. You heard Her Royal Majesty. We must *share* information. Would you disobey your sovereign?'

'When I have the intelligence, I will share it. As yet, I do not have it . . . my lord.' He loaded the words *my lord* with as much scorn as he could muster.

'Sir Robert, take your man in hand if you will. We must know everything if we are to fight and destroy this diabolical conspiracy. Is this man up to the task? Why, he has even managed to let Ovid Sloth slip from his grasp!'

Cecil smiled and nodded and listened. Occasionally he contributed a platitude. Shakespeare watched him with admiration, for he knew that inside he seethed. He knew, too, that Essex had shared no secrets of his own, and would not do so, whatever the Queen commanded.

At last Essex had had enough. He stood up from the table. 'We will convene tomorrow evening at Nonsuch Palace. One thing is certain: we must protect Her Majesty at all costs. Double the guard along the route and double it again at Nonsuch. No weapons, particularly pistols, will be allowed anywhere near the Presence Chamber or within a hundred yards of Her Majesty when she is out walking or at the hunt. No one but her innermost circle of courtiers must be admitted to the palace without my written authority as Master of the Horse, countersigned by the Lord Chamberlain. Ensure that all relevant officers understand that, Sir Robert. I will discuss the matter with Lord Hunsdon. And so I bid you goodnight, gentlemen.'

Essex nodded to Cecil then turned to Francis Bacon. 'Francis, come with me. I have a small task for you.'

Chapter 35

The cranes of Vintry Wharf stood stark against the darkening sky. The aroma of wine and aged oak hung like an intoxicating pall over the river bank where the great barrels were unloaded from the carracks to be taken into storage.

Boltfoot Cooper watched the men leaving work for the evening. He stood idly by in the shadow of a doorway like a crippled beggar hoping for alms. The dockers avoided him; they earned a shilling a day and had no intention of parting with a single farthing of their wages, however heart-rending a beggar's story might be.

One of the men was about to walk past when he looked again at the ragged beggar. He stopped, grinned and put out his hand.

'Well, well,' he said cheerfully, 'of all the ungodly creatures of the deep, if it ain't Boltfoot Cooper. Put it there, Mr Cooper.'

Boltfoot smiled from his battered face and shook the proffered hand. 'The pleasure is all mine, Mr Sands. I was hoping to find you alive and well.'

'Never been better, Mr Cooper. Can I buy you a gage of ale?'

'No, sir, you cannot, for I wish to buy you one. And see if I might pick some information from your brain.'

'To the tavern then, you old pirate. Handling casks of

Frenchie wine all day has given me a great thirst for honest English ale.'

They found a private booth in the King Hal and, after ten minutes' talking about old times and old friends from the days when they had sailed the western sea together, Boltfoot got down to business.

'I'm looking for a fellow named Ovid Sloth, a wine merchant who, I am told, has a counting house at Vintry Wharf.'

'Aye, true enough. But I don't believe I have seen him in three months.'

'Do you know where he might be?'

'Cardinal Quick? Up some apprentice wharfman's arse, I wouldn't be surprised. All the lads have to look lively to watch their backs when he's around. Mind you, he could be away. Travels a lot to his vineyards and on his other affairs. Even has interests in Spain, so I am told. When he is here, though, he has a house by Aldersgate.'

'No one there,' Boltfoot said. He had found Sloth's grand house closed and shuttered.

'Well, if he's in town, he'll not be able to stay away from the Bilge for long. Word has it that that's the stew he visits for his fresh meat.'

Shakespeare had no idea what function the room performed. She pulled him by the hand and closed the door behind her. There was no light, only utter darkness. He kissed her mouth and he felt her hand on him, tearing at his breeches. Now they were on the floor, which was strewn with rushes. She was pulling up her skirts and he was kissing the soft skin on the inside of her thigh. She clenched his hair in her hands and pulled him in closer.

'War and death, Mr Shakespeare.' Her whispered words were like a last soft breath; her fingers scraped at him with the ferocity of a cat. 'War and death . . .'

He wrenched his head away from her vice-like fingers and slid up along her thigh. Then he was inside her. Their gasps mingled into a muffled cry of pleasure.

Shakespeare was lost in the darkness. All thoughts of Frank Mills and his sordid end, of the intelligence Lucia had promised, of the gruesome death of Anthony Friday, were obliterated. The only thing that existed in this forgotten palace room was the electric touch of this woman's body. Shakespeare had never felt such heightened sensation. Even with his wife, there had never been a moment of more intensity. When it had finished, they moved apart, panting. He put his hand out and found the curve of her belly, but she pushed him away and began smoothing down her skirts.

'It builds up in you so you think you will go mad,' she said, as though thinking aloud. 'The weeks and months enclosed with her and the other women. The reek of their scented, unwashed bodies, their lewd whispered desires, the closeness of them all.'

'Can you not get out of here and come to me?'

'If she knew we were here, she would have us in the Tower. She cannot abide the pleasure of others.' She entwined her fingers with his. 'I will feign a common cold and come to you tomorrow before the court departs for Nonsuch.'

The word *Nonsuch* finally brought Shakespeare to his senses. He should not be here. The hour was late and he had much to do. And then there was the other matter.

He sat up. 'You have some intelligence.'

'It may be nothing. But Margaret of Cumberland said she believed Beatrice Eastley had been spotted near Susan Bertie's house at the Barbican, as brazen as a halfpenny whore.'

'Near?'

'Around the stables, I believe.'

'Is she still there?'

'Mr Shakespeare, have you not noted that I am cloistered here like a nun? I do not know whether she is still there or ever was there. Go and discover for yourself. And when you find her, you may tell her my mind. Now, we must leave this room without being seen. I shall go first. I pray she does not smell you on me.'

Shakespeare organised a five-man squadron to go to the Barbican and look for the woman known as Beatrice Eastley. If she was discovered, she was to be confined in the Counter prison in Wood Street.

'Use discretion,' he told the captain of the guards. 'We do not wish the Countess of Kent to suffer unwarranted alarm. Yet neither must we assume that she has nothing to hide in the affair of this woman.'

Another matter commanded his own attention: the matter of a man's life. Before midnight, he was at Knightrider Street in the city of London, a little way south of St Paul's, looking up at the tall, dark tenement building that was the home of Joshua Peace, the Searcher of the Dead. Shakespeare opened the door to the side of the six-storey lodging house and climbed the stone steps to Peace's rooms. The door was bolted, as he knew it would be, so he hammered at it with the haft of his poniard.

His other hand clutched the stock of one of the pistols in his belt. He had picked them up from Cecil's apartments before leaving Greenwich Palace for the short boat ride upriver.

'Who is it?' A wary voice from inside the locked door.

'Joshua, it is John Shakespeare. Let me in.'

There was a pause; then he heard the sound of bolts being drawn back. The door opened slowly. Peace clutched his chest in relief when he saw that it really was his old friend.

'Forgive me, John, I am mighty cautious these dark days.'

'With good reason, Joshua. Now in the name of God, give me wine and talk to me.'

Peace wore a long linen nightgown and cap. He was thinner than ever and there was something ghostly about his appearance. He poured two goblets of hippocras, sprinkling a little sugar in each one, and handed the larger vessel to Shakespeare.

'Thank you, Joshua.'

'Is this about Anthony Friday?'

'In a way, yes.'

'Shot dead. Ball through the back, straight to the heart.'

'But I believe he was probably killed by one or more of the same people who did for Garrick Loake, and it is the death of Mr Loake that interests me most.'

'I told you, it was the sailmaker needle through the jugular.'

'Yes, but what I want to know is whether Frank Mills's wife and the grocer, her lover, could have been killed in the same way.'

'Well, they died from wounds to the throat, and it was unusual. They were not slashed, but torn.'

'Could it have been a sailmaker that inflicted the wounds? If the needle had been pulled and manipulated with great violence, could it have been the murder weapon?'

Joshua Peace took off his cap, revealing the thin rim of his hair and bony bald pate. He frowned as he tried to recall the bodies of Anne Mills and Heartsease, the grocer. At last he shook his head.

'I could not say, John. That is the truth. And I am afraid they are both long since buried.'

'But it is possible?'

'Yes, it is possible, but that is all. But why do you think the murderer of Garrick Loake also killed Mistress Mills and her grocer?'

'Mistaken identity. I think the killers found them in Frank's bed and assumed Mr Heartsease was Frank. They are trying to kill every last one of this country's intelligencers.'

'But why hasn't Mr Mills defended himself?'

'Because he was already half deranged and he did not know whether he had killed them or not. He has desired to do for them for so long, he thinks he most probably did it. It is like a dream to him. As for the killers, it meant nothing to them; with Mills in Newgate awaiting the hangman's rope, he is where they wanted him – out of commission. My question to you, Joshua, is to beg you this one indulgence: express your doubts more firmly. Write a letter now that I can take to court to try to gain a stay of execution.'

'This is most improper.'

'It is a man's life.'

Peace exhaled slowly, then nodded. 'Very well. But you know that I would do this for no one but you.' He picked up a quill from his table and rifled through his papers for a blank sheet. 'John, you must realise that if someone wishes to kill all the intelligencers, that must include you.' He looked down at the two pistols in Shakespeare's belt. 'Forgive me, I see you already understood that.'

Shakespeare grimaced. He did not worry for himself, but the threatening note that menaced the lives of his daughters scared him. And yet, the threat seemed out of character for this enemy. These murderers did not bother to issue threats; they merely killed, as casually as a slaughterman at the shambles.

A slender young man with a smooth, naked chest leant against the wall by the entrance to the Bilge in Southwark. To his side there was a low doorway with stone steps that led down into a dimly lit cellar. The strains of a stringed instrument and a soft singing voice wafted up. The doorman spotted Boltfoot from fifty yards away, dragging his left foot behind him as he limped along. As Boltfoot came near, he tilted his chin.

'Help you, sailor?'

Boltfoot stopped and looked the young man up and down. 'Depends what you got to offer.'

'You look like you been home too long from the sea. Need a little company, do you . . . a little mariners' comfort?'

'I don't need a woman, if that's what you mean.'

The man chuckled. 'No women in this hole, master mariner. What exactly did you want?'

'You know what I want.'

The doorkeeper laughed again. 'But I want to hear you say it, don't I? Say the words without shame and you'll be welcome here.'

'I'll go elsewhere.'

'No you won't, because there ain't nowhere else betwixt here and Deptford.'

'Very well, I desire some male company this night.'

'Better come in then, master mariner. A sixpence for me and you can cheapen as you will when you're inside.'

Boltfoot handed over a silver coin and the doorkeeper stepped aside to let him enter. Downstairs, the room was warm and lit by beeswax candles. There was an exotic scent that Boltfoot recognised as the smoke of hashish. Boys and young men lounged around on cushions. A minstrel in red velvet was playing a soft ballad on his lute.

Boltfoot recalled the words Shakespeare had said to him more than once: *It is men's appetites that give them away. When a man has a hunger or a raging thirst, it must be satisfied, though his reason tells him there is a risk of poison.*

Another bare-chested young man, wearing only tight stockings that accentuated his manhood, sauntered across to Boltfoot and cocked his head inquiringly. 'I am Ariel. How may I help you, handsome stranger?'

'I am looking for a young man.'

'Now that *is* a surprise.' He smiled engagingly.

Boltfoot thought the young man looked kind, but you do not travel the world without discovering that the tiger's face can be beautiful until its teeth are bared.

'A particular young man, for my master. I am required to bring the young man to my master and I am authorised to offer a sovereign in gold.'

'Well, well, a sovereign! At that price, you may take your pick. What is the name of the lad you require?'

Boltfoot shifted awkwardly and scratched his tangled hair. 'That's the problem, you see. I fell among friends on my way here and drank too much strong ale. I have forgot the name. But I can tell you my master's name, for this young man is a favourite of his. His name is Ovid Sloth, though most of us call him Cardinal Quick. He is a fine gentleman of wealth.'

The youth did not lose his smile. 'Well, we all know the cardinal, but pray, why did he not come here himself?'

'He ails. His great weight drags him down. I think he has a wolf in the leg and the gout, too.'

'Indeed, he has looked slow.'

'Then I have at least found the right place . . . You have seen him recently?'

The youth called Ariel studied Boltfoot. 'Come, stranger, to another room with me. I have fine Italian brandy. Let us drink together a while and we can solve your puzzle to your satisfaction. In truth, I did not know the cardinal favoured any one of us. Perhaps it is me. Would you sample the wares on your master's behalf?'

Boltfoot shook his head hurriedly. 'Women only, me. Just doing my master's bidding.'

'Dear handsome sir, what is a woman and what is a man? I pledge you will not know the difference in the dark. Come, sir.' His soft, smooth fingers curled around Boltfoot's arm.

Boltfoot recoiled. His hand went to the hilt of his cutlass. 'I told you, this is not for me. It is for my master.'

The young man looked at Boltfoot's cutlass, still in his belt. He gave a nonchalant shrug. 'Then pick whichever you will. Take me, if you wish, but I'll need a mark before I go. I promise you he will be happy. Many is the time the cardinal has left my company with a smile upon his lips.'

'No. I will go to him and find the name he requires. He will have me beaten, but it is better this way.'

'Go then, stranger. But you have no notion of what pleasures you have forgone this night.'

Chapter 36

Sir Robert Cecil was not happy at being awoken in the early hours of the morning. 'Christ's blood, what is it, John?'

'Forgive me. I had to do this.'

Shakespeare held out the letter that Joshua Peace had written for him.

Cecil read it quickly. 'This proves nothing,' he said. 'It is one man's opinion that something might be possible. Any judge in the land would crumple it in his hand and throw it at you.'

'It is a man's life. I believe it is likely he is innocent. A man who has given much service to Walsingham, to you, and to his sovereign lady.'

Cecil paced around his bedchamber. From time to time he looked at the letter again, then at Shakespeare. He sat down on the edge of his bed and sighed.

'John, I have *heard* Frank Mills say that he would cut their throats. You have heard him say it. Even when he was apprehended, he did not deny it. He had the knife in his hand. How can there be more evidence than that to prove a man's guilt?'

'Does this letter not put doubt in your mind? Trott is dead by the sailmaker needle. So is Garrick Loake. Anthony Friday is shot dead – and there was a sailmaker at that scene, too. There is a pattern here, Sir Robert. Can there be no slender doubt in your mind that the death of grocer Heartsease and Anne Mills was a matter of mistaken identity? If they wished to kill all those others, why not Mills, too?'

And the rest of us.

Shakespeare had come back to the Palace of Greenwich as he had gone to Joshua Peace's lodging in Knightrider Street, with extreme caution: pistols loaded, eyes alert, sword ready. And all the time certain he was being watched. Even on the river he believed he could feel eyes upon him.

At last Cecil folded the paper and put it down, then walked over to his chamberpot and lifted his nightgown to piss in it. When he had finished, he smoothed down the gown and turned to his chief intelligencer.

'Yes, John, I can see why you harbour doubts. But I am sorry; it is not enough for a royal reprieve. I cannot wake her over this.'

'Could you not take it into your own hands to order a stay of execution? A reprieve until the matter is investigated further? There cannot be more than five or six hours left of Frank's life. A man who might just be innocent. A man who has given much service to this realm.'

Cecil laughed. 'You catch a man in his sleep and wheedle your way into his conscience like a worm. Go on. Tell my footman to fetch Clarkson. I will have the paper prepared for you.'

'Thank you, Sir Robert.'

Shakespeare bowed lower than he had ever felt the need to before.

Boltfoot waited in Mill Lane, just by Bartle Bridge. The youth named Ariel came out of the Bilge soon enough. He was no longer half naked, but attired in shirt, breeches and doublet. He looked about him briefly.

Boltfoot followed the young man as he sauntered through

the quiet streets. There was not far to go, for Ariel turned north into the maze of tenements that fronted the river to the east of the bridge, looking across towards the Bloody Tower. The young man entered the building and soon candlelight showed through a window-pane on the first floor. As Boltfoot had no way of seeing in, he settled down to wait once more and pray that this was the place where Ovid Sloth was hiding.

Had Boltfoot looked out on to the Thames, he might have seen the palace wherry carrying his master, John Shakespeare, as it was rowed slowly against the tide back from Greenwich. Shakespeare carried a leather bag over his shoulder, containing the precious parchment ordering a reprieve for Francis Mills, an assistant secretary to Sir Robert Cecil.

He urged the oarsmen on, glancing constantly back to the east, silently beseeching the morning sun to remain hidden behind the skyline. In his mind, he saw the malign black wood of the gallows and the coarse hempen rope that dangled so that men should dance and die. He knew that Mills would be awake, that there would be no sleep. Had the St Sepulchre's bellman started his mournful tolling yet? Would Mills be at prayer? Somehow Shakespeare doubted it. He would be waiting to be taken from his cell as soon as the sun was on the horizon. From there, he would be carried in a cart the long three miles to Tyburn, where he would ascend the ladder to the noose and a slow, choking death.

The rowers were strong men, but their arms began to tire and the wherry became so slow it hardly seemed to be making progress, so Shakespeare ordered them into land at Haywharf, just before the Steelyard. He jumped ashore before the boat was moored at the stairs and ran along the muddy river bank for Dowgate.

'Hold fast there!'

Shakespeare glanced sideways. It was a nightwatchman with lantern, staff and mastiff. He did not stop.

'Hold, or I unleash the dog!'

Shakespeare stopped. 'Queen's business! I am on urgent Queen's business, Mr Watchman.'

The watchman drew closer, his dog straining at the rope. Suddenly he stopped and tipped his cap with the top of his wooden staff. 'Ah, Mr Shakespeare, sir, I did not recognise you.'

Shakespeare raised his hand in acknowledgment. He was about to run on, but hesitated, to ask, 'How long until dawn?'

'Ninety minutes at most, Mr Shakespeare. Soon you will see the sky lighten to the east.'

He reasoned it would be quicker to fetch a horse from his stables at Dowgate, saddle up and ride for Newgate. He should be in time to save Mills before the cart clattered out from the prison yard on to the dusty road.

The house at Dowgate was in darkness, as were the stables. But there was a glow of moonshine to light his way – enough to saddle up his best grey mare and ride out into the waking London streets. He unlocked the tackroom, laid his leather bag to one side and pulled a harness from the hook. His foot struck something soft. He bent down. Even before his hands felt the whole form, he knew it was a body. A small, warm body. In the darkness he could not tell for certain of its sex, but instinct told him it was female and that she was dead. His mind went to all those he loved; Grace, Mary . . . Ursula.

He needed light. There was always a tinderbox here. He felt about on a shelf beside the harnesses. Without fumbling, he managed to strike a light and lit a stub of tallow candle. It was Sister Michael, the old nun from Denham, lying in a mess of blood. As he straightened up, he heard a sound and turned, but he was too slow, too late. He felt a sharp jab at the back of his head as he swivelled, and caught a glimpse of the face of Regis Roag, his hand on the stock of a gold-engraved pistol.

'Think'st thou I am your executioner? I will blow you to dust, Shakespeare.'

'Roag—'

The muzzle was pushed harder against his head. 'You know my name?'

'I know all about you, your grudge and your designs. I had expected to meet you.'

Roag's hand wavered. Another hand, from somewhere else in the flickering gloom, pressed against Shakespeare's throat with the razor-honed edge of a long blade. Roag pulled it away. 'Wait.'

The knife disappeared.

'You saw me in Cornwall. Mr Sloth said you described me to him. But how do you know my name?'

Shakespeare said nothing.

'It was Warner. Your spy Warner. Was that it? He sent messages, yes? What else did he tell you?'

'Warner? The name means nothing to me.'

'Disarm him.'

He felt hands pulling his weapons from him: his two pistols, his sword, his poniard. There seemed to be three of them, one very short, all with pistols and swords, and one with a butcher's knife. Shakespeare cursed himself for letting down his guard on this of all nights: if he was to die here, then he would never deliver the reprieve for Frank Mills.

The blow came like a smith's hammer, into his temple, and knocked him senseless. The last thing he knew was the crumpling of his knees as he pitched forward to the flagstones and darkness.

Boltfoot watched until late morning. It was a gruelling wait, but finally the youth named Ariel emerged from the tenement building and wandered off into the streets of Southwark. Boltfoot followed him. Ariel went into an ordinary where he ate a breakfast of manchet bread, ale and beef pottage, then came out once more into the sunlight and ambled back towards the Bilge. His way of life may have been profitable, but it was a dangerous one: the penalty for sodomy was death.

Grinding his teeth in frustration, Boltfoot returned to the tenement where the young man had slept. He walked in without knocking at the door and mounted the steps to the first floor. The lodging room consisted of a mattress, a coffer with clothes and some books. Nothing more – and, again, no indication that Ovid Sloth had been here.

It had been a wasted night. The young man clearly had no idea where Sloth was hiding, nor any interest in finding him. Boltfoot realised that watching him had been a long shot, but sometimes such ventures paid off.

He walked back through the streets to a tavern named the Hope, where seafarers gathered. The landlord was as surly as ever, but managed to tilt his chin at him in recognition.

'Not seen you in a year or two, Mr Cooper.'

'Bit far south for me, landlord.'

'Well, if you see any of your poxy old mariner friends, send them along and they'll have a free pint of ale from me. None of them come round here any more and, to tell you the truth, I could do with their custom, mangy company of rats though they be.'

Boltfoot was dejected. Nothing was going his way. It was the old seafarers he wanted, the sort of men who knew about sail-lofts, and they weren't here. He ordered a pint of small ale and some bacon and eggs and sat by the window that looked out on to the river. The landlord came over with his food.

'So what brings you across the bridge this day, Mr Cooper?

Want a fair view of Her Majesty's barge on its way to Nonsuch, do you? Stay here and you'll have no finer view.'

'I'm looking for sail-lofts. One in particular.'

'There's one or two, but they are a little way downriver from here, towards Deptford and Blackwall. You after work, then?'

'No, I'm looking for someone. A man named Regis Roag. I'm told he came from these parts; his mother was a seamstress, and she and her old man, the stepfather, ran a sail-loft here in Southwark some years ago. Want to know if they're still here.'

'Regis Roag, king of Southwark? He used to be well known in these parts. We'd watch him strut down to Paris Garden with his nose in the air like he was a nobleman. That afforded us all a few laughs. Now he's gone on to better things. I saw him playing the crookback Richard of Gloucester at the Theatre.'

'What of his mother?'

'Yes, she had a sail-loft, a little way east of Horsey Down, behind the Shad Thames Wharf. Not heard a word of her in recent years, but why would I?'

Boltfoot drank up and ate his food, then paid and left the Hope. As he wandered along the bank downriver, he heard the sound of ceremonial gunfire and the shooting of fireworks. The great spectacle of Her Majesty's journey from Placentia Palace at Greenwich to Nonsuch in Surrey had begun. Soon the river would be a mass of royal vessels, the most magnificent of all being the Queen's own barge, in which she would sit in state on cushions of gold, pulled by another barge with the finest rowers in all England. Behind her would come the vessels filled with courtiers, clerics, ladies and hundreds of other members of her retinue. Boltfoot paid it no heed; he was mighty tired and he had seen the great event more times than he cared to think on. It made him feel old.

There were a couple of sail-lofts behind Shad Thames Wharf.

'Aye,' the chief seamster at the first one said. 'This used to be Amy Roag's place. The plague took her to her maker two years ago. Her husband went some years before that.'

Boltfoot looked around the loft. It was a light, airy place with an expanse of floorboards laid across the top of the wooden frames of three houses. A large canvas sail was laid out flat, having the finishing touches applied to the hems.

'Does her son ever come here?'

'No. Why would he?'

'To buy needles. Sailmakers.'

The seamster gave Boltfoot an odd look. 'Now that *is* a strange suggestion, friend. Last I heard, Regis Roag was a player. What would he be wanting with sailmakers?'

'To kill people with.' Even as he spoke the words, Boltfoot realised he had made an error.

The seamster had a pair of shears in his hand. His grip on them tightened as he eyed up Boltfoot's weapons, estimating his chances against him. Other men in the sail-loft began to gather round.

The seamster turned to a boy. 'Go fetch the constable, Humphrey. I think we might have a felon here.'

Boltfoot backed off, unslinging his caliver. It wasn't loaded, but would these men know that?

He pointed the muzzle at the chief man. 'You got me wrong. I'm not after killing anyone.'

'We'll let the justice decide on that.'

'I mean you no harm, nor am I a felon. This is Queen's business.'

'If you're on Queen's business, then I'm a baked hedgehog. Now put down your fancy weapon.'

Boltfoot realised he had nothing to gain by staying here.

'Stand back easy and no one will be harmed . . .'

He turned and almost fell into the hatchway. He grabbed at

the rope handrail and stumbled down the steps in a clatter of weapons. Then he ran, as fast as his club-foot would allow.

He limped and tripped into the woodland of Horsey Down, and found cover behind a clump of trees. With as much calm as he could muster, he loaded his caliver with powder and shot, and waited. The moments stretched into minutes. No one was following. He leant against the main tree trunk of an ash grove and allowed his knees to collapse as he slumped into its folds. He was exhausted.

This was the way it had been on watches without number across the great oceans of the world. If a man slept on one of Drake's watches, he would have a dozen lashes. That was for the first offence. Caught a second time, he would face death. Boltfoot had never slept on a watch; he would not sleep now.

Painfully, he dragged himself to his feet. He left the caliver loaded and slung it across his back, its muzzle pointing at the sky, then limped slowly back into the streets of Southwark into a flood of people. They were all going in one direction – to the river bank to cheer their Queen as she was rowed past with glittering pomp.

Boltfoot was not far from the Great Stone Gate at the southern end of the bridge when he saw Ovid Sloth. He knew him instantly from his great bulk and his waddling gait as he shuffled westwards in the direction of St Mary Overy, the parish church of Southwark.

Sloth was with another man, who pushed a handcart. They were walking very slowly, away from the crowds, and were easy to follow. Boltfoot stayed fifty yards behind. Sloth did not turn, nor look about him. The cart-man, slender and lean, glanced around constantly. Was that one of the attackers from Falmouth? Boltfoot could not be sure. After the parish church, they turned south into the pleasure gardens around the Rose playhouse.

There were few people about. Almost all had gone to the river bank. It was less easy for Boltfoot to conceal himself here. His instinct was to walk up to the men, hold the muzzle of his caliver to Sloth's chest and order him to do as he was told. He could either take him across the river to Newgate, as Mr Shakespeare had instructed, or to the nearby Clink; they knew Boltfoot there and would incarcerate Sloth for him until he could be transferred under armed guard. But Boltfoot knew his master too well; he would wish to know where Sloth was heading, whom he was meeting. It was too good an opportunity to pass up. Also, there was the small matter of the man with the handcart; he might be armed.

The two men went into the Rose through the players' entrance, a double-width doorway that allowed carts to be taken straight in for deliveries. Boltfoot moved forward again, his caliver in his arms, his finger on the trigger. All tiredness was forgotten.

The Rose was a compact, timber-framed building, three storeys high, with a multitude of sides so that it was almost egg shaped. Boltfoot waited two minutes, then lifted the latch of the door by which Sloth had entered.

He walked in slowly, taking care to make no sound as he stepped on the boards, all strewn with fresh sawdust. He heard voices somewhere ahead and there, on the stage, stood Ovid Sloth, gasping for breath and leaning against a pillar. He was with three other men, one of whom Boltfoot recognised as Philip Henslowe, patron of this playhouse and attired in his court finery of gold and green. The cart-man and another man, in a wool jerkin, were holding up neatly hung costumes for Sloth's approbation. If he nodded, the article of clothing was put into the cart; if he shook his head, it was put aside.

'And you have not forgot the gilded vizards . . .'

Henslowe's assistant produced a wooden box and lifted the

lid. Sloth looked in, pulled out a golden face mask, then nodded and replaced it.

'They will do well.'

The box was added to the costumes in the cart.

Boltfoot watched in astonishment. What in God's name was going on here?

He looked at the cart-man again. It was no man, but a boyish young woman. Boltfoot tensed. A thought occurred to him: could that be the woman Master Shakespeare sought?

He watched and waited. When half a dozen costumes – men's rich doublets, hats, hose, robes and some armour – had been placed in the cart, Sloth pulled out a large drawstring purse from beneath his capacious doublet. He poured some gold coins into his hand, then held them out and let Henslowe count them. Henslowe seemed satisfied and took the money.

Boltfoot marched forward, dragging his left foot through the sawdust, the stock of his caliver held square into his chest. 'Hold fast. One move, Mr Sloth, and you will die.'

The four people on stage looked at him in shock. Then, like participants in an intricate dance, they began moving apart. The woman trundled the cart sideways. Henslowe and his assistant went wide, then moved forward as though they would encircle Boltfoot. Sloth backed away, towards the shadows beneath the canopy. He was pulling open one of the stage doors used for the players' dramatic exits and entrances.

Boltfoot recalled his master's words: *If you find Sloth, apprehend him. Haul him to Newgate, preferably alive.* Preferably alive. The implication of that was *Bring him in dead if all else fails.*

Boltfoot pulled the trigger.

Chapter 37

THE TOUCHPOWDER FIZZED and smoked, then burnt away. No explosion, no shot. Boltfoot looked at his weapon in dismay and uttered a low oath. This had never happened to him before. It was the poxy tiredness that had caused the error in loading and priming the caliver. He did not have time to reload before they were on him. He slung the gun over his shoulder and drew his cutlass.

Henslowe, unafraid and proud, strode up to him, chest thrust out. 'I know you. You're John Shakespeare's man. What do you think you are doing?'

Boltfoot tried pushing Henslowe aside. He had to catch Sloth. He lurched forward but Henslowe's hand shot out and grabbed his shoulder.

'You were trying to shoot the cardinal! Your gun misfired!'

'I must get him, Mr Henslowe. I beseech you, help me. And that woman—'

'No, God's death, I will not help you! You will not pass. Lend me assistance, Fontley! Bring him down.'

Fontley, who had the litheness and lean muscular body of a tumbler, thrust out a long, well-formed leg behind Boltfoot's knees. With the side of his arm, he pushed backwards against Boltfoot's chest. Boltfoot's lost his balance and his legs buckled. He crumpled backwards to the floor of the stage, his weapons clattering beneath him on the oak boards. Fontley leapt on him and pinioned his arms. Although Boltfoot was a strong, experienced fighter, he was encumbered by his caliver and cutlass. Fontley drew a dagger from his belt and held the tip to Boltfoot's throat. Henslowe stepped forward and eased Boltfoot's caliver from his shoulder.

'I think you have a great deal of explaining to do.'

'Let me up. I must catch Sloth—'

'You are going nowhere. Talk.'

'First hold Sloth, then I will explain all.'

'The cardinal has gone. What is this about?'

Boltfoot groaned in desperation. 'I am Boltfoot Cooper, here on behalf of Mr Shakespeare. This is Queen's business, Mr Henslowe. Ovid Sloth is a wanted man. I have been hunting him and followed him here. I beg of you, hold him.'

'The cardinal wanted? Wanted for what, may I ask?'

'He escaped. I was escorting him to be examined by Sir Robert Cecil and the Council. He escaped at Falmouth.'

'But what has he done? Why were you holding him?'

'He was freed by the Spaniards.' Boltfoot was struggling to think how to explain this. He realised he was making little sense.

'Well, Mr Cooper, you will have to be a great deal more convincing than that. Cardinal Quick is an old acquaintance of mine and has invested a great deal of money in the Rose and various other playhouse ventures. You cannot just go shooting at unarmed men, especially not respectable merchants like Mr Sloth. I fear you will have to answer for your actions in a court of law.'

Boltfoot fought to raise his head. There was no sign of Ovid Sloth, nor of his female companion with the cart. In the distance, he could hear the sound of trumpets blaring and guns being fired as the royal river procession passed through the dangerous narrows of London Bridge. A great cheer rose up.

Boltfoot was shut away in a dark props cupboard, which gave him little room to move and no hope of escape. He found what he took to be a pennant, which he rolled into a pillow. Like a cat, he curled up on the floor, placed his head on the flag and fell asleep. He was woken in the late afternoon by the opening of the door.

Henslowe was there, with the constable. Boltfoot began to repeat his plea that he was on the side of the law and that he was no threat. More than that, he had been grievously injured by those who had assisted in Sloth's escape.

Henslowe listened with interest and some amusement.

'If you cheat the rope, I might ask Mr Alleyn to find you a part in our next play, Mr Cooper, for you have something of the clown about you. The world would love a new Tarleton. He was a short-arsed wreck of a man like you, but he could make princes and paupers weep for mirth. I do believe you would be his equal, for you make *me* laugh.'

'Mr Henslowe, there is no amusement here. Only murder and treason. I must find Ovid Sloth! Mr Shakespeare ordered me to fetch him to Newgate. Why did he take those costumes? If you have doubts, come with me—'

'No, I will not go anywhere with you. As for the costumes, you will have to ask Mr Sloth. He asked for them some few weeks ago, named me a fair price, and so a deal was struck. Such things happen all the time. Great ladies and gentlemen stage entertainments for their great friends. And so I am happy to oblige. No one can afford to keep costumes unused if there is money to be made from them. As for detaining Mr Sloth and taking him to Newgate, I would say that trying to shoot a man is a strange way to arrest him.'

'I feared he was fleeing again, as he has done before.'

Henslowe laughed out loud. 'Cardinal Quick is the slowest creature on earth. He could not escape an earthworm, Mr Cooper. How could he possibly flee from anyone, even one as lame as you?' Henslowe shook his head and turned to the constable. 'He is yours to question, Mr Godfrey. Do with him as you think fit. I will happily testify against him, as will Mr Fontley.'

The constable had a squint eye and a mouth that turned down. His watery eyes looked at Boltfoot in turn, first the left, then the right. 'Are you a good man and true?' he demanded at last.

'Yes, Constable. I am in service to Mr John Shakespeare, an assistant secretary to Sir Robert Cecil. I work for him on behalf of Her Royal Majesty.'

'Then if you are a good man and true, why are you held here under guard?'

'It is an error.'

'In my experience, thieves, vagabonds and murderers are apprehended because they are guilty of crimes. Therefore a man apprehended must be a thief, vagabond or murderer. Which, then, are you – for *you* have been apprehended?'

'I am none of those, I pledge it.'

'Then you have committed some other felony. The chiefest of these are rape, rustling of cattle and treason. Choose your felony, Mr Cooper. The neck will stretch when the noose is about it, whichever you do decide on.'

'I have committed no crime!'

The constable rubbed his neck and stretched it this way and that as though he could feel the rope tightening.

'Why, I do believe there was one went to the Tyburn tree this very morning. Died well, the broadsheet sellers cry. Gave praise to God and the Queen and did beg mercy of the Lord for his manifold sins.'

*

✠ 333 ✠

The constable tied Boltfoot's hands with a leash of rope and led him out into the streets of Southwark to the Clink prison, fifty yards away.

'Hold this man, Mr Keeper,' the constable said, pushing Boltfoot forward at the heavy gate. 'He says he is a good man and true, but I say he is a most desperate felon and horse-thief, nor is he to be trusted. Have him brought before the justice in the morning.'

'Have you got sixpence for his keep?'

'He can pay you himself or starve.' The constable handed over Boltfoot's weapons to the keeper. 'Or you may sell these on his behalf. But I say observe him well, for he is most dangerous and ungodly. I wish you good day, Mr Keeper.'

The turnkey's long, grey-flecked beard straggled down to his waist. He tugged at it as he watched the constable march off, then looked at Boltfoot with a morose, puzzled expression. His tongue lolled out like a dog's on a hot day.

'Mr Cooper?'

'Aye, it's me behind these bruises.'

'Trug's arse, Mr Cooper, I know that each honest parishioner must do his duty and serve a turn as constable, but that maggoty son of a whore Godfrey is too much. I say he should be strung up for having the wit of a haddock. A *dead* haddock. He is a night-soil man, to which I think him better suited. Now then, Mr Cooper, what have you done?'

'Nothing. And I need your help. Free me and you will have gold.'

'Sadly, I cannot do that, as you must know.'

'Then get word to Mr Shakespeare for me.'

The first thing Shakespeare saw was a pair of eyes, glowing like fire. Through the cloud of his semi-conscious brain, he tried to look closer and realised that it was nothing but a black mastiff, sitting on its haunches a few yards from him. The dog's ears were pricked and it was alert, watching him closely. The light in the animal's eyes was the flickering reflection of a candle-flame.

He tried to step forward, towards the dog, then realised he could not shift at all, not even his arms. He was tied to a chair. His arms were bound down the sides of the high back and his ankles were fastened to the chair legs. Another rope was wound tightly around his chest, holding him back into the chair. There was a fragrant smell of incense in the air as well as some other smoke. A few feet away stood a small table with three dishes and a cup. He shivered, and realised that he was naked from the waist up.

'The demon awakes.'

He twisted his head at the sound of the voice and a thundering pain made him groan. Now he recalled: he had been clubbed at the stables in Dowgate.

'Where am I?'

'Are you in pain, Mr Shakespeare? Perhaps you would like to take a drink. I will bring you water.'

He could not see her, but he recognised that strange, smoky voice. It was Beatrice Eastley, born Sorrow Gray. She moved across his field of vision. Now she was standing in front of him with her pipe in her mouth, belching forth smoke that seemed to him like the fumes of hell. She picked up the cup from the table and held it out to him. He clenched his jaw tight and averted his lips.

'Drink.' Roughly, she put it to his mouth. He tasted a sip, then drank greedily, but she took the cup away too soon. 'Not too much. Food?'

'No.'

She clutched her arms about her slender body. 'It is cold in here, is it not? And yet outside, the day is warm.'

Her manner of speaking was spindly and curt, very unlike her sister's in Wisbech. He studied her closely. At first sight, at the Countess of Kent's home in Barbican Street, there had been an impression of fresh, faraway innocence in her unblemished skin, yet now he saw a strange, troubling absence in her eyes. She was garbed in a simple dress of dark red, and wore her hair uncovered. She had cut it most unusually short, so that it fell about her face like a helmet. It was the unblinking eyes that unsettled him.

'Release me, Mistress Eastley. This is a treasonous act for which you will hang. Release me and I will protect you.'

She sucked at her pipe.

'In the name of God, you have fallen into a conspiracy that can only help England's enemies!'

'Do not call on God. Call on the serpent. You are his fellow and your body is a temple to his demons.'

'I demand of you, where am I? Why have you brought me here?'

He looked around him now, his foggy eyesight clearing, and saw that he was in some church. A thin light of reds and blues streamed through soaring stained-glass windows. At the end of the nave there was a high altar with an enormous crucifix. But this church did not hold the comfort and tranquillity of God's house.

'To cleanse your body and free your soul, Mr Shakespeare.'

'Is that what Regis Roag told you?'

The name had an instant impact. He saw it in her wide eyes and realised it was the reason he was still alive, the reason his throat had not been ripped open at the Dowgate stables. They needed to know what intelligence he had. Whatever it was they were planning, they needed to be sure it had not been detected.

'What do you know of him?'

'Everything. This conspiracy will fail. You will all go to your doom. Release me. Save yourself.'

There was a pulse in her smooth brow. Her eyes narrowed. Carefully, she put down the beaker of water on a small table near by. Shakespeare saw the glint in her hand as a sailmaker needle slid from her sleeve into her palm. She raised it up and, with a scream that seemed to last a full minute, she plunged it down into his shoulder. The triangular point tore through skin and flesh until it hit bone. Shakespeare gasped with pain and his head arched back. She pulled the needle out, then stabbed it once more into his other shoulder. He gasped again. Blood streamed down his upper arms, chest and back in rivulets, a delta of scarlet, flowing over him.

She breathed heavily. Smoke spewed from her mouth and nostrils as she held the blood-streaked needle in front of his eyes. Her hand was shaking but her eyes were everywhere, as though watching a swarm of butterflies.

'See how they fly, screaming from you? See how your demons fly at my tender touch? We shall cleanse you of your demons. They have claws, but we have God's needle. God is mightier than you, mightier than the demons. You will tell me the truth before you die.'

He was utterly at her mercy. She was raving. And yet his thoughts were with Frank Mills and the rope from which he had failed to save him.

'. . . with this needle I shall pluck them all out like lice. I shall rid you of all your lewd devils. I am God's instrument. At the end, when your body is free, you will thank us, for we will not have let you die in thrall to the beast.'

High in the church rafters, a dazzling phantasm swooped. Shakespeare caught its shadow in the periphery of his vision. Was it angel or demon? He looked up and saw that it was a trapped jay. It landed on a rafter, defecated, then shrieked.

Chapter 38

Regis Roag sat at the front of the heavy draycart, whip in hand. His gaze seemed to be fixed straight ahead on the long dusty road, but he was watching constantly. He wore a cowl to conceal his face and ever-moving eyes, and to hide his fine head of hair. There was little chance of his being seen by anyone who could do him harm, but why take the risk?

The procession straggled for miles: horsemen and wagons as far as a man could see along the road south-west to the Palace of Nonsuch. Many of the wagons were the Queen's own, carrying her immense wardrobe and furnishings. Many more belonged to the hundreds of nobles and others who made up the royal court. Yet more were those of the hangers-on. Wherever the wealthy gathered, they attracted traders, beggars, jugglers and minstrels, just as meat left out will swarm with flies.

Roag's draycart was just one among many, trundling through the county of Surrey. It carried a striped pavilion tent and an array of playhouse costumes and props. His band of men either sat on the back or walked alongside the wagon. No one paid them any heed.

The journey here had been long and arduous, from a notion hatched in England, to the conspiratorial cloisters of southern Spain, and thence to the beaches of Cornwall. When Beatrice had entered his life, spouting her mad, half-formed ideas, he had not been slow to spot the potential.

'With one stroke, we could destroy them all,' she had said. 'Ten minutes of blood in God's name, and England will be saved.'

There was an elegant simplicity to her plan, but he had had to find the right men; he had had to find the right equipment. Her idea would not work without his exquisite attention to detail. Thanks to him, every obstacle had been bypassed or hurdled, every enemy removed. The recruitment of Ovid Sloth, with his terrifying debts and his contacts in England and Spain, had been the master stroke. It had been Sloth who had travelled to Toledo to commission the greatest of metalworkers to create the short, hard steel swords so neatly housed in their toy-like wooden frames.

All that was needed now was the extraction of a little information from a man named John Shakespeare and the way would be clear. Shakespeare was in good hands. The *best* of hands.

In nomine Patris, et Filii, et Spiritus Sancti . . .

The priest at the high altar intoned the words as he made the sign of the cross. He wore the long white gown known as an alb. Over this he wore a purple stole and then the chasuble, a sleeveless mantle.

John Shakespeare sat bound to the chair, unable to move more than his head. He closed his eyes and mouthed the Lord's Prayer, something he had not done for some time.

He could sense Beatrice Eastley behind him, and could smell the smoke of her burning tobacco. The dog's baleful eyes never left him.

Even before the priest turned, Shakespeare knew that it was Ovid Sloth. Englishman, Spaniard, merchant, traitor, priest: a man of many parts. He waddled slowly down the nave and stopped in front of the chair, gazing coldly at the captive.

'How do you know of Regis Roag?'

'He is the son of a king. How should I *not* know someone of such stature?'

'We are not here to make jest. Tell me how you know him. You mentioned such a man at St Michael's Mount, and then you knew him when you saw him. What do you know? How, too, did your man Cooper know where I would be this day?'

'Cooper? What do you know of Cooper?'

'What does he know of me? How did he find me?'

'We know everything about you. We all know of Roag, too, everyone who works for Sir Robert Cecil. Everyone in the office of the Earl of Essex. We knew he was coming to Cornwall. Do you think we would let such an enemy of the state enter the country unnoted?'

Since he had awoken in this malign place, Shakespeare had been thinking a great deal about the nature of Roag's entry into England. He was certain now that he had not come alone, that he had brought a band of mercenaries.

'We know exactly what he is about and whom he brought to England. We have spies aplenty in Seville and Sanlúcar.'

'Ah, yes, Robert Warner. A fine boy, by all accounts. Such a waste.'

'Warner? What are you saying?'

'Oh, I'm sure you know him. *Knew* him.'

'God damn you, Sloth. God damn you all. We know all about you. You will never walk free in England again.'

Sloth recoiled.

'He lies!' Beatrice's voice was a screech that echoed around the high vaulting walls of the old church.

'But he does know Roag. And that concerns me. *How* does he know him? How did Cooper find me?'

'It makes no difference. Regis can be anyone. You have seen him. He can transform himself. You know he can.'

Sloth ground his teeth so that the folds of his face quivered. 'Regis insists we must find out how this man knows his name. Well, we shall discover the truth. Satan cannot withstand the power of God.' He touched the corner of his purple stole to Shakespeare's bleeding shoulder. 'I do not like this man. I did not like him in Cornwall and I do not like him here. He is Satan's creature. He has serpents and clawed minions of the beast in his belly. They must be exorcised. Just as the devil inside the body of England must be cast down into fiery damnation. What are the signs, sister?'

'The chill air. He has no hunger. I see movement beneath the skin. Lesser demons have already flown. It is certain.'

Shakespeare struggled against the ropes. 'This is not about God. This is about temporal power. You are no man of God, Sloth – and you, Beatrice Eastley, are nothing but an assassin. You killed the old nun, Sister Michael. I had thought she was one of you. Did she not approve of your vile designs? Did you fear she would betray you?'

Sloth, who was clutching a crucifix, made the sign of the cross on his own breast, then on the breast, brow and lips of Shakespeare, who violently averted his face from the perverse ritual.

'*Oremus oratio . . .*'

Was this the way it had started for Loake and Trott and Friday? Did this woman and this man really believe in this gibberish, or was it some twisted entertainment, the way a child pulls off the wings of a fly, one by one?

'*Deus cui proprium est misereri semper et parcere: suscipe deprecationem nostram . . .* God who is ever merciful and forgiving, accept our prayer that this your servant, bound by the bonds of sin, may be granted pardon by your loving kindness.'

And so it went on. Verse after verse of the Latin rite of exorcism. Sloth called on God to crush the serpent, to cast him back down to hell where he belonged, having once fallen. He commanded Satan to be gone, to depart in fear with all his demons and servants, all this interspersed with flinging of holy water and signs of the cross.

All the while Beatrice watched Shakespeare intently, examining his torso and throat for signs of unholy creatures crawling within. Every so often, as if to keep him awake, she stabbed him with the needle in a different part of his body, whenever she believed she saw a clawed demon crawling beneath the skin. Even as he shuddered under the desperate and never-ending onslaught, Shakespeare could not help but think of the fishers in the fens, stabbing at the black water with their glaives in the hope of an eel. Like them, she was fishing . . .

As time wore on, Beatrice became more and more frantic and began foaming at the mouth. She made a guttural sound from her throat, her voice a growl, lower than a dog's, more disturbing than a wild beast's roar.

Suddenly a small cat appeared at the end of the nave, just inside the church door. Beatrice screamed, 'There it is! That is his kitling. Kill it, Sloth. Kill it!'

Looking about her, she saw a pile of wood lying close to the church wall. She picked up a long, crooked stick and began chasing the animal. Cornered, it bared its fangs and hissed at her. She lashed out at it, but the cat was too quick and dived for cover behind the lectern. The mastiff strained at its leash and barked.

'You see,' Shakespeare said to Sloth, 'she is insane. She is leading you all down to hell with this madness. Set me free and make your escape while there is still time. Make your way to Spain in safety.'

Sloth took a small box from beneath the folds of his gowns. He opened the lid and took out something brown and leathery. 'Light the brimstone, sister.'

Above them, the trapped jay flew about in panic, a flash of brilliance as it drove onwards from rafter to rafter, looking for its way out. Finally, as if summoning all its might, it flew for the light and collided with the ancient stained glass at speed. The impact must have stunned it, or broken its neck. It fell, spiralling black and grey and white, to the flagstone floor of the church and did not move.

Beatrice was on her knees stabbing at the cat, which was well concealed in the space beneath the lectern. Sloth's words broke her frenzy. She turned, still on hands and knees. Rising to her feet, she lit a taper from the altar candle and held it to one of the dishes on the table. After a while there was a sizzle and a burst of acrid smoke. Beatrice handed the dish to Sloth. He made the sign of the cross over it, then held it beneath Shakespeare's nose. Much as he wished to show no emotion, no physical distress or weakness to these people, the pungent fumes made him gag and choke. He gasped and coughed, using all his energy trying not to vomit.

'It is a demon in his throat, suffocating.' Ovid Sloth thrust forward the leathery brown object that he had taken from his box, pushing it into Shakespeare's mouth. Shakespeare gasped with shock. 'Oh, see how Father Sherwin's bone burns the beast. Oh, surely this relic is God's most potent weapon.'

Sherwin? Shakespeare recalled the name from many years ago. There had been a priest named Ralph Sherwin who died, butchered, on the scaffold along with Edmund Campion. Shakespeare could hold back no longer. He was sick, weakening fast, and knew he could not take much more before the blood loss made him slip into unconsciousness and death.

Beatrice thrust the sailmaker needle into Shakespeare's left leg. This time the surprise made him cry out.

'It is the devil that screams,' she shrieked. 'I hear the devil! He cannot last long. Baptise him, Mr Sloth, baptise the sinner, for that will burn the devil most wonderfully.'

Taking a pinch of salt from another dish, Sloth put it on to Shakespeare's tight-clenched lips and rubbed it in, as though coating a piece of meat. He wet his own fingers with the obscene dribble of his own mouth and smeared it on to his captive's eyes and lips. Then, from a little vial, he poured oil on Shakespeare's mouth and nose.

'*Vade retro satana*,' he intoned. '*Vade retro satana*. Begone, Satan. Return whence you came!' He held Shakespeare's head between his soft, grub-like hands and twisted it so that he spoke directly into his ear. 'Now tell me, John Shakespeare. Your life is ebbing. Tell me how you know of Roag. Do this and your family will live, though you die.'

The needle went in again, this time deep into his right thigh. Blood spat out on to the long white gown that Sloth wore beneath the chasuble and purple stole. Shakespeare did not even recoil this time. His body was growing colder, his life seeping from him like water through a colander. The surface of his body was now cloaked in blood. He had lost count of the times he had been stabbed. Soon, he knew, the mortal stroke would come: the needle through the jugular – if he survived that long.

Look after the little ones, O Lord.

He knew he could rely on Jane and Boltfoot, Ursula and Andrew, but he prayed that Sir Robert Cecil would watch over them, too. He closed his eyes. A vision came to him of his late wife, Catherine. Her dark waves of hair were tinged with a golden aureole, her eyes warm and serious, beckoning him, soothing him. The vision brought peace and acceptance, but faded like a sand picture under the incoming tide, only to be replaced by the carnal eyes of Lucia Trevail, beseeching him to live and join her in pleasure. But when he opened his eyes again they met the merciless gaze of Ovid Sloth and Beatrice Eastley, both staring at him with cold, deadly passion. They had no power over him.

Please God, he would be with Catherine soon.

Chapter 39

JANE COOPER AND Ursula Dancer hitched up their skirts and ran from the Cecil mansion in the Strand into the city streets. By the time they reached the bridge, Jane was out of breath and struggling to keep up. They both slowed to a brisk walk then began running again. They did not speak to one another as they manoeuvred their way through the late afternoon crowds down the lane between the houses that stood astride the great bridge. They did not notice the water rushing beneath.

At the south side of the bridge, they slowed to a walk again and caught their breath as they turned right, then began running once more, looking about them as they went.

Finally, they reached Clink Street and the dark oak door that held the gaol against escape or unwanted visitors. Both women leant against the wall, doubled over, exhausted by the two-mile race through waste-strewn streets, fighting their way past carts and traders.

'I thought my heart would pigging burst!'

Jane nodded at Ursula. Still gasping for breath, she banged on the door. From within, they heard slow footfalls and the clanking of keys. The turnkey pulled the door ajar a few inches and stared at them. Seeing two comely women, he opened it wider.

'How may I help you, fine ladies?'

He pulled back his shoulders, lifted his chin and smoothed his long bird's-nest beard as though that would somehow make him an attractive proposition. He licked his lips, leaving his tongue lolling out between his teeth.

'We want Boltfoot,' Jane said. 'Hand him over.'

'Boltfoot . . . Boltfoot?'

Jane was out of all patience. Mr Shakespeare was missing; their lives had been torn apart by the threat to the children, and the need to leave home and lodge in Sir Robert Cecil's house; and now Boltfoot was in gaol. Anger was barely known to her, but now it erupted like a blast of powder.

'Boltfoot Cooper. My cripple of a husband. Give him to me or you will suffer consequences the like of which you have never dreamt.'

The turnkey, taken aback by the sudden squall, shrank into the gaol, but Jane and Ursula were already inside before he could close the door on them.

'We have no one of that name.' He drew his short sword, which suddenly emboldened him. 'Think I'm frit of two drabs, do you?'

Ursula lunged at him and held him by the throat with one hand, while Jane pushed down on his sword arm. 'Where is he? Bring us to him or I'll have your balls for offal.'

Finding strength she did not know she had, Jane wrenched the sword from his grasp and held it out in front of her, pointing at him, its tip quivering. The turnkey tried to cry out but Ursula slammed her hand into his mouth.

'Can you read, Mr Keeper?' Jane said. 'We have with us a letter from Sir Robert Cecil, ordering the release of my husband. If he is not freed straightway into my custody, you will be brought before Star Chamber for impeaching the honour of Mr Cooper's person.'

She was not sure where the nonsensical words came from, nor the lie about the letter, but the keeper put up his hand.

'Very well, I will take you to him. But leave me be, ladies, I beg you.'

'Then take us to him. And if he's caught lice in this filthy place, I will make a bonfire of your stinking whiskers.'

Holding the sword at his back, they followed him through the cramped bowels of the ancient gaol. The other turnkeys stood back, trying to conceal their grins as their master passed them at the mercy of two women. The prisoners behind bars and in chains were not so restrained, openly laughing and jeering.

Boltfoot was standing with his arms folded in the centre of a small cell in which thirty men were crowded, some of them shackled and manacled. He had been here half a day or more, becoming more and more worried and frustrated as the hours passed. As soon as the cell door was opened, he stepped forward and removed the sword from Jane's hand.

'What is this, mistress? Why do you hold the keeper at swordpoint? Do you wish to be hanged?'

'He said you weren't here, Boltfoot. Anyway, he'll say nothing. The justice and jury would laugh so much that he was overpowered by women that he'd never be able to show his face in Southwark again.'

'He wanted garnish, that's all. It's how he lives, for no one else pays him for this dirty job he does.' Boltfoot handed the sword back to the keeper and apologised to him. 'You'll have your half a crown. Now hand me my cutlass and caliver and let me out of here.'

The tide was coming in, so they took the tilt-boat back to the Strand from St Mary Overy waterstairs. As they talked,

Boltfoot became increasingly alarmed to hear that there was no word from Mr Shakespeare.

'We have not seen him since you and he were together at Cecil House, which is more than twenty-four hours since,' Jane said. 'Sir Robert's steward sent messages to the palace at Greenwich, but now I am told they have all gone, headed for Nonsuch, so I don't know where he is.'

Boltfoot didn't like it. He badly needed to impart his new-discovered knowledge about Ovid Sloth and the playhouse costumes to his master. Should he ride for Nonsuch in Surrey or wait here? At least at Nonsuch he might be able to speak with Cecil or one of his assistants, even if Mr Shakespeare was not there.

In the event, the decision was made for him. As they arrived at Cecil's mansion, the door was opened by a servant who sighed with relief as he ushered them in. 'Thank the Lord you are here, Mr Cooper. You have a visitor.'

Boltfoot peered into the gloom of the hall beyond the door and saw a face from another place, from the watery wilderness of the Cambridgeshire fens. What in God's name was Paul Hooft doing here?

Pennants fluttered in the warm breeze of evening. Tents and pavilions of all shapes, sizes and patterns spread across the great park outside Nonsuch Palace. This was where many minor courtiers, administrators and other lesser mortals would spend their nights while the Queen and her favourites were in residence at the overcrowded palace. Even the city of tents had its hierarchy. The larger, grander pavilions were reserved for nobles and stood nearest the walls of the dazzling palace. Then came the senior officers of law, the bishops and government functionaries, followed by the gentry. And so it went on until, some quarter-mile from the palace, were to be found servants, cooks and the lower sort such as players and minstrels.

Hundreds of soldiers were in attendance, but they kept themselves apart. Many were stationed at the palace gates and inside its walls, for the Privy Council had ordered extreme security for this visit. The soldiers had their own camps, over-looking the city of tents, offering menace and protection at the same time.

The Ladies' Players were together in a large, striped pavilion that was in great need of repair, its canvas dirty and full of holes. Anyone stumbling into this tent in error would apolo-gise and stumble out again without a second thought. This was just another band of players, here by royal command.

Regis Roag held the book and directed his men. Suddenly he put up his hand. 'No! No! No! No! No!' He threatened to fling the pages to the ground, but thought better of it and smiled at his men like an indulgent father. His gaze alighted on Winnow. 'Have you lost all your wit, Dick?'

Winnow glared at him. Did these men know that Roag was leading them to certain death? He said nothing, merely turned his shoulder away.

Roag's voice did not betray his anger, only urgency. 'We are so close. This is about surprise and suddenness. If you do not convince, there will be no shock! Without it, we will fail.'

They all knew their parts, for they had been rehearsing since receiving the book. The Fitzgerald brothers, Hugh and Seamus, spoke with ease; they were natural players. Even the hirelings Ratbane and Paget, both of whom had non-speaking roles, were adequate. And what they lacked in style on stage, they more than made up for in their brutal skill with the short sword. But that was another rehearsal, one that had been perfected elsewhere.

Only the matters of John Shakespeare and Dick Winnow

caused Roag anxiety. No word had come yet from Beatrice. It was certain that Cecil's intelligencer knew his face from Cornwall – but how did he come by his name? They had never met, to his knowledge; and surely his brother William could not have made the connection. The case of Winnow was troubling, too. Until they sailed from Sanlúcar de Barrameda, he had seemed likely to be the strongest and most convincing member of the company. Since then, however, he had worried Roag; his heavy silences and truculence told of a man not to be trusted.

'When you enter, you fall to your knees in front of the Queen. Both knees, Dick, and you bow your head until your forelock almost touches the floor. This must be done with conviction. Is that clear?'

What was clear to Winnow was that he no longer wished to be part of this enterprise. It was not death that worried him, for it was in the cause of God. It was the thought of dying alongside Regis Roag that he could not stomach. He drew his short sword. It was housed in a slim wooden sheath that looked like a play-actor's prop sword. With cold anger, he thrust it into the ground and left it quivering there. Without a word, he strode from the tent out into the fresh air.

Roag cursed beneath his breath. Winnow was a danger to them all. With sun-bright clarity he realised he would have to do without Dick . . . and there *was* a way. He signalled to Ratbane and Paget, and spoke to them quietly.

'Go after Winnow. Take him to the river and send him downstream. I do not wish to see him again.'

He watched them go. Two sullen, brutish men, the sort who did the bidding of their masters with a will; the kind of men who in a past century would have slit the throats of Frenchmen bogged down in a muddy field at Agincourt without blinking. Slaughterhouse men. Just the men he needed. He would have dealt with Winnow himself, but he had other matters to attend to in an abandoned plague parish church a few miles north of this place.

Winnow ran for his life. He knew that Ratbane and Paget would be sent after him. He ran deep into the woods. At last he came to an area of dense bracken and sank into it, certain that he must be invisible. He turned on his back and looked up at the canopy of leaves, panting heavily, like a dog in summer. He would wait there all night, and survive.

Shakespeare was barely conscious. His head, the only part of him not coated in gore, was slumped on to his bloody chest. His breathing was shallow and rasping. His lips moved and he spoke a single word. *Live.* That was all. That was all he had left. *Live.* He had no idea whether the word was in his head or could be heard.

Sloth wrenched his head up by the hair. 'What do they know about Roag?'

'Everything,' Shakespeare said again, his voice faint and distant.

All he knew was that this man and this woman were all over him, crawling across him like clawed, frenzied reptiles, killing him bit by bit. Picking away at his body, scraping at his very soul.

'What, specifically? If you know the plot, explain it to me and I will finish you with a sword-thrust and your children will be saved.'

Somewhere, on a distant portion of his body, he felt the stabbing of a needle. He no longer even recoiled at the pain.

'He is full of demons, so full. They are without number.'

Beatrice was on the floor, on her knees, clutching at him with her long, narrow fingers, scratching the needle point along his skin until she thought she saw a demon, and then stabbing.

'He is alive with the creatures. I hear them talking to me.' She foamed and shrieked as she spoke. 'They cry out their names: Pippin, Maho, Modu and Soforce. These are the captains. They have under-demons each, numbering three hundred. I stab them and they growl and wriggle and laugh like girls. Except Soforce, which does not laugh. Why do they not flee? Even the lesser devils, Hilco, Smolkin, Hillio, Hiaclito, Frateretto, Hobberdidance and Tocobatto seem not afeared. Father Sloth, Father Sloth . . . give him more brimstone.'

Sloth was not listening. His face was so close to Shakespeare's that he was like a bear, open-mouthed, preparing to devour a piece of flesh from its prey.

'I will suck the truth from you. Speak, or be for ever cursed. Speak or your seed will die with you.'

Beatrice scratched her nails across the flagstone floor. 'Molkin, Wilkin, Lustie Dickie, Nurre, Killicocam and Helcmodon. But Maho is the tyrant. If we can burn Maho, then all will flee. And so I prick here . . .'

She stabbed again, in the sole of his foot.

Boltfoot Cooper stood inside the door to the little church with uncomprehending eyes. At his side was the slender young figure of Paul Hooft. Like Boltfoot, his blue eyes were wide in disbelief and horror.

'Have they killed him, Mr Cooper?'

Before them, in the centre of the nave, a blood-drenched figure sat, bound to a chair. It was impossible to tell who it was, or even if it was human. A large man, swathed in ecclesiastical robes, was almost on top of the figure, enveloping it. A woman had curled herself around his legs. The whole horrible tableau moved and squirmed like grubs in a fisherman's pot.

'I don't know, Mr Hooft. I pray he is alive. But I know this: it is time to put an end to this ungodly degradation.'

They had tethered their horses in the woods, then crept to the church. Pistols drawn and loaded, they had pushed open the door, unsure whom they would find, or how many. But there was no need for such caution. Beatrice Eastley and Ovid Sloth were too far gone in their lethal passion to notice the newcomers. Only the leashed dog saw them, wagging its tail and whimpering like a puppy.

Boltfoot limped forward and dragged Sloth off. He seemed surprised but did not resist. There was blood on his face, around his mouth. He looked at Boltfoot with recognition but no understanding. Boltfoot removed his weapons, then pushed him to the floor. Sloth tried to get up, but Boltfoot turned him over on to his front and placed a booted foot on his back.

Hooft pulled Beatrice away with surprising tenderness. She stood before him, shivering, full of loathing, but also triumphant. 'Fly, Maho, fly down to the depths. You are conquered! Go to your master in hell.'

'I am Paul. Do you not remember? You were to have been my wife.'

'Your devil's grease cloaks you in human form, Maho, but you do not deceive me. I escaped from you before. You will not snare me again. I am God's instrument now and I hold dominion over you and all your worms.'

Hooft gazed at her with a mixture of sadness and disgust, then turned to Boltfoot and raised his hands in a gesture of hopelessness. 'Look what the popish beasts have done to my bride, Mr Cooper.'

Boltfoot pulled her arm roughly and tried to wrench her down beside Sloth. 'Help me get her on the ground, Mr Hooft, then train the pistols on them.' He had a coil of cord slung around his body. He removed it and handed it to Hooft. 'Bind them tight. If they try to escape, shoot them. I must look to Mr Shakespeare.'

He took his dagger from his belt and began to cut the ropes that bound his master, all the time speaking to him, seeking some response.

'Can you hear me? All will be well now.'

He wiped the blood from Shakespeare's mouth and tried to give him a drink from his water bottle, but there was no response. He cupped his hand and poured a little water into it, then dripped some on to his master's lips.

He tried to decide what to do. They were four miles south-west of London, a third of the way to the Palace of Nonsuch. Mr Shakespeare was alive, but he was in a very bad way. He could not withstand a ride back to London, strapped across the back of a horse. This desolate ruin of a church stood in the middle of a field. The only other house they had seen in the vicinity was a farmhouse, half a mile away. That was their only hope.

'Are they bound, Mr Hooft?'

'Indeed.'

'Then bring the horses. We must get Mr Shakespeare away from this place. I will ride ahead and you can follow with these two fiends on leashes. We must trust there will be a barn where we can hold them.'

While Hooft went for their mounts, Boltfoot cut strips of cloth from Sloth's robes and, soaking them in water, cleaned as much blood as he could from Shakespeare's torso. Where the bleeding was not already clotting, he staunched the flow. There were so many needle wounds, so much blood.

Chapter 40

THE FARMWIFE WAS tall and strong, with power enough to restrain a struggling hog at gelding time. Though Shakespeare was six foot and well built, she took him in her arms and carried him like a child into the rambling old house, through to her own chamber. There she placed him on the large bed.

While Boltfoot and her children looked on, she began to tend to Shakespeare, cleaning and dressing the wounds with clean linen. After a while she turned to Boltfoot.

'Best thing you could do would be to fetch a physician, if you know one.'

'Is there one near here?'

'Not that you'd want to let loose on your master.'

Simon Forman was lying on his back, snoring and dreaming. He was always prone to vivid dreams, which he would recall and write down in the morning while he partook of his breakfast meat and milk. In this dream, Janey came to him with Alice Blague, the dean's lusty wife.

Both were wearing smocks of white linen and black shoes. About their hair, they had coronets of pearls. Both lifted their skirts and demanded he perform his duty as a man with them. Both wished to be first. They told him that if he chose correctly, something very good would occur; if he chose wrongly, then evil would befall him. As he looked from one to the other, trying to decide, their faces elongated like smithy's hammers and their white smocks turned black and became the handles. Giant fists seized them and began to pound him.

Suddenly he awoke. There *was* a hammering. Someone was beating at the front door of his house, in the middle of the night.

'Boy!' he shouted, but nothing would rouse apprentice Braddedge from his slumbers. Groaning, Forman slid from the bed and tripped downstairs in his nightgown.

'Who is there?' he called out through the heavily locked door.

'Boltfoot Cooper, Mr Shakespeare's servant.'

Cooper? Forman tensed at the name. Jane Cooper's husband. Had Cooper found out that his wife had been here? Did he plan violent retribution?

'What do you want, Mr Cooper? You have woken me. It is exceeding late at night, sir.'

'In God's name let me in and I will tell you!'

'Nothing untoward happened, I will swear as much on the Bible.'

'What? Open the door or I will break it down. My master is badly injured. He needs you.'

Forman scratched his balls and ran his fingers through his tangled hair, then, steeling himself for possible onslaught, opened the door. A squat, vaguely familiar man stood before him, speckled with blood and dust.

'Come in, Mr Cooper. You had better tell me what this is about.'

'I will tell you while you clothe yourself. There is no time to lose.'

*

They rode together through the night. A half-moon in a cloudless sky lit their way along the well-worn track through the fields towards the wealthy parishes of Clapham and Tooting. Forman had explained to Cooper that he might not be the right man, that he had no experience of surgery or wounds.

'You're all there is, so you are coming with me,' Boltfoot had replied.

Forman accepted the order and carefully packed a bag of everything he believed he might need. In truth, he felt nervous, but excited. Usually people came to him with commonplace complaints like gout, difficult pregnancies, melancholia and afflictions of the skin. At the worst, they might consult him about the palsy. Often they begged charts to know the chances of a marriage succeeding or love philtres to help gain a suitor's interest. But no one had ever called him out to attend a badly injured man.

Dawn was still some way off by the time they arrived. The house was in darkness. That had been Boltfoot's suggestion. If anyone came looking for Sloth or the girl, they would head straight for a house where the lights burnt.

Boltfoot wondered, not for the first time, about Paul Hooft's part in all this. The Dutchman said he had come to London looking for John Shakespeare, to press his case once more for subsidies to drain the fens. He had gone to his house in Dowgate and had seen him being attacked. Unsure what to do, he had followed the assailants out into the countryside to an old church. Unarmed and unused to the area, he had returned to London to seek help and had found Boltfoot. He did not explain how.

The tale did not ring true, but that did not concern Boltfoot for the present. He had fetched weapons for Hooft and had ridden with him to the church. All discrepancies in the Dutchman's story would be a matter for Mr Shakespeare to investigate when he had recovered. For the moment, Boltfoot was simply glad that Hooft had come to him with the information concerning Mr Shakespeare's abduction.

'Come in, come in,' the farmer's wife said in a low voice to Boltfoot and Forman. 'I would beseech you to be as quiet as possible.'

'Is he still alive?'

She nodded with a sombre smile. 'His breathing is more regular. He has lost much blood and his pulse is weak. I have fed him sips of water as he would take them and I have bandaged him as well as I could. But I have never seen a man in such a state, sir.'

'Take me to him,' Forman said.

As the physician followed the woman, a widow, through to her chamber, Boltfoot hung back with Hooft. 'What of our captives?'

'I have bound them tight and gagged them so they do not cry out.'

'Has anyone been to the church, to your knowledge?'

Hooft lowered his voice. 'I heard a horse and went over in that direction, as silently as I could. I saw a lantern light so I did not go too close. Whoever it was did not stay long.'

'How many?'

'One horseman. He let the mastiff loose. I think he was hoping it would lead him to his confederates and I confess I was terrified it would come straight for me, but it ran off into the woods and did not return. The horseman tried to follow it, but then gave up and went back to the church. He waited there ten minutes or so and finally rode off. I have never held a pistol so tight, Mr Cooper, fearing he would come here.'

'Did you see his face?'

'No. He was too far away.'

'Which way did he go?'

'It seemed south, but I am not familiar with this land, so I could not say that for certain.' As if reading Boltfoot's thoughts, he added, 'The mistress of the house has put out beer and some food for us in the kitchen.'

Boltfoot smiled. Yes, beer would be most welcome.

As he followed Hooft through to the kitchen, he wondered again about Simon Forman. *Nothing untoward happened*, he had said. What did he mean by that? Well, it was of no import. Beer and a pipe of tobacco were the vital things right now. And then, when the sun came up, they would transport Sloth and Miss Eastley to Newgate. But what most concerned Boltfoot was the intelligence he needed to impart to Mr Shakespeare: the connection between Ovid Sloth and Mr Henslowe at the Rose playhouse. He needed to tell him what he had seen, and quickly.

In Regis Roag's head, the words of Richard of Gloucester spun around like the sails on a mill. *I can smile and murder while I smile.* What had happened? The church floor by the chair was coated in gore and yet there was no sign of them. Had Beatrice and Sloth been disturbed in their work? Had they fled with their captive? If so, where? Or worse, had they been discovered?

He was halfway to Nonsuch when he reined in his horse; he had to go back to the church. He should have looked close by. There must be a house or a barn in the vicinity. He wheeled the horse's head around and set off.

Helped by the bright half-moon, the ride took him an hour. Tethering the horse at the church, he took another look around and examined the ropes that had been left around the chair. The ends had been cut, not untied. Why would Beatrice or Sloth have done such a thing? And why had they not taken the dog? This had to be the work of someone else.

He walked out of the church and gazed into the silvery

gloom. In the distance he saw the outline of some buildings, probably a farmhouse and barns. When he was here before, he hadn't noticed them. But now, the roofs were visible against the sky.

Leaving the horse, he walked at a steady pace across the fields. As he drew near, he saw that the farmhouse was in darkness. He moved on, then stopped. Was that the flicker of a candle against a window? For a moment it was there, then it was gone. Had it been his imagination or some reflection on the leaded pane of the window? No, it was a candle.

He drew his pistol from his belt. It was loaded.

Boltfoot was on edge. He did not believe they were safe; the house was too exposed and too obvious. He should never have brought Mr Shakespeare here, but there had been no alternative. He struck a light with his tinderbox, put taper to his pipe and drew deeply of the fragrant New World tobacco. Instantly, he snuffed the taper. That had been a mistake. Anyone out there might have seen the light.

He glanced out of the window. All he saw was moon shadows. It could not be long now until dawn, when they could fetch assistance. He wondered again about Hooft and began to think he understood him; he was out at the barn, standing just outside the door, listening out for the breathing of the woman he still loved.

Roag saw the face at the window. He could not recognise it from this distance, but it confirmed that someone was there and awake. It was possible, of course, that the farmer or his wife was rising, but it was possible, too, that his quarry was there.

He moved forward, more stealthily now. If Beatrice and Sloth were in the house, they would not be alone and they might not be in control. He steeled himself.

Remember your heritage; you are the son of a king.

As he came within fifty yards of the house, he saw movement at the side and stopped to watch. A man was walking from the large byre towards the house. From the shade of a clump of trees, he peered into the gloom. It was no one he knew. Perhaps it was the farmer, starting his day's work, or maybe he had been up all night, calving.

When the man had gone into the house, Roag crouched down and ran across the open ground to the barn. A dog barked, but he ignored it and pushed on. If these were simple farm folk, they would have no defence against him; if they were his enemies, he had the advantage of surprise. Either way, he would blow them away.

The door to the barn was padlocked. From inside, he heard movement. He called out softly and heard a muffled grunt. He called again a little louder and the grunt came again, panicky. Someone was in there, unable to respond.

Crouching double, he crept around the barn, looking for some other way in, or an open window, but the barn was made of brick and was sealed solid. Pushing the pistol back into his belt, he slipped the sailmaker from the pocket inside his sleeve into his hand and worked it into the keyhole. This was a trick he had learnt years ago from one of his mother's seamsters, a man who had once been apprenticed to a locksmith. His fingers were steady. He stood still, moving the needle about, feeling for the way the padlock was made up. He smiled. It was simple. This lock was made by fools, for fools. A firm twist of the needle and the bolt sprang open.

Silently, he placed it on the ground, replaced the needle in his sleeve, then took out his pistol again and opened the door. Two shapes lay on the floor in front of him. He could sense their movement without seeing them. They were live bodies, bound.

Roag knelt and tore the gag from Beatrice's mouth. She gasped for air.

'What has happened here?'

'Unbind me, Regis, I beg you.'

'What did you discover from Shakespeare? How much do they know?'

'We discovered nothing. He would not speak. He is dead. There were too many demons.'

'Is it safe? Can we proceed?'

'I beg you, Regis, I do not know. His body was a very city to the devil's spawn.'

Roag stared at her. If Shakespeare was dead, they must still take their chance, even though it meant the death of them all. He had to do this. He was born with teeth, which plainly signified that he should snarl and bite and play the dog. And if the dog must be whipped, so be it. But there would be many others who would be bitten along the way. They would die, every one of them, all those who denied his royal blood.

His voice softened. 'Tell me what has happened, Beatrice. Who is in the house?'

The bedchamber where Shakespeare lay was at the back. The windows were shuttered to keep in the light of the single candle by which Dr Forman worked.

At last he arched his aching back and sighed.

'Well, Mr Shakespeare, you will live. You are most fortunate for, as far as I can tell, none of the wounds punctured a vital organ or artery.'

Forman was talking to himself. Shakespeare did not make a sound. His eyes were closed and his breathing was steady. His upper body and legs were bandaged, and Forman had dripped a vial of herb essence into his mouth to aid sleep, nothing more.

Boltfoot knocked at the door.

Forman nodded to him. 'All's well, Mr Cooper. Keep these wounds bandaged with clean linen. Ensure that water is boiled and allowed to cool before you wash him. Do you understand?'

'Aye. How long will he be like this?'

'With sleep, plenty of clean water to drink and nourishment, he will build up very soon, though he may be weak and in pain for a day or two.'

'But when can I talk to him? I have information that I must impart to him. Can he be woken now?'

'No. He must have rest.'

'How long, Dr Forman?'

'Eight hours, seven at best. Sit with him and see when he wakes. Do not expect too much, though. I will leave you now. Stay here until he is strong.'

'No, *you* stay here. I will need you if anything goes wrong.'

Forman laughed. 'Mr Cooper, I have work to do. People have appointments; they will be coming to see me.'

Perhaps even your wife.

Boltfoot put his hand on the hilt of his cutlass. 'Stay. You will be well paid. Whatever you would earn this day, we will double it.'

Forman had not survived to the age of forty or more by tangling with piratical men with calivers slung over their backs and glittering steel blades at their waists.

He nodded. 'Very well,' he said. 'But I, too, will need nourishment. If the farmwife is up, please ask her to bring me food and ale.'

As Roag took Beatrice in his arms, she sank on to his chest and clung to him as though he would suckle her. Her short hair was wild, as were the shivers of her body. He looked past her in the emerging light to the dark, squirming bulk of Ovid Sloth. They had the play, they had the costumes, they had the props, they had the way in. Sloth was nothing but a risk, too visible and too slow to carry away. How would he cope under torture in the Tower? Not well. Not well at all. He would tell everything he knew at the mere sight of the iron tools in the burning cresset. The sailmaker needle, Roag's most precious jewel, slid down once more from his sleeve.

He wrenched Beatrice away and pushed her sprawling into a heap of hay. She tried to crawl back to him, but he shook his head and put the needle to his lips to hush her. Her eyes widened and she shied away from him into the corner. She clutched her hands about her knees and watched as he descended on the whale-like bulk of Ovid Sloth, clothed in blood-stained tatters. Cradling the bulbous head in his left arm, he quested around the enormous throat with the right hand until he felt the pulsing throb of the jugular. Sloth struggled, but he was bound tight. Roag kissed his sweating bald pate, then jabbed with the sailmaker and gasped with pleasure as the blood seeped over his fingers. Such were the powers of a king. The power of life and death.

Ego sum rex. Ego sum Deus. The devil's words. *I am king. I am God.* He waited, holding the bucking body firm against his chest, while the blood drained into the earth.

He stood up and held out his hand to Beatrice. Her eyes glowed in the new light of dawn.

Chapter 41

Tʜᴇʏ ᴡᴇʀᴇ ᴀʟʟ up and out by ten o'clock in the morning, meeting in the inner courtyard of Nonsuch Palace. The statue of the Queen's father, Henry, dazzled in the sunlight and the exquisite white plaster reliefs on the walls seemed to dance between rows of ornate red brickwork.

'Well met, sweetings,' said Lady Susan, the Countess of Kent, kissing the other three on the cheek. 'Let us venture out and visit our little troupe of players, to see that they are arrived safe and are well rehearsed.'

She took Lucia Trevail's arm, while Emilia Lanier linked arms with the Countess of Cumberland. As they walked forth, past the fountain and on to the outer court, and then through the majestic gatehouse to the parkland beyond, they knew that they cut a formidable dash. Four independent and proud women, the School of Day, in gowns of bright silk and worsted, their hair teased up and held with pins with diamond and pearl ornament, beneath small hats of felt. Each carried a fan and walked slowly so that all might gaze on them and admire them. Courtiers bowed low and swept their hats in great arcs by way of salute.

'Why, we might be a gaggle of girls on our way to the schoolroom,' Lucia Trevail said.

Emilia gazed at the array of armour and halberds on display

both inside and outside the palace walls. 'There are a great many soldiers about. Is there to be a tilt?'

'There is some scare, my dear,' the Countess of Cumberland said.

She might not have been as fetching as her three companions, but she was confident that her gown of cloth of gold and her long necklaces of rubies and pearls were a match for any of them.

'Not that I am complaining. You may send one or two handsome soldiers to *my* room tonight.'

'And what, may I ask, *is* this fright?' Lucia said. 'Why do they never tell us these things?'

Lady Susan glanced at Lucia with a questioning eyebrow and half a smile. 'They think such things beneath the feminine sex, which must bewilder Her Majesty, who is more learned than any man. But whatever it is, I would not be surprised if it involves the bold Mr Shakespeare in some way. What say you, Lucia? You know the delightful Mr Shakespeare well, I believe. Or is that mere tittle-tattle?'

Lucia tilted her chin and looked her straight in the eye. 'Do I detect a little envy, Susan?'

'What are you suggesting? I have a fine man-at-arms of my own. There is no want of a hard man in *my* bed. But one thing is certain. Mr Shakespeare is most keen to discover the whereabouts of our erstwhile companion Beatrice. I have received word that a squadron of men appeared at my house in Barbican Street late at night, wishing to apprehend her, but of course she was not there. Now, where is this grand pavilion? Where are our players? Let us see if they will do us proud. Mr Sloth has promised much. It is time to hold him to account.'

Roag spotted the four women approaching down an avenue of young oaks and grasped Beatrice by the arm.

'Slip away. Take off your vizard, go into the tent and put a coif about your hair. Then walk into the woods, keep your face down, and stay there, out of sight. Do not come back for an hour.' He pushed her in the back. 'Go . . .'

Without a word, she nodded and stepped into the tent.

As the women came closer, Roag pulled off his own golden mask and strode towards them, smiling broadly and extending his arms in welcome.

'Ah, the charming Mr Roag,' the Countess of Kent said as he bowed low before her and kissed her hand.

'Lady Susan, it is my pleasure to welcome you to our humble pavilion. And you, my Lady Trevail, Lady Cumberland and Mistress Lanier.' He kissed all their hands in turn. 'Might I offer you some refreshment? We have nothing but good English ale, I am afraid, but it is enough to quench a thirst.'

'I think we shall forgo the ale. We are here only to ensure that you are arrived as promised and that the masque is prepared for this evening's festivities, Mr Roag, nothing more. Is Mr Sloth not here? I had expected to see him, for he has done much work in preparing the entertainment.'

Roag affected a sigh. 'Poor Mr Sloth. He is indisposed with a summer sweat. And you are correct, Lady Trevail, we could not have done without him. However, all is now in place. I believe we are to perform when the hour strikes eight or there-abouts – sometime between the jesters and the banquet. I pledge that we shall produce a spectacle of great passion and vigour, one to be remembered for many a day.'

Lady Susan clapped her hands. 'Good. Play your heart out, sir, for if you do well, the Queen will wish to see you again . . . and again. And your star will surely ascend in the firmament.'

In her hand, she had a rolled document, which she handed to Roag.

'Here is your pass. You will be asked to produce it at the

gatehouse. It has been signed by the Earl of Essex and countersigned by Lord Chamberlain Hunsdon. You are expected.'

Roag took the pass and bowed. 'Thank you, my lady. You have no idea what an honour this will be for me.'

Margaret, Countess of Cumberland, a woman with a remarkable eye for detail and a dedication to the sciences, pointed to the sword at Roag's waist. 'I fear you will not be able to bring *that* into the palace, Mr Roag. No armaments of any kind within the presence of Her Majesty. It will not get past the outer wall.'

Roag laughed and drew his wooden sword from its scabbard. 'It is nothing but wood, my lady, and fragile, too. A child's play-thing or toy. You would be hard-pressed to harm a mouse with it.' He waved it about, as though engaging in a mock sword-fight.

'And who else have you here, Mr Roag?' Emilia swept her arm around the gathering of players, all standing awkwardly about, still in their golden masks. 'Are there any players we might recognise?'

'You will see them when they take their bows, mistress. I pledge that the audience will gasp with amazement.'

The Countess of Cumberland looked upon the players, who certainly seemed a fine little group of men. 'I am sure you will all do very well, Mr Roag. It is always a pleasure to see you. I trust you have had time enough to prepare yourselves, for I know you have been absent from London some little time.'

'A death in the family, in the North, my lady. I had much to settle in the matter of probate.'

'Come, ladies,' Lucia Trevail said, 'let us leave poor Mr Roag to his labours. I do believe Her Majesty will soon have finished with Council business and will require us to join her for her morning volta and cards.'

*

Regis Roag watched them walk away and smiled with relief. God was with him, there could be no doubt. This was his destiny, this day. Would they have recognised Beatrice in man's attire, with the mask about her face? Probably not, but there was no point in taking chances before it became necessary.

In his hand he held the toy wooden sword. Slowly, he withdrew the true sword housed within. A thin, flat blade of finely crafted Toledo steel. This was no toy; this was an instrument perfectly devised and honed for one specific task: the killing of a Queen and her entire court.

John Shakespeare woke at six o'clock in the evening to find himself in a strange bed, in darkness. He lay still for a few moments, his eyes open, trying to make sense of his surroundings.

'Mr Shakespeare?'

He turned towards the voice and let out a low, involuntary scream of pain.

'Do not try to move, sir, you have suffered grievous injury to your body. Every movement will cause you great anguish.'

A face had appeared before his eyes. At first it was too close for him to focus on, then it moved back. It was a face he recognised. But in the name of God, what was Dr Simon Forman doing here – and where were they, anyway? This was not his own bedchamber, nor the one he had been assigned in the house of Sir Robert Cecil.

'Dr Forman, what is this? Where am I?'

'You are in a farmhouse. You were tormented almost to death by a woman who has been identified to me as Mistress Sorrow Gray and by a man, now dead, named Mr Ovid Sloth.'

'Boltfoot? Where is Boltfoot?'

'Close by. He brought me here to tend you. But I must insist that you lie quiet and still. You have lost a quart or more of blood. If you rest, you will regain your health; if not, then there is still danger. Here, let me give you some sips of water, sir.'

'Get Boltfoot.' In his mind he shouted the words, but in truth they were as faint as the illicit whisperings of a Cistercian. 'I must speak with him – alone.'

'Very well.'

Shakespeare's whole body was alive with pain. His torso and legs were bandaged as tightly as a corpse in its winding sheet. The slightest movement made him grimace. Even the simple act of breathing was agony.

Boltfoot came in and stood by the door. Forman stayed outside.

'Come closer, Boltfoot. I cannot move easily to see you.'

He limped over to the bed. 'I thank God you are alive, master.'

'Not God alone, I think.'

'Dr Forman has played his part, as has the goodwife whose farmhouse you are in. She has nursed you and fed us.'

'Us?'

'Dr Forman, myself and Mr Hooft.'

'Hooft is here? Why?'

'He discovered where they had taken you. You must talk to him when you have your strength back, but, in short, he says he came to London to find you, for he had hopes you might lead him to Sorrow Gray. I confess I am not certain of his story, but it is fortunate he followed you, for you were close to death when we found you.'

The events came back in a rush. The weird melding of exorcism and torture. But perhaps exorcism and torture were one and the same thing, both born of religious insanity. Beatrice had been there and Ovid Sloth, and then Boltfoot, wonderful Boltfoot with the astonishing tenderness of his callused hands.

'What of Sloth and the woman?'

Boltfoot ground his teeth and shut the door before returning to Shakespeare's bed.

'I confess I am not certain, master,' he said quietly. 'They were both bound and locked in the barn. But at first light when I went to them, Sloth was dead, his throat stuck through, and the woman was gone.'

'How? How did that happen?'

Boltfoot glanced back at the door. 'Mr Hooft was with them. I fear he might have freed her. It is all I can think. But he denies it, says he would never kill.'

Shakespeare was struggling to rise from the pillow, but fell back, breathing heavily.

'There was another matter, master. As commanded by you, I went in search of Mr Sloth. I found him at the Rose playhouse, with Mr Henslowe. He was buying or hiring costumes and certain props. It seems it was a long-standing agreement between the two men.'

'Why did you not take him then and there?'

'My caliver misfired and I was overpowered while Sloth made his escape. There was a young woman with him, pushing a handcart. Now that I have seen her, I believe it was Beatrice Eastley.'

'Have you no idea why they wanted these things?'

'Mr Henslowe said it was the practice of great men to put on plays for their friends, that is all. Whatever Sloth's part in all this, I think Henslowe an honest broker and innocent of crime.'

Shakespeare struggled to make sense of this new information. Sloth could not be staging a play; he had made himself a renegade. So why would he wish costumes and props?

The answer broke upon him like thunder from a darkening sky. Anthony Friday had been writing a play, though no one knew whom it was for. Of course, it was clear now: he was writing it for Sloth. This had always been about the Theatre and about players. Most of all, Roag. Regis Roag, the man who believed himself the son of a king and who had played Richard of Gloucester, a man who killed to be king. This was about a play – and it was suddenly clear whom the intended audience must be.

The words of his brother Will slid like an ice blade into his spine. *This golden ray, this English goddess, this nonsuch of our hearts . . .* The words he ascribed to Anthony Friday's play, the paean to Her Majesty. It was the word *nonsuch* that dealt the blow. The Palace of Nonsuch. That was the place. It would happen there. The Queen must be there by now.

'What is the date, Boltfoot?'

His man frowned and tried counting on his fingers. 'I believe it to be the twenty-third, master. August the twenty-third.'

The twenty-third. The number in the Wisbech letter. He had believed it referred to the landing of the Spanish galleys in Mount's Bay. That had been July the twenty-third. But that was not the vital date at all. *This* was the day. This was the day they would stage their play before the Queen.

But what bloody surprises were they preparing to unleash? The thought was too dreadful to think on; he had to act, whatever the pain.

'Boltfoot, get me out of this bed!'

Chapter 42

THE CAPTAIN OF the guards put up his hand. Two halberdiers crossed their weapons, barring the way to the six players and their handcart. 'Hold fast. Who are you?'

Roag stopped and smiled. 'We are the Ladies' Players, Captain. We are to perform our humble entertainment before Her Royal Majesty.'

The guard had the hard look of a soldier who would not blink as he cleaved a skull in two. He ran the forefinger of his right hand down a list. 'I have you. Where is your pass?'

Roag handed over the paper. The captain studied it carefully, then looked up and stared hard into Roag's eyes. 'Have I seen you before? You look familiar.'

'I played with Lord Strange's Men before the Queen some time ago. It is possible you saw me then.'

The captain grunted. 'What's on the cart?'

'Our costumes and props.'

'I see you wear a sword at your belt. Take it off and leave it here.'

'It is a wooden sword, a prop for the play.'

'No weapons. Order of the Council.'

Roag laughed. 'But it is not a weapon.'

The captain held out a hand. 'Show me.'

Roag drew his wooden sword and handed it over. The

captain tested it and weighed it in his hands. It was light, for it was made of soft wood, and there was no hidden blade within, unlike all the others. The guard ran a finger down the thick, blunt blade, then handed it back.

'Are there other toy weapons?'

'Just what you see. A wooden sword for each of us. And there is also a white staff of office, the symbol of the Lord Treasurer, if you consider that to be a weapon. We need it because we are to represent the great men of the Queen's court, to pay tribute to her. Could you imagine Ralegh without his sword or Burghley without his white staff?'

The captain nodded to two of his men. 'Search the cart.'

'I beseech you to take care. Those costumes and masks are hired; they cost more gold than I could earn in a lifetime.'

The guards sifted through the costumes and masks but found nothing suspicious.

'Now search the players. Every inch of them.'

Roag looked at Beatrice. She wore doublet and hose and a velvet hat, but it seemed to him that she was shaking. She was the weak link in the chain. She was slim and her hips were narrow enough to pass for an effeminate youth, but a cursory examination would quickly detect her true sex. And even if, by some chance, they did not discover her secret, she was at the edge of her undoing. It would not take much to push her over.

'Captain, is this necessary? We have much preparation to do to set our scene.'

The guard stared at Roag again. Suddenly he nodded, then turned to a guard within the gatehouse. 'Take them through, Corporal.'

Roag breathed out and bowed his head to the guard in gratitude. He was nearly there now; he could almost taste the fear and the blood. He would likely die this day, but they would know who he was. *For yet I am not look'd on in the world.*

Oh, they would look on him. Never again would they deny his parentage, never shun him as though he were a scraping on their golden shoes.

He followed the corporal into the outer courtyard. Striding purposefully ahead of them, he caught sight of a small knot of courtiers, among them Essex. His former employer was looking in the other direction, but nonetheless Roag hurried by, head down, gaze averted.

There was a delightful intimacy about the inner courtyard of Nonsuch Palace, which made it perfect for the performing of entertainments on a warm summer's evening such as this.

A mighty noise of talking, laughter and music already filled the balmy air. The sun was low, and there were long shadows, but pitch torches and lanterns added lustre to the space. Scores of courtiers stood or sat or milled about, conversing and arguing. At the far end of the courtyard, beneath the windows of the Queen's Privy Chamber, a bank of seats had been erected for Her Majesty and her private party, protected from the weather by a large canopy of gold and green stripes. Directly opposite it, ranged behind the central fountain, was a low stage where a company of tumblers flipped their lithe and graceful bodies through the air.

The Queen was already in her place, seated on sumptuous cushions, idly sipping at a silver goblet of hippocras, watching the gymnasts and listening to some scandalous tittle-tattle that Henry, Lord Hunsdon, the Lord Chamberlain, dripped into her ear. Suddenly she laughed and struck him with the edge of her fan.

Essex sat on her right, his face imperiously sullen as he talked with Southampton. Cecil and his father, Lord Burghley, were seated near by, as were Heneage, Egerton and Puckering. Most of England's senior nobles and holders of the offices of state were here for the occasion. The entertainment did not interest them a great deal; their real purpose this evening was to jostle for favour and preferment while doing their rivals down.

From the window of their appointed tiring room, Roag looked out and noted the positions of these men who held England in their fists. Each of his players had his task; each knew whom he was to kill first. At the sign – the utterance of the word *Nonsuch* – he would lunge forward and strike Essex to the ground; Paget would kill Sir Robert Cecil, and Ratbane would see to frail Burghley. The Irishmen, Seamus and Hugh Fitzgerald, had orders to slaughter Southampton and Egerton, then turn on Puckering and Heneage. They would do the court in one by one, as many as God allowed.

And Beatrice? She would stab the Queen through the heart.

He spotted Richard Topcliffe, the white-haired torturer, crossing the courtyard, towards his Queen. Two guards appeared and shook their heads, turning him back. So Topcliffe was out of gaol; Roag laughed. He might be free, but it did not seem as though he was back in favour. It occurred to him, however, that Topcliffe could be dangerous. Despite his years, he was strong and deadly. Given the chance, he would delight in playing the man of action here. Well, Roag would not give him the chance. After Essex, he would attack the white dog.

In the second tier of seats, he saw his patrons, the four ladies. What would he have done without such useful, hapless fools? They had been his passport to this occasion; he doubted they would enjoy the evening.

John Shakespeare blacked out and slid from his horse two miles short of Nonsuch, crunching down on his shoulder. The pain shook him back to groggy consciousness. He rose to his hands and knees and tried to gather his thoughts.

Boltfoot dismounted instantly and knelt at his side. 'Master, you cannot go on.'

'I must.'

'I will go alone.' Boltfoot turned to Hooft, who had also reined in. 'Mr Hooft, stay here with Mr Shakespeare. If you can summon help, do so, but do not let him try to follow. I will return for you both when I can.'

Shakespeare nodded. 'You are right, I slow you down. Go, Boltfoot. Ride!'

Boltfoot remounted his horse and kicked on into a canter. The going was easy from here, lush countryside and parkland. He should be at Nonsuch within ten minutes, God willing.

They were ready. Every man primed: ready to kill and die. They were in their court costumes, each man attired as an English hero of Elizabeth's long reign. The words were well learnt; they would declaim in turn, and act out the great events of the past thirty-seven years, until the audience was lulled and unprepared, and the guards dozing. Roag was Burghley in his red velvet gown, his black, ermine-lined cape, his black velvet hat and his white staff of office. His *deadly* white staff.

The likeness of Drake was there, Essex and Hatton, too, Leicester and Sidney. And all with masks of gold and swords of finest Toledo steel hidden in their wooden toys. With hearts of iron, they walked from the tiring-house, through a series of passageways to the back of the stage. They waited until, at a signal from the Master of Revels, they strode out and took their bow. This was the beginning; they would say their lines of poetry, act out their parts, until the fell moment came that they would descend upon their enemies like wolves. Surprise would win them the day. In battle, surprise was everything.

Leading his companions, Regis Roag took his bow, then looked up, ready to embark on his great enterprise. But instead of an appreciative audience, agog with anticipation, he was faced with two solid lines of soldiers, separating them from their quarry. Two lines of men armed with swords, hagbuts and crossbows.

'You will drop your weapons!' a captain called, marching towards them. 'Drop them now, then fall to your knees with your hands above your heads.'

Roag looked about him at his five gold-masked companions, all staring at him through the eye-slits in their vizards, desperate for guidance. This was not how it was supposed to be. He drew his thin rapier from the white stick of office.

'Nonsuch!' he shouted. 'Attack!'

He drove forward, sword held out like a lance. Around him he heard the twang and whisper of a dozen crossbow bolts. Beatrice lunged forward at his side and crumpled with a dull gasp, a bolt embedded in her chest. Roag launched himself at the middle of the line of soldiers, roaring and snarling like a great cat of the Africas. The shock and ferocity of his charge tore the soldiers apart at their very heart, and he pushed through, stabbing at one with his rapier and ripping the short sword from his hand. And then he was there, facing his foe, the entire royal court of England, all now standing, looking at him in astonishment. He hesitated, suddenly overwhelmed with the power that lay in his hands.

Unsheathing their swords, the Queen's senior courtiers ran down the steps from the royal gallery to confront him. All of them – Essex, Southampton and the rest – were skilled swordsmen, having studied the art since early childhood. He had no hope against any of them. The soldiers at his back had already turned on him. He glanced this way and that, rapier in one hand, short sword in the other. He saw that his band – the Fitzgerald brothers, Paget, Ratbane, Beatrice – had all fallen, riddled with bolts or hacked down with swords. Roag was alone. His eyes fell upon the four women whose pass had gained him entrance to this place. They were but two paces away.

As a sword-thrust came at him from a soldier, he lurched sideways, dropped the rapier and grasped the wrist of the nearest woman, Lady Lucia Trevail.

A strong man with the rage of battle in him, he dragged her into the crook of his arm and thrust the short sword at her heart so that it slashed into her damson and gold gown and nicked her flesh. 'Stay back or she dies!'

They did hold back and he began to inch away from them. Roag's only hope now was escape, yet it was slender enough with a dozen or more soldiers and courtiers advancing on him.

Lucia struggled against him, but his arm was curled tight about her throat. He pulled her back into the outer courtyard, then increased his pace, wrenching her into a stumbling backward run towards the gatehouse.

As he came over the rise of a hill and steadied his mount, Boltfoot realised that something was amiss. A bugle was blaring and soldiers were streaming in through the main gatehouse. He dug his heels into the horse's flanks and urged it on towards the avenue of oaks that lined the approach.

Through the wind at his ears, he heard shouting, then two gunshots and screams from somewhere within the palace grounds.

Suddenly, there was movement at the gatehouse. A man in a golden mask and lavish robes emerged on foot, stumbling backwards like a stag at bay. He had his arm around a woman's neck, a short sword poised to strike her, holding a squadron of soldiers at arm's length.

Boltfoot slid down from his horse and drew his cutlass. He had no plan, but he saw a man with a sword to a woman's breast and knew he had to stop him. The man was not looking behind him, so he did not see Boltfoot loping towards him, dragging his club-foot along the soft grassy path.

Out of the corner of his eye, Boltfoot saw soldiers approaching from the left and right. They halted, uncertain what to do, but Boltfoot did not hesitate. As he came up behind the man and the woman, the man turned and rasped, 'Get away!'

Boltfoot slashed down with his cutlass on to the man's sword arm. The action dragged the swordpoint through the woman's gown, but the man had already lost his grip. The blade flew up into the air and spun away from him. The man screamed, his forearm shattered by Boltfoot's crushing blow.

The woman fell to one side, out of the man's grasp. Boltfoot was immediately on to him, wrestling him to the ground. 'Assist me!' he shouted to the soldiers.

As he struggled, Boltfoot saw the glint of a blade out of the corner of his eye. Suddenly the woman was on her knees beside him, a dagger in her hand. As Boltfoot held the assailant down, she lunged forward and thrust her dagger deep into the man's throat.

Chapter 43

S HAKESPEARE HAD HAD his fill of Newgate. It was a place of pain, the ante-room to slaughter. He had visited Father Robert Southwell there, and then Frank Mills. Each time the stench of death and ordure grew stronger. Yet now he was there again, to talk with the one called Dick Winnow, the only survivor of the band of assassins. He had been picked up five miles from Nonsuch and after initial denial had confessed all.

He lay in chains, his body broken by the rack. In the morning he would face the bloody passage to death known as hanging, drawing and quartering – godly butchery, as some would have it.

Shakespeare looked on him with pity and spoke softly. 'I believe you are a sea captain, Mr Winnow.'

'I was. Yes.'

'Tell me your story . . .'

Winnow's voice was faint but clear. 'My father was a fisher out of Yarmouth in Norfolk, but he and my mother held to the Catholic way, the true way, and were ever harangued by the parish priest and the justice with fines for recusancy. From an early age – from birth, almost – I was cut adrift from the society of my fellows. After my father was lost at sea, a mocking letter arrived, unsigned, that said his boat had been deliberately holed before he sailed. "*So drown all papists*," it said.'

Shakespeare listened in silence. The tale had the ring of truth; many had been persecuted for their religion. His own family had suffered at the hands of Topcliffe and others. He nodded.

'I inherited money on my father's death, but I knew that I could stay no longer in Yarmouth without committing murder or being murdered, so I invested it all in a bark to take me away from Norfolk. I desired only to live in peace and hoped to earn my wealth trading between the coasts of England and the countries of Europe. But it was not easy, for my faith seemed to follow me like a slavering dog. Mariners did not like to serve with me, nor pilots. Then I heard tell that money was to be earned bringing sherry wines and tobacco from Andalusia, to break the embargo. But it was an ill wind that sent me there, for I was seized by the Inquisition and condemned as an English spy. That is, until Regis Roag and Ovid Sloth came to my aid. They said I could help them rid England of the Protestant tyranny.'

'What did Roag promise you?'

'He said that many thousands of lives would be saved by a simple act of justice. Good English men and women, now suffering under the yoke of a heretical dictator, would be set free. I knew what he meant, for I saw how my family had suffered. It was not spoken of, but I think I knew all along that my own survival was impossible. Yet it seemed a worthy use of my worthless life.'

'Who was behind the conspiracy?'

'I am not certain of its origins, but Roag was the leader and Sloth had the means. He was desperate for gold. He owed a great deal to Spanish moneylenders and was being threatened. The crafting of those swords of fine, sharp Toledo steel that we concealed within wooden toys: that was Sloth's doing. He also provided lodging, and assistance for us to perfect our skills as players and swordsmen. But authorisation had to come from the *casa de contratación*. A man may not fart on that coast without the house of trade's permission. The *casa* dithered and debated the matter for many weeks, but their decision never seemed to be in doubt and we departed at the allotted time. I suppose they reasoned that the death of Elizabeth could do nothing but enhance the claims of the Infanta Isabella to the throne of England.'

'Did the conspiracy begin in Spain?'

'No, here in England, that is all I know. I was told no more than I needed to know. None of us was.'

'Who were the others, the men who died at Nonsuch?'

'The Fitzgerald brothers, Hugh and Seamus. Ovid Sloth found them in the Irish College at Salamanca, where they were training for the priesthood. They were obedient and too stupid to know fear. They wanted nothing more than to fight and kill.'

'There were two more men . . .'

'Ratbane and Paget. They were lower than dogs, dredged up by the Spanish from the barrel of the renegade English regiment of the Low Countries. They would do what they were told and would not blink in the face of enemy fire. They spent their days fighting and their nights whoring and drinking. They are better dead.'

Winnow was in great pain. As well as the rack, he had been beaten without pity. He shifted position and groaned.

Shakespeare pressed on. 'Tell me about the College of St Gregory. Did you meet Persons? What of his assistant, Joseph Creswell? What was their part?'

'They came to me when I was held by the Inquisition. I could not swear what they knew of the plot, but I can tell you that Roag visited them often. He needed Father Persons's influence with the *casa*. But though Roag needed him, he did not trust him or anyone else at the college. He thought there were spies in their midst.'

'Was there talk of one particular spy?'

Winnow looked up at Shakespeare through a watery, blood-lined eye. 'I heard of one young man, caught writing a coded letter and taken to the Castillo de Triana. Was he yours?'

'What was his name?'

'I don't know.'

'What became of him?'

'You must know what the Inquisition does to heretics.'

Shakespeare felt sick at heart. Poor Robert Warner. A mere twenty-one years of age, he had been so courageous in agreeing to work under cover at St Gregory's. Revulsion welled up in Shakespeare at the thought of the Inquisition. It was a perversion of everything that Christ had stood for. And as for the traitor Persons, the Englishman who had blessed the Armada, he *must* have known everything. He had connived at cold murder – the killing of Loake, Trott, poor Ambrose Rowse, Anthony Friday, and the Queen of England herself.

'Mr Winnow, does the name Garrick Loake mean anything to you?'

'No.'

'Anthony Friday?'

'Yes, I was there at his death. It became clear to Roag that Friday had realised what we intended to do with the play he had written. He had to be silenced.'

'There was a paper there, one you left. It had three words on it: *They are cousins*. What does that mean?'

'I don't know.'

'What of Wisbech Castle and the priests imprisoned there? Men such as William Weston and Gavin Caldor? Do you know of them?'

As he asked the question, a sudden thought occurred to

Shakespeare. He would look more closely into Loake's family background . . .

'Again, no. I repeat, Mr Shakespeare, I know nothing of Wisbech nor the origins of the plan. All I know of this is what little I was told in Spain and what we did when we landed.'

'Ah, yes, the raid on the Cornish villages. What was the purpose of that?'

'We had to come into England as one and stay together. It was Roag's suggestion to attack Cornwall as a cover for our landing. The *casa* seized on the idea and provided a small fleet. I think it amused them to burn parts of the west country from where so many of their tormentors hailed – Drake, Hawkins, Grenville, Ralegh. They were astonished by the lack of defence put up against them. Why, we even said mass on the clifftop and the Spaniards promised to build an abbey there when they returned.'

Shakespeare shook his head. He would take this information to Cecil without delay; Cornwall must be reinforced.

'Who helped you in England?'

'Sloth again, but also the girl Beatrice. They had everything organised for us. We avoided inns and slept in the open air as we came to London.'

'Did you stay at a great house in Cornwall? Trevail Hall?'

Winnow shook his head. 'We had a tent. Sloth provided it for us and made us appear a genuine company of players. He had commissioned a play for us to say, and costumes and masks to wear. He used his influence with certain ladies to arrange our performance before the Queen.'

'Did you have any contact with Lady Trevail?'

'No. I know nothing of her.'

The suspicion was like an angry wasp in an enclosed room: impossible to ignore. Perhaps he had been taught too well by Mr Secretary Walsingham. Always looking for *the plot behind the plot.* Shakespeare could not get away from the doubts he harboured. Why did Lucia Trevail go down to Cornwall? Why did she go with Beatrice Eastley? And yet Lucia had been held by Roag at the point of a sword and was now the heroine of the day.

'What did you know of these ladies?'

Winnow was shackled by neck irons. He shook his head and his mouth opened in a rictus of pain. 'Nothing. I believe they knew Roag from his days at the Theatre, but we were to meet them only on the day of the performance.'

'Tell me more. Confess your crimes. Beg forgiveness of your maker before you meet him and hear his judgment. There were two more deaths . . .'

Winnow closed his eyes and grimaced with pain. 'I heard that a man and a woman were killed. Beatrice told the story to us. She said they were naked in bed together and she laughed. They had been Cecil's spies, she said. All his intelligencers were to be eliminated.'

'Their names?'

'She told us, but—'

'Mills? Was it Frank Mills and his wife?'

'Yes, that name sounds familiar. Mills. She told me Mills . . .'

Shakespeare sighed. Mills had indeed been innocent all along. The murders of his wife and her lover had been a matter of mistaken identity.

So much death and pain, and for what? Far from easing the lot of England's Catholics, these conspirators had probably made their lives much harder. Somehow they all needed to cross the divide, as he had once done, when he married Catherine. They had to realise they shared the same God and the same holy book; only the politics of vain, angry men divided them.

Chapter 44

THE BED IN Shakespeare's chamber was hot and damp with lust. Two bodies sprawled upon it, one tall and angular and adorned with bandages, the other slender and soft. Lucia Trevail turned over on to her front and exhaled deeply. Shakespeare sat up against the bedhead, catching his breath, all spent.

There was no tender dealing here. Their couplings were nothing but wanton greed and hunger. A brutal, desperate collision of bodies. There had been no time for small murmurings and fragrant kisses; they had merely pulled off each other's clothes in a frenzied tearing of stays and seams.

She reached out her slender arm and touched the bandages that still decorated his chest and shoulders. Her hand was light and warm.

'The wounds are healing well,' he said by way of conversation. 'I have my energy back.'

Food and plenty of water, along with herbal preparations from Dr Forman, had helped him recover more quickly than he might have dared hope.

'So I see.'

He laughed. She had been showered with diamonds by the Queen and fêted by courtiers. All had expressed awe and wonder at her courage when dragged away at swordpoint by a murderous savage.

'You know, Mr Shakespeare, you might have saved everyone a great deal of trouble and fear if you had allowed us ladies some intellect. Had you but entrusted us with information about your inquiries – your search for Mr Roag and Mr Sloth – we would have known straightway that there was something rotten about their plans to stage a masque for the Queen. But no, you would not have it, so how were we to know anything was amiss? None of you men will credit us with any wit.'

It seemed that her little group, her School of Day, as Lady Susan liked to call their intellectual gatherings, had been used most cynically by Ovid Sloth. And yet, at the end, it was this very same group that had proved the conspirators' undoing.

In particular, it had been the good sense of Margaret, the Countess of Cumberland, that had been decisive. There had been something about Roag that had roused her suspicions when they met him rehearsing at his pavilion in the park of Nonsuch.

'Instinct, sir,' she had told Shakespeare later when he called on the group at the house in Barbican Street. 'As a wild animal senses a hunter, I smelt it on him. He had the unholy stench of impending death. That, allied to the fear raised by the powerful military presence, alarmed me greatly.'

The intense feeling had stayed with the countess all day, but she had not acted on it. It was only as the evening drew on, and as fear gnawed at her, that she had confided in Emilia Lanier.

Emilia had known exactly what to do. She had gone straight to Lord Chamberlain Hunsdon and told him of the countess's fears. By this time, Roag and his group were inside the palace, closeted in the tiring room where they were putting the finishing touches to their costumes, donning masks of gold and checking their weapons in readiness for their blood-drenched performance.

Hunsdon did not waste a moment. He called out the

Queen's Lifeguard. The confrontation between the guards and the would-be assassins had been a moment of high drama: enjoyed immensely by Her Majesty but less so by her chief ministers, Burghley and Cecil.

In the fray that followed, a young Lifeguard had suffered a cut to the ribs from the assault by Roag, but his life was not in danger. The only other blood shed was that of Regis Roag's mercenaries. All had died on the stage. A hue and cry had immediately been set up for confederates and Winnow had been caught within the hour.

Shakespeare had asked Cecil in vain that he be spared the rack. 'He will die horribly, Sir Robert. Is it necessary to have Topcliffe break him first?'

'As squeamish as ever, John?'

'I would not treat the lowest creature on God's earth the way he treats his prisoners.'

'And yet *you* were tortured by this unholy band. For that was what your so-called exorcism amounted to, did it not?'

Shakespeare nodded.

'Fear not,' Cecil continued. 'Topcliffe might be out of gaol, but he is not back in favour. He will be consigned to his country estates where he can devote his energies to his peat and ironworks. Mr Winnow will face the rack, but it will not be Topcliffe who operates it.'

Shakespeare had his doubts. The thought of Topcliffe forgoing the pleasure of persecution was like a swift giving up the air: it would happen only at death.

Here in Shakespeare's chamber, however, such dark thoughts were very distant. He stretched and yawned. Lucia Trevail nestled closer to him and began to stroke him once again.

He gasped. 'You are a wanton, Lady Trevail.'

'Thank you, Mr Shakespeare.'

Again, he wondered about her. *You shoot at Spaniards and*

you stab a man to death with a dagger to the throat. Your skin is soft, but your heart is steel, mistress. What was he, John Shakespeare, to her?

'Am I nothing but a scratching post on which to pleasure yourself as the need takes you?' he asked her.

'You are indeed a fine post. Wood, strong and hard.'

He thought back to Cornwall. The way he had gone to Trevail House to spy her out. He thought of confessing the suspicions he still held, but decided against it. *Never reveal more than you need, John.* That had been one of Sir Francis Walsingham's first strictures.

Instead his hand went between her thighs and he pulled her to him once more.

In the evening, when Shakespeare woke, she was gone. There was no note. He smiled to himself. She was an uncommon woman.

With the sun slanting in from the west through the leaded pane, he rose from the bed, dressed at a leisurely pace and wandered downstairs. He longed for his family to come home from the Cecil mansion; yet the outcome of the conspiracy left many questions unanswered and he could not risk the girls' lives until all was settled.

The warning had been clear enough: little Grace and Mary would die if Shakespeare did not cease his inquiries. Who remained out there to exact revenge?

One question above all still troubled him: why had they killed the old nun, Sister Michael? He had put the matter to Dick Winnow in Newgate.

'We found her body at the same time as you did, Mr Shakespeare.'

'We?'

'Roag, Paget, Ratbane and me. The body was there, warm

and newly dead. Stabbed through the heart. Roag did not seem surprised; he merely laughed.'

'Did Beatrice do this?'

'Possibly. She was mad enough.'

And then there was the matter of Paul Hooft. Shakespeare wished to know more about his movements, but that could wait.

He drew a cup of ale from the keg in the kitchen and sipped it, then spat it out. It was stale and foul. It was time for Jane to come home and organise them all; brew some fresh ale and beer, and fetch good food from the market. He was longing to hear the chatter of Grace, Mary and Ursula, and once again turn this house back into a family home.

There was a knock at the door. He opened it, hoping to find Lucia again, but a young woman stood before him. She looked vaguely familiar.

'Yes?'

'I want to talk to you, Mr Shakespeare.'

'I know you, don't I?' he said, searching his memory.

'You should know every inch of me,' she said and gave him a look of brazen amusement.

Her audacious look brought back his memory. She had been Dr Forman's bedmate when he had called at the house in Fylpot Street before travelling to Cornwall.

'It's Janey, isn't it? May I ask what this is about?'

At Forman's house he had thought her rather plain, though full of sensual promise. Now, fully clothed and with her hair untangled and combed back from her face, he found her quite striking. As he looked at her, his eye was suddenly caught by a small mark above her right eyebrow. It was faint, but he would swear it was shaped like a new moon – a crescent moon.

Her hand went to the mark and she nodded. 'You know about that, I take it.'

Oh yes, he knew about the crescent moon.

He nodded. 'Yes, yes I do.'

'Then you must know that my name is not Janey, but Thomasyn.' She met his gaze, looking for his reaction. 'Thomasyn Jade. I believe you have been looking for me.'

Shakespeare smiled. 'I am very glad to make your acquaintance, mistress. I doubt you know how glad, for it enables me to fulfil a promise I made to a good man.'

'That fool Southwell—'

'Why do you call him a fool?'

'For getting himself killed for a childish superstition, that is why.'

'Perhaps he was misguided, but he was a good man for all that. And he wished well of you. Now, if you would care to repair to the Swan with me, I have a thirst that must be quenched and a hunger that must be satisfied. Step inside while I fetch my purse.'

The tavern was crowded with drinkers, but they pushed past some drunks and found a corner for themselves in a tiny partitioned booth.

'This place is so small it's like being locked away in a cupboard,' Thomasyn complained. 'And no one knows better than I what a cupboard is like, for they kept me prisoner for months, moved me from house to house, locked me in cupboards and cellars. Every day from dawn to dusk and beyond, they kept me tied to chairs and assailed me with their wicked rituals until I did come to believe I had demons within me.' She smiled ruefully. 'Buy me a gage of Mad Dog, Mr Shakespeare, for I have a desire to get as cup-shotten as a constable this evening.'

Summoning the potboy, he ordered a quart of spiced beer for Thomasyn and a flagon of Gascon wine for himself, as well as a trencher of cold beef pie, eggs and salad, for he had a mighty hunger.

'I trust you will excuse my ill manners in eating while you merely drink, mistress?'

'Fill your belly, Mr Shakespeare.'

'You have a story to tell, I think.'

She nodded. 'I do, if you wish to listen. But first I have an apology to make. You see, I have known for quite some time that you have been looking for me and I have done my best not to be found. I was worried that you had come to spy me out, so I tried to frighten you off.'

The potboy arrived with their beer and wine. Shakespeare watched her as she supped a deep draught of beer and waited for her to continue.

'It was me that left that note with the girl you keep, Ursula.'

Shakespeare frowned. 'What are you saying?'

'I wrote that letter that threatened you. I never meant it. I wouldn't harm a rat. Well, I would harm a rat, of course, but not a little girl . . .'

'You did that?'

'Yes.' She said the word very quietly.

Slowly, as the enormity of her words dawned, anger welled up within him.

'So that was you all along, the vile letter? We have all been scared out of mind for nothing?'

She nodded again and looked down into her beer.

'You even put their names, Grace and Mary, and all in the shape of a cross. In blood!'

'It was unforgivable.'

'But why?'

'Because I was scared myself. I thought you had sent your servant Jane Cooper to Simon's house to spy me out. I couldn't let you find me and I didn't want to run again.'

'But you threatened my children! In God's name, you sit here and drink beer with me, and tell me you sent a letter in blood threatening that my young girls would be harmed or even killed! Why would you do such a thing?'

She put a hand to her forehead and clenched it. Then she shook herself, took another sip of beer and placed her hands flat on the ale-sticky oak table. Taking a deep breath, she looked around as though they might be watched or overheard.

'Whatever it is, you *will* tell me.'

'Yes, I will. I say just this in my defence. I have known such fear and horror that I cannot bear to even think on it. I know you have done many brave things, Mr Shakespeare, but they were manly feats of arms. I know, too, from Simon Forman that you suffered one night at their wicked hands. But what I endured was the destruction of my soul, piece by piece over many months.'

'The exorcisms?'

'I thought you were sent by them to bring me back. I thought this time they would finish what was started and kill me.'

'But, Mistress Jade, your tormentors were all captured. Many were executed. Father Weston languishes in Wisbech Castle. Why would you think he could harm you from there? Indeed, why did you ever run from the safe harbour you had found in the home of Lady Susan, the Countess of Kent?'

'Because I saw her and knew I was in danger.'

Shakespeare's food arrived and he pushed it away irritably. 'Whom did you see? The old nun, Sister Michael?'

'Oh no, Mr Shakespeare, you do not understand at all. Sister Michael was my one friend in the world. She persuaded Father Southwell to intervene and put an end to the exorcisms. It was she who took me to safety in London and found me refuge. I could not have survived without her. Why do you think she hid away at Denham? Why do you think they killed her in your stables, Mr Shakespeare? Because they knew what she had done and she refused to tell them where I was. They wanted to get me because I was the only one that knew the truth. Poor Sister Michael was not the one I saw. The one I was fleeing was the one who ran it all, the one who was always there, urging them on, doing filthy things to me, stabbing me with needles, sticking bones and other disgusting things into me, forcing my legs apart and squirting strange liquids into me. And as soon as I saw her at Lady Susan's house, I ran.'

All Shakespeare's appetite had dissipated. He drank a goblet in one swallow. The horror unfolding was too much to hear.

'You know her name, Mr Shakespeare, for I saw her leaving your house this very day. I know all about her and her evil desires. The one I am still not sure of is *you*.'

Chapter 45

Shakespeare was disappointed and horrified, but not shocked; he had never lost his suspicions of her, even as she lay in his bed. He had not even persuaded himself that his suspicions were false; he had simply put them to one side.

So Thomasyn Jade fled from the sanctuary of Lady Susan's house because she saw Lucia Trevail.

Shakespeare was silent a few moments as he took in the story that Thomasyn Jade had told him.

'When you saw Lady Trevail at Lady Susan's gathering, why did you not simply report her if she was your tormentor?'

'To whom?' Thomasyn demanded. 'I was terrified.'

'To the other ladies in the group, the justice, the sheriff – even the Privy Council.'

'I didn't trust any of them. As far as I knew, the whole of England was of one mind. All bent on my destruction. You should have seen the gentlemen and nobles who crowded into the exorcisms. What power did I, Thomasyn Jade, the dirty common harlot from Denham, have against such men and women? Who would listen to me if I reported them? I was cornered like a bear at the baiting. Sister Michael was the only one who showed me kindness. She tried to persuade Weston and the other priests to be more gentle with me, but she had little influence with them. She was the only one I could trust and so I ran from London back to Denham, for I knew she would still be there and hoped she would shelter me.'

'What happened next?'

'Poor Sister Michael had no idea what to do for me, for I was close to madness. She needed a safe place for me – and she needed a healer. Eventually, she recalled hearing that Dean Blague had given refuge to another victim of exorcism – a girl servant much vexed with spirits – and approached him on my behalf. Blague is a good man and took me in without question. His wife knew Forman well and she took me to him. I went there many times.'

'How did he help you?'

'He cast my horoscope. He gave me soothing herbs – and he talked with me. Dr Forman brought me back to health. He may be a goat or a satyr, but he is a true healer of bodies and souls. Gradually I became well again. Simon Forman is a good man, though many speak ill of him.'

Shakespeare nodded. The doctor had helped save his life.

All London now knew of the deadly events at Nonsuch, but there was still one question that had to be asked.

'Do you believe Lucia Trevail was part of the conspiracy to assassinate the Queen and her courtiers?'

'I am certain of it, but that is for you to find out and prove, Mr Shakespeare. I also believe she killed Sister Michael – or ordered her killing – to silence her. I consider her capable of anything. Men testified that they saw demons running up my leg into my womanhood and others crawling, defeated, from my mouth. I saw but one demon in all the exorcisms I endured, and its name was Lady Trevail.'

Shakespeare froze. So at the end she had killed Roag not out of rage at being taken hostage, but to silence him, too; he was the one man who knew the truth about her. But he, Shakespeare, had suspected the truth, too – hadn't he?

I had my eye on her, and then I took it off. Now she is heading back to Nonsuch Palace, trusted by the highest in the land, with unfettered access to Gloriana herself. None would think to search her gowns for a long-bladed dagger or a wheel-lock pistol . . .

Nonsuch glowed in the night as he rode up to the gatehouse. The captain of the guard was in no mood to admit anyone without first scrutinising his letters of pass with meticulous care, and then checking them again.

'Who are you?'

'John Shakespeare, as it says on my pass. You have seen me a dozen times or more, Captain.'

'Why are you here? The palace is asleep.'

'I have urgent business with Sir Robert Cecil.'

'I will have to have these letters checked.'

'Captain, I believe you erred once before in admitting men with swords disguised as toys. I suggest you do not make another deadly error by barring me. Now let me in.'

The captain seemed put out. 'Very well, Mr Shakespeare, I will escort you in myself. But you must first hand me your sword and dagger.'

Shakespeare removed his weapons and held them, hilt first, across his palms.

The captain took them and handed them to one of his men. 'Look after these.' He nodded to Shakespeare. 'Come with me.'

They marched quickly through the outer courtyard and thence to the inner quad, which was ablaze with cressets of burning coals and lanterns by the walls. Three minor courtiers stood by the fountain, drinking themselves into oblivion. Otherwise, all was quiet.

'In here,' the captain said as they approached a door.

They entered a small ante-room where a steward immediately jumped up from his seat and stepped forward.

'This is John Shakespeare, assistant secretary to Sir Robert Cecil. He wishes to see him. Says it's urgent.'

The steward bowed to Shakespeare. 'Sir Robert is asleep, sir. Is this urgent enough to wake him?'

'Yes.'

'Then come with me, if you will.' He turned to the captain. 'That will be all.'

'Can you vouch for this man?'

'Yes, Captain, I know Mr Shakespeare well. Now return to your post.'

Cecil was not asleep. He was at the desk in his chamber, working on documents by the light of half a dozen candles. His eyes were dark with fatigue and his fingers were stained with ink.

'Come in, John.' He signalled to the steward. 'Fetch wine and some food for Mr Shakespeare. He looks as though he needs it.'

The steward bowed and departed.

'Now then, John, what is it?'

'It is Lady Lucia Trevail, Sir Robert. Is she in the Privy Chamber?'

'Why?'

'Because I have discovered reason to suspect that she was part of the conspiracy against the Queen's person.'

Cecil put down his quill. 'Well, she is not here. I know this because Her Royal Majesty was asking after her this evening. She wished to play some hands of primero with her. The Queen was exceeding displeased at her absence.'

'Thank the Lord . . .'

'John, sit down. I think you had better tell me exactly what you have discovered.'

Chapter 46

ON THE DAY of the homecoming, Jane immediately set to cleaning the house. Bustling about, she opened the windows, organised the laundry, dusted the floors and put down new rushes. Ursula forsook her stall for the day and helped her with the housework. Little John tagged along, trying to help but merely managing to be disruptive. Boltfoot, meanwhile, hid in the stables with his pipe, cleaning his caliver and oiling his cutlass.

Shakespeare spent some time with Grace and Mary, telling them about Andrew's new ship, the *Defiance*, with its figurehead shaped like a lion. He told them, too, of the day the Spanish had landed in Cornwall and how the brave Cornishmen had thrown them back into the sea whence they came. Finally, he tested them on the lessons they had learnt in Cecil's household and was pleased to discover they had been taught well.

He then told the girls to go and help Jane and Ursula, while he retired to his solar to catch up on reading intercepts and correspondence. More than anything, he longed to have word of young Robert Warner, the intelligencer he had sent incognito to the College of Gregory in Seville, but there was nothing. After a while there was a knock at the door.

'Come in.'

Jane stepped in with little John at her heels. Shakespeare noted how the boy was blossoming, as was she, back to her old, comely self. He found himself staring at her bosom, which seemed riper and fuller than he could recall in recent months. He looked up at her face. 'Forgive me . . .'

She smiled.

'Jane, are you—'

She nodded and her hand went instinctively to her belly, though there was nothing showing as yet.

'That is good news. I am delighted for you both.'

'I haven't told Boltfoot yet.'

'Well, I won't say a word.' Shakespeare turned back to his paperwork.

'I do believe that Dr Forman's potions have helped. He has made me believe the baby will come to term.'

Shakespeare had to laugh. 'I am sure Boltfoot had some part to play in your good fortune. In the meantime, I will pray for you.'

'But he also said that I would experience a death.'

'I think it the nature of astrologers that as many of their predictions are in error as correct. God alone is without fault.'

Jane hastily delved into her apron pocket. 'But it was not about me that I came to you, master. It was for this.'

He looked up and saw that she was holding a large needle.

'A sailmaker?'

'I found it while I was changing your bedding, master. It was beneath the cushions, pinned into the mattress.'

She put the needle down on the table in front of him.

He picked it up and turned it in his fingers. In the wrong hands it was a diabolical implement, as his perforated body testified. Had Lucia Trevail and Beatrice Eastley used this to kill Garrick Loake when they suspected he was about to betray their approach to him? Or perhaps it was another needle, just like it.

The thought of Beatrice and Lucia, killing together, both soaked in blood, sent a shiver to his heart. Poor Loake, deep in debt and a Catholic: he must have seemed a certain recruit to their cause. And, as Shakespeare now knew from his inquiries into Loake's family connections, he would have been recommended to the conspirators highly, for he had a cousin at Wisbech Castle: a young lay brother by the name of Gavin Caldor, connected to the Theatre just as Loake had been. The nervous young man who had pissed himself with fear at the thought of his own torture and death – surely that callow, terrified youth could not have had the diabolical brilliance to devise such a plot, unless he was a play-actor of uncommon gifts? Yet he was certainly involved.

That was what Anthony Friday had been trying to tell him with his scratched message: *They are cousins.*

'Does the needle mean something to you, master?'

'Yes,' he said.

Had Lucia meant to kill him before changing her mind? Was it a warning, or merely a little farewell gift?

'It is something I mislaid. A thing of no value. Thank you, Jane.'

He put it to one side.

There had been no word of Lucia Trevail. None of her friends from the School of Day had any idea where she might be, and all had been utterly shocked and bewildered by the secret side of her that they had never known.

'I simply cannot believe that Lucia had anything to do with those devilish people,' Lady Susan, the Countess of Kent, had told him.

'Which of you had the idea of putting on the masque for the Queen?'

The countess had thought for a moment. 'Why, yes, that was Lucia's notion.'

'And which of you commissioned Mr Sloth to organise it?'

'Well, I am sure that must have been Lucia, too.'

Shakespeare had sighed and said no more. Had Father Weston sent Beatrice to Lucia when she fled Wisbech? It seemed mighty probable. They had been partners in treason all along. Lucia had brought her into Lady Susan's circle, believing she would be protected from suspicion there; perhaps she had even introduced her to Regis Roag.

And then Lucia and Beatrice had travelled down to Cornwall together to await the arrival of Roag and his men, and to assist them in the initial stages of their mission. But something had happened to unsettle them before they reached Trevail Hall, and they had decided to part and meet again later. Perhaps someone got word to them that Shakespeare was on their trail with orders to apprehend Beatrice. Perhaps one of Lucia's servants had been watching him? Was it perhaps the same servant who told them later that Ovid Sloth was to be taken by sea to Falmouth? This was all surmise, but it made sense.

The ladies of the School of Day would come to their own conclusions about Lucia. Cecil had raised a hue and cry, ordering searchers and pursuivants to all her properties and any known haunts. The ports had been alerted. Word had been sent post-haste to Godolphin in Cornwall to seize her and bring her to London, should she arrive at Trevail Hall, but Shakespeare knew she would not be found.

He would never know the truth about Lucia and Roag. Something told him they had been lovers, but, again, this was nothing more than instinct and surmise.

*

Jane was leaving the room. He called her back.

'I will be away for a few days, but when I return, we will have a feast. There will be nine of us – ten including little John. This includes you, Jane. You are to commission the Swan Inn to provide food and servants – and then leave the work to them. *All* the work. You are to do nothing towards it, is that understood?'

'Yes, master.'

'I want good Gascon wine and fresh beer. There are to be three roasts – a sirloin of beef, a turkey cock and a leg of mutton. There will be salads, sweetmeats, fruit pies and sylla-bubs. If they can manage a subtlety of jelly, I would like that, too. In the shape of a lion as a tribute to Andrew and his ship. And, remember, their best potboys will serve us. Tell them they will be well paid, so take no disobedience from them. Is that clear?'

'Yes, master.'

He wasn't convinced. He knew Jane too well. She would never relax. The novelty of sitting at table, being waited on, would be simply too great.

'Send Boltfoot to me, if you please.'

'Sit down, Boltfoot,' Shakespeare said. 'Light your pipe.'

Boltfoot looked about him suspiciously, as though someone were trying to gull him.

'I want to thank you for saving me, and I want to ask you once again about Mr Hooft. What did he say when he came to you?'

Boltfoot limped to the settle and sat down.

'He said he had been following you, master. He had ven-tured to London, believing you might lead him to Sorrow Gray, the maid he was to have married. That is all he said.'

'Did you believe him?'

'I thought it mighty strange, but most welcome. Without him, I would never have found you.'

Paul Hooft, short-trimmed beard, fair and austere, smiled stiffly at Shakespeare as he welcomed him to his abbey farm home on the edge of fens. The waters had receded now, leaving dry land where once there had been a sea.

Shakespeare did not smile back.

'Can I offer you refreshment, sir?'

'No, I am not staying.'

'That is a great shame. I would welcome some company. We have much to talk about. Please, come through to my with-drawing room and sit awhile.'

'No. I will stand here. I owe much to you, Mr Hooft. Not only did you save Mr Cooper and me from the flooded fens, but you led Boltfoot to the place where I was lately held captive. So I thank you twice over.'

'It was my duty and pleasure, sir. For as I have said before, I owe my life and liberty to your great Queen and country.'

'And yet there is much that I find troubling and puzzling—'

'Mr Shakespeare, please, I am a simple soul. I was besotted with that woman and came to find her. I now know how wrong I was to follow you as I did. I should have come to you and told you my business straight. But I must thank the Lord that I was enabled to save your life.'

Shakespeare raised his hand. 'Let me speak. I have been thinking long and hard about the role you have played and it seems to me there is only one conclusion to be drawn.'

Hooft frowned. 'What are you saying, sir?'

'You know very well what I am saying. When first we met you on the road near Waterbeach, there was a suggestion that you had come from Cambridge, where we spotted you at the

Dolphin Inn. At the time we took you for a traveller, like us. Is that still your version of events?'

'Why, yes, I always stay at the Dolphin when I am in Cambridge. I was there for my trade.'

'Yes, you have told us of your business interests. You are a man of *many* interests. Farming, engineering, trading with the Low Countries.'

Hooft nodded.

'But, Mr Hooft, I suggest your journey did not start at Cambridge, but in London. What do you say to that?'

Hooft said nothing.

'I suggest not only that your journey started in London, but that you were following us all the time, and that was the sole purpose of your journey. I suggest, too, that you knew my name even before we met and that you knew where we were heading.'

'Why would I have followed you? I do not understand what you are suggesting. I am a farmer and a trader, nothing more—'

'But you have another interest: you are an intelligencer in the employ of the Dutch estates. You are engaged in espionage, sir. You may not be hostile, but you are still a spy. You are in the pay of a foreign power and have been trained in the role to a high degree. That is why I could never spot you, even though I knew I was being followed.'

Hooft shook his head, but it was a feeble, half-hearted denial.

'You have not merely engaged in observing and reporting back to your masters, but have actively fomented religious dissent here in the East of England. I say, Mr Hooft, that you have caused unrest in the fens among the more severe Calvinist and Puritan elements. You have stirred up rabble-rousing outside Wisbech Castle and you have undermined public order in the commonwealth. You may have saved my life, but you did so because it suited you.'

'Mr Shakespeare, everything I have done has been in the interests of England and Queen Bess.'

'No, it has been in the interests of the Dutch estates. It is mere coincidence that our requirements correspond with yours at the moment. Whose side would you take in a dispute between our two nations?'

Hooft rose from his seat, his back stiffened in a pose of defiance. 'This is preposterous. You come into my home and then accuse me of betraying you! Without me, you would be dead!'

'Betrayal. Yes, that is the word I was looking for. How do you think the Queen or Sir Robert Cecil would react if I told them about your double dealings?'

'They would thank me.'

Shakespeare snorted. 'You would be fortunate to be thrown out of the country with your life. Her Majesty likes Calvinists even less than she likes the Church of Rome. Her friendship for the Dutch estates is a mere convenience: two peoples joining forces against a mutual enemy, Spain. Least of all does she like strangers disturbing the peace of her realm.'

As he spoke, Shakespeare saw something in Hooft's face that he had not noted before – a sullen hardness. The soft features had been replaced by the ruthless, clever aspect of the assassin. Shakespeare had encountered many such men in his years as an intelligencer. Normally, he could spot the signs. Why, he had even seen them in Lucia Trevail. So why not in this man?

He stepped forward so that his face was a mere six inches from Hooft's.

'You are to leave England.'

Hooft did not back off. 'This country is my home—'

'No longer. You have two days to sort out your affairs and then you will be gone. I will come for you and accompany you to Tilbury, whence you will depart for the Low Countries aboard a vessel of my choosing.'

'No, sir, this is wrong! I am a friend to England. I can do you much good service. I have *already* done you good service. I am your friend—'

'Very well. If you are my friend, tell me the name of the man who ordered you to follow me.'

Hooft was silent. He bit hard at his lower lip.

'If you fight me on this, Mr Hooft, then I shall bring the full force of the law against you.'

The Dutchman was breathing heavily through his locked teeth, like a dog at bay. 'You do not know what you are doing, Shakespeare, nor who you are dealing with. I am God's vessel.'

Shakespeare had had quite enough of people believing they were God's instrument. His voice let slip his anger.

'I could have you incarcerated in the Tower and questioned under duress until you told me what I wished to know. But I will not because I remain indebted to you for my life.'

'*He* wanted you dead.' The words came out like the rasp of steel on flint. 'I thought you might have value alive. He was right; I was wrong.'

Shakespeare's body went rigid with anger. He might have many enemies, but only Richard Topcliffe, the Queen's own torturer, a man so severe in religion that he would drain the blood of every Roman Catholic in England – man, woman or child – wanted him dead with such slavering intensity of purpose. The white dog had sworn to destroy Shakespeare and his family. So even behind the dank walls of the Marshalsea, he had wielded power. And now he was out, and free to do his worst again.

Shakespeare raised his right hand and pointed his finger at Hooft.

'You are not God's vessel, but Topcliffe's.'

A fine pairing of zealots he and this hard-bitten Dutch intelligencer made.

'You said the name, not me. He wanted me to ensure you brought Weston back to the Tower and execution, but you could not stomach it. And he wanted me to be there when you hunted down the papist whore Sorrow Gray.' He snorted. 'Mr Topcliffe will kill you rather than lose my services.'

How had Topcliffe heard of Shakespeare's plan to go to Wisbech? It must, surely, have been someone from his own office: Mills, perhaps? Or even Cecil himself? It didn't matter now.

'And what did you plan to do with her when you found her? What would you have done had she not escaped?'

'What do you think? I would have taken her to Mr Topcliffe so that he could extract all her diabolical secrets and the names of every last papist traitor infecting this realm. I should have taken her straight to him – and left you to die.'

'You would have done this to the woman you claim to have loved?' Shakespeare did not wait for a reply, but strode towards the door, then turned briefly. 'Good day, Mr Hooft. I will come for you in two days' time. If you are not here, ready for me, you may consider yourself an outlaw and subject to the law of England.'

Thomasyn Jade stood alone beside the mound of earth in the churchyard of St Mary-at-Lambeth. The grave was beneath an old yew tree at the very edge of the field, well away from the tombs and vaults of the great men and women who were buried there. It was a peaceful, disregarded corner, set apart from the church and the archbishop's palace.

Dean Blague had secured permission for Sister Michael to be buried in this ground. He had not told the incumbent nor the archbishop the truth about her faith, merely saying she was a Christian friend who needed a final place of rest.

Thomasyn, too, had compromised on Sister Michael's behalf. She was well aware that, as a Catholic nun, she might not have liked the Protestant prayers that were said over her, but this was a holy place, whatever sect you belonged to. The church was named after the mother of Christ and it would have to do. Perhaps it might have amused the ragged old nun to lie so close to the graves of dukes and duchesses – even the grandmother of Queen Elizabeth. For herself, Thomasyn could not take seriously the doctrinal distinctions so beloved of the clergy. Did Protestants and Catholics not worship the same God and read from the same scripture?

The day was warm. In her purse, Thomasyn had a great deal of money, given her by John Shakespeare. He would say no more about it, other than that it had belonged to Sister Michael and had been impounded. Thomasyn could do with it what she wished, for he was certain the old nun would want her to have it. She had spent some of it on this funeral, and she had plans for the remainder. And should she need it, there was a promise of more to come, from the family of Father Southwell in Norfolk.

Bending down, she placed a posy of wildflowers at the head of the grave beside the little stone she had bought. She knelt awhile and said a prayer, knowing that Sister Michael would have liked that. It had been many years since Thomasyn had prayed. Back then, the ritual had been meaningless; her words and thoughts had merely wafted away into empty air, never to be heard. Now she expected no more, but she said the paternoster all the same.

The way from Waterbeach to Wisbech was a great deal easier than on Shakespeare's last visit. Now the floods had gone and the sky was clear. Gangs of parishioners were hard at work repairing the causeways and paths. It was a simple, gentle ride through a flat landscape. So this, he thought, is how it will look all year round if engineers such as Paul Hooft ever have their way and dig drainage channels to run off the floodwaters.

When he arrived at Wisbech Castle a little before dusk, he knew immediately that little had changed. From deep within the prison walls he heard shouting and banging: the seminary priests and the Jesuit faction were still at each other's throats.

'Mr Shakespeare,' keeper William Medley said, the surprise in his eyes evident. 'I had not expected the pleasure.'

'Is all in order?'

'Indeed, it is. The castle is now run with severe discipline and rigour, as befitting a prison for traitors. And it is a great deal more secure with the guards sent by Sir Robert.'

'What are those shouts I hear?'

'A minor disturbance, I am sure.'

'Well, we will talk of that in due course. For the moment, you will find me food and lodging, then bring Gavin Caldor to me in your rooms in an hour's time. Let him know he is to appear before me. I would like him to sweat awhile.'

Before this journey, Shakespeare had conversed again with Will about Caldor: Jesuit lay brother, builder of hiding holes and servant to Father Weston. His brother recalled him as an intense young man who spent more time trying to convert the players than he did on building sets.

It was clear that Caldor was the man with the connections at the Theatre. He was cousin to Garrick Loake and must have encountered both Lucia Trevail and Regis Roag. It was young Caldor who had given Beatrice papers of introduction to their furtive world of papist intrigue. But was the plan his? Was he the one with the simple idea of how to get a band of armed men into the presence of the Queen and her senior government officers by staging a play?

While Weston would never talk – and while Cecil insisted he be denied his martyrdom – Caldor most assuredly would. Fear would loosen his tongue.

Medley's face creased into a grimace. 'He is dead, Mr Shakespeare.'

'Dead? How?'

'Hanged himself a week ago.'

Shakespeare saw again the young man drenched in sweat, pissing himself with fear. He remembered how he had used that fear against Caldor – fear of the Tower, of the rack, of Topcliffe and his devilish irons, of the scaffold – and imagined how terrified he would have been when the news of the failure of the plot at Nonsuch reached him.

Shakespeare felt sick to his stomach. He very much wished to see Father Weston once more to tell him what he thought of him, but he was not certain he could stand to be in his presence again.

It was time to go home, to his family.

Chapter 47

Back in London, with Hooft duly sent on his way aboard a Dutch trading vessel, Shakespeare had a meeting with Sir Robert Cecil.

'Still no news of her, John?'

'Nothing. Not a single word.'

'Where do you think she is?'

Shakespeare gazed out of the window. The sun was full in the south. He supposed that she must be somewhere in that vague direction, certainly across the narrow sea. 'Spain, perhaps, or some nunnery.'

Cecil recoiled in disbelief. 'Lucia in a nunnery?'

Shakespeare laughed. 'Perhaps not.'

'Well, if she turns up at the Spanish court, we shall hear soon enough.'

'With every despatch that arrives, from Madrid, Seville, Valladolid, Paris, Rome, even Prague and the Germanies, I expect to hear of a sighting. Surely, she will grace some royal court with elegant tales of her clever plan to bring a band of assassins into the very presence of the Queen.'

'*Her* plan?'

Shakespeare had thought this over, time and again.

'I no longer believe this conspiracy was devised at Wisbech, Sir Robert. It began in the heart and mind of Lady Lucia

Trevail. As a lady of the Privy Chamber, she had intimate access to the body of Her Majesty. The power of life and death. But she had no desire to sacrifice her own life, so she devised a plan by which she would use her influence to allow half a dozen armed assassins to gain access to the Queen. I believe she took the idea to Wisbech, perhaps to Father Weston or others there . . .'

He thought again of the young man Gavin Caldor, hanging dead in his cell, and sensed a bitter taste in his mouth.

'I doubt she could have made that journey in secret, even under cover, John.'

'If not herself, then she sent a trusted minion. She knew she needed help and she knew of no better place to go than the Catholic seminary of Wisbech Castle. Maybe it was that other Jesuit in our midst, Henry Garnett, who went for her. And whom did they send back to assist Lucia, but Weston's own prize convert, his acolyte Sorrow Gray. You may think this is mere conjecture, but I believe it was all Lucia's doing. She played the part of the Protestant as well as any player at the Theatre.'

'But why did she do all this?'

'Like so many secret Catholics she felt helpless in the face of the religious settlement. I suspect that for years she attempted to subsume her feelings, but they could not be contained for ever and eventually burst forth like the lid on a kettle.'

Or perhaps it was simply the devil within her, a lust for pleasure and evil that could not be contained.

'So we were all taken for fools? The Queen and all her court-iers, the Countesses of Kent and Cumberland, and all their circle?'

'All of us. Myself included.'

'Do not be too hard on yourself, John. It was the work you had already done that alerted Margaret of Cumberland. It was your warning that made us ready.'

Shakespeare nodded graciously, then continued to unload his thoughts. 'Lucia kept up her façade perfectly, even reading to Her Majesty from that great Protestant tome Foxe's *Book of Martyrs* – without ever once disclosing that she considered the burning of heretics by Queen Mary to have been entirely laudable. Yes, we were all fooled. One day, I am certain, she will appear at the Escorial with a fan at her face, jesting at our expense to her new friend the Infanta.'

'Perhaps you are right. But, John, I hope not.' Cecil sat back in his chair and, for the first time in months, almost seemed relaxed. 'I like it the way it is. Utter silence. I think the fate of Lady Lucia should remain a mystery for all time. You know Her Royal Majesty feels betrayed and has no wish to hear of her again.'

Shakespeare looked hard at the young statesman. 'It would suit everyone, I suppose, if she had somehow met an accidental death, do you not think?'

'Such as falling from the back of a packet boat from Dover to Calais, you mean? Yes, you are right, that would be most convenient. But if such a thing had happened, none would ever know, would they?' He stood beside Shakespeare and together they gazed out of the leaded window at the empty sky. 'None but the seagulls and the fishes . . .'

John Shakespeare's table had never been so heavy laden. Almost every inch of the large, oak refectory board was covered with platters of fine food and flagons of wine and beer. He stood at the head and looked at his guests with warmth, satisfaction and a little impatience. One of them was late.

Grace and Mary sat side by side, giggling about the turkey,

which they said was the biggest chicken they had ever seen. The time at Cecil's house had been an adventure; they had been overawed by the size of the place and the dozens of servants who ran the household, but they were clearly happy to be home.

Next to them, Thomasyn Jade was talking to Ursula, who was just glad to have everyone back in the house. As soon as she heard they were returning, she had thrown over her swain because she had decided she really could not abide his mother.

Then there was Simon Forman, tousled and stocky, beaming at everyone through his bushy beard and holding his knife at the ready for when the eating began. His eyes swivelled from the food to the delectable Ursula and back to the food again. Why did Shakespeare not just say grace and get on with it? He had a mighty hunger on him, and his belly was rumbling in anticipation.

Beside him sat Jane with her promise of a swollen belly. She was plainly nervous of Forman's presence here, but Forman was playing his part, as was Thomasyn. They had shaken hands with Jane like strangers and were keeping up the pretence well.

Boltfoot stood awkwardly behind his chair, seemingly more bent and shrunken than ever. But for all that, the cares in his face had fallen away, now that they were home again and he no longer had to chase around England at his master's behest. Shakespeare wondered whether he suspected the good news that his wife had held back from him.

He wondered, too, whether it might not be time to start eating. The reason for the delay was the empty space at the other end of the table. Shakespeare did not wish to begin until the final guest arrived, but they could not wait for ever and he was just about to say grace when there was a knock at the door.

Jane stood up to answer it, but Shakespeare stayed her.

'Not tonight, Jane. You are no servant tonight. I will go.'

*

Francis Mills stood before Shakespeare like a ghost. His skin was grey, his eyes deep and his body gaunt; his clothes hung like long jute sacks from his thin shoulders. He brought to mind an ill-fed jackdaw.

'It is a fine thing to see you, Frank.'

'And you, John.'

'Welcome. We were about to start without you.'

They did not embrace, nor even clasp hands. Such gestures of affection would have seemed out of place to both men. But even at a distance, Shakespeare could tell that Mills had washed himself and returned to the world of the living. He had even trimmed his hair and beard. For the first time in many months, Shakespeare felt there was hope for him.

'Come in, come in.'

Mills stepped into the house; Shakespeare showed him to his seat and then said grace.

The two potboys from the Swan hovered behind the diners like mayflies, pouring wine, clearing platters and bringing more food as required. Soon, the strong drink and convivial atmosphere had everyone talking and laughing as though they were all old friends. Simon Forman held everyone's attention with his bawdy tales of patients and their problems.

'Enough,' Shakespeare said, banging the table and standing up as the laughter died away. 'I have asked you here this evening to celebrate our safe return home.' He looked down the table. 'First, it is my pleasure to welcome Mr Mills – Frank – back from the dead, as it seemed. He was an innocent man almost brought to the gallows for a heinous crime that we now know for certain he did not commit. Frank, you have suffered terribly. Your loss has been great and we must all pray that you can find a way to live again.'

Mills nodded, but said nothing.

'It seems that Her Royal Majesty could not sleep the night

before you were meant to hang. You were on her mind, because she knew your story – and she knew you to be a good and faithful servant. In the early hours, when the palace slept, she summoned Lord Chamberlain Hunsdon from his slumbers and ordered him, personally, to carry a royal pardon to Newgate. From what I am told, there were no more than a few minutes to spare . . .'

Mills nodded again.

Shakespeare turned and held his goblet up to Thomasyn. 'But more than anything, this evening is about this young lady, who has endured such horrors in the name of superstition that few could bear to imagine it. And so, I would ask you all to drink a toast. To life.'

Thomasyn smiled and looked around the group of friendly faces. In her hand she clasped a pearl, sent to her by the Queen of England. She raised her goblet, her demons all gone.

Acknowledgments

I am indebted to many people for their support and help. I would particularly like to thank Christine Clarke for giving me access to her scholarly work on the Wisbech 'stirs' – the infighting among Catholic priests held prisoner at Wisbech Castle in the late sixteenth century. As always, my heartfelt thanks go to my wife Naomi, editor Kate Parkin and agent Teresa Chris.

Books that have been especially helpful include: *The Medieval Fenland* by H. C. Darby; *Liable to Floods* by J. R. Ravensdale; *From Punt to Plough: A History of the Fens* by Rex Sly; *A History of Wisbech Castle* by George Amiss; *Ladies in Waiting* by Anne Somerset; *St Gregory's College, Seville, 1592–1767* by Martin Murphy; *The Spanish Inquisition, 1478–1614*, edited and translated by Lu Ann Homza; *The Spanish Inquisition: An Historical Revision* by Henry Kamen; *James Archer of Kilkenny* by Thomas Morrissey, SJ; *History of Penzance* by A. S. Poole; *Sex and Society in Shakespeare's Age* by A. L. Rowse; *The Elizabethan Renaissance* by A. L. Rowse; *Tudor Cornwall* by A. L. Rowse; *Eminent Elizabethans* by A. L. Rowse; *The Life of Robert Southwell* by Christopher Devlin; *William Weston: The Autobiography of an Elizabethan*, translated by Philip Caraman; *Popish Impostures* by Samuel Harsnett.

Historical Notes

Exorcisms at Denham

The sordid story of the exorcisms carried out by Father William Weston and other priests is still a matter of controversy more than four hundred years later.

That the rituals happened is not in doubt. Weston himself mentioned them with some pride in his autobiography, saying, 'out of many persons demons were cast . . . before my own eyes'.

What is in dispute is the nature of the exorcisms.

The chronicler and sceptic Samuel Harsnett documented evidence against a group of twelve priests who gathered at the houses of fervent Catholics around London and who, he claims, performed a series of disturbing and unsavoury rites.

The hub of all this activity in 1585–6 was the home of Sir George Peckham at Denham in Buckinghamshire. His son Edmund was the prime mover in allowing the priests to use the house.

Those present included the would-be assassins Father John Ballard, Anthony Babington, Sir Thomas Salisbury and Chidiock Tichborne. All four were executed later that year for conspiring to kill the Queen in the Babington plot.

The atmosphere at Denham was feverish. Harsnett names some of those who were exorcised over many months: these include three sisters – Sara, Alice and Frances Williams; and three men – Richard Mainy, Francis Marwood and a servant named Trayford.

There was much violent shrieking, banging of walls and ceilings, flinging of holy water and scratching the names of demons on the walls. The 'possessed' men and women were stuck with pins, forced to inhale burning sulphur and had relics applied to them.

On one occasion the priests were said to have applied a relic 'to the secret place' of a maid in the service of Lord Vaux when she was having menstrual problems. These relics were often the bones or clothes of martyrs.

Father Weston, a stern Jesuit, owned various relics of Edmund Campion, who had been executed at Tyburn in 1581. They included parts of his body, especially his thumb, which, said Weston, 'did wonderfully burn the devil'.

Sara Williams, who had become possessed in her mid-teens, was frequently bound to a chair and given potions, one of which consisted of rue, wine, oil and various other substances. Brimstone and feathers were burnt in a dish under her nose.

'At one time she was so extremely afflicted with the said drinks and smoke as that her senses went from her and she remained in a swoon. At her recovery, she remembers that the priest said that the devil did then go down in the lower parts of her body.

'Also, she remembers well, that at one time they thrust into her mouth a relic, being a piece of one of Campion's bones, which they did by force, she herself loathing the same.'

Harsnett says, too, that the priests 'caused a woman to squirt something by her privy parts' into Sara's body, 'which made her very sick'.

Sara's sister Frances claimed that the priests told them they needed to be baptised anew to be rid of devils. They were baptised this time with salt in the mouth, saliva on the eyes and oil on the lips.

Cats were seen as devilish creatures. Once, a group of priests whipped a cat around the room until it fled.

Father Richard Sherwood, who was later martyred, would pinch Frances until she was bruised all over and say it was done by the devil. He also thrust pins into her shoulders and legs, seemingly to stab and trap the devils that were supposed to crawl beneath the skin.

A young Catholic gentleman in the service of Lord Burghley testified that he saw the exorcisms and said, 'You could actually see the devils gliding and moving under the skin. There were immense numbers of them, and they looked like fishes, swimming here, there and everywhere.' This tale is related by Weston himself.

Dozens of demons were named. They included Modu (described as the dictator of the demons), Cliton, Bernon, Hilo, Motubizanto, Killico, Hob, Portirichio, Frateretto, Fliberdigibbet, Hobberdidance, Tocabatto, Lustie Jollie Jenkin, Lustie Dickie, Delicat, Nurre, Molkin, Wilkin, Helcmodson and Kellicocam.

But how much of Harsnett's account was a true reflection of events?

Weston's involvement is accepted as 'ill-judged' by Philip Caraman, a Jesuit priest who translated Weston's autobiography from Latin into English in 1955. He adds, however, that in the sixteenth century exorcism was 'considered a universal remedy for all cases that would now be classified as hysteria, mental derangement and obsession'. He describes Samuel Harsnett's book as 'worthless as historical evidence', used only to discredit the priests who had taken part, adding that 'the book contains charges of such gross immorality both against

Weston and the other participant priests that it must be rejected as Protestant propaganda'.

However, Father Caraman, writing in the introduction to his translation, fails to mention that Harsnett also attacked Protestants for carrying out exorcisms. Some Protestants did a roaring trade in the theatre of exorcism – and got equally short shrift from the disbelieving quill of Harsnett in an earlier volume, *The Fraudulent Practices of John Darrel* (a Puritan exorcist who attracted large crowds to his rituals), written in 1599.

Harsnett had sat on the commission that condemned Darrel for fraud. His volume exposing the Catholic priests, *Popish Impostures*, was written four years later in 1603 and was probably read by William Shakespeare, for he used the names of demons such as Hobberdidance and Flibbertigibbet in *King Lear*.

It should also be mentioned that some of the older priests in the company of Weston disapproved of the exorcisms. They had heard of similar goings-on in Europe and did not want them in England.

After his arrest, William Weston remained imprisoned in Wisbech Castle and the Tower of London until he was exiled during the reign of James I. He went to Spain where he wrote his autobiography.

Harsnett went on to become Master of Pembroke College, Cambridge, and later Archbishop of York.

The True Story Behind Sorrow Gray

The character in this book named Sorrow Gray was inspired by the true story of Ursula, the daughter of Thomas Gray, keeper of Wisbech Castle in Cambridgeshire when it was an internment camp to Catholic priests in the 1590s.

Ursula and her husband, already parents and expecting

another baby, were leading members of the Puritans, a strict Protestant movement considered heretical by the Catholics.

She was so zealous that she was considered almost a prophet among the Puritans of Wisbech and the surrounding fens of Cambridgeshire. She and her husband did their best to convert the Catholic priests to their religion.

Though the priests were held captive, they were allowed a degree of liberty and were permitted to argue with the Puritans who would flock to the castle to heckle them.

There was, too, infighting among the Catholic priests themselves. The inmates had split into two ill-tempered factions – the majority led by the unbending ascetic William Weston (who reveals the tale of Ursula Gray in his autobiography – see the Acknowledgments), the rest by his sworn enemy Dr Christopher Bagshawe, a seminary priest who despised the Jesuit order and resented Weston's assumption of power among the thirty or so priests held in the castle.

But it was the debates between the Catholics and the Puritans that enthralled Ursula. According to Weston, she was particularly struck by her husband's impotence in trying to refute the priests' arguments.

She converted in secret to Catholicism, the faith she had once loathed, and sometimes spoke out in favour of her new religion. Her father Thomas Gray, described as a 'vigorous Puritan', began to harbour suspicions.

As it became clear that she had converted, he became enraged and started to threaten her. 'Nothing was left him,' says Weston, 'except to show openly his implacable anger and hatred and his solid alliance with the devil.'

Her father and her husband joined forces against her. Though she was pregnant, they would not allow her the services of a midwife. Subsequently, she suffered a miscarriage, narrowly escaping with her life.

She left her husband and went home where she had to put up with daily barracking from her father. Even her mother, who still loved her, argued with her constantly.

When they tried to make her to go to the parish church, she refused and they attempted to drag her there by force.

Tempers boiled over and a public row ensued. Her father was heard to call her a 'base woman'. In a fury, he drew his dagger and ran at her. Ursula tried to flee but her father caught her. There was a struggle against a door in which she managed to wrest the knife from him. She ran off into the town but could find no refuge. The locals were terrified of her father. 'But an honourable and wealthy woman having pity on her took her in for the night,' wrote Weston. 'Then, with the help of Catholics, it was arranged for her to ride off on horseback as quickly as possible to a certain Catholic house.'

Not only did she leave behind her parents and husband, but also her own children. She is believed to have never seen her family again.

Though Ursula is long dead, it would be wrong to suggest that my character Sorrow Gray is based on her, nor would it be right to impugn her reputation in any way. It was merely the idea for Sorrow that came from the young woman's story.

The Deaths of Drake and Hawkins

In August 1595, the great mariners Sir Francis Drake and Sir John Hawkins set sail from Plymouth on what would prove to be their last voyage. They both died at sea while attempting to capture Panama from the Spaniards.

Hawkins, whose brilliant reputation as a seafarer and treasurer of the navy has been tarnished in recent times by his activities as a slave trader, died first, on 12 November of that year, after a two-week illness. He was sixty-three, and was buried at sea near Porto Rico. He was largely credited with having built the fast, nimble warships that defeated the Spanish Armada.

Drake followed two months later, dying, as he had lived, in a most dramatic fashion. The seemingly immortal admiral caught dysentery in January 1596 while refitting his ships at the island of Escudo.

He put to sea again, but his condition worsened and by 27 January, as they approached Porto Bello, it became clear he would die soon. An unseemly battle over his property and will then broke out between one of his captains named Jonas Bodenham and his brother Thomas Drake.

Sir Francis ordered the two men to shake hands to make up. In the early hours, sensing that death was close, he rose from his sick bed and had his servants dress him in his armour so that he might die as he had lived, as a warrior.

But he was too weak to remain on his feet and returned to his sickbed, where he died within the hour at 4 a.m. on 28 January, aged fifty-six. He had asked to be buried on land, but he was buried at sea in a lead coffin off Porto Bello.

His heroic place in history was guaranteed by his defeat of the Spanish Armada, but it was his circumnavigation of the globe – the first by a sea captain (Magellan died en route) – that was his greatest glory.

Three Early Feminists

Queen Elizabeth was not the only powerful and highly educated woman in England in the sixteenth century. Three of the very finest minds of the age appear as characters in this book . . .

Lady Susan Bertie, Countess of Kent (born 1554)

Susan Bertie spent her early years in exile in Poland with her parents Catherine Willoughby, Duchess of Suffolk, and Richard

Bertie. They were outspoken Protestant radicals who returned to England only when Elizabeth succeeded to the throne. Susan was educated to a high degree. Miles Coverdale, the translator of the Bible, has been named as her tutor. At sixteen, she married Reginald Grey, who was raised up as Earl of Kent, but she was widowed three years later, aged nineteen. Susan joined the court and was taken into Elizabeth's orbit. In 1582, she married the soldier Sir John Wingfield and went with him to the Low Countries where their son Peregrine was born in 1589.

Back in England, she became a patron of the arts and a mentor to the young Emilia Lanier, who was greatly influenced by Susan's Protestant humanist circle of friends. Lady Susan greatly valued and emphasised the importance of young girls receiving the same level of education as young men. Emilia Lanier called her 'The mistress of my youth, the noble guide of my ungoverned days'.

Emilia Lanier (1569–1645)

One of the first Englishwomen to be a published poet, Emilia has been suggested as the Dark Lady of William Shakespeare's sonnets. She was the daughter of Baptista Bassano, a court musician. On his death she entered the household of Susan Bertie, Countess of Kent, where she received a humanist education, learnt Latin and developed a love of poetry. She became the mistress of the great courtier and patron of the arts Henry Carey, Lord Hunsdon, who was forty-five years her senior and held senior office as Lord Chamberlain. When she became pregnant at twenty-three with his son Henry, Hunsdon paid her off and she married a musician named Alphonso Lanier.

She was clearly a beautiful woman and it is possible she met William Shakespeare about this time. The identification of her as his 'Dark Lady' – seemingly the object of the author's affection in his sonnets – was first suggested by the historian

A. L. Rowse. Much of what is known about her is revealed in the diary of Dr Simon Forman, who seems to have had a sexual interest in her but was rejected. He says she had several miscarriages and tells us much about her happy relationship with Lord Hunsdon and her subsequent unhappy marriage to Lanier. 'The old Lord Chamberlain kept her long,' says Forman. 'She was maintained in great pomp . . . she had £40 a year.' Not so with Mr Lanier. 'Her husband has dealt hardly with her and consumed her goods and she is now in debt.'

In 1611 her proto-feminist poem *Salve Deus Rex Judaeorum* was published with dedications to both Lady Susan Bertie and the Countess of Cumberland. It tells the story of Christ's passion almost entirely from the point of view of the women around him. Emilia makes a point of denying the subservience of women.

Margaret, Countess of Cumberland (1560–1616)

The countess was widely read with an inquiring mind that led her to embrace many subjects in the arts and sciences, including alchemy, medicine and mining. Born Margaret Russell, the daughter of the Earl of Bedford, she was given an extensive education – a benefit she would pass on to her own daughter, Lady Anne Clifford. At the age of seventeen, Margaret married George Clifford, the Earl of Cumberland, but eventually left him because of his continual adultery.

One of the talented women she helped was the poet Emilia Lanier, who had also been befriended and mentored by Lady Susan Bertie. In the early 1600s, Emilia spent some time at Margaret's home in Cookham, and in turn dedicated poetry to her. Margaret's daughter described her mother as having a 'very well favoured face with sweet and quick grey eyes and a comely personage'. She tended towards Puritanism and was deeply pious.

The Dean of Rochester's Wanton Wife

Alice Blague might be described, kindly, as a fun-loving girl. Married at fifteen to an ambitious clergyman named Thomas Blague, who was twice her age, she spent the rest of her life having affairs with other men and spending far too much money.

She doesn't appear in *The Heretics* as a character, but she is mentioned by other people. In truth she could easily be made the subject of a book in her own right.

Much of what is known about her comes from the secret diaries of Dr Simon Forman, who used the word 'halek' as code for having sex. He certainly *haleked* with Alice Blague on at least two occasions – in June and July 1593 – and earned a fortune from her by providing medical and astrological consultations for a wide range of conditions and personal problems.

Forman gives us a very clear description of her character and appearance: 'She had wit at will but was somewhat proud and wavering, given to lust and diversity of loves and men; and would many times overshoot herself, was an enemy to herself and stood much on her own conceit. And did, in lewd banqueting, gifts and apparel, consume her husband's wealth, to satisfy her own lust and pleasure, and on idle company. And was always in love with one or another. She loved one Cox, a gentleman on whom she spent much. After that, she loved Dean Wood, a Welshman, who cozened her of much: she consumed her husband for love of that man. She did much overrule her husband.

'She was of long visage, wide mouth, reddish hair, of good and comely stature; but would never garter her hose, and would go much slipshod. She had four boys, a maid and a shift [miscarriage]. She loved dancing, singing and good cheer. She kept company with base fellows of lewd conversation – and yet would seem as holy as a horse.'

Alice came from a well-to-do family, as did Blague, who had been schooled in the household of Lord Burghley, Queen Elizabeth's most senior minister.

Dr Blague, a Cambridge graduate, evidently believed he was destined for the very top of the church tree – for both he and his wife consulted Dr Forman about his chances of success when bishopric vacancies arose.

But perhaps it was his wife's activities that held him back. One of her lovers was, like her husband, a church dean. She was utterly infatuated with Dean Owen Wood, who was married to a wealthy widow, and she was desperate to know whether he was in love with her.

However, Dean Wood's eye was as roving as hers. We know this because a maid from his house consulted Forman (as did many great ladies and gentlemen of the court). This maid told Forman of the day she saw her master with another man's wife, having seen him 'occupy Wem's wife in her own house in the garret. He did occupy her against the bedside, her mistress being abed in Tottenham.'

Maybe Forman thought it wise not to pass on this bit of tittle-tattle to Alice Blague.

Alice gave Forman substantial amounts of money for her frequent consultations. For instance, she wanted to know whether her supposedly good friend Martha Webb (another patient that Forman took to bed) was having an affair with Dean Wood behind her back; she also wanted to know if she should have a child with Dean Wood. These two consultations cost her £1 3s 3d and she promised the huge sum of £5 if Forman would use magic to ensure that Wood would be hers alone.

Belief in magic and demonic possession were commonplace in the Elizabethan era. The Blagues knew all about supposed possession by devils, for one servant girl had been 'much vexed with spirits in her youth'.

Many of Alice's consultations concerned physical ailments. She and her husband were given expensive medicines for a whole host of illnesses and pains.

During the plague year of 1603, she became frantic with worry and went time and again to Forman. He said her only problem was that she was afflicted 'with melancholy, and much wind. It makes her heavy, sad, faint, unlusty and solitary; and will drive her into a melancholy passion'.

She survived the plague and continued her wanton way through life for many more years.

Did the Dean of Rochester know about his wife's philandering? He once asked Simon Forman 'whether she be enchanted by Dean Wood or no'. But the answer he got was evidently 'no', for Dr Blague never forsook her. On his deathbed in 1611, he made her executor of his will and praised 'her wisdome and fidelitie'. Little did he know. Or perhaps he simply turned a blind eye to her activities.

As for Alice, a mother of four, she went on to marry a prison keeper named Walter Meysey. They soon separated.